SWEET SAVAGE INNOCENCE

"Do you feel affection for me, Nicholas?" Alanna questioned.

His body tensed, and she could feel him pull away. "Of course I feel affection for you, Blue Eyes."

"Then will you show me how to kiss?"

He was silent for a moment, then he bent forward to place his lips on her forehead.

Alanna pulled back. "That is not a kiss," she replied scornfully. "You kissed Grace Flemming on the lips."

He sighed in resignation. "You won't be satisfied until you have your way, will you?" He grasped her by the shoulders and pulled her into his arms.

Nicholas was taken by surprise as his lips pressed against hers. Her mouth was so soft and sweet, and his desire for her broke all bounds of consciousness. His hand drifted down to her waist, and he pressed her tighter against him. The heat of passion racked his body.

"Blue Eyes, what are you doing to me?" he whispered hotly in her ear. "I am only human, and you are so desirable. I thought never to find innocence again in a woman."

She trembled at the feather-light kisses he sprinkled on her eyelids. "You will teach me," she breathed, not thinking past the wild yearning she was feeling.

"Yes," he whispered in a deep voice. "I will introduce you to a world of pleasure. . . ."

CHEYENNE SUNRISE

CONSTANCE O'BANYON

ZEBRA BOOKS
KENSINGTON PUBLISHING CORP.

ZEBRA BOOKS

are published by

Kensington Publishing Corp.
475 Park Avenue South
New York, NY 10016

First printing: August, 1990

Printed in the United States of America

To you, Jim, dear friend, kind adviser and husband. Your strength and support have guided me, your shoulder has been available to me when I needed comfort, your patience has been unending.

Prologue

Montana Territory, June 20, 1876

In only eight days the United States would celebrate its one-hundredth birthday. In Washington, D.C., and in towns and villages all over the young nation, the banners had already been hung as the government prepared to commemorate the country's centennial.

But hundreds of miles away, in a seemingly peaceful Cheyenne Indian village situated along the banks of the Powder River, an uneasy calm settled over the people. To the untrained eye, it might appear as if it was a day like any other. But there were undertones of uncertainty and fear in the eyes of the Cheyenne as they watched the western horizon with troubled eyes.

Something out of the ordinary was happening, something that would change forever this peaceful Indian village and the Cheyenne people who dwelled therein.

Since gold had been discovered in the Black Hills, the white man had been coming in large numbers to the once forbidden Indian lands. Cheyenne warriors

7

were ready to grab up their weapons, don their war bonnets, and join their Sioux brothers to drive the white invaders off their land!

In five days a confrontation would erupt that would involve Colonel George Armstrong Custer and every man, woman, and child of this Cheyenne village.

Chapter One

The soft rain that had fallen earlier in the morning had washed the land clean with its freshness. Now the day was blessed with the rainbow brightness of the sun, and still, dewy drops clung to the wide, leafy plants that graced the side of the swollen stream. On the western horizon, low clouds hovered above the distant mountains. A fresh breeze swept through the low hills that flanked the Cheyenne village to the east, stirring the leaves of the pine trees and the short grasses of the prairie. It was a tranquil world almost untouched by man.

In a nearby meadow, just out of sight of the Cheyenne village, a young Indian maiden moved past the young boy who tended her grandfather's horses. She hesitated as she approached a giant buckskin-colored stallion, the latest addition to her grandfather's large herd.

The maiden's graceful movements had not gone unobserved by Gray Falcon, a young war chief who had been riding by and dismounted, moving out of the maiden's view, so he could watch her. For Gray

9

Falcon had long had a yearning for this girl, and he was not alone in this desire, for her beauty was such that many warriors of the Cheyenne Nation sought her as a wife.

The maiden was called Alanna, and she was the half-white granddaughter of Wolf Dreamer, the tribal council chief and wise shaman. Alanna's grandmother, Blue Flower Woman, was sister to the mighty chief of the Cheyenne, which made Alanna a Cheyenne princess.

Since Wolf Dreamer had no living sons or grandsons to help tend his horses, that honor belonged to Alanna. It was said by many that the horse had never been sired that Wolf Dreamer's granddaughter could not break. Her ability was legendary among the Cheyenne, who boasted that she had the gift.

Alanna continued to move closer to the stallion, even though it snorted and pawed at the ground. She spoke softly while reaching out her hand, but the horse backed away, perking up his ears suspiciously.

"Now, beautiful one," the young girl said soothingly, "you know you want me to ride you. What good is a horse that cannot be ridden?"

Something in the girl's voice stilled the untamed animal's nervous movements, and he lowered his head. Though still suspicious, he allowed her to touch his neck.

"Easy, beautiful one," the girl said, running her hand down the sleek neck and across the stallion's back. "I am going to ride you, and you are going to like it," she whispered next to his ear.

Gray Falcon watched with naked yearning in his dark eyes as Alanna stroked the animal. He could not tear his eyes away when she slipped the halter over the horse's head and spoke to it softly. "There, that was not so bad."

The horse shook its silky mane and tried to back away, but Alanna kept a firm hand on the reins. She led the reluctant animal forward, first pacing him in a small circle; then, as the stallion grew accustomed to the feel of the reins, she guided him into a wider course.

Behind the wide trunk of a tree, Gray Falcon followed Alanna with his eyes. She was better at this dangerous task than any warrior he knew.

"Now for the real contest," Alanna said under her breath, gingerly mounting the horse. For a long moment the animal did not move; then, in one big lunge, he shot into the air as though he had been propelled from a cannon. The magnificent stallion twisted and turned in an attempt to dislodge the persistent rider on his back, but her muscled legs gripped his sides, and he was unable to unseat her— no horse ever had.

Gray Falcon stood speechless as the horse and rider became as one. Never had he seen anything more beautiful than the maiden and the stallion that now raced across the prairie grasses with graceful precision.

Alanna maneuvered the animal over a small hill and then back again before returning to the herd. Dismounting, she quickly removed the halter and slapped the stallion on the rump, laughing as he raced away. She then turned to the young boy and handed him the reins. "That will be enough for the first day. But the horse is not so dangerous now."

The young boy looked up at the beautiful maiden in admiration. "Do you think your grandfather will allow me to ride the stallion?"

"No, you must not do that. The stallion is still too dangerous to ride."

11

"But you rode him, and you are only a girl," he protested.

She ruffled the boy's dark hair and laughed at his observation. "And you are but a boy, but that will change. Wait until you are older."

Alanna then moved away toward the distant village, her midnight-black hair streaming down her back and past her waist. She did not know that Gray Falcon had been watching her. When he stepped out into her path, her eyes widened and her heart fluttered inside her breasts.

"You did well today, Alanna. You have brought much honor to your grandfather's lodge."

"It is I who am honored by my grandfather," she replied, looking into the dark eyes of the tall warrior and feeling warmed by his praise.

For several years their eyes had spoken of the admiration they felt for one another, but until today, the handsome war chief had not spoken directly to her, and it would have been unseemly for her to approach him.

Gray Falcon had always known that the warrior who won Alanna would have to offer Wolf Dreamer many horses, for the old man loved her well and would be saddened to see her leave his lodge. Thus far, all offers of marriage had been brushed aside by her grandfather, with Alanna's approval, for the wise old man insisted that he would not give his granddaughter to a man who was not of her own choosing.

Alanna smiled up at Gray Falcon, noticing everything about him—the way his dark hair was sectioned off into three braids, two of which fell over his shoulder and one down his back. His bronzed skin glistened in the sunlight, and his eyes held a most serious expression.

"I have been watching you for some time," he admitted at long last.

"I know," she replied without the pretense of maidenly coyness.

"Do you know why?" he asked, and his voice deepened. "Can you guess?"

Now she did feel shy. "How can I know what is in your mind?"

Suddenly his dark eyes softened as they moved across her features. Her face was lovely, with high cheekbones that enhanced the slenderness of her neck. Surprisingly, her eyes were a deep sapphire blue, and he realized that if she had not been exposed to the sun, her skin would be white, like that of her father's people. She was small-boned and delicate, yet her arms and legs were muscled and strong from years of riding and training her grandfather's horses.

"Alanna, I wonder why you do not know what is in my mind, when everyone else in the village seems to." His voice deepened. "How could you not know?"

She felt his strong hand clasp hers, and her heart began beating a rapid tempo. Was it possible that he wanted to offer for her at last? she wondered, her blue eyes questioning and hopeful. She would force him to put his thoughts into words. "Tell me what you are saying, Gray Falcon."

Suddenly he released her hand, his eyes going to the hill just beyond. "I know Wolf Dreamer is considered one of the wealthiest men in the tribe because he owns so many horses." His eyes came back to her, and she saw uncertainty there. "I am hoping he will increase his herd by twenty today."

Her eyes widened, and joy filled her heart! "Twenty horses, Gray Falcon?"

Almost hesitantly, he reached out and touched a

13

strand of her midnight-black hair. "Do you think he will accept the horses from me, Alanna?"

She closed her eyes at his gentle touch. "He would have accepted fewer if I had asked it of him."

He raised his broad shoulders proudly. "With less, I would not have asked for you. Now all will know what value I place on you, and how proud I will be to have you walk beside me for all our lives."

For a moment, doubt clouded her eyes. "Have you never cared that my father was a white man?"

Softly he caressed a strand of her hair between his fingers, and he was lost in the blue of her eyes. "I would have you no different than you are."

She wondered if anyone's heart had ever burst from happiness. What a glorious day this was. Did it seem the birds sang a little sweeter in the nearby pines?

Gray Falcon stepped away from her, wishing he could take her in his arms and hold her next to his body. She would never know how hard it had been for him to gather up twenty horses. His friends had sometimes made him the object of their jests, because they knew he loved the shaman's granddaughter so deeply and had strived for so long to present a gift to Wolf Dreamer that was worthy of her.

It seemed to him that it had taken a lifetime to accumulate the bride price, and he had watched apprehensively during that time as each hopeful suitor had approached Alanna's grandfather. His mind would be at ease each time his rivals were turned away.

"I will leave you now to prepare for my meeting with your grandfather. If he will allow it, you will soon be mine, Alanna. It is hoped that he will not send me away as he has sent so many away before me."

14

"He will not send you away," she said with assurance. "My grandfather has always cared more for my happiness than the bride's price."

"Then I was not wrong when I sensed that you might favor me, Alanna?"

Her eyes glowed with the light of a woman in love. "You were not wrong, Gray Falcon."

She watched as his throat throbbed with emotion, just before he turned and walked away, as if he did not want her to see how much her admission had affected him.

In her heart she had known for a long time that Gray Falcon wanted her, but she did not know why he had never approached her until today. The thought of him working so long for the bride's price made her heart swell with tender feelings for him.

Soon she would be the wife of the man she had loved since she was a young girl. Although he was several summers older than she, she had watched Gray Falcon obtain greatness in the tribe. He was young to be a war chief, but his bravery was talked about around the council fires, and she would be proud to be his wife and bear his children.

The whole village seemed to be caught up with the excitement in the air. It was a spectacular sight as Gray Falcon rode through the village leading twenty horses. He was wearing his ceremonial finery, and his head was held high, his chin thrust out proudly. Many warriors ran along beside him, offering him words of encouragement, while children laughed and tagged along behind them.

As Gray Falcon dismounted, his friends wondered if he too would be sent away as so many others had been. The shaman had not thus far looked on any one

15

of his granddaughter's suitors with favor.

Alanna was seated near the back of the lodge with her grandmother, Blue Flower Woman, when her grandfather invited Gray Falcon to enter. Alanna looked into her grandmother's eyes and found them filled with happiness.

"I am glad, my granddaughter, that you have such a fine warrior offering for you. I began to think you would not find a husband who pleased you."

Although Alanna was not supposed to look at Gray Falcon, she could not keep from doing so. "I have waited a long time for him to ask for me."

The old woman smiled. "I know. I have seen this coming for some time."

Wolf Dreamer motioned for the welcome visitor to sit with him before the lodge fire. Already he knew that this young war chief had Alanna's heart. "It is a fine day," he said, observing how the young man's eyes kept moving to his granddaughter.

"Yes, a fine day," Gray Falcon muttered. Now that he was here, he was less certain that his suit would be accepted. How could Alanna, who was looking so delicate and lovely, love a man such as him?

Wolf Dreamer lit his pipe and smiled knowingly. "You have something you wanted to discuss with me?" he asked, passing the pipe to Gray Falcon.

"Yes, wise shaman. I have come to talk to you about something important." He took a drag on the pipe, hoping it would help to restore his courage. "I have come to offer you twenty horses for your granddaughter Alanna."

Undaunted, Wolf Dreamer nodded. "Twenty horses is a respectable number. There was a Sioux chief who offered thirty horses for her, and one from the Blackfoot tribe who offered forty. What makes you think I should accept your offer?"

Gray Falcon drew himself up proudly, but still his courage was ebbing as he looked into the sagacious old eyes of the shaman.

"Because I will treat her with gentleness and honor her always as my only wife. I am building a fine lodge for her, and I promise you that as my wife, she will never know a hungry day." His eyes met Alanna's, and he smiled tenderly. "I love your granddaughter; I cannot remember a time when I did not."

For a moment the shaman was silent and thoughtful. He looked toward his granddaughter and then back again. "If I did not believe that, I would not give her to you."

The young man's eyes brightened with hope, but then he looked doubtful. Could he have heard the shaman correctly? Could the old man have just given Alanna to him as his wife? "Then will you accept the horses?" he asked, hardly daring to breathe.

The old man smiled. "Have I not said so? I have been wondering when you would gather the courage to approach me."

Gray Falcon looked astonished. "You knew how I felt about Alanna?"

"Of course. And so did everyone else." His smile deepened. "I have watched you grow to manhood, and I have been proud of your accomplishments. I believe you will make a worthy husband for my granddaughter."

Gray Falcon stood up slowly. He tried to speak but found that a lump had formed in his throat.

The shaman stood up, took the pipe from the young man, and waved him toward Alanna. "Take your intended bride for a walk. I am certain you have many things to talk about."

Alanna came to her feet and moved to her grandfather. The old man's eyes softened when they

17

rested on her. The old man embraced her. "Take care of her, Gray Falcon. She is my greatest treasure."

His confidence restored, the young warrior boldly reached out and clasped Alanna's hand. "Now she will be my greatest treasure."

Alanna caught her grandmother's eyes, and the old woman smiled and nodded. Alanna thought she would burst with happiness because her grandparents approved of the man she loved.

Gray Falcon's dark eyes deepened with intensity, and Alanna trembled with excitement. "Come," he said, in a voice steeped with emotion, "walk with me."

Chapter Two

The stars twinkled in the ebony skies as Alanna walked along beside her future husband. Her hand rested in his, and she felt like she already belonged to him. They had passed out of the village, and he led her toward the woods, where they could escape well-wishing friends. They wanted to be alone, for they had much to discover about one another.

When Gray Falcon pulled her beneath the shadow of a tall pine tree, Alanna readily went into his strong arms. It felt wonderful to lay her head against his chest and hear his heart thumping against her ear.

"You are mine," he said in a voice soft with awe. "For so long I have watched you, wanting you, yet fearing some other would have you before I could approach your grandfather."

She looked up at him, her heart reflected in her eyes. "How could you not know that I was waiting for only you? None of the others mattered to me."

He laid his cheek against hers, filling his senses with her nearness. "My heart is so full, I can hardly speak of it."

She touched his face, lost in the wonder of his love. "We shall have a lifetime to speak of such things," she assured him.

His hands drifted down to rest against her tiny waist, and with gentle pressure, he moved her so her back was resting against the trunk of a tree, taking care to cushion her with his hands.

She gasped with surprise when he pressed his hard, lean body tightly against hers. With eyes filled with wonderment, he spoke: "So long have I desired you, and now that you will be my wife, I find myself impatient to have all of you."

"It will not be long," she said, wisely pushing him away.

"I want to take you to my mat and fill your body with fine sons," he said with feeling. "The lodge will be finished in three days' time, and then you will come to me."

She smiled shyly. "That will give my grandmother time to finish the gown she has been making for me."

He raised his hand and allowed a finger to drift across her cheek. "I have dreamed of how it will be between us, Alanna." His finger drifted across her lips and down her neck. "In my mind I have taken your body to me many times." His finger now boldly moved forward to trace around her breasts, and she shivered with newly awakened desire.

When Gray Falcon saw that he had aroused her, he pulled back, not wanting to ignite her untested passion into a flame. He had waited a long time to possess her; he would wait three days more.

"Come," he said, holding his hand out to her. "We will go back."

She was not experienced enough to hide her disappointment. "I want to be with you," she said.

He almost weakened when she reached out to him, but this was not the place he would choose to take her body for the first time. "And so you shall, but not now. I find some things are the sweeter for having waited for them."

"I do not understand," she said in confusion.

He took her hand and led her back toward the village. "I waited for you, and the sweetness of your body will be my reward."

There was a promise of pleasure in his dark eyes. "Yes," she agreed, "it will be better to wait."

When they reached her grandfather's lodge, Gray Falcon again encircled her in his arms. Pressing his cheek to hers, he felt the softness of her fill his being. "Sleep well, my heart, for soon we will be together."

Before Alanna could throw her arms around him, he stepped back, and without a word, moved away to disappear into the darkness. She stood for a long time as though lost within a frightened premonition of things to come. Suppose something happened to tear her and her love apart? She pushed those troubled thoughts aside. Nothing would happen. She and Gray Falcon were destined to walk among the stars together.

Everyone was aware that there was trouble with the white man since many of them had crossed into the sacred Cheyenne and Sioux territories looking for gold. The men of the Cheyenne nation were attending a council meeting to decide what was to be done about the long knives who had been sent to protect the invaders.

Alanna sat in the lodge beside her grandmother, watching Blue Flower Woman's nimble fingers weave the blue and green beading into the soft elkskin gown that she was to wear tomorrow when she became Gray Falcon's wife. "The gown is lovely, Grandmother. I shall always keep it."

21

The old woman smiled. "My mother made me such a gown when I married your grandfather. See," she said, pointing to the green beading across the sleeve, "I have used the same pattern as the one on my gown."

"Grandmother, did you love Grandfather when you were married?"

Blue Flower Woman's eyes glowed with a special light as her mind turned back in time. "Yes, he was much sought-after, because he was not only handsome of face, but from a wealthy family that owned many horses. Out of all the maidens he could have had, he chose me. I was not bad to look upon myself, and I was the sister of the chief."

"And you have been happy, I know this."

"Yes, my granddaughter, as you will be happy. I know that Gray Falcon will—"

Suddenly the sound of many horses and war whoops filled the air. Alanna's face whitened, and she jumped to her feet.

She turned bewildered eyes on her grandmother, who had come to stand beside her. "What can this mean?" Alanna asked, although she already knew the answer. The war paint on the faces of the warriors indicated that the Cheyenne were going to war!

Frantically, she looked for Gray Falcon, but she could not find him. Running from lodge to lodge, she asked if anyone had seen him, but no one had. At last she reached the lodge he had built for her, the one she was to share with him beginning tomorrow.

Going inside, Alanna found Gray Falcon standing as if in a daze. Unlike the other warriors, he wore no war paint. When he turned to face her, there was sadness in his eyes.

Holding out his arms to her, she ran to him, and he enfolded her in a warm embrace, burying his face in her hair. "I worked all night so I could finish the lodge. Now it is ready to receive you," he whispered brokenly.

She could not speak, her heart was so full of love for him, and there was such a fear deep inside her. How could she bear it when he painted his face and donned his war bonnet to ride off to war?

"You know, do you not?" he asked, resting his lips against her cheek.

"It is war."

"Yes."

"I wish . . . I wish . . ." She raised her face to his. "I do not want you to go away."

He looked at her regretfully. "I must go because it is my duty."

Alanna knew that she must not make it difficult for him to fulfill his duty as war chief, so she smiled bravely. "I will be waiting here for you when you return."

He pulled her to him so tightly she could scarcely breathe. "I have a feeling—" He pressed her even tighter to him, as if he could make her a part of his body. "If I do not come back, Alanna, do not grieve for me."

"No!" she cried, shaking her head in desperation. "Never say that. I will not hear it," and she covered her ears with her hands.

He took her hands and held them in his, his eyes tender as they swept her face. "Forgive me, I was only talking foolishly. I will return to you because the Great Father meant you to be my wife."

"When will you leave?" she asked, feeling as if her heart would break.

"Now."

A pitiful sigh escaped her lips, and she buried her face against his chest. For a long moment they stood there, locked in each other's arms. Finally he held her at arm's length. "Will you do something for me?" he asked.

She was ashamed that tears were gathering in her eyes, and she brushed them away, hoping he had not noticed. "Anything," she answered.

He reached up and unfastened the silver falcon that he wore about his neck and slipped the leather strap over her head. "Keep this for me, and I will feel you are close to me, even in battle."

Now she could not keep the tears from falling as the cold metal rested against her breasts. "I will keep it for you, Gray Falcon, until you return."

Suddenly his eyes were filled with agony, and he cupped her face, looking over every delicate feature. "You are my love, Alanna, and my one desire is that you will always be happy. Promise me you will."

She clutched at his arm, reluctant to let him go. "Promise you will return."

His eyes were filled with sorrow, but just for a moment. He pressed her to him once more and then released her abruptly.

"Remain here until after I am gone," he told her, moving toward the door. "Let me take with me the memory of you here in our lodge."

She nodded as he moved outside, and she waited until his soft footsteps faded away. Tears choked her as she clutched the silver necklace he had given her. "Oh, please come back to me, my love," she sobbed. "Please come back!"

Alanna entered her grandfather's lodge to find it empty, her grandmother gone. It had been three days since Gray Falcon and her grandfather had ridden off to war, and she had spent that time anxiously watching and listening for their return.

She bent down to turn the spit over the cookfire where the hindquarter of a deer was roasting, in case her grandfather arrived unexpectedly. Feeling the cool breeze on the back of her neck, she turned to see her grandmother, who had just entered the lodge.

"Because of our mild winter, the berry season came early this year," Blue Flower Woman remarked, showing her granddaughter the basket of black-berries she had gathered. The old woman's brow became furrowed with worry for her absent husband. "Blackberries are a favorite with your grandfather. I have gathered these for him."

Alanna placed her arm around her grandmother's frail shoulders, knowing she was distressed because they had heard no word of how the war with the long knives was going. In a voice that sounded much more confident than she felt, Alanna said: "I will make the sweet berry cakes so grandfather will have them when he returns."

Blue Flower Woman eased her body wearily down on a blanket and stared into the dancing flames of the cook-fire. "I know it is warm, and yet I feel cold inside. I feel something is very wrong."

Alanna shivered with unknown fear. "Perhaps the Sioux decided to talk peace with the long knives and there was no confrontation."

"No, there will be no peace." Blue Flower Woman saw the fear in her granddaughter's eyes, so she changed the subject. "I am told that today you finished taming the wild stallion. Your grandfather will be pleased."

Alanna shrugged modestly. "Anyone can ride the horse now."

"There are those who laughed at your grandfather when he trained you, a girl, to ride his wild horses.

25

But they do not laugh any longer. Your grandfather had much faith in you—your grandfather was right." The old woman's eyes flashed with pride. "I believe that you have a special gift with horses, a gift that was sent by the Great Father. You have been blessed."

"I wish I had the gift to see what was happening with my grandfather and Gray Falcon. Like you, I feel something is very wrong."

"This is a difficult time for you, Alanna." As always, the old woman stumbled over her grand-daughter's English name. "And I know what you are feeling. It has always been a woman's place to stay at home and worry while her man goes to war and faces danger. To watch and wait is like having a hundred arrows in your heart. Since you are about to be a wife, you must prepare for many days like this."

Alanna stared at her grandmother, who carried herself tall and proud. Blue Flower Woman's face was surprisingly unwrinkled, and her dark eyes were softened with kindness. Her gray hair was braided and circled with a plain leather band, and her hands were roughened from hard work.

Alanna's eyes darkened with apprehension. "Has there been no news of the battle, Grandmother?"

The old woman looked into the clear blue eyes of her granddaughter. "I have heard only that our warriors and chiefs have joined the Sioux in pursuit of the hated Yellow Hair and his long knives."

"Oh, Grandmother, I am so frightened of what might happen."

"War is always bad, Alanna, but this one will be worse than most. Your grandfather says that there is no way we can win against the white eyes. They are as many as the wildflowers in the field, and like the wildflowers, they are ever-increasing in number."

With deliberation, Alanna pushed a strand of black hair from her forehead, while her blue eyes flashed with smoldering anger. "I curse the white blood that runs in my veins. I wish it were possible to cut it away."

Blue Flower Woman looked at the lovely young girl with a speculative eye. Alanna was of a proud nature, and she was touched with beauty, not only of face, but of spirit, no matter who her father's people had been. The old woman knew that Alanna was ashamed to admit she was half white.

Blue Flower Woman shook her head sadly and said, "The white blood in you should not cause you shame. Your father is an honorable man, and he was a friend to our people."

Alanna thought of her father, who had once filled her whole world. She remembered laughing blue eyes much like her own. Colonel Anson Caldwell had been tall, but to a child of ten summers, all grownups are tall. Her mother, White Fawn, was little more than a vague memory to Alanna, because she had died when Alanna was in her eighth year.

Her thoughts returned to the present, and she decided that if she kept busy she would not worry so much about her grandfather and Gray Falcon. She mixed up ground corn, then added water and crushed berries. But the question was still nagging at her: "If my father is such a fine man," she asked, "why did he leave me? And why then has he not come back for me?"

Blue Flower Woman bent down beside her granddaughter and pinched off a piece of dough which she then formed into a flat cake by pressing it into the palm of her hand.

"It was always difficult for me to see into your father's head and know his thoughts. I only know that he loved my daughter, and when she died of the white man's smallpox, your father was wild with grief." Her eyes turned inward. "He left you with me and went off by himself for many moons. When he returned, he was a different man, cold and distant. He told me he was returning to his home in a place called Virginia, and—" Blue Flower Woman's eyes softened with love, "—he wanted you to remain with me and your grandfather. I was glad to have the daughter of my daughter to raise in my husband's lodge."

"Although I am glad he did not, I have often wondered why my father did not take me with him."

"Your father once told me this from his past: he had quarreled with his father, who was a very powerful man in the white man's government. Your father became a soldier to get away from his father's domination. At the fort, just two days' ride from here, is where he met your mother."

"And they loved one another?"

"Yes, they loved each other almost at once and were married according to white and Indian law. Since your father was an officer at the fort and could not live with your mother openly, he built her a fine house, away from prying eyes. In that house your father and mother were very happy, and that is where you were born. But then the big war came that divided the white man, and Anson Caldwell was sent away to fight against his own kind, while your mother honored his wishes and stayed with you in the house he had built for her so you could be schooled with the children of the other officers."

Blue Flower Woman's eyes deepened in color as she remembered the death of her only daughter. "The rest you know. Your mother became ill and sent for me. By the time I reached her, it was too late. I brought you back to the village with me, and this is where your father came after the war was ended. It fell to me to tell him about the death of my daughter."

Alanna stared across the lodge as if she were reliving something in her mind. "I remember seeing my father for the last time. He told me he had been married to a woman of his race before he met my mother and that he had another family in Virginia, a son and a daughter. He said he must go to them, but he would one day come back and take me with him. I was ten years old then—I am now sixteen—where is my father? Can he love his white son and daughter more than me?"

Blue Flower Woman sat back on the mat, taking her granddaughter's trembling hand in hers. "Anson Caldwell once told me that he had married as a young man to a woman of his father's choosing, and that she died after giving him two children. He did not love the woman as he loved your mother, but he did care for the children."

The sharp pain of feeling rejected by her father was reflected in Alanna's blue eyes. "That does not explain why my father abandoned me. Is he ashamed of me, or has he just forgotten all about me?"

"I do not believe either of those explanations is true. I did not know him very well, but this is what I believe: Anson Caldwell loved your mother so greatly that he did not want anything to remind him of the pain of his loss."

Alanna raised her chin proudly. "It does not matter about him, because I have forgotten him, too. My life is here, and I will soon be with the man who is to be my husband. I do not need a father."

Blue Flower Woman tightened her grip on Alanna's hand. "The time may come when you may most certainly need your father, my sweet child."

Fear tightened the muscles in Alanna's stomach. "What do you mean, Grandmother?"

Before Blue Flower Woman could answer, the

rumble of horses' hooves cut through the quiet of the village, and she and Alanna exchanged frightened glances.

"The warriors have returned from battle," her grandmother said with eagerness.

They both jumped to their feet and hurried outside. Alanna drew in a painful breath and reached for her grandmother's trembling hand as they watched in horror while the battered and bloody warriors returned from battle, some leading riderless horses, others leading horses that carried dead bodies. Many familiar faces were missing.

Alanna searched frantically for Gray Falcon and her grandfather. At last she saw her grandfather, but when his eyes met hers, there was a deep sadness reflected there. She clutched her hands together tightly, fearing for her beloved. Where was Gray Falcon? she wondered with fear in her heart.

Wolf Dreamer dismounted wearily, and after greeting his wife, went to Alanna and took her hand. "I have not seen your Gray Falcon since this morning when he fought with a bravery you can be proud of."

Her eyes were seeking as she watched the last of the warriors enter the camp. "Where is he, Grandfather?" she asked with fear rising in her voice.

"There are those who were more severely wounded who are coming along slower. Perhaps he is one of those who stayed behind to bring them home."

Alanna strived to push aside the dread inside her. "Yes," she said, with hope gleaming in her eyes, "that must be where he is."

The old man put his arm around his tiny granddaughter and led her into the lodge. It was good for her to have faith that Gray Falcon was alive. For her sake, he hoped the assurances he had given her were true.

Chapter Three

Silence filled the lodge as Wolf Dreamer stripped off his war bonnet and hung it on the lodge pole. Alanna waited tensely for him to speak of what had happened in the war with the long knives.

Finally, his eyes sought those of his wife, and he said in a soft voice filled with regret, "The battle lasted only as long as it would take a man to smoke a pipe. Custer, the Yellow Hair, and his soldiers are no more. Today we have lost by winning, and every Cheyenne—man, woman, and child—shall pay for this victory, and go on paying for many sunrises."

Alanna could not understand how a victory could be called a defeat. "Why is that, Grandfather?" she felt compelled to ask.

"Now the white eyes will not stop until they have driven us into the dust. There are too many of them and too few of us. Today, I fear we have loosened the hungry wolves upon our flesh."

Blue Flower Woman helped her husband out of his battle gear, then handed him a wet cloth to wash away the war paint from his face. "If you felt this way, why did you fight the white man, my husband?"

"I fought because my people fought." His eyes

rested on his granddaughter, and he smiled. "Come here, Blue Eyes," he said, holding out his arms to her. "Blue eyes" was his name for Alanna, because he refused to call her by the white name that had been given her by her father.

When Alanna was in the circle of her grandfather's arms, she leaned her head against his shoulder. This man had taken her to his heart, and growing up in his lodge she had known much joy and kindness. "I pray with you that Gray Falcon will return unharmed."

Her eyes were swimming with tears. "I hope so, Grandfather."

He looked at her questioningly. "Does the white blood in you rebel against the battle that was won today, Blue Eyes?" he asked.

Taught always to speak the truth, Alanna examined her mind for the answer. "I find no joy in knowing men died today, whether they were long knives or Indian warriors."

Wolf Dreamer sat down on the mat, pulling her down beside him. "If only there was a world where all the people thought as you do." He drew in a deep breath. "But not in this world, Blue Eyes, and not in my time or yours will we see the hatred between the white and the Indian wiped out. There will be terrible recriminations against us after today. Your grandmother and I are old—we have lived our lives, but I wish the ugliness would not have to touch your life."

Fear widened her blue eyes. "What will happen to us, Grandfather?"

"Our chief does not believe me, but there will come a time when, like all other tribes who have tried to defy the white man, we will be forced to live on a reservation. The white man will think they are saving our children by giving them the white man's education, while our warriors will either be slain or forced to give up their pride and live like dogs, begging handouts from some dishonest Indian agent."

Alanna listened to her grandfather's words. She did not doubt that his prophecy would come to pass, for was he not the shaman? But what would it mean for her and Gray Falcon? She could not bear to think they would be punished for defending what by rights belonged to them.

Already she could hear the wailing of the death chant as her village prepared to grieve for the dead. Sadness had descended upon them, and Alanna ached for the many lives that were lost—the fathers, husbands, and sons.

She shivered, feeling uneasiness close in around her. Since she was half white, should she not also grieve for the white soldiers who had lost their lives today?

She walked to the door and looked out into the night, her eyes searching the western horizon for Gray Falcon's return. Turning to her grandmother, Alanna knew what she must do. She would be waiting for him in their lodge when he returned. "Is my wedding gown completed, Grandmother?" she asked.

The old woman nodded, and picked up the soft elkskin gown that she had sewn with such love and handed it to Alanna. "What will you do?" she asked.

"I will wear this and go to the lodge Gray Falcon built for us." She hugged her grandmother and smiled at her grandfather as she hurried out to make herself ready for the return of the man who had promised to make her his wife.

Alanna had bathed and dressed in her wedding

gown, and now waited for her beloved to come to her. All night she sat cross-legged, with a prayer on her lips that Gray Falcon would return safely to her. When the sun came up and spread its light over the village, there was still no word from him.

Alanna's eyes were locked on the doorway, and she scarcely dared breathe as she waited, each passing moment lending fear to her suspicions that something had happened to Gray Falcon.

At last a shadow fell across her doorway, and Alanna held her breath as hope ignited within her heart. Coming to her feet and standing on shaky legs, she watched her grandfather enter the lodge, his face etched with grief. One look in his eyes and she knew he was the bearer of bad tidings.

Her hand went to her heart to still the thundering there. She shook her head as tears ran down her cheeks. "Grandfather, please, no," she moaned. "He is not dead. He promised he would return."

Wolf Dreamer took her in his arms and held her trembling body. "I would rather tear out my own heart than to see you grieve, but you must hear that Gray Falcon is dead!"

She rolled her head from side to side as he supported her limp body. "Then I am dead also, Grandfather, for one cannot live without a heart."

His eyes were filled with pain for this lovely girl that was his whole world. "Cry, Blue Eyes, for he was worthy of your tears."

Deep sobs made her body tremble, and her grandfather held her while she cried out her grief. She clung to him, until at last her tears were spent.

Alanna refused to leave the lodge Gray Falcon had built for them. As she sat on the mat that was to have been the place where her beloved would have made her his wife, her grief was unendurable.

Soon her grandmother came to sit beside her. After

a moment of long silence, Blue Flower Woman spoke: "I was told by Gray Falcon's brother, who brought us the sad news, that Gray Falcon's last thoughts were of you."

Alanna held onto her grandmother's hand as if it were her only lifeline. "Did he . . . have any words for me?"

"Yes."

"W . . . what were they?"

"Gray Falcon said you were to remember the promise you made him."

Alanna lovingly reached up and touched the necklace he had given her. "He made me promise that if anything happened to him, I was to be happy." Again her eyes filled with tears. "But how can I ever be happy again, Grandmother? How can I go on without him?"

The old woman gently touched her granddaughter's cheek. "There is a time for grieving, and a time for living. Each will come in its own time. Right now, you can grieve, but one day, you will again know happiness."

"Never!" she said with conviction. "I will never love another man, and I swear I will hate all white men, for they killed my love."

Blue Flower Woman bent over to lay her cheek to Alanna's. "You cannot hate what is a part of you. But you are too young to know this." She felt Alanna catch her breath as a deep sob was building within her. All she could do was to hold her granddaughter while the girl's tears washed the grief out of her soul.

November, 1877

Wolf Dreamer burst into his lodge to find his wife and granddaughter huddled near the fire to keep

35

warm. Both women knew something was wrong, and they waited for him to speak.

"Gather what you can and prepare to leave. My prediction has come true. When word of the battle at the Little Bighorn reached the white government in Washington, the soldiers were ordered to punish the tribes involved in the war."

Blue Flower Woman tensed. "Must we leave our home, my husband?"

"Yes. Already several Sioux villages have been put to the torch, and many innocents were killed. Some of the Sioux have escaped to Canada, but many of the survivors were rounded up like cattle and forced onto reservations. The same will be the fate of the Cheyenne."

"What shall we take with us?" his wife asked. "We cannot take everything."

"Bring only what you can carry," he said, rushing to the lodge pole and removing his war bonnet. "Hurry, the long knives are almost upon us!"

Before Alanna could spring into action, the sounds of pounding hooves were heard throughout the village. There were shots fired, and the screams of terrified women and children filled the air.

"It is too late to flee," Wolf Dreamer acknowledged, arming himself and standing at the entrance of his lodge to defend his wife and granddaughter.

Alanna screamed and screamed, her anguish a deep void of horror as she watched her proud grandfather crumple to the ground to lay in a pool of his own blood. She ran to him and tried to take him in her arms, but one of the long knives, wearing the hated blue uniform, grabbed her about the waist and shoved her outside with a force that sent her sprawling to the ground.

"Grandmother!" she screamed, trying to get back

inside the lodge. She kicked and fought like a wildcat to reach her grandmother. Finally something hard came down on her head, and she fell to the ground unconscious.

Alanna did not see the long knives as they went about the village, capturing the women and children and shooting the warriors who tried to protect their families. The soldiers' swords were red with blood as they sought revenge for the Cheyenne's part in the massacre of the Seventh Cavalry.

When Alanna regained consciousness, she found that she and her grandmother were tied to several other women. They were all dazed. Everything had happened so quickly that there was a feeling of unreality about the whole situation. The soldiers had made them watch their village go up in flames, then the women and children were force-marched away in the snow.

Blue Flower Woman stumbled many times, but Alanna always managed to draw her up and support her weight. They were cold and hungry, and the ropes cut into their flesh, but they did not complain. There was too much grief—too much hatred.

The women did not have to be told where they were being taken. They knew they would soon face the cruelty of reservation life. They clung together in their grief and misery, as they trudged mile after weary mile. Once they reached the white man's fort, they were placed in wagons which transported them many miles from their homeland.

There was so much to think about that Alanna was unable to deal with it, so she sank into silence while her hatred for the white man festered and grew in her heart.

She tried to remember her grandfather as the proud man he had been, because she could not bear to think

37

of him as dead. She wondered where her grand-mother got the strength to suffer in silence when her gentle heart was broken. Alanna was determined to follow Blue Flower Woman's example because Gray Falcon would have expected it of her.

In the unfamiliar surroundings and in a land that had been set aside by the government and known only as Indian Territory, the still proud but beaten Cheyenne people had been resettled. Most of the warriors had either fallen in battle or been confined in an area separate from the women and children. The young boys had been dressed in uniforms and sent away to boarding schools so they could learn the white man's ways. They were encouraged to speak English and to forget their native tongue.

The Cheyenne did not feel at home in this land that was foreign to them. They were forced to depend upon the government rations allotted to them by an Indian agent, and that they did not like.

In their old life they had been able to tell a man's wealth by how many horses he owned. Now the horses had been taken from them, and they considered themselves destitute. The government tried to encourage the warriors to farm the land, but stubbornly they refused—was not farming woman's work?

The mighty Cheyenne had been stripped of their heritage and driven into the ground, while the white man tried to mold them in his own image. But still they held their heads high and faced their tormentors with pride and with what dignity remained to them. They grew closer together as a people and learned to depend on one another.

Chapter Four

December, 1877

Alanna huddled in her blanket while she watched the sun rise over the distant snow-covered hills. In her quiet times, like this morning, she would remember every word Gray Falcon had ever spoken to her. Even though their marriage had not been celebrated, she felt as though she was his widow, and her life felt empty without him.

There was no joy in her heart as she faced this new day, for now, one day was very much like the last. She remembered how good life had been in the Cheyenne village before Gray Falcon and her grandfather had been killed and she and her grandmother were forced to live here in this harsh land.

Life was hard here, with no man to provide for them, and since winter was upon them, Alanna and her grandmother often went hungry. So far they had managed to survive on the meager beef rations that were allotted them, but even that was almost gone.

Though the Cheyenne were not farmers, Alanna knew that when spring came she would plant the corn and squash seeds the Indian agent had given her. Perhaps it would make next winter more tolerable—if they survived this one.

Never had Alanna felt so alone. She had no one she could turn to now in her desperation, for the others of her tribe were no better off themselves.

Many of their people had already died from hunger because of their refusal to take anything from the United States government, but Alanna was determined that she would do whatever was necessary to feed her grandmother.

With a worried frown, Alanna turned her eyes to the drafty wooden shelter that housed her and her grandmother. Lately Blue Flower Woman had not been sleeping well, and there was a dullness to her eyes and a hesitation in her step that she had not been able to hide. Alanna was forced to admit that her grandmother was ill and getting weaker with each passing day. If they could just endure the cold weather, she was sure the spring would bring new hope for them both.

With one last glance at the sunrise, Alanna hurried down the hill, clutching the armload of wood she had managed to uncover from beneath the frozen snow. As she trudged along, the imprints left by her moccasin-clad feet were quickly covered over by newly fallen snow. The wind intensified, howling across the prairie, and snow swirled around in a blinding blizzard, making her existence even more wretched.

When Alanna entered the dark one-room structure, she found her grandmother's condition had worsened in the short time she had been away. Blue Flower Woman was still huddled on her mat, as she had been when Alanna left. Alanna's concern deepened. Never had she known her grandmother not to be up to greet the sunrise.

Dropping down on her knees, Alanna's eyes were troubled as she felt the wrinkled forehead and found it hot to the touch. Her grandmother was very ill indeed.

"Do not worry for me, my child," Blue Flower Woman said, attempting to smile, but her eyes were lusterless, and the hand that rested on Alanna's arm trembled.

"Grandmother, why did you not tell me that you were ill? I will get the medicine woman at once."

Blue Flower Woman shook her head. "No, do not trouble Wannah, she has too many sick to look after now. I will be better soon."

Alanna held the water jug to her grandmother's lips so she could take a cool drink. She then placed the last precious slice of beef in the boiling pot, knowing her grandmother needed the nourishment.

Alanna tried to hide from her grandmother the tears that were gathering in her eyes. She had to keep her spirits up.

In the time it took the beef and water to bubble into a thin broth, she saw her grandmother weaken even more. Raising Blue Flower Woman's head and supporting it, Alanna spooned the nourishing broth into her mouth, wondering what they would do for food when this was gone.

Suddenly the older woman clamped her lips together, a look of defiance in her eyes. "I have known for some time that you have been giving much of your portion of food to me. I will not have it. Food is for the living; do not waste it on me, my child."

Alanna shook her head. "Do not say that! Nothing is going to happen to you; I will not let it."

"Child, I would like to spare you this one last grief since you have had so much to bear, but you must be

41

strong and face the truth. I cannot stay with you."

Now the tears made a trail down Alanna's face. "I will keep you warm, Grandmother, and I will go to Mr. Chappell, the agent, and beg him for food. You will see, you will get stronger right away."

Blue Flower Woman's eyes flamed. "My one regret is in leaving you alone, Alanna. What will become of you?"

The young girl covered her ears with her hands. "I will not hear this, Grandmother. Too many people I love have died already. I will not let you go." With a firm resolve, she raised the spoon to her grandmother's lips. "Please eat more," she urged.

Blue Flower Woman pushed the spoon away and grasped her granddaughter's hand. "Listen to me, Alanna, for there is not much time. Back in the summer months, when I first felt ill, I sent word to your father through Mr. Chappell, telling him of our plight and urging him to come for you as soon as possible. I do not know if the word reached your father, but if it did, I believe he will see to your future."

"No!" Alanna cried. "I will not leave you. I am a woman now. I do not belong to my father, and he does not belong to me."

The old woman closed her eyes, reaching deep inside herself to draw air into her lungs. She could feel herself growing weaker. It did not matter about her—she had lived a long life, and much of it had been filled with happiness, but now she was weary; life was not good. The thing she feared most was that she might linger for many days or even weeks, thus further adding to Alanna's burdens.

Blue Flower Woman had lost her husband, two infant sons, and her only daughter—she would not be sorry to leave this world for a better one where she would dwell with the family that had preceded her in death. But, oh, she did fear for her granddaughter. What would happen to Alanna if Anson Caldwell did not come and take her home with him?

Captain Nicholas Ballinger stepped out of the stagecoach, pulling his greatcoat tightly about his neck to protect himself against the blistering cold. Grim-faced, he glanced up at the sign that swung over the rustic porch, WILEY CHAPPELL, INDIAN AGENT.

Wearily, he climbed the icy wooden steps that led to the building. He felt certain he had come on a fool's errand, but nonetheless owed it to Anson Caldwell to attempt to locate his daughter.

Pushing open the door, he entered, noting that several Indians were huddled around the potbellied stove, their gaunt faces grim evidence of their hunger, their dark eyes brimming with hostility when they saw his army uniform. Since Captain Ballinger had been stationed in Indian Territory for the last year-and-a-half, he was accustomed to hostile glances. He was glad his hitch in the cavalry was up and he could now return to his home in Virginia.

Nicholas glanced about him, seeing sacks of flour and corn stacked against the wall, and dried meat hung from the rafters. The shelves were filled with blankets, but very little food. Behind a chipped and battered desk sat a white-haired man he suspected was Wiley Chappell. The man rose to his feet and smiled a greeting.

"Thank God you've come," the agent said, relieved. "I feared the storm would delay you and I'd have more starving Indians on my hands."

The captain removed his gloves, unbuttoned his

43

coat, and faced the man. "I am Captain Nicholas Ballinger. I believe you have mistaken me for someone else, because you couldn't possibly have been expecting me."

The man looked befuddled. "Aren't you from Fort Sill? Didn't you bring the cattle?"

"No, I have come on an entirely different matter."

"How in the hell am I supposed to feed three hundred Indians if the army doesn't get the beef here on time? Already this winter I have lost sixty-two women and children to hunger and cold. If something doesn't happen soon, I'll lose twice that many before spring."

Nicholas glanced at the barren shelves that lined the walls. "I can see you don't have much food here. Surely you have cattle penned up in your corrals?"

"No. We slaughtered the last of the herd two weeks ago." The man stuck his hand out. "Name's Wiley Chappell, and I'm the Indian agent."

Nicholas shook hands with the man. "So I gathered. Pleased to meet you."

"If you didn't come with supplies, Captain, can you influence those in authority and convince them that we are in a desperate situation here?"

Captain Ballinger felt sick inside at the government's neglect. It was nothing new. The plight of the Indians reminded him of the destitute people of the South after the war. Many had starved or died. There were even those who had been cheated out of their land by dishonest Yankees.

From what he had observed, many of the Indians suffered because some dishonest agent misused the precious foodstuffs that were intended for the Indians. That did not appear to be the case here, however. Wiley Chappell seemed to be genuinely concerned for the welfare of those under his control.

44

"I may be able to help when I get back to Washington. I'll see what I can do."

"That may be too late."

"Perhaps, but there is nothing I can do until I get home," Captain Ballinger said regretfully. "I'm on my way now. I am only here to inquire about a half-breed Indian girl by the name of Alanna Caldwell. Can you tell me of her whereabouts?"

The agent's eyes brightened with interest. "Why do you ask?"

Nicholas pulled a letter from his breast pocket and held it out for Chappell's inspection. "Alanna Caldwell's father, Anson Caldwell, is a neighbor of mine back in Fairfax County, Virginia. He received this letter from you, informing him that his daughter was in trouble. Since I was stationed nearby, he asked me to do what I can for her."

"Yes, I wrote the letter at the request of the girl's grandmother. The old woman fears she is dying and is worried about her granddaughter's future. If you look around, you can see she has good reason to worry."

"How can I see her?"

"I'd take you out myself, but I can't leave the station just now. I can furnish you with a horse and give you directions, or you could wait until tomorrow morning and I'll show you the way then."

"I can't wait. As you know, the stage leaves later this afternoon, and I intend to be on it. I'll take you up on the offer of the horse and the directions."

Wiley nodded. "I just hope you aren't too late. What are you going to do, take her to her father?"

"No, I thought I would see that she and her grandmother have adequate shelter and food. Beyond that, I have no further instructions from her father."

Wiley snorted. "I thought Blue Flower Woman would get no help from the girl's father. She's such a pretty little thing; it don't seem right that she will soon be left alone. Up to now, her grandmother has kept her safe, but after Blue Flower Woman dies, one of the young bucks will probably take Alanna Caldwell as his woman."

Nicholas pulled on his gloves. "That's not my concern. I am only doing a favor for a neighbor."

"Yeah," Wiley murmured, "the Indian is no one's concern. The government would like to pretend they don't exist, and Washington, in particular, would like to drive them from sight."

"The horse?" Nicholas reminded the agent. "And the directions."

Alanna's frosted breath came out in puffs, and her hands were so cold she could no longer feel her fingers. The icy wind stung her face, and her feet would no longer obey her commands. Soft whimpers came from her throat as she pushed the shovel into the frozen earth. Somewhere in the back of her mind, she knew she was not being rational, but she was compelled to dig her grandmother's grave.

Sobbing in grief for her dead grandmother, and frustrated because she could not penetrate the frozen ground, Alanna stayed at her task. She did not hear the rider approach, nor did she notice the shadow that fell across her face as Captain Ballinger stood before her.

It took only a moment for Nicholas to realize the grim truth. He had found Alanna Caldwell, but too late. Apparently her grandmother was already dead. He realized the girl was in shock, because she did not acknowledge his presence or offer any resistance when he took the shovel from her. His hand tightened on the handle, and with powerful thrusts, he soon had dug a hole deep enough for the old woman's grave.

When Nicholas turned back to the girl, he could see nothing but a small face peeking out of the tightly wrapped Indian blanket. "Do you speak English?" he asked at last.

She stared at him as if she did not comprehend his meaning, so he moved past her and into the shabby dwelling, where he suspected he would find her grandmother's body.

Suddenly Alanna came to life. She remembered it had been the white soldiers who had killed Gray Falcon and her grandfather and forced her and her grandmother from their village and brought them here to this barren land. This man was also a soldier, and he represented everything she hated. Fearing what he would do, she ran after the stranger, placing herself between him and the dead body of her grandmother.

"Leave us alone," she said in Cheyenne. "Do not touch my grandmother."

"Do you speak English?" he asked again. "I do not understand your language."

She shook her head, her blue eyes defiant as she refused to speak in English. Without a word, she stood before him, blocking him from her grandmother's body.

Nicholas looked about the pitifully furnished room, thinking he had never seen such privation. The fire had gone out, and it was freezing inside. He saw no food, and only two blankets lay on the bare floor. He felt anger toward Anson Caldwell for allowing his daughter to live in such poverty.

He tried once more to get through to her. "Miss Caldwell, your father sent me. My name is Nicholas Ballinger, and I have come to help you," he said in a

47

sympathetic voice.

Alanna's bottom lip began to tremble, and she found herself crying out her grief. Deep sobs racked her body, and she dropped to her knees beside Blue Flower Woman. She gently touched the wrinkled face that looked so peaceful and serene in death.

Now the army officer was beside her, and she stared into compassionate green eyes.

"You have nothing to fear from me. Let me help you," he said, pulling her forward and allowing her to cry against his shoulder. For a long time Alanna wept while the stranger held her. At last he spoke in a soft voice. "It's time to bury your grandmother."

Alanna was too weak to protest, so she allowed him to pull her to her feet, and then stood stiffly while he wrapped her grandmother in one of the blankets. He gently lifted the body in his arms and carried it outside.

In a daze, Alanna followed the white man. She watched with a strange detachment while he laid her grandmother in the shallow grave. She stood stiffly beside him when he removed his hat and bowed his head for a moment of silence.

Suddenly Alanna remembered the blue skies and golden hills of her homeland, and she wondered if her grandmother now walked there with Wolf Dreamer. Perhaps the spirits were kind, because now her grandmother did not have to feel pain, hunger or cold—she was free.

Alanna reached out her hand as the ground swirled around her, and she felt herself falling forward, only to be caught in the stranger's strong arms. Blackness enveloped her, and she floated in a silent world where, like her grandmother, she was no longer cold or hungry.

48

Chapter Five

Nicholas wrapped the unconscious girl in one of the blankets, carried her out of the lodge, and mounted his horse. By now the snow was coming down in a frenzy of white, making it difficult to see where they were going, so Nicholas gripped the reins and nudged the horse forward, hoping that the animal would know its way home.

His eyes darkened with anger as he realized the disgusting conditions in which this girl and her grandmother had lived. How was it possible that a daughter of Anson Caldwell, a wealthy and influential man, was forced to live such a dismal existence?

Nicholas was tempted to take this poor creature to her father and demand he do right by her, but he did not want to get involved. Anson Caldwell would certainly be told about his daughter's deplorable living conditions, and he would have to answer to Nicholas for his neglect of the girl.

For now he would take her to the Indian agent so the man could nurse her back to health. After all, Wiley Chappell was responsible for the well-being of the Indians.

With irritation, Nicholas realized the stage would have pulled out hours ago, and he was not pleased that Alanna had caused him to delay his trip to Washington by a week. He glanced down at the wretched-looking girl. Her face was drawn, her eyes sunken; he doubted she would live. He cursed himself for allowing Anson Caldwell to pull him into this situation. This girl wasn't his responsibility. It was not up to him to see if she lived or died.

Digging his heels into the flanks of the horse, he raced forward, knowing, in spite of his resolve not to be burdened with the girl, that if he did not get her to a place of warmth, she might die in his arms.

Alanna slowly regained consciousness, but at first she did not have the strength to open her eyes. It was apparent to her that she was no longer in the cold dwelling, because she was laying in a soft bed, and for the first time in weeks she felt really warm. Too weary to care where she was, she heard the murmur of voices. Again she endeavored to open her eyes, but she was too weak to make the effort. She snuggled down under the warm blankets and drifted off to sleep.

Some time later, two men stood over Alanna, discussing her condition.

"When she first come here she was a mighty pretty little thing," Wiley observed regretfully. "I always thought she looked more white than Indian, but the Cheyenne didn't have no trouble accepting her as one of their own. She's considered a princess of the tribe, you know."

"She doesn't look like royalty to me," Nicholas observed.

"Maybe not, but she is, all the same. Didn't seem right to me that her father never saw to her welfare. It's a pity, but she's probably going to die of starvation. I'm not a doctor, but I've seen people with her symptoms before, and they're all dead. It would appear she hadn't had anything to eat in a long time—for more than a week, I'd say. Judging from the way she looks, most likely she won't live past today."

Alanna's face was as white as the pillow she lay upon. Dark circles fanned out below her eyes; her cheeks were hollow, her face drawn, and her breathing shallow.

When Nicholas touched her forehead, he discovered she had fever. "She's so weak, and she doesn't seem to care about getting better," he observed grimly.

Wiley nodded sadly. "Yeah, most likely she don't care to live now that her grandmother's dead. She doesn't have anyone else."

Captain Ballinger removed his blue jacket, rolled up his sleeves, and moved to sit beside the girl. "She's not going to die, damn it! Not if I can help it." He then picked up the bowl of food which Alanna had thus far refused to eat. "She's going to eat this if I have to force it down her throat. By God, she's going to live so she can one day confront her father for the way he's neglected her."

Wiley shook his head. "There ain't much you can do for her, Captain, just prolong her misery, I 'spect."

Nicholas set his jaw stubbornly. "I have a week before the next eastbound stage comes through; I'd say that was just enough time to see her on the mend."

Wiley watched expectantly while Nicholas lifted the girl's head and placed the spoon at her mouth, but she clamped her teeth together and turned away weakly.

"I told you she ain't going to eat, Captain. I already tried to feed her."

Nicholas laid the girl's head back against the pillow. With a firm grip on her cheeks, he forced her mouth open and forced the spoon inside.

Alanna opened her eyes and stared at the white man who had been tormenting her. On tasting the foul substance he had pushed into her mouth, she spit it out and closed her eyes once more as anger began to slowly burn within her. Even if the long knife had helped her bury her grandmother, she would not take nourishment from him. All she wanted was to be allowed to join in death the people she loved.

"Oh, no, you don't," Nicholas insisted. Again he forced the girl's mouth open and fed her a spoonful of gruel, only to have her spit it at him again. This act was repeated several times before Alanna opened her eyes and glared at her tormentor. Her sapphire eyes locked with his determined green eyes.

"You will eat, Miss Caldwell," Nicholas insisted. "You will save us both a lot of trouble if you understand that I won't give up until you do." To make sure she understood, he had Wiley repeat what he said to her in the language of the Cheyenne.

Alanna realized it would take far less effort to swallow the horrible-tasting food than to match wills with the obstinate captain. The next time he put the spoon to her lips, she took the food and swallowed it, hoping he would leave her alone.

Nicholas knew enough to realize that since the girl had been half-starved it would not be wise to feed her too much this first time. Thereafter, every two hours, he would awaken her and feed her several spoonfuls of the gruel before allowing her to drift off to sleep again.

At last he was satisfied that she would not die from hunger, but he was concerned about her fever and the dry cough that had developed in her chest.

Somehow Wiley came up with a flannel night-gown, and Nicholas, with a feeling of detachment, removed the girl's buckskin gown, tossed it aside, and pulled the soft, warm nightgown over her head.

All day and into the night Nicholas remained at the girl's bedside, administering cool cloths to her forehead and forcing sips of water between her parched lips.

Each time the white man with the green eyes awakened Alanna, she would resent his intrusion into her lethargic world of darkness. He was forcing nourishment on her when all she wanted to do was be allowed to be wrapped in the warm arms of nothingness.

Just before sunrise, Nicholas fell into an exhausted sleep, feeling that he had done all he could to ensure that the girl would survive.

Alanna awoke feeling strangely sad as her mind cleared and she remembered that her grandmother was dead. It hurt to think she would never see Blue Flower Woman again. What would she do without her grandmother's love and wise counsel?

Turning her head toward the window, she observed the way sunlight bathed the room. As she watched dark snow clouds gather on the distant horizon, it filled her heart with a sense of dread. Everyone she loved had died—why was she still alive?

Her eyes moved to the open doorway, where she heard the sound of voices. She recognized one voice as

Wiley Chappell's, and she knew the other belonged to the cavalry officer who had been forcing her to eat against her will. Had the long knife said that he had been sent here by her father? Everything was so hazy in her mind, she could not remember. Alanna slowly became aware that the men were discussing her.

"Now that the girl is going to live, will you be taking her to her father, Captain Ballinger?" Wiley was asking.

"No, I have to report directly to Washington before going home to Virginia. I could hardly show up at the capital with a half-breed Indian girl in tow, now, could I? If only there was some way I could know she would be safe."

"If you leave her here, she'll soon die. The other women won't take her in—they have it hard enough to look after their own families—they won't welcome another mouth to feed. Even marriage won't help her now, because the men aren't allowed to live with their families—leastwise, not yet."

"Damn it, she isn't *my* trouble," Nicholas said in an irritated voice. "You're the Indian agent; do something about her future."

Wiley shook his head. "Now, Captain, I can't do no more for her than I have already. I wrote to her father, and you came here as a result of my letter. It's up to her father to see to her well-being, not me." Wiley saw Nicholas's jaw clench at the mention of Alanna's father. "Yep, it sure would be a shame to see her die after all the trouble you took to bring her along. But she won't survive on her own—you saw that for yourself."

Nicholas drew in a long breath. It was becoming more and more apparent to him that he had made himself responsible for the girl. "Damn you, Chappell, you know I can't leave her here to die, but I can't

54

take her with me either. Until I discharge my duties in Washington, I am a soldier, and I have orders, which don't include playing nursemaid to a starving half-breed girl."

Nicholas paced the floor angrily. "There must be someone who would be able to help. Do you know of a white woman around here that might be persuaded to look after the girl? Maybe take her into her home."

"Nope. The only white woman I know in these parts is Miss Frances Wickers, the missionary's spinster daughter. She came out here to teach school to the Indians while her father goes about trying to save their souls. She won't be of any help to you, though. I heard tell she would soon be going back to her home."

The men were quiet for a moment, and then Wiley jumped to his feet. "Say, Captain!" he said excitedly, "if I remember correctly, the Wickers are from Richmond, Virginia."

Nicholas's eyes brightened. "If she's going to Richmond, Anson Caldwell's estate will hardly be out of her way. Do you think that Miss Wickers could be persuaded to take the girl with her?"

Wiley scratched his head thoughtfully. "I can't say. But what's the harm in asking her?"

"If she would consent, it would solve many problems. Tell me where I can find her."

"The mission is a far piece from here—a two-day ride. If you've a mind to, you could write a letter, and I'll see that it gets to Miss Wickers. Course, no one will make the trip until this snow melts."

Alanna closed her eyes, attempting to ignore the two men. Her proud spirit rebelled at the thought that they were planning her future without consulting her. She had no intention of going to her father. She certainly was not Captain Ballinger's concern, and for that matter, she wasn't the Indian agent's concern either.

An idea began building in Alanna's mind, and she sat up slowly. It was time for her to escape!

Looking around the bedroom, she saw that her elkskin gown was draped over the back of a wooden chair and her moccasins had been set near the fireplace.

Carefully, Alanna moved to the edge of the bed. By the time she swung her legs over the side, weakness washed over her and she had to grasp the bed post to pull herself to a standing position. With a strong determination, she forced herself across the room on unsteady legs.

She had just lifted the nightgown over her head, so she could get into her buckskins, when the door opened and she turned to see Captain Nicholas Ballinger standing in the doorway with a disapproving glare on his face.

With a gasp, she pulled the nightgown in front of her to hide her nakedness. There was a fire of resentment burning in her eyes as Alanna frowned at the man, daring him to try and stop her from leaving.

Nicholas paid little heed to the girl's nakedness; after all he had put the nightgown on her in the first place. Besides, with her small white face and the midnight black hair that hung limply about her shoulders, she was a homely little creature—skinny and pale. He could see by the pallor on her cheeks that she was still quite ill and should not be out of bed.

With long strides Nicholas crossed the room and towered above her. It took little effort to pry the nightgown from her grasp, pull it over her head and lift her in his arms. Alanna was too weak to protest when he laid her back in bed and pulled the blankets up to her chin.

"You aren't going anywhere until you are well enough," he said, staring down at her furiously. "Are you such a little savage that you don't understand I'm trying to help you? By God, you are going to get well and go to Virginia to live with your father, where you belong. This is no life for a young girl, even if she happens to be only half white."

Alanna managed to gather enough strength to strike out at the irritating man. As he ducked out of her range, his soft laughter told her he was only amused by her puny efforts.

"I'll bet you are a regular little hellion, aren't you?" He eyed her assessingly. "You certainly are a sickly little creature." He frowned. "It's a good thing you don't understand English, Miss Alanna Caldwell. You would never forgive my unflattering assessment of your shortcomings."

Alanna turned her back to the white man while hot scalding tears gathered in her eyes. Why was he saying such cruel things to her when he had so tenderly nursed her back to health? She had no understanding or liking for the white race, and this man in particular. Did he truly think she was ugly? Perhaps to a white man she was unattractive, but to Gray Falcon, she had been beautiful. And had not her grandfather turned down numerous marriage offers for her?

Alanna closed her eyes, wishing she had the strength to fight this hateful man. At that moment she became determined to get well. She had to escape! She did not think about where she would go; Alanna only knew she would not allow this man to force her to go to her father.

Her eyes focused on the window where sleet was pelting the glass. She could feel a trap closing in

57

around her. There was nowhere she could go, no one to turn to for help.

Nicholas read the letter he had received from Miss Wickers. Yes, she would be delighted to escort Alanna Caldwell to her father, but only if Nicholas could get the girl to St. Louis where she would resume her homeward journey after staying with friends for two weeks. If Captain Ballinger would bring Alanna to her in St. Louis, she would accompany her to her father.

In irritation, Nicholas handed the letter to Wiley. "It seems we have a dilemma on our hands."

After Wiley read the letter, he spoke. "As I see it, you have the perfect solution to your problem. In another week the girl will be well enough to travel, so you can take her to Miss Wickers in St. Louis."

"I had not intended to wait around here for another week. You know I am expected in Washington."

Neither man was aware that their voices were carrying to the bedroom where Alanna was listening to her future being decided.

"I don't see any other solution, do you?" Wiley asked. "If you have any ideas, I'll listen to them."

"Damn it, I have told you repeatedly that she isn't my problem," Nicholas stated sourly. "Why should I be saddled with her?"

Wiley shrugged his shoulders. "Look at it as doing a favor for a neighbor."

"I feel certain Anson Caldwell will not consider it a favor when the girl shows up on his doorstep. He only wanted to see to her needs, not have her in his home."

"That bothers you, doesn't it?"

"Of course it bothers me. The girl should have been shown the same consideration as Anson Caldwell's children by his first marriage."

Wiley Chappell looked at Nicholas with interest. "Tell me about the girl's father. What kind of a man is he that he would leave the care of his daughter to others?"

"Very respected," Nicholas snarled. "The Caldwells were one of the first families to settle in Virginia. Anson Caldwell's daughter, Eliza, is pretty enough, I suppose. The son, Donald, was running for some office in the federal government when I left. The Caldwells are a proud family, and I can't see Eliza and Donald taking to their half-breed sister with open hearts."

"Then perhaps we're not doing her a kindness by sending her to Virginia," Wiley observed.

"What do you suggest we do, let her stay here and starve to death? You saw what a sad condition I found her in. No, she will be safely placed in her father's keeping, and he can do with her as he will. After I get her to St. Louis, I wash my hands of any responsibility where she is concerned. Let's hope her father will recognize his duty to her. I'm sure there are several proper schools for young ladies where he could place her."

Alanna felt resentment building up inside her. She would not go anywhere with this hateful man, and he could not make her. Who did he think he was that he could take it upon himself to arrange her future?

With fever-bright eyes she listened to the storm rage outside, glad that as it intensified, it drowned out the sound of the two men's voices.

Chapter Six

The mirror was cracked and dusty, but still Alanna could see her reflection well enough to discover that she was all skin and bone and looked like a walking skeleton. She shuddered, wondering if she would ever be pretty again.

Her eyes moved across the floor to where the blue print gown and cotton undergarments Captain Ballinger had miraculously provided for her lay discarded in a heap.

She hastily dressed in her own elkskin gown, feeling it would provide her with the needed courage for the battle that surely lay ahead. Turning sideways so she could see her reflection better, she realized that the gown that had once been so flattering to her, now hung loosely about her small frame. Captain Ballinger had been right in his judgment of her—she was pathetic looking.

What did it matter? she thought bitterly. Her life was over anyway. She had nothing but darkness in her future—everyone she loved was dead. With quick efficiency, and a resigned sigh, she grasped her midnight black hair that hung limply about her face and braided it in two long braids which trailed down her back.

When the knock sounded at the door, she did not acknowledge it, so after a second knock, the door was opened and Captain Ballinger stood there silently assessing her. He took note of the discarded blue gown on the floor, and Alanna cringed inside as his strange green eyes ran over her from head to toe. She had been prepared for his anger, so therefore was totally thrown off guard by the sardonic smile he bestowed upon her.

"So, Miss Caldwell, you will not wear the gown and undergarments that were so carefully selected for you. It might interest you to know that those niceties came all the way from Fort Union, just for you. One of the officers' wives, on a plea from me, generously agreed to provide you with the clothing."

Alanna turned away, still unwilling for him to discover that she spoke and understood English. How could she ever allow him to know she had understood all the unflattering remarks he had made about her? His cruel words still echoed in her mind, and she would never forgive him for his pity.

When Alanna felt him behind her, she did not turn around.

Nicholas suddenly spoke in exasperation: "How can I make you understand that you must discard your Indian way of life if you are going to make a place for yourself in the white world? You will never be accepted as you are."

Now, unable to contain her anger, she felt her spine stiffen, and she slowly turned to face him. It was on the tip of her tongue to tell him that she had no intention of going to his white world, but the words were never uttered, for she was suddenly lost in the depths of his green eyes. She was unaccustomed to looking into green eyes, since she had only known

61

men with dark eyes, and she found it unsettling.

In a whirl of emotions that dazzled her mind and made her head swim, she became aware for the first time that Captain Ballinger was a man. He was tall, taller than Gray Falcon had been. The blue uniform he wore fit snugly across his wide chest, and she examined the golden captain's bars on his shoulders.

She became aware of many things about him that she had not noticed before: his controlled strength, the cleft in his chin, the slight scent of shaving lotion that clung to him from his morning shave. Why had she never noticed that Captain Ballinger was handsome and very manly?

Angered by her sudden attraction to this man who should have been her enemy, Alanna turned away from him, calling on all her composure to come to her rescue. A deepening feeling of disloyalty to Gray Falcon crept into her consciousness, and she wanted to cry out in anguish. Why was her heart racing so rapidly, and why was her throat so dry she could hardly swallow? What was happening to her?

"Damn it!" Nicholas exclaimed in frustration. "You don't understand one word I have said to you. Your father could have at least had the foresight to see that you were instructed in English. I was told that you were with your father for the first few years of your life—how in the hell did you communicate with each other?"

Alanna took a step away from him and then another, needing to put some distance between them. She was unprepared when he reached out and whirled her around to face him.

"The coach is preparing to pull out, and you will be on it with me." His features hardened. "You will wear the gown I provided for you." With a firm grip on her arm, he led her across the room, scooped up the gown and thrust it at her. "Either you put the gown on, or I'll dress you myself—I've done it before."

Her blue eyes sparked with defiance, and she threw the gown on the floor and stomped it under her foot. At least this was something she could understand, something she could react to. She needed the anger to take her mind off the conflicting emotions she felt for this white man.

With hard-fought patience, Nicholas tried reasoning with her again. "I wish I could make you understand that you cannot go about dressed as you are. You would be the object of hatred and intolerance."

She turned away from him, and to show her defiance, she kicked at the gown once more.

With a hiss of anger, he pulled her forward. When she realized he intended to dress her himself, as he had warned, she quickly dipped down and picked up the gown. Her heart was pounding as she backed away from him.

Nicholas's anger melted away when he saw the fright in the girl's eyes. He had not meant to be so harsh with her, but he knew something she did not know—he knew that since George Custer's rendezvous with death, hatred and deep resentment was rampant for the Indian. This girl could not know that it was for her own good that he could not allow her to travel to St. Louis looking like the half-breed that she was.

Alanna took another tentative step backward, knowing she would have to wear the hateful gown. She was helpless against this man's overpowering strength, and she resented the fact that he seemed to think he could control her life. She had to find a way to get away from him—she must!

Thinking she was at last submissive, and with a nod of approval, Nicholas crossed the room and paused at the door. "You can pack your belongings in that leather satchel Wiley provided for you. I'll be back for you in five minutes. I suggest you be quick, because the stage driver will not like being kept waiting." He smiled at her look of apparent unconcern. "But then you don't understand me, do you? Where's that damn Chappell when I need him?"

As the door closed behind Captain Ballinger, Alanna wasted no time in stripping off her buckskin gown and slipping into the blue print. Her fingers were awkward as she hooked the neck and stepped back to survey herself in the mirror. This gown did no more to hide her emaciated body than her own had.

"Look at you," she said, speaking in English for the first time in many months. "Will you pass for a white woman, do you think?"

With a shrug of her shoulders, she scooped up her gown and delicately touched the blue and green beads her grandmother had so lovingly sewn across the bodice and threaded through the fringe at the bottom of the skirt. She set her chin stubbornly. No one could force her to leave this gown behind; it was the only thing she had left of her grandmother. It was a reminder of the life she should have had as Gray Falcon's woman.

For a moment, daring flared in Alanna's eyes. Why did she allow that man to order her about? She shook her head, knowing that for now, his was the position of strength. It would be better not to provoke Captain Ballinger until she knew she could win. She placed her gown in the satchel, as he had instructed, and walked to the door.

With one last sweeping glance at the room where she had spent the last three weeks, she knew she would feel no regret at leaving here. There had been times, in the first few days, when she had thought she was going to die, indeed had wanted to die, but Captain Ballinger had pulled her back from the jaws of death. Well, she was not going to thank him for it!

Cautiously she opened the door and stepped out to find Captain Ballinger talking with Wiley Chappell.

"I'm only going to escort her as far as St. Louis, then I will be well rid of her, thank God."

"I hope her father will appreciate what you have done for his daughter," Wiley said, pulling on his pipe and watching the smoke circle his head. At that moment he noticed Alanna and smiled at her. In the tongue of the Cheyenne he spoke: "You were a very sick girl, but you look well now, Alanna. I hope you have a good life with your father."

She looked into the compassionate eyes of the Indian agent and glared at him because she felt as if he had betrayed her by turning her over to Captain Ballinger. "I will not be going to my father," she stated flatly.

Wiley chuckled. "You are strong-willed, Alanna," he nodded at Nicholas, "but this white man has a stronger will than you do. I am afraid you will lose in this instance. Trust him to know what's best for you."

"I thank you for your kindness to me, Wiley Chappell, but you will see me again before long." She stiffened her back and marched out the door without a backward glance.

Nicholas stared at her curiously. "What was that all about?"

Wiley's eyes danced with humor. "What it translates to is, you are going to have a fight on your

65

hands, Captain. Don't turn your back on that cunning little miss for a moment, or she'll be gone. Mark my words, she is going to be nigh on impossible to control."

"Well, then, I shall be thankful to turn control of her over to Miss Wickers once we reach St. Louis. What I shall do with her until then, I cannot imagine."

In a gesture of camaraderie, Wiley Chappell clapped Nicholas on the back. "I have been pleased to know you, Captain. I'd be mighty grateful if you would write and tell me how this all comes out. After all, I have an interest in that young lady's future."

The two men shook hands, and Nicholas moved out the door.

Alanna waited outside, glad that she and Captain Ballinger appeared to be the only passengers leaving from the reservation. Since the drivers were occupied with hitching the horses, she moved around the coach, curiously peering in the window. With a slender finger, she traced the highly varnished red trim on the door. Suddenly she wondered what it would feel like to travel in this wondrous mode of transportation.

Hearing footsteps behind her, Alanna spun around to find Captain Ballinger peering down at her. He reached around her and opened the door. Before she could protest, he lifted her inside and plopped her on the seat.

Alanna whirled to face him as he dropped onto the seat opposite her. With his usual amused smile, he tossed a woolen blanket in her direction.

"This will keep you warm until we reach St. Louis; then I'll buy you a warm cape," he explained.

66

"You have been very ill and cannot go running around in the dead of winter improperly attired."

She merely gave him a haughty glance, but it was cold, so she pulled the blanket about her for warmth.

When the coach started off with a jerk, he spoke to her. "Are you ready to start on the first leg of your journey, little savage?"

She had the strongest urge to tell him that she was not a savage, but instead, she sank back in the soft seat, turning her face away from him, knowing the moment would come when she would get even with this overbearing man. She had visions of sticking a knife between his ribs or pushing him off the edge of a cliff. The thought of seeing him suffer brought a smile of satisfaction to her lips.

As if Captain Ballinger had read her mind, he raised his eyebrow and shook his head. "You would be well advised not to try anything foolish," he warned. Then, pulling his hat down over his face, he propped his booted feet on the seat beside her and appeared to drift off to sleep.

Alanna glanced out the window, watching the scenery, wondering if their journey would take them near Cheyenne country. She would not be sorry to see the end of this harsh country that had robbed her of her grandmother. She yearned for the tall pines, the lush green meadowlands, and the rushing streams of her home.

She was confused. Where did she belong, in the land of her birth, or in this land where her grandmother was buried? One thing that was certain, she did not belong in Captain Nicholas Ballinger's world, and she never would.

She glanced across at the sleeping white man, puzzling over his character. Why had he nursed her back to health when he so obviously did not like her?

No matter where life took her from here, it would never be the same, now that Nicholas Ballinger had entered it.

Trying to clear her mind, she relaxed against the seat, while her head rocked back and forth with the movement of the coach. Soon she was lulled into a dreamless sleep.

The stage had been clipping along at a fine pace when the driver failed to see a deep rut in the road and Alanna was jostled awake by the careening of the coach. Grabbing out to steady herself, she flew off the seat, and her body slammed against Nicholas Ballinger's.

For a moment she was too stunned to react. Strong arms went about her to brace her, and she was clasped so tightly against him she could actually feel the rise and fall of his chest. They were so close she could feel his breath on her cheek.

With rounded eyes, she glanced up at his face. His features were bold and handsome. When she stared into those disturbing green eyes, she felt a strange weakness wash over her, and all she could do was tremble. She tried to think of Gray Falcon, but the vision of him was clouded by a pair of piercing green eyes.

Somehow needing to feel this man's closeness, yet frightened of that need, she pushed away from him so quickly that she tumbled onto the floor.

With amused laughter, Nicholas reached down for her, only to have her push his hands away.

"All right," he laughed, raising his arms in a gesture of surrender. "I promise not to touch you." His amusement deepened when he saw her scowl at him.

Alanna climbed onto the seat, her eyes watchful and alert for any sudden move from him. She wished someone would tell her what had just happened to her. Why, even now, did she want to lay her head on those broad shoulders and have him assure her that everything would be all right?

Misreading her expression, he spoke: "You are an uncivilized little savage, ready to tear a man's heart out and feed it to the buzzards, aren't you? You don't trust me at all, do you? I wonder what caused you to be so suspicious of everyone, or is it just the white race you mistrust?" There was compassion in his eyes. "Chances are your life has been hell."

She wanted to ignore him, but his warm gaze kept drawing her attention. She suddenly wanted to know all about Nicholas Ballinger. What kind of life could there be waiting for him in Virginia? A disturbing thought came to her. What kind of woman would it take to make those unusual green eyes soften with love?

She stared across at his strong hands and dared to speculate on what he would be like as a lover. Embarrassed and unsettled by her daring thoughts, Alanna glanced quickly out the window, looking at, but not seeing, the passing scenery. What was the matter with her? Had she no loyalty in her heart for her dead love?

Like every young girl who'd grown up in the Cheyenne village, Alanna knew something about the relationship between a man and a woman, but she had never thought much about it, at least not until she had prepared to marry Gray Falcon. He had awakened many new emotions within her, and when he had been killed, she had thought those emotions had died with him. It was troubling to learn that was not the case.

She had known Captain Ballinger for a few short weeks, and already he had turned her world upside-down. Since he had insinuated himself into her life, he had controlled her every move, and thoughts of him dominated her mind.

Glancing in his direction, she noticed that the captain seemed to have lost interest in her and had once again pulled his hat over his face.

Alanna felt the icy winds seep under the door of the coach. Reaching for the blanket that lay on the seat beside her, she wrapped it about her, feeling cold in the very depths of her soul.

She remembered her grandmother once telling her about one of the old women who lived in their village. The poor woman was always moaning and complaining about how bad her life was, and Blue Flower Woman had explained to Alanna that the pathetic woman had winter in her soul.

Staring at the bleak and desolate countryside, the trees stripped of their foliage, icicles hanging from their bare branches, Alanna shivered inside, thinking she was like that poor woman, and wondering if spring would ever come into her own soul again.

Chapter Seven

On the level stretch of road the six stage horses were running full-out. Alanna had been traveling with Captain Ballinger for three days, and the two of them had settled into an undeclared truce.

Alanna still looked for any opportunity to get away that might present itself, but so far Captain Ballinger had made escape impossible.

Each night when they stopped at a way station, Alanna would go directly to the room that was assigned to her and stay until the next morning when it was time to leave again. And each day Captain Ballinger would meet her at breakfast and escort her to the stagecoach to resume their seemingly endless journey.

At that moment Alanna could feel Captain Ballinger's eyes on her. She concentrated on the hill the coach was climbing, so she would not give in to the urge to look at him.

Nicholas glanced at the Indian girl while her face was in profile to him. The setting sun cast a soft pink hue on her features, and he was suddenly touched by a beauty so deep that it left him breathless.

Shaking his head to clear it, he spoke more to

himself than to her. "We are coming to the way station where we will spend the night."

Alanna turned to look at him and caught him staring at her with a strange expression in his green eyes. Their eyes locked, and she could not look away. She was not conscious that she had stopped breathing, she only knew that his eyes were pulling at her. Her lungs suddenly filled with air, and she forced herself to look away, knowing she would be lost if she allowed this man to gain control of her heart.

Nicholas laughed softly as he watched her shrink from him. "There is more to you than surface beauty, little savage."

At last the way station loomed ahead of them, and Alanna was glad when the stage came to a halt in front of a long sod building. Before the driver could climb down to help her Alanna pushed the door open and jumped to the ground.

As she moved away, she could hear the driver's voice. "You'll find most every comfort here, Captain Ballinger. The Buckners set a mighty fine table. Though the food's not fancy, it does go down mighty good."

"What time will we pull out in the morning?" Nicholas queried, more interested in continuing the journey than in the promise of food.

The driver stroked his beard thoughtfully. "We'll head out at first light, like we always do, Captain. Just see that you and the little lady are on time."

Alanna entered the station with dread and apprehension. Civilization was crushing in on her, and she was frightened by the many unfamiliar things she had seen. She examined the room with deliberation: the lamp with the red globe, the braided rug near the fireplace, gleaming copper pots and pans that lined the wall near the cook stove.

Feeling Captain Ballinger just behind her, she knew there were many questions whirling around in her mind, but she would not voice them since she had convinced him that she neither spoke nor understood English.

Now, as the motherly Molly Buckner smilingly introduced herself to Nicholas and Alanna, it made it even more difficult for Alanna to remain silent because she was warmed by her hostess's kindness. There was something about the elderly woman which reminded Alanna of Blue Flower Woman. Perhaps it was the way her eyes twinkled, or the gnarled hands that attested to the hard labor she performed in her everyday life.

"I'm just laying supper on the table," Mrs. Buckner pattered on, wiping her hands on her apron. "I hope you're hungry, because I got fresh biscuits, fatback, gravy, beans, and molasses. Just come along now, me and my husband ate hours ago, but you won't have to eat alone. Got a family to share the meal with you. They arrived just ahead of you."

Mrs. Buckner led the way to the crude wooden table where three other people were already seated. "This is the Flemming family, and they are on their way to Fort Union." Mrs. Buckner looked first at Nicholas, then at Alanna. "Captain Ballinger, Miss Caldwell, make the acquaintance of Mr. and Mrs. Flemming and their daughter, Grace."

Soon Alanna found herself squeezed in between Mrs. Flemming and her daughter. Nicholas was seated across the table beside Mr. Flemming.

Niceties were exchanged while Nicholas explained to the Flemmings that Alanna could not speak English. Right away they lost interest in her, which allowed Alanna time to study them in detail.

Mr. Flemming seemed a jolly man, with a round

73

face and body. Alanna could not help noticing that when he laughed, he both shook and quivered. Mrs. Flemming was the opposite of her husband, tall and thin, with a dour expression that hardened her features and made her hooked nose prominent. The daughter was surprisingly pretty, with soft brown hair and equally brown eyes. It was clear that those dark eyes glistened as Miss Fleming turned them on Captain Ballinger.

Alanna then directed her attention to Nicholas Ballinger, seeing a different side of him. With the pretty Grace Flemming, he was gracious and polite, using manners he had never bothered to use in his dealings with Alanna.

Alanna could not hide her curiosity as she peeked sideways at Grace, who could not be much older than she, and who, in a fashionable gown of yellow print with a matching bonnet, was the most beautiful girl Alanna had ever seen.

At the other way stations Alanna had always taken her meals in her room. She had not dined at a table since her childhood with her father, and was unaccustomed to eating with the utensils that had been placed beside her plate. She glanced across at Nicholas, and as if he understood what she was feeling, he encouraged her with his warm smile. Picking up his fork, he indicated that she should do the same.

It suddenly became clear to Alanna that she knew little of the white world. She could see how attentive Nicholas was being to Grace Flemming, and she found herself wishing for the same treatment. But why should she have these feelings? She hated Captain Ballinger, didn't she?

All of a sudden it became important to her that she not shame herself before these people. Each move

Grace Flemming made was mimicked by Alanna, and no one was the wiser, with the exception of Nicholas, who knowingly arched his brow at her.

Alanna was so caught up with imitating Grace Flemming that she hardly tasted the food and was glad when the meal was over and everyone had moved away from the table and into the sparsely furnished sitting area that had been set aside for the use of the guests.

The conversation between the men revolved around the reconstruction of the South, and something called carpetbaggers, which Alanna did not understand at all.

Grace and her mother were seated near the front window, both sewing dainty patterns on fragile pieces of material. They did not make any effort to include Alanna in their conversation—of course they had been led to believe she could not understand English.

It soon became apparent to Alanna that Grace Flemming was preoccupied with watching Captain Ballinger, and even though her eyes appeared to be downcast, the girl observed his every move.

Alanna was fascinated with the subtle tactics the white girl employed to engage the captain's attention. She was amused when Grace batted her eyelashes and simpered coyly every time Nicholas looked in her direction.

Nicholas, however, appeared to be totally unaware of the girl's admiration, since he and Mr. Flemming were deep in a conversation about the futility of trying to regain one's self-respect after losing a war.

At last Mrs. Flemming insinuated herself into the men's conversation. "Tell me, Captain Ballinger, where is your final destination?"

"First to Washington, Madame, then on to my

home in Virginia."

"Saints preserve us," Mrs. Flemming said, beaming. "A fellow Virginian." Her brow furrowed in a frown as if she was vexed about something. "Of course, I *am* puzzled as to why you are wearing the uniform of the Union, Captain. Could you so easily throw off the gray of the South—assuming you fought with your fellow Southerners?"

Nicholas's eyes were expressionless, his voice dull. "Yes, I fought for the glory of the South. But there is no longer a Confederacy, Mrs. Flemming. The government in Washington would have us believe we are again united as one country. Many of us have been forced to put the hostilities behind us."

Mrs. Flemming peered over the rim of her spectacles indignantly. "I hope then that your home came through the war unscathed, because we were not so fortunate, or so forgiving toward our enemies, Captain. Our home in Richmond was gutted by fire, and has only recently been rebuilt, but not in the grand style it was before the war. Nor will it ever be. We were ruined, as were so many of our friends."

Nicholas's eyes became cold, as if he were remembering something unpleasant. "I suppose you could say I was fortunate, Madame. Even though my home is outside Arlington, where some of the heaviest fighting took place, it sustained very little damage."

Mrs. Flemming's eyes gleamed with a sudden realization. "Are you perchance from Fairfax County, Captain?"

His tone was dull, for he knew what was coming. "Yes, Madame."

"Why, then you must be one of the Ballingers of Ballinger Hall," she said in astonishment. "Can that be true?"

"Yes, Mrs. Flemming, I have that distinction," Nicholas admitted guardedly, somewhat on the defensive now. "My home is Ballinger Hall."

"One of Virginia's proudest families . . . until . . . until . . ." Mrs. Flemming stammered, and then her voice trailed off when she remembered what she had heard. Her face reddened before she continued. "Captain, I . . . that is we . . . do not believe a word of the scandal attached to your family."

Her eyes gleamed and she hurriedly continued, "It is said that the man who was executed by the Yankees was the head of the Ballinger family. As I recall, he came home unexpectedly one night and found his faithless wife in a very compromising situation with a Yankee officer. The poor man, enraged at the betrayal of his wife, shot the Yankee, thus bringing Northern justice down upon his head."

The foolish Mrs. Flemming was unmindful that Nicholas had tensed and that his eyes were growing colder by the minute.

When Nicholas glanced at Alanna, she could see pain in the sparkling depths of his green eyes, and she wondered what tragedy had touched his life. What was the white woman talking about? What had happened in the captain's family to cause the pain she saw etched on his face?

Mrs. Flemming was thoughtful for a moment. "As I see it, that Mr. Ballinger was within his rights to shoot the Yankee; but as I was told, he was placed before a firing squad by the Yankee officer's men without benefit of a trial." Her mouth opened in excitement, and her eyes were bright with curiosity. "Was the man involved in the shooting a close relative of yours, Captain Ballinger?"

Nicholas's eyes were cold and penetrating as he glanced at the woman. "Yes, you might say that. He

77

was my father. As for the truth—there are truths and half-truths, Mrs. Flemming. I find people will believe what they want to believe."

"Then that means the woman was your moth . . ." Grace Flemming was shocked into speechlessness.

"What *was* the truth of that incident, Captain?" Mrs. Flemming pressed, eager to have the whole story.

"It depends on which version you want to believe, Mrs. Flemming," Nicholas said in an embittered voice. "Your version was, of course, an embroidered one. Very few people know what really occurred that night, myself included." He smiled at the shock on the faces of mother and daughter. "I'm sure the real truth would appall you even further."

"Does your mother still reside at Ballinger Hall, Captain?" Mrs. Flemming questioned.

Now Nicholas was angered by the woman prying into his private life. "I do not know, Madame. I never went home after the war—I have not been home since my father was executed."

"Now, see here," Mr. Flemming spoke up, a note of reprimand in his voice for his wife and daughter. "A man's business is his own, and he doesn't need prying females pestering him with rumor and innuendo."

Alanna saw a muscle twitch in Nicholas's jaw, and she could only speculate as to what was going on in his mind. She observed Grace Flemming when, with compassion in her eyes, the girl reached out and placed a small gloved hand on Nicholas's. "Papa is right, Captain Ballinger, I am sure you must know that Mama and I never meant to dredge up painful memories for you."

Nicholas's expression did not soften. "Do not give it another thought, Miss Fleming. I have faced curiosity and questions about my family many times since my father shot my mother's lover!"

If he had meant to shock the occupants of the room, he succeeded admirably. Silence hung heavily in the air, and Grace Flemming's face drained of color as she quickly withdrew her hand from his arm. "How . . . horrible of you, Captain."

Mrs. Flemming folded her sewing and stood up. Avoiding Nicholas's eyes, she spoke: "I believe it is time for us to retire. Tomorrow will be a long day."

"Not just now, Mama," Grace insisted, not wanting to let the evening end in a misunderstanding. Now that she had time to digest what had happened to Captain Ballinger's family, she was further intrigued by this handsome and arrogant man. "Could we not talk of something more pleasant, Captain Ballinger?"

Nicholas understood her completely. Some women wanted to mother him; others thought they could change him for the better. For whatever the reason, women seemed to flock around him, and he was not one to turn away from a beautiful lady, whatever the reason for her attraction to him.

"We could turn the conversation, and I could ask *you* questions," he said, giving her a devastating smile.

"Such as?" she responded flirtatiously, much to her parents' dismay.

"Such as . . . why you are so far from home, Miss Flemming?"

She dimpled at him. "We are going to visit my married sister, Franny. Her husband has a trading post near Fort Union. I confess I am already weary of this journey and cannot wait to get back to civilization, especially with all the trouble concerning the Indians. What are *you* doing so far from Virginia, Captain?" she asked, her brown eyes sparkling with interest.

"I am not here by choice. I was assigned to Indian territory, along with many fellow Southerners. I suppose the government was at a loss as to what to do with us and thought we would cause less trouble if our time was spent trying to keep peace with the Indians." He glanced at Alanna. "You see, the United States government found a solution for both former Confederate soldiers and troublesome Indians; the first they put in uniform and banished to obscurity; while the other they drove onto reservations, where many starved to death because of neglect."

"You sound as if you have empathy for the Indians," Mr. Flemming observed. "I can assure you that my family and I do not. I would sooner see them all dead. Of course, I have very little sympathy for Colonel Custer, since he was a Yankee, but the attack was brutal and wanton. Even a Yankee should not have suffered such a fate. It was completely inhuman."

Nicholas glanced at Alanna. "One need not be of the white race to experience inhumanity. I have seen firsthand what we have done to the Indian, and I have come to believe that the attack on Custer was provoked." No one was more surprised by that admission than Nicholas himself. Alanna looked into his eyes as if searching for the truth.

Mrs. Flemming shivered. "Let's not talk any more about Indians, Captain." Her eyes were probing. "I was just wondering . . . isn't it true that in order to serve as a soldier for the Union, you would have had to sign an oath of allegiance to the United States?" she asked, her small pinpoint eyes gleaming.

Nicholas was impatient with the woman's prodding. "It seemed the sensible thing to do under the circumstances," he answered. Suddenly he stood up and moved to the fireplace, putting an end to the inquisition. His eyes wandering again to Alanna, who sat demurely, hands folded in her lap, looking as if she was uninterested in the drama that was going on around her.

Mrs. Flemming's attention now turned to Alanna as her new target, and she could no longer contain her curiosity about the silent girl who seemed oblivious to her surroundings. "Tell me, if you know, Captain Ballinger," Mrs. Flemming puffed up her small bosom with indignation, "how is it possible that this young girl is traveling alone? We all know it's not at all proper for a young lady to go about the country without a proper chaperon."

Alanna merely looked into the woman's eyes, and then glanced away, as if she had not comprehended her meaning.

Mrs. Flemming tapped Alanna on the shoulder. "Where is your traveling companion?" she said, thinking that if she spoke slowly and in a loud voice, perhaps the girl would be able to understand her.

Alanna's eyes burned with anger as she glared back at Mrs. Flemming. With a violent shrug, she threw the woman's hand off her shoulder and stood up, moving toward the bedroom Molly Buckner had placed at her disposal for the night.

"Well, I never," Mrs. Flemming declared. "Such lack of manners. She's . . . nothing but a . . ."

A faint smile curved Nicholas's lips as he watched Alanna sail out of the room and slam the door behind her. "Your criticism is lost on Miss Caldwell. As I explained to you, she does not speak or understand English."

The woman's face whitened. "More the reason she should not be traveling alone. Is she from one of those heathen countries where they aren't educated in English?"

"You aren't far from the truth," Nicholas admitted. "You see, Alanna Caldwell was raised by the Cheyenne."

The color drained from Mrs. Flemming's face, and her daughter gasped, words of disbelief pouring out. "Do you mean to say she was abducted by savages?"

"No, Miss Flemming, I don't mean that at all. You see, Miss Caldwell is half Indian, and was raised by her mother's people, the Cheyenne."

Grace stared blankly at the door which Alanna had disappeared behind moments before, obviously horrified by Nicholas's confession. She swallowed with revulsion. "How horrible. What an unworthy creature she is. She shouldn't be allowed to travel on public conveyances with decent folks. Why, she could slit our throats while we sleep!"

"Disgusting," Mrs. Flemming admonished. "How could her father, a white man . . . be with an Indian?"

"Poor little creature," Mr. Flemming said with more tolerance than his wife and daughter displayed. "She doesn't look like an Indian."

Mrs. Flemming was watching Nicholas closely. "How is it that you know so much about her, Captain? Do you know her destination?"

Alanna could hear the conversation taking place on the other side of the door, and her sapphire eyes sparkled with anger. Why did it seem that Nicholas Ballinger was deliberately exposing her to the ridicule of the Flemmings? Did he gain some twisted pleasure from tormenting and belittling her?

Nicholas's voice was calm as he spoke. "You might be interested in knowing that Miss Caldwell is under my protection, Mrs. Flemming."

"Do you mean she is traveling with you?" the woman questioned in horror. Grace Flemming could be heard to gasp, a habit she had that was beginning to annoy Nicholas.

"Yes, I am her escort, at least as far as St. Louis. You must have observed that Miss Caldwell and I are two of a kind; we are both social outcasts, although you have been less charitable to Miss Caldwell, who is innocent of any wrongdoing, than to me, and I'm more deserving of your contempt."

The silence that followed Nicholas's declaration was tension-filled. Alanna realized that Nicholas had not intended to shame her, but rather to hold himself up to ridicule. What had happened in his past that had caused him to have so little regard for the opinions of others? Why was he so cynical about life? She knew it had something to do with his mother and father, but she had no pity for him. He did not deserve her consideration—he was a white man.

She turned away from the door to stand at the window, where heavy snowflakes were drifting out of an ebony sky. She would not soon forget the humiliation she had felt tonight. She had been forced to stand by silently while her people were criticized by the Flemmings, who, if the truth were known, had never met an Indian, much less a Cheyenne.

If they were an example of what one could expect of white people, Alanna dismissed the whole race, especially Captain Ballinger, whose thoughtless remarks continually hurt her.

Alanna stared down at her moccasin-clad feet, wishing she had insisted on wearing her elkskin gown so that everyone would know that she was proud of her Cheyenne blood.

She was not ashamed of her people, at least not of her Cheyenne mother. She was not so sure about her white father, or the family that waited for her in this place called Fairfax County, Virginia.

Chapter Eight

Alanna tossed and turned on the lumpy bed while sleep eluded her. Realizing her mind was too filled with questions for her to find any peace, she slipped out of bed and moved across the cold floor to stand at the window. She was accustomed to an airy lodge, and this room seemed hot and stuffy. It took her only a few moments to locate the latch on the window, and she pushed it open wide. Breathing deeply, she filled her lungs with the icy, fresh air.

It had stopped snowing, and from the position of the full moon riding high in the indigo sky, she judged it to be midnight. It was so quiet that she could hear the coach horses softly neighing from the nearby barn and icicles falling off the roof.

Alanna watched as her breath came out in puffs of frosted mist, and wondered what tomorrow would be like; she would again be forced to share the coach with Captain Ballinger. At least she would be away from the Flemmings, with their hateful remarks and accusing glances. She suddenly felt the chill of the night wind and shivered.

Tonight Alanna had discovered that she was entering a world she was ill prepared for, one where she did not know the rules. There were many things she did not understand about the white race; their lack of kindness was foremost in her mind. For no reason at all, she had felt the sting of Mrs. Flemming's sharp tongue, although the woman did not know her or anything about her situation.

Alanna frowned when she thought of Grace Flemming. She would never act foolish with a man as Grace had done. She had found the whole episode distasteful, as well as deceitful. For some reason she could not understand, she was annoyed with Nicholas Ballinger because he had apparently encouraged Miss Flemming's absurd attempts to attract his attention. She thought back to when she and Gray Falcon had declared their love for one another. There had been no sly glances or flirtatious movements. There had been only honesty and openness between them.

Suddenly fear struck at Alanna's brave heart. The world as she had known it had crumbled into nothingness, and the unknown future was far more frightening to her than anything she had thus far had to endure.

With a resigned feeling of dread, Alanna realized that if she were going to escape, it would have to be soon. If she waited much longer, she might never find her way back home. Inside her there was an ache for her old way of life, when she had known the security of her grandfather's and grandmother's protection and the wonder of Gray Falcon's love. She longed for the comforting arms of Gray Falcon. But that was in the past and lost to her forever. Even if she did manage to escape, she would never be able to return to the home of her childhood, she could never recapture what had been lost.

Feeling desperately alone, she wiped away the tears

that trickled down her cheek.

Suddenly Alanna's senses became alert, and she drew back into the shadows. With a practiced ear, she listened to the sound of crunching footsteps on the frozen snow and wondered who would be about at this time of night. When the shadowy figure moved into her view, she recognized Nicholas Ballinger.

Apparently he had not detected her presence, because he casually leaned against the hitching post outside her window and stared into the night. It was obvious that he could not sleep either.

Alanna studied Nicholas's silhouette, wishing she could guess what was on his mind.

If only he would turn around, she could see the expression on his face and she might be able to read his thoughts. Was he troubled about memories of his mother and father?

Now a new sound could be heard—the sound of the front door opening. Nicholas must have heard it too, because he turned in that direction. Alanna heard Grace Flemming's high-pitched voice, and she watched Nicholas stiffen as the woman's footsteps approached.

"Captain Ballinger, I had no notion you were out here. I just came out for a breath of air."

He turned and the faint light fell on his face. Alanna saw his sardonic smile. "You have a tedious journey ahead of you tomorrow, Miss Flemming. Shouldn't you get some rest?"

Grace now moved into Alanna's view, and Alanna could see she was all bundled up in a heavy cloak with nothing but her pale face peeping out.

"To tell the truth, Captain," Grace confessed daringly, "I heard your footsteps when you walked past my room. I followed you here because I wanted to talk to you." She moved closer to him. "Does that

86

surprise you?"

He did not answer at first, but assumed a stance that showed his aggravation. At last he said: "Your coming here can cause trouble for you and me, Miss Flemming. Neither your mother nor your father would approve of a midnight rendezvous. If you return at once, they will not be the wiser, and you will have saved yourself a severe rebuke, and save me having to proclaim my innocence in the matter."

Grace placed her hand on his arm and stared up at him with a wistful expression. "I don't care what anyone thinks, I wanted to talk to you. I am aware of what you were feeling when we were discussing your parents tonight. I just want you to know that it makes no difference to me that your parents disgraced the Ballinger name. I will not think any less of you because of their sins."

Nicholas shook her hand off his arm while a muscle in his cheek knotted. "So you have decided to be magnanimous, have you? And what have I done that I should climb so high in your esteem?"

Grace raised her face to him, intrigued not only by his handsomeness, but by his aloofness as well. "I think . . . I think you are hurting and need a woman who understands you."

Alanna watched as Nicholas grabbed Grace by the shoulders and brought her closer to him. "Do you think so?" he asked in a stiff voice. "Do you fancy yourself in that role?"

"I . . . would like to comfort you."

"I find no comfort in a woman's arms." He arched an eyebrow. "Nor do I want to."

"No one could understand you like I do," she persisted.

"I can assure you I have had many women in my life, and none of them understood me—I doubt that

87

you would either, Miss Flemming."

"I . . . could try," she said breathlessly. "I want to help you."

"Miss Flemming, you have no notion what goes on inside the mind of a man like me. If you did, you would run for your very life."

Slipping her hood from her head, Grace Flemming tossed her hair in an attempt to be flirtatious. "I am not frightened of you. I never could be."

He drew her even closer. "Well, you should be afraid."

Her breath came out in a puff of frosted air. "Why, Captain?" she asked breathlessly.

"It's very simple. I have little trust for your sex. Anything I would feel for a female would only be short-lived and leaves me unencumbered afterward." He paused, allowing her to ponder his words. "Do you get my meaning?"

Grace gasped at his bold words. "I . . . don't really understand."

"Exactly. But you were so certain you understood me a moment ago," he reminded her.

"I don't care what you say to me, or what your reasons are, I want to be with you," Grace insisted, throwing her arms around his neck. "When I first saw you today, I knew you were an exceptional man and different from all the men I had ever known. Now that I know your background, I know why."

"What could there be about me that would possibly interest you?" His tone was insolent, his stance arrogant, as if he was accustomed to dealing with women who threw themselves at him. "Could it be you are intrigued with the scandal that is attached to the Ballinger name? Or perhaps it is the money and property that goes with that name that interests you."

"Neither," she insisted, undaunted. "I care only about you. I want to help you get over the tragedy in your life. I want to help you forget about how your father died. I could, if you would only allow it."

"Ah, I see. You think I need mothering, and you're just the one to do it. Well, I don't need a mother. You forget I have a mother, tarnished reputation and all."

Alanna knew she should not be watching, but she was fascinated by what was taking place. She sensed that Grace was foolishly ignoring the danger signs, but Grace did not seem to be aware of the threat, and plunged on.

"No, I don't want to be your mother, Captain, but I can help you forget your sorrows."

In a quick, fluid move, Nicholas pulled Grace's face up and lowered his head until his mouth crushed hers, robbing her of speech and stealing her breath away.

Alanna watched, unable to turn away, while Nicholas held Grace Flemming in his arms. She had never seen a kiss before, and marveled at this strange custom. She felt her body tingle all over when she wondered what it would feel like to have Nicholas Ballinger's lips touch hers. Reaching up, she touched her mouth, shocked that she should want such intimate contact with him.

When Nicholas released Grace, she stumbled backward, her eyes round and luminous. "I knew this would happen between us," she said in a breathless voice. "Surely you can see that I would be good for you."

Nicholas's laughter came out in a cruel snarl. "Be warned about my feelings concerning women. There is only one reason I would attach myself to you or to any other woman. And believe me, you would not like my reason. You got what you came for, so run along to bed and thank whatever Providence you owe it too that you have escaped so easily."

As if he had already dismissed her from his mind, he seemed to glance right in Alanna's direction. "Get this through your head, Miss Flemming: I don't want your help or anyone else's to straighten out my tangled life."

Grace took another short step backward. "You . . . you hateful man. You deliberately misled me and humiliated me. I . . . I . . . hate you. I will always hate you!"

His laughter held a sinister note. "Alas, hate where moments ago love was in full bloom. How very fickle the feminine heart is. Is there any doubt as to why I am so weary of your sex?"

Grace was now out of Alanna's view, but she could hear retreating steps as Grace ran away. Moments later she heard the opening and closing of the door. Alanna knew enough about a woman's heart to realize that Nicholas Ballinger had wounded Miss Flemming deeply. Grace Flemming was a silly fool, but even so, Alanna felt pity for her.

"So, you couldn't sleep either, Blue Eyes," Nicholas spoke up as he moved to the window.

She was so astonished that Captain Ballinger should call her by the same name her grandfather had given her as a child, that she stared at him for a moment.

He loomed before her now. "Perhaps you were asleep and the little drama outside your window awakened you."

Alanna was embarrassed because he had caught her eavesdropping, but there was no rebuke in his voice, only regret in his eyes.

"You don't understand a word I'm saying, little Blue Eyes, so I can confess to you that I am weary of

90

females who think they can either reform me or make me happy. I can assure you the woman has not been born that can make a husband out of me, much less touch my heart."

She stared at him, still unwilling that he should discover that she understood his words only too well.

"You were hurt tonight by the Flemmings, weren't you?" he asked. "Perhaps it's my fault that we are both in disgrace, but I detest smugness and self-righteousness, and perhaps I went too far in my lame attempt to chastise Mrs. Flemming."

Alanna was disturbed by his confession and looked away.

"You don't know it yet, little Indian, but the world is full of ignorant but well-meaning people like the Flemmings. I fear you will meet with far more cruelty when you reach Fairfax County."

When Nicholas saw Alanna shudder, he wrongly assumed it was from the cold, so he closed the window partway and smiled at her. "People can be extremely ignorant of anything they don't understand. But I suspect you already know that."

Alanna shook her head, not because she did not understand his words, but because his meaning was unclear to her.

"Ah, well, perhaps your father will be able to deal with the Flemmings of the world. I certainly hope so, for your sake."

Alanna had many questions she wanted to ask the captain, but the words stuck in her throat.

"Go to sleep, Blue Eyes, and dream of a better world than this one."

With a shrug of her shoulders, she turned away, and heard him close the window all the way.

Lying down on her bed, she stared at the notched log ceiling overhead, her mind whirling with questions. Why had Nicholas touched his lips to Grace Flemming's? Surely anything so intimate as two lips touching was a show of affection. Why then had he turned Miss Flemming away so cruelly?

With a heavy sigh she turned on her side, dreading the next day, when she would have to be in the coach with Nicholas Ballinger. His presence was becoming very disturbing to her, though she did not know why.

She knew sleep would continue to elude her for the remainder of the night. She would be glad when the stage pulled out at first light. After that, she would not have to face the Flemmings again.

Chapter Nine

The jingle of the horses' reins was soon drowned out by the howling of the wind. As the day progressed, the blizzard intensified and pounded mercilessly against the stagecoach, which swayed drunkenly against the punishing onslaught.

Alanna huddled beneath the wool coverlet, feeling miserable and travel weary. She thought of the two men perched atop the coach and wondered how they were enduring the bitter cold. She hoped it was not far until they reached the way station so they could all be warm.

She took a furtive glance at Nicholas Ballinger, who appeared to be lost in thought as he stared out the window at the frozen landscape.

Since leaving the Flemmings behind three days ago, he had been silent and brooding, hardly sparing a glance in Alanna's direction. But then, she reminded herself, she did not want his attention.

Nicholas felt Alanna's eyes on him, and he looked at her reflectively.

"If only you could talk, Blue Eyes, what tales you could relate to me! No doubt you could entertain me endlessly until we reached St. Louis." His eyebrow arched. "But perhaps it's best you can't. Perhaps you would only bore me like all the others." His smile was sardonic. "More than likely you would sting me with your anger. You don't like me very well, do you?"

Alanna turned away from his probing glance, wondering when she had stopped disliking him. Certainly he had done nothing to win her approval, especially after the episode with the Flemmings. But still he intrigued her, and she wanted to know more about him.

She did not have long to speculate about her new interest in Nicholas Ballinger, because at the moment the coach came to a sliding halt and angry voices could be heard above the howl of the wind.

"Throw that money box down and be quick about it," a loud voice demanded. "Don't reach for your gun, or you're dead where you sit."

Nicholas tensed, his hand moving to the holster he wore at his waist. "Damn it," he swore in irritation. "We're being robbed."

Alanna watched Nicholas unhook the holster flap and withdraw his pistol. With a quick motion, he shoved her down on the floor of the stagecoach and threw a blanket over her head. "Stay put, and don't move or make a sound," he ordered in a voice of authority.

From her position under the blanket, Alanna could not see what was happening, but she clearly heard the gunfire erupt, followed by an oath uttered in pain. Another volley of shots resulted in a loud groan of anguish, and she knew both stage drivers had been shot!

The cold air alerted her to the fact that Captain Ballinger had opened the stagecoach door, and she quickly threw aside the blanket, needing to know what was happening. He was nowhere in sight, but she heard his voice issuing orders to their unseen assailants.

Apparently Captain Ballinger had the outlaws in his gunsight, because his voice was cold and threatening. "Drop your guns and stand back."

Alanna moved forward and cautiously slipped out the door and around the back of the stagecoach, where she would have a view of what was happening. She was horrified to see the prone bodies of the two stage drivers. They lay face up on the ground, where the snow was dyed red from their blood. From the looks of their sightless eyes staring blankly at nothing, she knew they were both dead.

Her eyes moved to the two outlaws, who held their hands in the air as Nicholas trained his pistol on them. The lower portion of their faces were covered with bandannas to hide their identity, and it gave them a sinister look.

From her vantage point, Alanna saw something Nicholas could not see; a third man was moving up silently behind him with his gun drawn!

"Captain Ballinger," she cried out as she watched the third man take aim at Nicholas's head. "Look out behind you! There is another one!"

When Nicholas turned, the man fired, and the bullet struck! Alanna reached toward the captain as the impact of the shot sent him staggering backward, where he slammed against the coach. With a look of amazement, he dropped the gun and slumped to his knees. With a sorrowful glance at Alanna, he collapsed and lay unmoving on the frozen ground.

Without thinking of the danger to herself, Alanna raced to Captain Ballinger's aid. She quickly dropped down beside him, feeling for a pulse—to her relief, she found a strong one. Deep inside, her anger was building. How dare those men shoot Captain Ballinger!

Her hand brushed against his pistol, and she quickly shoved it into the folds of her gown, wondering what to do next. She heard Nicholas moan, and she glanced down to see him watching her with a quizzical expression on his face.

The scrawny little girl bending over the fatally wounded captain seemed of little interest to the three outlaws. One of them gathered up the loot and searched the coach for valuables.

"Throw those bodies over the cliff, then push the coach over. That'll give us more time to make a clean getaway. I figure we got two-days' head start as it is," the man who seemed to be in charge speculated. "Chances are it'll snow and cover up the tracks anyway."

The other two men readily obeyed their leader. Alanna shuddered when they picked up the dead bodies of the drivers and shoved them over the embankment.

When one of the outlaws moved toward Alanna and she saw his intention was to throw Nicholas over the cliff with the others, she brandished the gun and aimed it at his heart.

"I do not care what you do with the others," she said with feeling, "but you will not touch this man. Go about with what you were doing, but leave him alone." Her eyes defied the man to take one step closer. "I warn you, white man, I never miss what I aim at."

At first the man was surprised that the skinny girl had so much courage. Something in her eyes made him believe she meant what she said, and he hesitated, looking to the leader for instructions.

"Leave her be," came the spoken command. "She

ain't worth fooling with, and she can't last long in this cold anyway. She'll be dead within hours. Unhitch the horses, and you and Bob push the coach over the cliff. We need to get going."

"What about the man?" the outlaw questioned.

"Leave him be, too. He's done for."

Alanna did not lower her weapon, but kept it trained on one man or another as they performed their tasks. The stagecoach soon disappeared over the sides of the icy cliff, crashing into the gully below. She felt momentary compassion for the two men who had lost their lives, but they were beyond her help now, whereas Captain Ballinger still lived, though for how long she could not guess.

When the outlaws were mounted, the one who was leading the coach horses drew reins beside Alanna. "I'd advise you to use that gun on yourself, little gal. If the wolves don't get you, the cold will. And there's always the Injuns, who may come to investigate the gunfire. Yep, if you're wise, you'll save a bullet for yourself." He nodded down at Nicholas, and for a moment the two men's eyes met—Nicholas's cold with contempt, the outlaw's coolly amused. "Your friend ain't going to make it. Serves the man right for trying to be a hero."

"Leave us alone," Alanna said, placing her body between Nicholas's and his tormentor. "Just ride on. We'll manage just fine."

The man shrugged, and she watched with a feeling of helplessness as all three of them rode away. She knew in her heart that their chances for survival were very slim indeed.

In the distance, the howling of a timber wolf reminded her of their vulnerability, and it seemed that already it had turned colder. She wondered how far it was to the next way station, but it did not matter, Captain Ballinger could not walk, and she would never leave him. After all, she owed him his life. If it had not been for her, he would be in Washington now. It was because he stayed behind to nurse her that he had found himself in this dreadful situation.

Glancing down, she saw that Nicholas was trying to speak, but no sound issued from his lips. She noticed he was having trouble focusing his eyes. With a soft moan, his head fell sideways and he lost consciousness.

She tried to think what her grandfather would do if he were faced with these grim circumstances. Instinct alerted her to the fact that they would need shelter above all else, and there was no time to waste, because it would soon be dark.

Her Indian upbringing had prepared her well, and she now sprung into action. Obviously their best means of shelter would be the coach, if she could just find a way to get Captain Ballinger down the hill.

A quick assessment of his wound revealed a gaping hole in his shoulder. It could have been worse—the bullet could have hit his heart. Already his blood-stained shirtfront was frozen with the congealed blood from his wound. Perhaps the cold was working in their favor, for it had slowed the bleeding.

Alanna realized she still had the blanket wrapped about her, so she quickly removed it and tucked it around Nicholas to keep him warm until she could decide how best to get him down the slope.

Moving to the edge of the ravine, she looked first for the bodies of the two men that had been killed. She spotted them further down a deep gully, sprawled out like lifeless dolls. She could not think about them now—there was no time. She saw that the coach had mercifully landed right side up, but it was

98

halfway down the slope, resting against a wide ledge.

Cautiously she slipped over the side of the ravine, taking care not to fall on the icy surface. After looking around for a short time, she finally located the wide board which had once served as the driver's seat on the stagecoach. It would be perfect to use as a sled to transport Nicholas down the slope to the shelter of the coach.

The ground was icy and slippery as she made her way back up the cliff, and the going was slow. She lost her footing many times, but she would always gain her feet and continue on. Fear was her armor against the cold.

Concentrating on the task at hand, she struggled toward the top and had almost made it when her foot slipped on the frozen snow and she went sliding back down the hill. With firm determination, she grasped the board and scrambled upward.

It seemed to her that the sounds of the wolves were coming closer. With difficulty, but a great deal of fortitude, she finally made her way up to the road where Captain Ballinger lay, looking as pale as the frozen snow.

"Can you help me?" she asked, dropping down beside him. "Can you rise enough to move onto this board?"

He moaned but did not acknowledge her urgent plea. Alanna struggled with the heavy body until at last she thought he could safely be moved down the embankment. Anyway, she reasoned, it would be far better to die of a broken neck then to freeze to death or be torn apart by hungry wolves.

With the sound of wolves drawing ever nearer, she pushed and tugged at the makeshift sled, until she had drawn it to the edge of the cliff. Aiming for the path that had been smoothed when the stagecoach had gone over, she slid the board over the side, jumped on, and pressed her body against Nicholas's to keep him from falling off. She had no control over where the sled would end up, but she tried to direct it toward the coach. Down they slid until, with a soft thud, the sled propelled itself against the side of the stagecoach, spilling her and Captain Ballinger onto the ground.

Alanna quickly scrambled to her feet, fearing Nicholas had been injured further. There was no time now to examine him, and she tugged and pulled until she finally maneuvered him inside the coach. She had never realized what a big man he was until she tried to fold his long legs inside the small space.

She quickly made the captain as comfortable as possible, knowing her ordeal was not yet over. She climbed out of the coach and quickly went through the scattered trunks and valises, looking for useful items. She took every article of clothing she found, because they could use it to keep warm. She found a leather bag that contained bandages and instruments and realized they would be useful in tending Nicholas's wound.

At last, frozen and thoroughly exhausted, she made her way back to the coach. She climbed inside and placed several wool jackets over Captain Ballinger, who was shivering with cold.

She examined both doors and was thankful that neither had been damaged when the stage had gone over the cliff. Closing them firmly, she paused for a moment to gather her thoughts.

The afternoon was almost spent, and there were dark storm clouds gathering in the eastern sky. It was getting colder, and Alanna knew it would not be long until the wolves would be upon them.

She dropped to her knees and felt around the floor

of the coach, searching frantically for Captain Ballinger's gun, but it was not there. She would need the gun to defend them in case the wolves broke through the door!

How close were the wolves now? Would she have time to climb back up the embankment and search for the gun? The captain's wounds needed tending. Which should she do first? How she wished her wise grandmother were here to advise her.

Since the captain's wound was not bleeding, Alanna decided the gun was the most urgent matter to attend to, so she tucked the blanket about him, eased herself out the door, and closed it firmly behind her.

Alanna knew she was the captain's only hope for survival. He was in no condition to take care of himself. If anything happened to her, he would have no chance at all—but then he probably would not survive anyway. Most probably neither of them would.

With Alanna's Indian training, it was not in her nature to give up hope or to leave anything to chance. With her eyes on the top of the embankment and her ears trained on the sound of the wolves, she made her way up the slippery incline. Going down on her knees, she searched until she found the gun. She then jumped to her feet, hurrying back down the hill, just as the wolves broke out of the woods nearby. She slid down the slope, hoping she would reach the safety of the coach before they got to her.

With trembling hands, she slammed the stagecoach shut, moments before the snarling beasts reached her sanctuary. She cringed inside, and her body shook with fear when the hungry animals hurled their bodies against the door with a force that rattled the windows.

After a while, Alanna could hear the wolves moving away. Soon after that there was loud snarling just beyond the stagecoach. With a shudder she realized that the wolves had discovered the bodies of the dead white men and were devouring them.

With a firm determination, she closed her mind to the wolves and pushed her fear aside—she had to tend Nicholas's wound. Going down on her knees, she ripped open his bloody shirt and examined him in the waning light. He was bleeding again, and she knew she had to remove the bullet at once.

Willing herself to remain calm, Alanna opened the black bag and took out one of the sharp instruments. With a steadying breath, she probed the wound, steeling herself to have courage. When she probed deep, Captain Ballinger winced in pain, even though he was unconscious. At last, relief washed over her as she found and withdrew the offending bullet.

If she were in her village, she would know just which medicines to apply to an open wound, but she was confused as she looked at the many bottles of medicine in the black bag. With uncertainty, she chose a brown salve and applied it to the wound. Then she bound the captain's shoulder with a snowy white bandage. She had done all within her power to help him, now all she could do was wait and see if it was enough.

He had not stirred since she had removed the bullet, and that was not a good sign. Touching his lips, she felt his faint breath on her hand.

For a long time she sat there with her hand resting on his chest, feeling his steady breathing. Surely it was a good sign that his breathing was not impaired. But he was weak, and he was still unconscious.

Alanna had a chance to reflect on the two men who had so senselessly lost their lives today. Perhaps they

102

were after all the fortunate ones. They would not have to slowly freeze to death or risk being torn apart by hungry wolves.

Later, during the night, Captain Ballinger's body began to tremble, and Alanna lay down beside him, hoping to lend him some of her warmth. She was cold and hungry, but that was nothing new; she had been cold and hungry before. Right now the most important thing to her was that Captain Nicholas Ballinger live.

Here, in the foreboding darkness, with the wolves and the biting cold wind howling outside the stagecoach, death was held at bay by a thin thread.

Chapter Ten

The night seemed to drag on forever. Alanna pressed her cold body tightly against Captain Ballinger's, drawing not only warmth from him, but courage as well, because several times the wolves returned to claw on the door and hurl themselves at the coach. She had heard nothing of them for some time, and she hoped they had given up and gone off in search of more accessible prey.

The pistol was never far from her hand as she strained to listen for any noise that would alert her that the wolves had returned. Alanna had been brought up to respect the wolf, and she would never wantonly kill one, but if it came to protecting herself and Captain Ballinger, she would not hesitate to shoot. She reached out her hand and touched the frosty window, knowing it would be little protection from any animal that wanted to gain entrance.

Now as she shivered and moved closer to Nicholas to borrow from his warmth, she heard him moan. Fearing she had hurt his wound, she drew back as his voice came out thick and questioning.

"Where am I? What in the hell has happened?"

"You are safe, Captain Ballinger. Go back to

sleep." Touching his forehead, she realized he was feverish. "You must save your strength, for you have been wounded." The English words came slowly to her lips since she had not spoken the language in a very long time.

"Who . . . are you?" he questioned, searching the darkness, and wondering where he was.

"I am Alanna, remember? Go back to sleep now, and I shall watch over you."

He tried to fight his way back to reality, but nothing seemed real in this world of darkness. Suddenly he remembered the outlaws and Alanna Caldwell fiercely protecting him from them. "Blue Eyes?" he asked. "Is it you?"

Her answer was whispered. "Yes, it is I. Please go back to sleep."

Easier in his mind, he sighed deeply and drifted into a shadowy world of sleep.

At least Captain Ballinger had awakened, and Alanna took that to be a good omen for his recovery.

Just before morning he roused again, but this time his muttering made little sense. "Damn you Yankees for killing my father! You punished the wrong person! It was my mother who was to blame! She is the one who needs to be punished!"

Alanna knew it would take more than her puny strength to hold Nicholas down to keep him from reopening his wound, so she talked to him in a soothing voice, hoping to assuage his fears with words. "Tomorrow, when you are better, you will worry about your mother and father. For now you must rest."

"All women are vixens. They will tear a man's heart out and betray him to his enemies."

"Do not think about that now," she soothed. "Think of something pleasant that happened to you

105

as a boy."

Nicholas felt the cool hand on his forehead and began to relax, his demons chased away by a soft-spoken word and an equally soft body. "I have sworn never to love a woman," he muttered to himself, "and I never will."

Alanna carefully clasped him in her arms and rested her cheek against his. "Sleep, Captain, sleep," she soothed. "Tomorrow will see you better."

Alanna did not know how long she had been asleep, but when she opened her eyes, the sun was slanting through the frosted window, making a dull pattern of light on the wall of the stagecoach. A quick glance told her that Nicholas still slept, though now his breathing was more even and the rise and fall of his chest was consistent.

Extracting herself from underneath his body was no easy task, for his head was cradled in her arms. With slow deliberation, so she would not disturb his much-needed sleep, she moved away from him. When she was free, she paused to look into his face.

His square jaw was testimony to his stubborn nature. His dark eyelashes lay against the shadows on his cheeks, long and silken, but not feminine. He was muscled and firm, tall and every inch a man. Never having been this close to a man, not even Gray Falcon, Alanna felt her face flush, but still she did not look away. The stubble of a beard amazed her, for she had never seen a man who needed a shave. Of course, there had been the white trappers with long beards, but they did not count. She touched his face gingerly and found the stubble scratchy, but in a pleasant sort of way. When was it that she had grown to appreciate his handsomeness?

Daringly, she touched his lips, wondering if he would awaken should she bend and press her lips to his. Deciding against such a bold act, her eyes wandered downward, past the white bandage on his shoulder to his bare chest.

Seeing the dark curly hair that covered his chest, she was amazed. She had not known that a man had hair on his chest—the Indians did not. This too she touched, finding it soft to the palm of her hand.

When he moved slightly, she quickly moved back and looked away, not wanting him to find her staring at him so closely. She held her breath, glad that he did not awaken. Pulling the blanket up to his chin, she resisted the urge to touch the dark hair that fell across his forehead.

Chiding herself for needless delay, she eased herself off the seat, still taking care not to disturb Captain Ballinger. Deciding it would be foolish to go about without a weapon, she retrieved the pistol from where it had fallen on the floor. Looking carefully out the window, she saw no sign of wolves, so she opened the door and breathed in the clear morning crispness. The clouds had moved away, and she was greeted by a clear blue sky.

Fresh snow had fallen during the night, and when she stepped down from the coach her leg was buried in snow up to the calf, making her glad she still wore her knee-length moccasins.

With a tentative look around, she knew her first task would be to forage for food. This did not concern her, for she had been taught to hunt from an early age.

She decided it would not be wise to fire the pistol, because she needed to save bullets should any real trouble arise, and she did not want to risk alerting any hostile forces of their whereabouts. The Indians of this land could well be enemies of the Cheyenne. It was best not to find out if they were friend or foe—another lesson taught her by her grandfather.

A surprisingly warm sun shone down on Alanna as she made her way down the incline toward a small stream in the distance. She knew it was always easier to catch small game at their watering place.

Standing with the sun on her face, breathing the air of freedom, she felt almost happy for the first time since Gray Falcon had been slain. That Captain Ballinger would recover, she now had little doubt, so she was not concerned for his health. Fate had stepped in and prevented the captain from taking her to her father, and she was not sorry for that, although where she would go from here, she did not know.

Her Indian-trained mind was sharp as she crouched down behind a tree. The stream was swift, and chunks of ice floated with the current. She waited and watched, blending into the scenery, as she had been taught.

It took only a moment for her to recognize and target her prey. A cottontail rabbit hopped unknowingly within the range of her carefully-aimed stone.

When Alanna returned to the stagecoach, she found Captain Ballinger attempting to rise.

"Damn it," he muttered, as weakness overcame him and he had to clutch the back of the leather seat for support. "Where have you been?" he asked, disgruntled, because he had been concerned for her safety when he'd awakened to find her gone. "Did it occur to you that I might need your help?"

She held up the rabbit for his inspection. "More than that, I thought you might be hungry."

"Hungry, hell. I forgot how food tasted." Suddenly his features froze, and he looked at her suspiciously. With effort he stood up and slipped out of the coach. "So, it wasn't a dream; you can speak English."

She leveled her gaze at him. "Yes, I always have. Actually, I am told it was my first language. I am also told that I speak my mother's language with an accent."

Weakly, he leaned his head back against the seat, trying to recall if he had ever said anything he should not have in her presence. "You could have told me," he said sourly. "Why did you think you had to be so secretive?"

She shrugged. "It seemed to suit you to think of me as an ignorant savage, so I indulged you."

He closed his eyes and moaned. "God, you sound just like your father. He could always turn a situation to his advantage."

She was now curious. "Was I doing that?"

"You were."

He stared at her tumbled appearance, her uncombed hair, the little face with the big eyes, which made her appear far younger than she was. "You have several of his traits. Like the way you hold your head, so sure of yourself. And he was always good with a quick answer to any question."

"You do not know me well enough to liken me to my father," she said stiffly. "I do not want to be like Anson Caldwell."

"You already are."

"I still say you do not know me well enough to say such things," she repeated stubbornly.

He glanced up the steep incline, and then at the wilderness beyond. "No, but I will, Blue Eyes. Before we get out of this, I will know you very well."

109

Alanna retrieved a knife from inside her moccasin and began cleaning the rabbit expertly, while Nicholas looked on, impressed with her unusual ability. Her certainly knew of no other woman who could so aptly skin a cottontail.

"I am told I look like my mother," she announced.

"Maybe so, but your eyes are definitely blue, like your father's."

She turned away, not wanting to hear that she was anything like the man who had abandoned her after her mother's death.

After a long moment of silence, Nicholas moved away, and Alanna went about her task, even though her first instinct was to rush to help him, but she thought better of it. She had already learned that he was a proud man, and proud men did not like to depend on a woman for help.

Setting the rabbit aside, she cleared the snow away, laid a fire, and soon had the rabbit roasting on a wooden spit.

When the captain returned sometime later, she could see he was pale, and his usual arrogant stance was hampered by pain, which caused him to stoop. In spite of his wound, he had managed to shave and dress himself in a fresh uniform, and he looked every inch the dashing young cavalry officer.

As his tall shadow fell across Alanna's face, she was aware that her hand trembled when she turned the spit.

"That smells good," he said, dropping down on a smooth rock and bracing his back against a narrow birch tree.

"My grandmother would have stuffed it with dried berries, wrapped it in leaves, and buried it in hot coals to roast for several hours." She sighed. "But of course, that is not possible here."

"You miss your grandmother, don't you?"

She avoided his gaze while thoughts of her grandmother and grandfather, and of course painful memories of Gray Falcon, flooded her mind. "You may not understand this, but I try not to dwell too much on my old life because I lost so much. There are times when I wonder what my life would have been like if it had not been for the war."

"The war?" he questioned.

She gave him a guarded look. "I forgot, you are a white man and a soldier, so you would refer to the incident as "the massacre." I wonder what you would have called it if your side had won—a victory?"

"Knowing Washington, yes, they would probably have called it a victory." He caught and held her gaze. "Did you lose anyone in the . . . war?"

Her eyes were fever-bright. "Oh, yes. That terrible day my whole world tilted upside down, and it has not righted itself since."

"Who did you lose?"

She was silent for a moment, as if she was reluctant to discuss her personal life with the enemy. But she needed to tell someone. Anyway, perhaps it would not matter, since they might both soon be dead. "After the war, I lost my grandfather, who was a wise and noble man." Her eyes softened. "And I lost . . . my . . . Gray Falcon was killed in the war."

She turned troubled eyes to him. "Were you in any way responsible for that war?"

He felt her sadness like a heavy hand on his heart. She was so young, so vulnerable, to have suffered so much. "No, Blue Eyes, I was not in any way connected with your war. You see, my war was lost, as was yours in the end."

111

Chapter Eleven

Nicholas watched Alanna as she focused her attention on preparing their food. He could tell that she was preoccupied, and he wondered what painful memories he had stirred up for her. He found himself thinking about the man she called Gray Falcon, and against his will, he realized he had to know more about this Indian warrior and what he had meant to Alanna.

"I saw many husbands, fathers, and sons fall in the Civil War, Alanna. There are women all over the South who can identify with your loss," he said, knowing that she was remembering Gray Falcon.

"I suppose. But that does not help me, nor does it diminish the torment I live with every day. It is hard to think that I am alive while he is dead."

Nicholas could not mistake the pain that was etched on Alanna's face. "Was this Gray Falcon a suitor, or perhaps a husband?"

"He was . . . he was to be my husband. He had given my grandfather the bride's price of twenty horses, and had built a lodge for us to live in." Her blue eyes seemed to be swirling with tides of pain now. "I was to have gone to him as his wife the very day he was k . . . killed." She lowered her eyes and stared at the tip of her moccasin. "I am told that he died with honor and . . . that his last thoughts were of me."

He could feel the turmoil of her soul, but for some reason Nicholas did not want to think of her with some brave young Indian warrior. "Your Gray Falcon was very fortunate to have a woman love him enough to grieve at his passing. I wonder if I will be so fortunate when it comes my time to die."

When she looked at him now, her eyes were filled with hostility. "Death seems to be something you soldiers take so lightly. It is because of you that Gray Falcon is dead."

"It wasn't me, Blue Eyes. I already told you I wasn't in your war."

"No, but men just like you were."

"I don't think you are being fair. Just because an Indian killed George Custer, I do not accuse you of the deed because you are Indian."

Her eyes darkened with hidden rage. "He deserved to die!"

Their conversation was giving Nicholas further insight into Alanna's life, but since it caused her such pain, he thought it would be best to speak of other matters. "Blue Eyes, why did you really allow me to believe you could not understand English?"

"I . . . did not like you, and I did not want to talk to you. My heart was so filled with hurt and rage, I just wanted to be left alone to die."

After a long silence, he answered: "I see. I suppose there is no reason you should hold any white man in high esteem after all that has happened to you."

Suddenly she glanced up, her eyes locking with his. "I certainly do not hold my father in high regard. He has not cared about me before now. I do not

113

welcome his concern now. His interest comes too late to help my mother or my grandmother."

There was nothing Nicholas could say to defend Anson Caldwell, so again he steered the conversation onto a safer subject. "Your English is exceptionally good—better than most people I have known who were educated in the language."

She smiled slightly. "My father insisted that I speak English well. When he left my mother and me to fight in one of your wars, I was sent to school with other officers' children. I liked school and found learning about your world fascinating. I wanted to do well, to please my father. Now I want to do well to please myself. There were times when my great-uncle, the chief, would call on me to be a translator for our tribe, but my dealings were mostly with hunters and trappers. I know I spoke better English than they did." She was thoughtful for a moment. "It seemed to irritate most white men when they had to ask me to explain some English word I had spoken, for which they did not know the meaning—I took pleasure in that. After a while, it became a game with me. I would learn new words in English just so I could confuse them."

He suppressed a smile. "I can only imagine what a shock you must have been to some poor trapper."

"Do not expect me to be grateful to my father for teaching me English. I have always considered it as unimportant—I still do."

"You might want to credit your father with giving you life."

She shook her head. "Do you thank your father for giving you life? Or have there been days when you cursed him for a happening of human nature that nurtured a baby?"

Nicholas smiled to himself. Oh, yes, her speech

114

was correct, but her reasoning would be controversial in Anson Caldwell's drawing room. He could see how this little Indian girl would upset the serene world the Virginians dwelled in.

His eyes twinkled. He was finding her fascinating. "Well said, little Indian."

A mischievous smile played on her lips. "Do you number many Indian women among your acquaintances, Captain?"

"No," he smiled, "one is quite enough." He quirked his eyebrow. "Ever since I have met you, you have had me dancing to your tune. I can only wonder what you must have done with the men you knew in your village."

She raised her head and looked down her nose at him. "I have already heard what you think of my looks." Her voice was edged with hurt. "I would like you to know that in my village, I had many suitors before I agreed to become Gray Falcon's wife."

His eyes clouded. "You overheard me talking to Wiley Chappell."

"Yes, and you were not very flattering." She shrugged her shoulders. "But I do not care about your opinion of me."

"Nonetheless, you have my apology, Blue Eyes. My only excuse is that I was irritated at being delayed in my journey and I was not responsible for what I said."

She wanted to ask him if he still thought her pathetic and homely, but she dared not, fearing his answer. "As I said, I do not care what you think of me."

"I think you are an exceptional young woman."

She concentrated on the roasting cottontail. "I do not care."

He smiled to himself. "Did I forget to say 'thank

115

you' for saving my life? I would be dead now if it was not for your intervention."

"Your thanks are not necessary, white man. You saved my life; I have done likewise. From here on out, I owe you nothing and you owe me nothing."

"Noblesse oblige, Miss Caldwell."

"I do not understand those words," she admitted, staring at him with curiosity.

"It translates to something like, nobly born, noble deeds."

"That is still unclear."

"Wiley told me you are a Cheyenne princess."

"Yes, I am."

He smiled before he turned away. "Thus you are nobly born."

Alanna was not sure of his meaning. Had he insulted her or paid her a compliment? Knowing his low opinion of women, she decided he had meant to insult her. She shrugged it off, wondering why she should care so much what he thought of her—but she did. She cared very much.

"I do thank you for saving my life," he drawled. He was thinking that she might not be a beauty, but she was an enchanting little minx all the same, and he was finding her wonderful to talk to. He had not been bored since he met her, and that in itself was a revelation.

"Captain Ballinger, if I have judged you correctly, you do not value your life; why should you thank me for saving it?"

"Perhaps you are right." His lips thinned. He was startled by her acute perception. She was correct, he did not value his life. In the unit he had commanded, he was often thought of as a brave man, when in truth he had rushed into danger because he had not cared if he lived or died. Disgrace is a bitter pill when one comes from a proud family, as he had. He had no illusions left, and he certainly set no value on life.

His eyes moved over the young girl, and he thought that in spite of the fact that she had almost been a wife, she was a long way from being a woman. Would the so-called "civilized world" strip away her innocence and make her into a scheming female like all the rest? That would be a pity.

Poor little thing, he thought, she looked so bedraggled, with her torn print gown, and her thin little face peeping from behind a strand of midnight-black hair that had fallen limply across her forehead. More than likely, her spirit would not survive the bigotry that existed in the social world her father and his other children inhabited.

"Are you going to cook that meat all day, Blue Eyes? It looks done to me."

A rare smile lit her face. "It is ready." She tossed back her head and gave him an enigmatic glance. "Will you eat it like an Indian?" she challenged. "Or will you need the white man's implements?"

His jade-green eyes flickered with amusement. "It might surprise you to know that soldiers often eat under adverse circumstances." He ignored the pain in his shoulder and reached for the spit. As if to prove a point, he rolled the sizzling meat in the snow to cool it, then tore it apart and handed half to Alanna.

She watched as he bit into the meat with strong, white teeth, while he fixed her with a look of triumph. "Does this meet with your approval, little Indian?"

She took a bite of the delicious meat, knowing Grace Flemming probably never ate with her fingers. She paused, trying to ignore the sudden longing she felt inside. She wished Captain Ballinger would look at her the way he had looked at Grace Flemming.

117

Never mind that he had insulted the poor girl, he had still treated her with a certain amount of consideration. Again she remembered him pressing his lips to Grace's, and she felt a weakness wash over her. Why did she want to feel this white man's lips against her?

Alanna became angry with herself because she felt that she was betraying Gray Falcon's memory. Gray Falcon had been her only love, and he always would be. So why did she have to keep reminding herself of that fact?

All other thoughts left her mind as she watched the captain lean back and clutch his shoulder, while his face paled beneath his tan. "Does your wound hurt?" she asked with mounting concern.

"It hurts like hell," he groaned. Then he managed a stiff smile. "You did a good job patching me up. I assume you took the bullet out."

"Yes, it was very deep. You were fortunate that the wound was not more serious."

"I have you to thank for that, too. When you called out to warn me that the man was about to shoot, and I turned, it probably foiled the man's aim."

Alanna shrugged, as if it was unimportant. She had finished eating, and she dipped her hands in snow, rubbing them vigorously until they were clean. "Do you suppose someone will come to look for us?"

With a speculative glance at the clear blue sky, Nicholas shook his head. "Not right away, and even if they did, they may not find us since there was a heavy snow to cover our tracks."

He glanced around as if searching for something. "I will need to find the bodies of Mr. Harden and Mr. Yance, so I can bury them."

Alanna shuddered. "There is no need. There was a

118

wolf pack roaming about last night," she said with meaning.

His eyes widened with understanding. "At least I will see that their remains are buried."

"You are not well enough, and you might tear your wound open," she protested.

He stood up with considerable effort. "You stay near the stagecoach. I will do what has to be done." Before she could object, he moved away.

"You are a stubborn man, Captain Ballinger." She called out after him. "I will not help you if you bust open that wound."

His laughter was amused. "I will keep that in mind, Blue Eyes."

In irritation, she stood up, dismissing him from her mind. She walked in the direction of a clump of trees to collect more firewood. Alanna knew she must use only wood that would not smoke, so it would not attract the attention of unwelcome visitors.

When she returned to camp later, she heard the sounds of digging, and she knew Captain Ballinger had located the remains of the two white men and was laying them to rest.

What a fragile thing life was, she thought. Sometimes one could only hold on by a slender thread.

If fate had been more kind, she would be a wife by now, and perhaps even a mother. That thought opened up old wounds and made her very sad.

Chapter Twelve

When Nicholas returned, he made no mention of the gruesome task of burying the two stage drivers, and Alanna did not ask him about it. Watching him with anxious eyes, Alanna feared he may have opened his wound, but when she questioned him about it, he brushed aside her concern.

It was still mid-morning when he trekked off through the bushes, saying he would provide the evening meal, since Alanna had provided breakfast. Now it was late afternoon, and Alanna was troubled because he had not returned.

As the afternoon shadows lengthened, Alanna's concern turned to anger. Where could he be? Did he not know that she would worry about him? What if the wolves had returned and caught his scent? He had left the gun with her, so he had no weapon to defend himself.

"An Indian would be wise enough to know he must rest after being shot with a gun—but no, not this white man. He does not consider anything or anyone," she said aloud, airing her frustration. "If he does not return soon, I suppose I will have to go in search of him."

She watched with dread as the warm sun disappeared behind a threatening mass of dark clouds. A new storm was impending, perhaps even another blizzard. She decided to keep busy and forget about Captain Ballinger, so she rummaged through the strewn contents of the splintered trunks, searching for any useful items that might have been left by the outlaws. There was no way of knowing how long they would be here before help came.

Amid the bounty, she found a cake of soap and a hairbrush. She also found a knife and two blankets that she had missed the previous day, and carried them to the stagecoach.

Alanna then moved downstream so she could bathe. She shivered as she dived into the icy water, but she gloried in the feeling of lathering her hair and body with bubbly suds.

Rushing out of the water, she shook with cold while she dressed in her elkskin gown. She took great pleasure in abandoning the soiled and ripped gown she had been forced to wear. Not only was the soft leather gown warmer and more practical, but Alanna felt she needed it to remind her that she was Gray Falcon's woman.

She brushed her long hair, then braided it and retied it with leather strips. Even braided, her hair hung below her waist.

Now she felt more herself and ready to face whatever came her way. No matter what Captain Ballinger said, she would not dress like a white woman.

"Blue Eyes, you are once again the Cheyenne princess."

Alanna was startled. The captain had come up behind her so quietly that she had not detected his presence. The surprise must have shown on her face,

121

because he laughed when he handed her the game he had provided. "So, little Indian, you did not know that a white man can walk with the silence of an Indian?"

"How long have you been spying on me?"

His laughter was amused. "Fear not, Blue Eyes, I came upon you when you were braiding your hair." He shook his head in disbelief. "I find it impossible to believe anyone would bathe in that water."

She shrugged with indifference. "It is no great feat for an Indian." Scorn crept into her voice. "I suppose a white man would be too soft to venture into water that had not been heated to his body temperature."

Nicholas refused to be baited by her. "I see you have changed your gown."

She gave him a scathing glance and turned her back. "I will not wear that other gown," she announced with determination. "My grandmother made this gown for me, and I will wear it."

"As you wish," he stated. "I admit you look charming in your buckskins."

She turned and bestowed on him a dubious look, then turned away and moved downstream to pluck and clean the turkey he had given her. "I had the gun. How did you kill this bird?" she asked.

"How did you kill the rabbit this morning?" he countered.

"I struck it with a stone."

"Well, I was not so artful in my kill. In fact, I can hardly take credit for it at all. You see, a flock of turkeys was frightened by my appearance, and this one got itself tangled in the branches of a tree." He smiled at her surprised glance. "I had only to untangle it."

She looked doubtful. "That is not the truth."

He held his hands up. "I assure you that's just the

way it happened."

By now she had deftly skinned and gutted the fowl, and she moved toward the campfire.

Walking behind Alanna, Nicholas noticed that her gown clung to her soft curves, and her hips moved gracefully as she walked. He wondered why he had not noticed her gracefulness before. He shook his head, reminding himself that she was little more than a child. The bullet that had struck his shoulder must have also addled his brain.

In no time the bird was sizzling over the campfire, and Alanna glanced at Captain Ballinger. His color was not good, and she could see that his shoulder was bothering him.

"I will change the dressing on your wound," she said, reaching for the bag which held the bandages. She motioned for him to be seated near the campfire.

"No, it's all right."

"I said sit down, Captain Ballinger. I will change that dressing." Although she had spoken in a soft voice, the tone left no room for dissent.

For a moment, a frown appeared on his face, and then he shrugged in defeat, giving in to her demand. "You can be a hard woman, Blue Eyes," he observed. "Did you learn how to handle men from your grandmother?"

When she cut away the soiled bandage, she was rougher than she needed to be, and he winced in pain.

"My grandmother did not have to handle anyone. She was married to an understanding and wonderful man."

His eyes narrowed thoughtfully. "How old are you? Thirteen—fourteen?"

Her features hardened. "This wound is healing nicely."

123

"Come on, tell me how old are you," he urged.

Again, she was not gentle as she applied salve and bound his shoulder with a clean bandage. "Captain Ballinger, if you are attempting to be humorous, you have failed with me."

His eyes clouded with pain as she tied a knot in the bandage. "Are you younger than thirteen?"

Her eyes narrowed at the insult. "The way you white men tell birthdays, I will soon be eighteen."

He looked at her doubtfully. "How can that be? You look much younger."

"Well, I am not. At least I am not old, like you are, white man."

He tried not to smile at her obvious retaliation. "How old do you judge me to be?"

"Somewhere in your late thirties, I'm sure. Perhaps forty. Far past marriageable age. Your best years are all used up, and you would be no bargain for any woman."

He buttoned his tunic and smiled. "What if I told you I'm closer to fifty?"

"You are not," she said in disbelief.

He merely shrugged.

"You could not be older than twenty-five," she said accusingly.

Satisfied laughter rolled off his lips. "Close, Blue Eyes. Actually, I'm twenty-eight."

"You tricked me!" she exclaimed, putting the campfire between them. "You are a devious man, but that is what I would expect from your race."

"You deserved it."

She smiled, at last realizing that he had out-maneuvered her. "Yes, perhaps I did. I knew you were not fifty."

Without either of them realizing it, they had begun to form a bond, and she was beginning to trust him, something she swore she would never do with a white man.

"Shall we declare a truce, Blue Eyes? If you like, it can last only until we are rescued, then you can go back to hating me again."

"I do not hate you."

Nicholas knew that that in itself had been hard for her to admit. "Truce then?"

"I . . . yes."

Alanna bent down to turn the roasting spit. "It is not long until dark, and there is a snowstorm coming. We should be in the stagecoach before it hits."

He studied the tip of his boot. "I have heard it said that Indians can predict the weather. Is it true?"

"My grandmother was never wrong when she foretold the weather. If she said it would storm, it always did."

He studied her delicate features, realizing that she was actually pretty. "Did you have a happy childhood, Blue Eyes?" he wanted to know. "I cannot imagine what it would be like to grow up wild and free."

"I recall the early years when I lived with my mother and my white father. If I was unhappy then, I was too young to know. In my grandfather's lodge, there was much happiness. Both my grandfather and grandmother were loving, and they raised me with kindness. They cared so much for my happiness that my grandfather allowed me to choose my own husband." She was silent for a moment, remembering the loved ones she had lost. Then she continued softly: "You cannot imagine the beauty of the Cheyenne lands. Game was plentiful, the streams and rivers were filled with fish. Life was good . . . before . . . before. . . ."

"I am sorry if I invoked painful memories for you, Blue Eyes." He reached forward, tested the turkey, and found it to be done, thus putting an end to their conversation.

They ate in silence, and when they were finished, Nicholas went off to bury the remains so they would not attract wild animals to the camp.

The wind hit without warning. It swooped down the gully and swirled the dry snow, blowing out the campfire. Suddenly it was as if the heavens had opened up and giant snowflakes had fallen earthward, whipped up by the wind and whirled around in a blinding white haze.

Alanna raced toward the shelter of the stagecoach with Nicholas in close pursuit. When they were safely inside, he pulled the door shut while Alanna sat shivering in the corner.

"You were right, Blue Eyes. That's one hell of a snowstorm."

Then he looked at her mockingly. "I beg your pardon; I guess I'll have to be more careful what I say around you, now that I know you can understand me."

She pulled a blanket across her legs and snuggled down in its warmth. "I fear this storm will not let up for hours. But at least it will keep the wolves away. And we are fortunate that we have this shelter."

Nicholas leaned back and stared into the gathering darkness. "If someone had told me a month ago that I would be stranded with an Indian girl in a snowstorm, worrying about marauding wolves and how to get back to civilization, I would have thought them addle-brained. I am still wondering how I got myself into this."

She was thoughtful. "We are each accountable for our own actions; you must have walked into the situation with your eyes wide open."

He burst into boisterous laughter. "Where did you learn to strip a man of his dignity? You speak with the authority of someone twice your age."

For some reason she was pleased by his observation. "I would think a woman would have to be very wise to deal with you, Captain Ballinger."

A sudden gust of wind seeped through the cracks in the door, and Alanna shivered. "The weather is going to get worse, Captain. We can hope we do not freeze to death before morning."

"Come here, Blue Eyes," he told her, holding out his arms. "We shall just have to keep each other warm."

"No," she said through trembling lips, as a sudden thrill went through her body at the thought of being close to him. "I will not."

"Why not? You slept beside me last night," he reminded her.

"That was different; you were unconscious most of the night. And we did not have these extra blankets."

He was quiet for a long moment. "Blue Eyes, you don't have anything to fear from me. Don't you know by now that I would never harm you? I thought you trusted me."

"I do trust you," she admitted, unwilling to tell him that it was her reaction to him that she was worried about. "But last night you thought I was a child. Tonight you know I am a grown woman."

She could not see his smile. "So you are. I'll tell you what. If you get cold during the night, come on over and I'll make you warm."

"I will . . . if I get cold."

The darkness had closed in around them like a

gentle friend. It seemed to Alanna that they were the only two people in the world.

"Does your shoulder pain you?"

"It's much better."

"Captain Ballinger?"

"Why don't you call me Nicholas?"

"Nicholas, would you tell me about your mother and father? I know something happened to them that distressed you very deeply."

A sharp intake of breath was followed by a long silence, as if the subject was painful to him. At last he spoke. "You heard the remarks the Flemmings made about my family?"

"Yes, but I did not really understand what they were talking about."

"It's very simple, Blue Eyes. My mother had a lover—a Yankee lover. My father came home and found them together and shot the man. My father was later executed for defending his honor. My mother still resides at Ballinger Hall."

"In the white man's war, your father and the Yankees were on opposite sides, were they not?" She asked, trying to understand the war that had separated the white people.

"My father was not a soldier, but yes, they were on opposite sides. I suppose you could better understand if you thought of a woman of your tribe being with a man from an enemy tribe."

"Perhaps your mother had a reason to do what she did. Have you asked her?"

"No. You see, she admitted that she had been in love with the Yankee."

Alanna heard the bitterness in his voice. "Surely you must feel something for your mother?"

His eyes were reflective. "I can remember a time when, like all little boys, I thought my mother was

128

the center of the world. I can remember a cool and gentle hand when I was feverish. She was lovely—an angel. I can close my eyes now and still see her as she was then." Suddenly, as if coming out of a daze, his eyes flickered. "I was too young to judge a person's worth."

"Perhaps if you went home and talked to her."

"I have been away from Ballinger Hall for a long time. Even now I do not want to return."

"How very sad."

His voice was cynical. "Yes, isn't it."

"Captain Ballinger—"

"Nicholas."

"Nicholas, my grandfather once told me that all men have their warts. Even great men."

"You have me at a loss. What is that supposed to mean?"

"It means simply that no one is perfect. Everyone has faults—you, your mother, perhaps even your father."

His laughter lent a lighter mood to their conversation. "Did your grandfather have warts?"

"If he did, I never saw one."

"So you think he was perfect?"

"I think he was, and so did my grandmother, and that was all that mattered."

Nicholas shifted his weight and lay back on the seat, pulling a blanket over him. "I thought Indian maidens married young."

"Most of them do. All my friends were married long ago."

"But not you."

"No, I was waiting for Gray Falcon to admit that he loved me."

"Why did Gray Falcon wait so long?"

"Because he wanted to pay my grandfather a high

bride price for me. Gray Falcon was a very proud man, and he wanted me to know that he held me in very high regard."

"If I recall right, you said he gave twenty horses for you."

"Yes, twenty." She suddenly felt sad. "It seems a pity that he labored so long and hard, never to know me as his wife."

Nicholas tensed at the longing in her voice. "There are other things in life besides marriage," he said. "Now me, I never intend to marry."

"So you can spread yourself around to all the women?" she taunted.

He laughed in amusement. "You little vixen, you would lead any man who was fool enough to marry you a merry chase."

When she spoke, it was with earnestness. "I shall never marry. I will always feel as if I belong to Gray Falcon, even though I never knew him as my husband."

Nicholas found himself envying the dead Cheyenne warrior who was the recipient of so much love and devotion even after death. "Perhaps you will one day find a man who will change your mind."

"No, I never will."

"Are you sleepy, Blue Eyes?"

She yawned. "Yes. I hardly closed my eyes last night."

"Since you kept watch over me last night, it seems only right that you sleep tonight while I keep watch over you."

She tried to ignore the intense cold as her eyelids drifted shut. She had been cold many times on the reservation. She had endured it then, and she would endure it now.

Alanna did not know how long she had been

asleep, but she suddenly became aware that her body was shivering from the cold. She felt Nicholas lift her in his arms and bring her next to him. With a contented sigh, she sought the warmth of that hard body and sank into a peaceful sleep, feeling warm, safe, and protected.

Nicholas held the slight girl in his arms, thinking of her courage. Not once had she complained about what had happened to her. Yesterday she had saved his life, and last night she had kept watch over him. He came closer to admiring her than any woman he knew.

"Sleep, little Blue Eyes," he murmured. "I will not allow anything to harm you."

Chapter Thirteen

Alanna was awakened by the sound of thundering hooves. Disoriented for a moment, she made her eyes focus on the brass door handle, and she remembered she was in the stagecoach. Trying to gather her wits, she realized that Nicholas was not beside her and wondered where he could be.

Now she could hear the jingling of harnesses that alerted her to the fact that several riders were making their way down the embankment. Hoping the riders would be their rescuers, she shoved the door open and leapt to the snowy ground, taking in the situation with one long, sweeping glance.

Nicholas was by the stream, and there were twelve Indian warriors bearing down on him!

When Alanna saw Nicholas reach for his gun, she realized she had to stop him before he made the mistake of firing at the Indians. By now she knew the warriors were Sioux, and they certainly had no reason to love any white man. Fright gave wings to Alanna's feet as she raced across the uneven ground, hoping she would reach Nicholas ahead of the intruders.

When she reached his side, she urgently whispered:

"Put the gun away. Do it now!"

Nicholas, trusting that Alanna knew what she was talking about, immediately obeyed. "Who are they?"

"They are Sioux. I will try to speak to them and find out what they want."

By now the warriors had paused in front of Alanna and Nicholas and were silently surveying them. With a feeling of uneasiness, Nicholas watched the Indians glance first at him, then at Alanna. He knew the Sioux would not hesitate to kill him, but he did not know how they would feel about Alanna, a Cheyenne princess.

Alanna raised her arm in greeting. "It is good to see my brother, the Sioux. I am of the Cheyenne, niece of Chief Yellow Wing, and granddaughter of the council chief, Wolf Dreamer."

"Yellow Wing and Wolf Dreamer are both dead," the warrior who seemed to be the leader spoke up. "Dead men cannot deny your claim."

"This is true. They both died in battle, defending our village from the white soldiers."

The Sioux leader regarded her with dark, suspicious eyes. "I knew Wolf Dreamer very well, but how can I know you are his granddaughter?"

She did not lower her eyes, but met his dark gaze without flinching. "Ask me any question about my grandfather, and I will answer it, thus proving who I am."

The Sioux warrior was thoughtful for a moment. "What was the name of Wolf Dreamer's woman?"

"My grandmother's name was Blue Flower Woman, and she is now also dead."

The Indian nodded. "I believe you are who you say you are, because Wolf Dreamer once told me of his granddaughter who had eyes the color of the sky, just as your eyes are."

"May I know your name?" she asked.

"I am Chattering Squirrel. We saw the smoke from your campfire and came to see who was intruding on our land." He glanced at Nicholas, and his eyes hardened. "Why are you with the long knife?"

Alanna knew she had to think fast and be convincing or Nicholas might yet die. "I am his woman." She nodded toward the stagecoach. "We were traveling when the coach was attacked by three white men. They killed everyone but us, although my husband was wounded."

Chattering Squirrel glanced at the stagecoach and then back at Alanna. "You have no way to continue your journey."

"That is so."

"It would be wise not to stay here in my land for very long, granddaughter of the Cheyenne. The long knife is not welcome here."

Alanna took Nicholas's hand, knowing Chattering Squirrel had decided to let him live. "Can we buy a horse from you so we may leave?"

"What have you to offer?"

She quickly took Nicholas's pistol from the scabbard, and when he would have protested, gave him a warning glance. Smiling, she held the gun out to Chattering Squirrel. "We have this to trade."

The Sioux Warrior backed his horse away, shaking his head. "Since the battle with the Yellow Hair, we have all the guns we will need." His eyes were suddenly piercing as he assessed her. "I would take you in trade, granddaughter of Wolf Dreamer, and give the long knife a horse in exchange."

She quickly shook her head. "I cannot belong to anyone but this man. I have given my word."

Chattering Squirrel looked regretful for a moment. "It is good that you keep your word, little

Cheyenne. Even if it is to a long knife."

Without a backward glance, the Indian turned his horse and rode back up the slope, followed closely by the other warriors.

After they disappeared over the rise, Nicholas let out a sigh of relief. "What was that all about?"

"You can be thankful for the respect that the Sioux have for my grandfather that you still live."

Nicholas nodded. "I saw the hatred in the Sioux's eyes. There were moments when I wondered if I would see sunrise tomorrow. What were you saying to the leader?"

"I had to tell him I was your woman. He wanted to trade you a horse for me."

Nicholas laughed as his eyes roamed over her face. "Not a bad bargain at that. Had you told me, I might have accepted his offer."

She gave him a scalding glance. "I do not think you have a good humor, white man. I told you before that my price is twenty horses."

His amusement showed itself as his sea-green eyes danced. "Twenty horses—a high price indeed." His glance ran down the length of her body. "But a price well-spent, I would say, little Indian."

She turned away toward the stream, her long braids swaying with each graceful movement. The amusement died away when he remembered how soft and warm she had been in his arms at night. He thrust his hands in his pocket, not liking the direction his thoughts were taking. This made twice she had saved his life, and he was slipping further into her debt.

With the encroachment of late afternoon, the temperature dropped and the air turned bitterly cold.

135

Alanna blew on her hands to keep them warm as she lay on her stomach, peering down into the swift current while Nicholas looked on quizzically.

She grasped the sharp-pointed spear she had whittled earlier and was poised and ready to strike should some unsuspecting fish swim within her range.

Nicholas shook his head. "I don't think you are going to catch a fish like that. Pity a hawk carried away the remainder of the turkey."

"*Shh*," she cautioned.

He lapsed into silence. Moments passed while he watched her. He was taken by surprise when she suddenly lunged forward, stabbing the spear into the water. She jumped to her feet and sang out triumphantly as a fat trout wriggled on the point of her spear!

"We shall have fish tonight, doubting Nicholas. I never did care much for turkey anyway."

When Alanna finished the last morsel of trout, she licked her fingers and looked at Nicholas as if wanting his approval. "The fish was good."

He nodded. "Yes, splendid. I am beginning to believe that there is no end to your talents. Perhaps someday you could teach me to fish with a spear."

She added another log to the fire and watched the sparks sizzle onto the snow. "Pooh, any child or girl in the Cheyenne village can fish with a spear. It is no great accomplishment. The warriors do the really difficult feats."

"So any girl can do it, huh?" She did not miss the twinkle in his eyes, but she did not see when he reached back behind him and picked up a handful of snow. Forming it into a ball, Nicholas propelled it forward, and laughed when it hit her right in the face.

At first Alanna was startled. Brushing the snow away with the sweep of her hand, she stared at him in amazement. When she saw the smile on his lips, she realized he was playing a game. Drawn into the spirit of fun, she quickly gained her feet and leaped behind a wide tree trunk just as another well-thrown snowball whizzed past her head.

After forming the feather-light snow into a ball, Alanna let fly her missile, catching Nicholas in the jaw just as he made a dive for her and dragged her down on a soft bed of snow.

"So, Blue Eyes, you complain about eating my turkey and claim that your fish is superior?"

She tried to wriggle out of his grasp, but he held her firm. "Yes, my fish was the best, and you know it."

His brow creased as he smiled down at her. "That's your word against mine."

She suddenly felt the closeness of his body and could hardly catch her breath. "Let me up," she pleaded.

He arched his brow. "And if I don't?"

Her eyes met his, and she could not mistake the warmth she saw etched there. "I . . . promise to teach you to fish with the spear if you will let me up."

Nicholas stared at her, wondering how she could have woven herself so thoroughly into his life. How would he feel when the day came that he must let her go? "Done," he said, releasing her arms. "You strike a difficult bargain."

Alanna rolled out of his reach, gathered up a handful of snow, and pelted him again. Scrambling to her feet, she raced toward the sanctuary of the coach with Nicholas in pursuit, two steps behind her.

She dived inside and shut the door, but he wrenched it open, grabbed her wrists, and pulled her forward. "I've a good mind to toss you in that icy stream," he threatened good-naturedly.

She tossed her head. "I would not do that if I were you, white man."

He released one of her wrists and flicked her braid. "And why not?"

"Because you have to sleep sometime, and you would never feel safe enough to close your eyes if you did that to me, fearing I would retaliate—and I would."

Unconsciously, he pulled her closer and his arms went around her. "Would you sneak up to do mischief on a man when he was asleep?"

She glanced up at him. "Yes, but I do not think I could do that to you."

He saw the sincerity in her eyes, and he had the urge to tighten his hold on her, to cherish her. That thought was so troubling that he immediately released her and stepped back. "It's getting late. We need to prepare for another cold night."

Alanna watched Nicholas move away, his broad shoulders straight, his head with the proud tilt, his blue uniform a perfect background for the whiteness of the snow. Glancing down, she watched his footprints fill with newly fallen snow and wondered why she felt a sudden emptiness inside.

It was long after dark, and still Nicholas had not returned. Alanna climbed under the blankets to wait for him, her senses attuned to every sound. Why had he not returned? she wondered.

The silence of the night was interrupted only by the distant call of a wolf and the gentle pelting of the snow against the window.

When Nicholas finally appeared, he caught Alanna unprepared. The door opened, and a blast of snowflakes swirled inside. It was dark, and she could see only his outline, but she knew from his movements that he was half frozen.

When he dropped down in the seat beside her, Alanna pulled the covers over him. Taking his cold hands in hers, she rubbed them vigorously while she snuggled close to him, trying to lend him her warmth.

"I was beginning to be concerned. Why were you gone so long?"

"I was leaving signs to show our position to anyone who might come searching for us. I used heavy logs to mark a trail, hoping they would easily be seen."

Alanna felt a warmth spread over her. She liked being this close to him. She felt his breath against her cheek, and a weakness tightened her nerves. "You . . . you did not hurt your shoulder, did you?"

"No. But it's so cold I don't think I'll ever feel warm again."

She took another blanket and spread it over him. "I will keep you warm tonight."

His head drifted slowly down to rest against her shoulder. "So tired, Blue Eyes. Don't know when I've ever been so . . . tired."

"You have done too much. You must sleep and give your body time to heal."

He made no further sound, for he had fallen into a deep sleep.

Chapter Fourteen

In the darkness of the storm, Alanna held Nicholas in her arms. She was overcome when a rush of feelings swept through her mind that left her stunned and breathless. What was happening to her? Why was she having a woman's longings for Nicholas Ballinger when she was Gray Falcon's woman?

She was besieged by thoughts of guilt and disloyalty. What would her beloved think of her if he knew she had these feelings for a white man, and a long knife at that?

She remembered Gray Falcon making her promise that she would be happy. Well, she was not happy— she was miserable.

Alanna felt Nicholas take in a deep breath, and her arms tightened around him. She knew in that moment that she held Nicholas Ballinger as no woman had ever held him before. She was seeing his weaknesses and his strengths. She knew just how to make him angry, and what amused him. She was learning the things about him that he tried to hide from the world. She had witnessed his anguish about his mother and father, and she had felt his pain. She had not wanted to like him, but the more she came to

140

know the real person behind the mask, the more she cared for him.

Her mind drifted back to a conversation where her grandmother had tried to explain to her what it meant to become a wife. If she closed her eyes, she could almost hear her grandmother's voice. . . .

"You must be prepared to put all childish ways aside," Blue Flower Woman had told Alanna.

She had not understood. "But when shall I know that I am a woman, Grandmother?"

"Your body will tell you first, and then soon your heart will agree."

"But what shall I do? I love Gray Falcon, but I do not know how to be a wife."

"Do not worry, my child. Your husband will instruct you on how to be his woman."

Alanna now sat pondering the words her grandmother had spoken so long ago. What her grandmother had failed to tell her was what to do about her feelings once the man she loved had been slain. And what was she to do about these feelings that she was having for Nicholas Ballinger? She tried to resent his intrusion into her life, but she could not. She had wanted to keep Gray Falcon's memory fresh and sacred, but already it was beginning to fade in the wake of piercing green eyes.

Hours passed as Nicholas slept with his head on her shoulder. In spite of her reluctance, Alanna cherished those moments, for now he belonged to her alone. Soon they would be rescued, and she would probably never seen him again after that.

Suddenly Nicholas's head snapped, and he tensed just as the clouds moved away, leaving a brilliant moon to illuminate the countryside. Bright prisms of

141

light shone through the streaked window. After a moment, he reached out and grasped Alanna's arm in a tight grip.

"How long have I been asleep?"

"Not long. You are warmer now."

His hand moved down her arm, and he clasped her hands, finding them cold to the touch. "You are like ice. Why didn't you awaken me?"

"I have been colder."

He shifted his weight, pulling her down beside him until her head rested on his arm. She found herself penned between him and the back of the seat. His body was like fire to her, and she gasped in wide-eyed wonderment.

When he felt her body become rigid, he laughed. "Relax, Blue Eyes, I want no more than to get you warm."

The bright moonlight fell across his face, and she felt a lump in her throat. He was a handsome man to look upon, even moreso than Gray Falcon. When she trembled with some yet untapped emotion, Nicholas thought she was shivering from cold, and he pulled her even closer to his body.

With slow deliberation, he ran his hands across her cold arm, up to her shoulder, and back down again. "I was a brute to fall asleep while you were freezing, Blue Eyes. Will you forgive me?"

His lips were not far from hers, and they drew her gaze.

"I am warmer now," she told him.

His face was half in shadow, half in light, so she could not make out his expression. "Good. Go to sleep, you have earned your rest."

"I am not sleepy."

His firm lips curved into a smile. "You will be tired tomorrow if you don't sleep now. God help me if you awake in a bad temper."

"I am tired," she admitted.

Her eyes locked with his, and she could not look away. As if she had no control of her speech, she heard herself ask: "Why did you touch your lips to Grace Flemming's?"

Astonished by her question, his hand paused in its quest to warm her arm. "Oh, yes, you did witness that little fracas between me and Miss Flemming that night, didn't you?"

"Nicholas, what was it called when you pressed your lips to hers?"

His expression softened. "That was called a kiss, Blue Eyes."

"A kiss?"

"Um-hum. Didn't you ever see your father and mother kiss?"

She searched her memory. "No." She looked into his eyes. "I have never seen a man touch his lips to a woman's lips. Do all whites touch their lips together in the kiss?"

Nicholas was not in the least amused at being forced to explain to an innocent girl the relationship between a man and a woman. "Most of them do. It is merely a way to show affection." He hoped his vague answer would put an end to her questioning.

"It is all very puzzling to me. If you did not like Grace Flemming, why would you give her affection with the kiss?"

His brow furrowed. "It was not affection you saw, Blue Eyes. It was something else entirely. Had I not known that you were watching, it might have gone . . ." His voice was sharp, and he wanted to put an end to this conversation. "It was merely a man touching a woman. Surely you know about that?"

Her eyes were wide with wonder. "I have never

143

touched a man in that way."

He saw the innocence clearly reflected in the depths of her blue eyes. "Nor should you, until you are married."

"But you were not married to Grace Flemming. As you said, you did not even like her."

"Love has little to do with what went on between me and Grace Flemming, Blue Eyes," Nicholas said in exasperation.

Suddenly her stomach muscles tightened at the thought of his lips on hers. "Do you feel affection for me, Nicholas?"

His body tensed, and she could feel him pull away. "Of course I feel affection for you, Blue Eyes. But a man cannot go around kissing everyone he feels friendship for."

Her face fell, and she lowered her eyes to his lips. "I would like to know how a kiss would feel."

Nicholas, who had been slowly moving away from her, paused and stared at the wistfulness in her expression.

"One of the first things you must learn of the white world, Alanna, is that a lady from a good family does not put her self forward with a man."

It had not escaped her notice that he had not called her Blue Eyes as he usually did. "But Grace Flemming was—"

"I said a *lady* of *good* family. Miss Flemming does not qualify for either, but you do."

He now became aware of the way the moonbeams danced across Alanna's midnight-black hair. Suddenly she was not the little girl that he had made himself responsible for, but a soft, desirable woman. Her tantalizing lips parted, and her blue eyes seemed to have caught the stars in their shimmering depths.

144

He shook his head to clear it. "You are a bold little baggage, Alanna Caldwell. If I had any doubt before, I believe you would benefit greatly by learning how a proper young lady should act."

"You could teach me."

He laughed nervously. "I am afraid the lessons I want to teach you at the moment are better left untaught."

She stared at him. "Nicholas, I find many things about your world confusing, but nothing more confusing than how a woman should behave with a man."

He raised a skeptical eyebrow at her. "You seem to learn quickly." He rolled away from her and sat up. "Too quickly."

"Will you not show me the kiss?"

He was silent for a moment, then bent forward to place his lips on her forehead. Once his lips touched her soft brow, his arms slid around her, and he had an overwhelming feeling that he wanted to absorb her into his body. She had belonged to him, in a way, and she always would, because he had saved her life and she had saved his. Their lives had intertwined as few others ever would.

Alanna pulled back. "That is not a kiss," she said scornfully. "You kissed Grace Flemming on the lips."

He sighed in resignation. "You won't be satisfied until you have your way, will you?" He grasped her by the shoulders and pulled her into his arms. She could not see him in the darkness, but she could feel his intake of breath. She could hear her own heartbeat.

Slowly he lowered his head and his lips brushed lightly against her trembling lips. Alanna felt something akin to pain shoot through her body, and she moved forward boldly, wanting to deepen the kiss.

Nicholas was taken by surprise as her lips pressed against his. He would have pulled away, but her mouth was so soft and sweet that his desire for her broke all bounds of consciousness.

Deep hidden emotions came to life within Alanna when she instinctively pressed her body against the heat of Nicholas's hard frame.

His hand drifted down her waist, and he pressed her tighter against him, feeling her firm young breasts against his chest. His hand drifted across her well-rounded hips and the heat of passion racked his body.

"Blue Eyes, what are you doing to me?" he whispered hotly in her ear. "I am only human, and you are so desirable."

He moved her back against the seat and lay beside her. With trembling anticipation, he reached out and touched her cheek. "Are you frightened of me, Alanna?"

"No, not of you." But she was frightened by the strange yearning she felt within her young body. She ached for him to hold her, to fulfill her as a woman.

He touched his lips to the corner of her ear. "You are so sweet. I thought never to find innocence again in a woman."

She trembled at the feather-light kisses he sprinkled on her eyelids. "You will teach me," she breathed, not thinking past the wild yearning she was feeling.

"Yes," he whispered in a deep voice. His hand drifted down to lightly cup her breasts, and a tremor shook his tall frame. "Yes, I will introduce you to a world of pleasure."

He moved her gown aside so that her breasts were

146

exposed. With a sharp ache in his loins, he bent to press his hot mouth against the swollen nipple. "So sweet," he murmured. "So innocent."

Alanna threw her head back, experiencing pleasure beyond anything she had ever felt before. She wanted to be a part of this man, to belong to him, to have him belong to her.

Her voice came out in a throaty whisper. "I did not know that the kiss could be so pleasurable, Nicholas. Will you kiss me again, please?"

Suddenly the swirling fog of passion cleared, and Nicholas was horrified by what had almost occurred. He pulled her gown together and moved away. "My God, what have I done?"

"Hold me, Nicholas," she pleaded, needing to feel close to him.

He fought the temptation to do just that. He was responsible for her safety, and he had almost become her spoiler. He tried to gather his thoughts. "Alanna, I am sorry for what happened. I lost my head for a moment. If I had taken advantage of you, I would never have forgiven myself."

Always taught to speak her mind, Alanna did so now. "Nicholas, did you not feel the pleasure of the kiss? The touching. Was it . . . enjoyable to you?"

He moved away from her. "It is better forgotten, Alanna. Again, I can only apologize."

She was confused as he opened the door and stepped out into the frigid air. His next words confused her still more. "I will long remember the taste of your sweet lips, Blue Eyes. But this happened between us only because we have been thrown together in such an intimate situation. You have my word it will not happen again."

With deep disappointment, she lay alone, the bright moonlight making shadowy patterns across

147

her face. Alanna remembered Nicholas insulting poor Grace Flemming the night she had sought him out. Perhaps she would never understand the white world.

With a heavy heart, she listened to Nicholas's footsteps moving away into the darkness. She had driven him out into the cold by her actions. She felt sad inside, wondering if he had been repulsed by her.

It was at that moment that she knew she would no longer fight him about going to her father. If she lived with her father, she might be able to see Nicholas sometimes.

Chapter Fifteen

Cold air fanned Alanna's cheek, and her eyes fluttered open. She found Nicholas bending over her, shaking her shoulder gently.

"Gather your wits about you, Blue Eyes, we have been rescued!"

She sat up slowly, shaking her head to clear her mind. "Who? When?"

"The Overland Stage is here. It seems many people have been searching for us. The roads have been closed because of heavy snow, and they just now got through." He tugged on her braid. "You have but a short time to make yourself ready, so hurry."

When he moved away, Alanna sprang into action. Lacing her moccasins, she hurried down to the stream to wash her face. She then brushed out her hair and braided it tightly.

Three men accompanied Nicholas to the graves of the two stage drivers. He then took them to inspect the overturned stagecoach.

The two men with the scuffed boots and baggy trousers were with the Overland Stage, but the third was a heavy-set redheaded man, dressed in a wrinkled black suit and carrying a bulky camera. He was from a

149

St. Louis newspaper, and just happened to be in the area when the search was launched for the missing stage and its passengers. He walked around setting up the camera until he had it just right, then with a blinding flash of light captured for posterity the images of the wrecked stagecoach and the two forlorn graves.

"You're damned lucky you weren't killed," the redhead exclaimed as he took another picture of the coach. "It would seem you have that little Indian gal to thank that you are alive. I would like to take her picture for the newspaper also."

"No," Nicholas said blocking the man's path. "You will not put her in your newspaper."

When the three newcomers turned their attention to Alanna, she shyly moved up the slope and out of their view.

Her heart was pounding with undetermined feelings as she neared the stagecoach. She had begun to wonder if she and Nicholas would ever be rescued. Now that help had come, she was not sure that that was what she wanted at all.

She ran a smooth hand over the flank of one of the coach horses and was rewarded with a soft whinny. Peeping in the window, she was glad to find there were no other passengers, so she would not have to endure curious stares as she had with the Flemming women.

Hearing voices, she turned to see Nicholas move up the hill. "Are you ready to seek civilization, Blue Eyes?"

"I . . . am ready to leave here," she admitted, glancing at him and wondering if he was thinking of last night. The cool smile he gave her indicated that he had put the incident behind him. Perhaps the sooner they parted company, the sooner she could sort out her feelings.

Nicholas grasped her about the waist and settled her inside the coach. After he climbed in beside her, they were joined by the redheaded man. The stranger settled his heavy bulk into the seat opposite them and stared at Alanna with curiosity in his blue eyes.

"Will you introduce me to your friend, Captain Ballinger? I am most anxious to know more about her."

Alanna sensed a reluctance in Nicholas, but at last he made the introduction. "Miss Caldwell, may I present Mr. Shelby? He works for the *Missouri Republican* in St. Louis. It seems he was gracious enough to join in the search for us." In a softer voice, he said, "Mr. Shelby conveniently had his camera with him at the time."

"What is a camera?" she asked.

"It is that black box," Nicholas told her. "It can make an exact image of you on a piece of paper."

Mr. Shelby extended his hand to Alanna. She was unaware of how to react to his gesture, so she merely stared back at him.

Not knowing how well the Indian maiden understood English, he spoke lowly and distinctly, so she would understand his words. "I am proud to meet you, Miss Caldwell. I was informed at the way station that you are a half-breed, and were raised by the Cheyenne. It's not every day I meet such a brave young lady."

She raised her head, not knowing how to answer him. "It was not bravery that motivated me, sir. It was merely the will to survive." She did not bother to respond to his other assertions.

His mouth gaped in shocked surprised. "Good Lord, you speak better English than I do. Where did you learn my language?"

151

"Your language, sir? English was in existence long before you were born; therefore, it does not belong to you exclusively," she said airily, taking an immediate dislike to the man, though she could not have said why.

Mr. Shelby's eyes became seeking. "Yes . . . well, what I meant to say . . . was how did you learn to speak the English language? Of course, I noticed your blue eyes, and I'm sure—"

"My father was a white man," she interrupted him. "I did not know it at the time, but I have come to realize that he taught me very well."

The man's interest intensified. "You are amazing, Miss Caldwell. Where did you come from? Where is your destination, and where did you meet Captain Ballinger?" His eyes deepened in color as his excitement intensified. "What a story I will write about you! Of course, I'll need your picture, and your interpretation of what occurred. I want to know every detail."

"No," Nicholas said. "I already told you, no story, and no pictures."

"But I could make Miss Caldwell famous," he persisted. "People from all over the country will read about her. She might even be asked to travel to Europe. Those foreigners are always wanting to meet a real live American Indian."

Alanna saw Nicholas's jaw set in a stubborn line, and she knew his anger was building. She did not fully understand what the man wanted of her, but Nicholas did, and he apparently did not approve.

"No." There will be no story about Miss Caldwell in your newspaper, and that's final."

At that moment, the stage driver called down to them. "Make ready, we're under way." Six horses lurched forward, and the stage leaped into motion.

Alanna turned her head to stare out the window. She was not sorry to be leaving this place, for here she had met with her greatest challenge. She had fallen in love with a man who would never return her love. As the bleak countryside flashed by the window, she felt a loneliness settle heavily on her shoulders, and she shivered.

Nicholas took her hand. "Are you cold?"

She regarded him with troubled eyes. "No, I do not think I will ever be cold again—at least not like we were back there."

Nicholas pulled a blanket over Alanna, tucking it about her chin. When he looked up, he found Mr. Shelby studying him with a knowing, self-satisfied smile.

"It must have been convenient, Captain Ballinger, to have this little Indian to keep you warm back there. I wouldn't have minded being lost myself, if she was with me. No, indeed, not at all."

Before Alanna had time to analyze the man's words, Nicholas had reached across, grabbed the man by the shirtfront, and yanked him forward. Through clenched teeth, he spoke: "You will apologize immediately to Miss Caldwell for what you insinuated," he hissed. "Do it now, or I'll toss you out the door, so help me, God."

The man's eyes bulged out, and he stammered. "I'm sorry, ma'am . . . I didn't mean any disrespect."

Nicholas flung Mr. Shelby back against the seat, and the man seemed to bounce forward several times before grasping the handrest to steady himself. Immediately he shrank away, quickly turning his attention to the passing scenery.

Alanna wanted to ask Nicholas what Mr. Shelby had said that he should apologize for, but she dared not. Again she could see the muscle twitching in

Nicholas's jaw, and she knew he was angry, but she did not know if his anger included her, or just the luckless newspaper man.

There was no further incident between Nicholas and Mr. Shelby the rest of the day. But the air between them was thick and tension filled, and Alanna would be glad to see the last of the odious Shelby. She was relieved when they finally stopped at a relay station for the night.

Twilight lingered in a wide golden sphere as Alanna walked outside the relay station. Hearing the horses neigh, she walked slowly toward the corral. Nicholas had been cold and indifferent to her, and it cut her deeply. Had he forgotten they had been through so much together?

Her heartache was so acute that she did not hear the heavy footsteps, or notice Mr. Shelby setting up his black box.

She was suddenly blinded by a flash of light. When she regained her sight, Mr. Shelby tipped his hat and nodded. "Thanks for the pose. Don't tell Captain Ballinger, but I'm going to make you famous."

She stared after the newspaper man when he carried his camera into the barn. Moments later he rode past her on a big bay mare. "See you in St. Louis," he called back over his shoulder.

Alanna thought the incident strange, but soon put it out of her mind. She was glad he was gone, and she hoped she had seen the last of him. There was no reason to tell Nicholas what the man had said; it would only make him angry again.

Night had fallen, and Alanna sat alone before the

big fireplace, picking at the food that had been served to her. Nicholas had left word that he would not be joining her tonight, and she felt lonely with only the aged dog that slept by the hearth to keep her company.

After finishing the meal, but tasting nothing, Alanna silently went to her room. Lying on the hard, lumpy bed, she almost wished herself back in the wilderness, lying in the stagecoach where she would now be huddled up with Nicholas.

It was strange, but since the incident involving Mr. Shelby, Nicholas seemed to be ignoring her, and she did not understand why.

Tomorrow they would reach St. Louis, where she and Nicholas would part company. He would go on to Washington, and she to her father.

Her heart was heavy at the thought of not seeing Nicholas again, and she dared not think of the meeting with her father and his white family, for it was too frightening to contemplate.

St. Louis was like nothing Alanna could have ever imagined. As she followed Nicholas through the hoards of humanity pressed together on the boardwalk, she glanced at the massive buildings, some of which reached three stories in the air and blocked out her view of the horizon. The streets were filled with women in strange gowns which were bustled in the back, and men in suits or filthy buckskins.

She was surprised to see that Indians mixed with the white people and no one seemed to notice or care. She could not identify their tribe, but the Indians seemed unconcerned by their surroundings. No one seemed to notice that Alanna was dressed as an Indian.

Nicholas took Alanna's arm and led her into one of the shops that displayed female apparel in the window. Pulling her forward, he approached the woman behind the counter.

Alanna was busy looking at the wondrous items she saw: gowns of lace, ribbons, shoes with pointed toes, bonnets, and shawls. There were trinkets and jewelry with different colored stones that were displayed on a shelf behind the counter.

Nicholas spoke to the woman in a commanding voice. "I am Captain Nicholas Ballinger, and this is Miss Alanna Caldwell. She will need everything to make up a wardrobe. I am leaving her in your care, hoping you can accommodate her needs. I shall return for her shortly."

The woman was at first indignant at the thought of the captain buying clothing for someone who was not his wife, but then her eyes sparkled at the thought of such a large purchase. "I am Mrs. Lee, and I shall do my best to see to her needs, Captain Ballinger."

Nicholas nodded slightly, and Alanna watched his retreating back. In confusion she turned to the elderly woman who stared at her with brazen curiosity.

Mrs. Lee came around the counter, sizing Alanna up. "You are very slender, but with padding, we can take care of that." She looked in disgust at the elkskin garment Alanna wore. "You don't look like an Indian." Her face froze in horror. "Were you abducted by the savages, dear?"

Alanna raised her head and glared at the well-meaning woman. "No, I am one of those Indians you call savages."

"Oh . . . I . . . meant no disrespect. It's just that you have . . . blue eyes . . . and—"

"May we proceed with this, please?" Alanna

returned, her tone even. She was resigned to the fact that she would have to dress as a white woman, but she did not like it one bit, nor did she like this woman.

Mrs. Lee was silent as she hustled Alanna into the back room, took her measurements, and began bringing gowns for her to try on.

What seemed like hours later, Alanna stood before a mirror, staring at the stranger reflected there. Her waist had been cinched in by some strange contraption that made it very difficult for her to breathe. She now wore a pair of pointed slippers that pinched her toes. The gown she wore was of a soft brown material that came together in a soft bustle in back. On her head was a matching hat with feathers. Alanna had to suppress a smile, wondering what Blue Flower Woman would think if she could see her granddaughter now.

Alanna observed that she was still too thin, and her face looked pale and pinched. It came as a shock to her that she was no beauty. In her village she had been considered beautiful, but not here—not in the white world, not dressed in this unflattering gown that hid the shape of her body.

Hearing Nicholas's voice calling from the outer room, she glanced one last time at her reflection and tottered out to meet him, trying to keep her balance in the strange new shoes she wore.

Nicholas's eyes glowed when he saw her. "Very nice," he complimented her. "Just the proper attire to blend in with your new life."

"I am not pretty," she said sadly. "I once thought I was, but now I know I am not."

His eyes softened as he noticed how large her blue eyes were in contrast to the thinness of her face. Her hair, still in long braids, lent nothing to her mode of dress. The drabness of the brown frock made her skin-tone appear yellowish. "There are better traits in life besides a pretty face, Blue Eyes, and you have the most important—a kind heart."

The pain of his words was like a knife thrust in her heart. She did not care to be perceived as kind by him. She wanted to be beautiful so he would desire her as a woman.

Nicholas had turned to Mrs. Lee to settle the bill, and he did not see the tear that trailed down Alanna's face before she brushed it away. He made arrangements for the rest of her new finery to be delivered to the hotel.

He then hurried Alanna outside, down boarded walks, past the stench of the muddy streets, stopping before the door of a huge building with shining windows. Taking her arm, he ushered her into the hotel.

Alanna was awed by the way her feet sunk into the plush floral carpet as they climbed the stairs. In a whirl of color, she saw shiny mirrors, crystal chandeliers, and brass statues.

When Nicholas led her down a wide corridor, he paused before a door, inserted a key in the lock, and led her inside.

"This is your room, Alanna. Mine is directly across the hall."

Alanna was speechless as she stared at the spacious bedroom, with its soft rugs and a fine blue covering on the bed. She had never known such luxury existed. She did not see that the carpet was frayed around the edges, or that the lace curtains at the windows were a bit tattered.

Her voice was breathless. "Nicholas, this is truly wonderful."

He tried to see the shabby room through her eyes,

but only shrugged. "You will find it much grander at your father's home, Blue Eyes."

She was skeptical. "How could anything be more wonderful than this?"

"You have much to learn, little Indian." His tone was almost regretful. "But once you arrive in Virginia, your father will be your teacher."

She placed her hand on his arm. "Will you not take me to my father?"

"No, I cannot. I have other matters to attend to. You know about Miss Wickers, who has kindly consented to take you on to your father."

Her heart was heavy at the thought of being parted from Nicholas. "What matters must you see to in Washington?"

"For one thing, I am going to the Bureau of Indian Affairs to see if I can get some help for your people at the reservation."

Her eyes rounded with warmth. "You would do that for the Cheyenne?"

He smiled at her affectionately. "What I do is for you, Blue Eyes."

"After you leave, will I ever see you again?" she asked him forlornly.

He took her hand so he could reassure her. "Of course. Fairfax County is not that large. We will be neighbors."

Alanna turned away from him, wondering how she would ever live with the heartbreak of their parting. In just a few short weeks he had become her whole world.

Chapter Sixteen

Nicholas tossed his jacket on the bed and loosened the neck of his shirt. It had been a long, tiring journey thus far, and he was anxious to see it end. He was in the process of removing his boot when a soft rap came at the door.

Crossing the room, he flung the door open to find a small, birdlike woman dressed in black, peering at him over the rim of her bifocals.

"I'm Frances Wickers," she said, her eyes darting about nervously. "I believe you were expecting me, weren't you, Captain Ballinger?"

"Yes, of course," he said with relief. "Won't you come in, Miss Wickers?"

She clasped and unclasped her hands nervously. "I . . . do not think that would be wise. The gossips . . ."

"I see. I'll just leave the door open, and that will still any tongues that might wag at the impropriety of your being in my room." He rebuttoned his shirt, then moved to the bed and pulled on his jacket once more.

At first Miss Wickers took a tentative step forward, then another. Finally she got up enough courage to move out of the doorway, but she still stood rigid and watchful, as if she thought Nicholas was going to pounce on her at any moment.

For many years Frances Wickers had been in awe of the Ballinger family, as many Virginians had. Now that she was facing the master of Ballinger Hall, Nicholas Ballinger himself, she was nervous and uncomfortable.

She twisted her handkerchief into a knot. "In your letter, you stated that I would be escorting a young girl by the name of Alanna Caldwell to her father in Fairfax County, Captain Ballinger."

Nicholas, by now aware that he was the reason for the woman's agitation, moved farther away from her to stand by the window. "That is correct, Miss Wickers. How soon can you leave?"

The woman frowned. "The reason I came is to inform you that, in view of what has happened, I cannot be of service to you and Miss Caldwell."

Nicholas frowned. "One of the reasons I thought you would be an ideal escort for Miss Caldwell was because you had worked with Indians. I hope you are not prejudiced against her because her mother was Indian."

Frances Wickers drew herself up as if offended. "I have nothing against her parentage, Captain Ballinger." Her gaze hardened. "I am referring to what happened between you and Miss Caldwell. And to think you were bold enough to allow the *Missouri Republican* to flaunt your indiscretion on the front page!"

He eyed her with bafflement. "I have not seen a newspaper since arriving in St. Louis, Miss Wickers. What are you talking about?"

"I am sorry you and Miss Caldwell had such a horrendous and dangerous adventure, but I am

161

appalled that you would allow it to be printed in the newspaper for all to see. The innuendoes are made plain by the reporter, who said he was quoting you."

"What are you talking about, woman?" Nicholas demanded.

"That reporter, Frank Shelby, put the story of Alanna Caldwell's ordeal on the front page of the *Missouri Republican*. It was most shocking."

Nicholas arched his eyebrow. "More of a nuisance, but hardly shocking, Miss Wickers. If you have never been marooned in the wilderness in the middle of the winter, you cannot imagine the hardships we faced. However, Miss Caldwell handled herself admirably, and even managed to save my life twice."

Miss Wickers looked doubtful. "The article called her a half-breed, and as I told you, I have nothing against the Indians since it is my father's mission in life to bring Christianity to them, but I will never consent to being an escort to anyone who is of a loose moral character, Captain Ballinger."

Before Nicholas could say anything, Alanna entered in a flurry of flimsy white nightgown, her young body clearly outlined through the transparent material.

Frances Wickers gasped in horror while Nicholas groaned to himself.

Alanna had not seen the woman as she moved toward Nicholas. "Look at this. The woman at the shop said this was to sleep in, but must I? I would much rather sleep without anything on."

Alanna turned around when she heard a gasp. Staring at the older woman, she wondered who she was. There would be no introduction, however, for the woman backed out the door, declaring how shameful the world had become and how some

162

people had no morals at all.

"Who was that?" Alanna wanted to know. "Was she here to see you?"

Nicholas drew in an angry breath. "That, my dear, was your escort to your father's house. I can only guess what she thinks went on between you and me." He nodded at her nightgown. "That must have fueled her imagination."

"Well, she did seem to leave in a hurry."

Nicholas jerked the coverlet from his bed and draped it about Alanna's shoulders. "Go back to your room, and never come out dressed as you now are."

"But I . . ."

"Do you have any notion what you have done?"

She could see he was perplexed, but could not see why. "No, but—"

He took her by the arm and led her into the hallway. "Just do as I say, Alanna. Go to your room. I must see if I can convince Miss Wickers that she is wrong about you, but first I need to buy a newspaper so I can find out what the woman was raving about."

"But Nicholas, I did nothing to offend that woman. You saw . . . we did not even speak."

He pushed her into her room and closed the door behind her. How could anyone with Alanna's gentle and trusting nature ever survive in a world that was ready to condemn her at every turn? She would be expected to walk a very fine line to prove herself worthy of people far less worthy than herself.

Nicholas stared at the newspaper where Alanna's likeness jumped out at him from the front page. When had Frank Shelby taken that picture? He thought he had protected her from that man, but

163

obviously he had not. With his anger rising by the moment, his lips hardened in anger as he began to read:

Half-Cheyenne and half-white, Alanna Caldwell, daughter of Anson Caldwell, who is from a socially prominent family from Fairfax County, Virginia, was the heroine in a true, but unbelievable adventure. As a passenger of the Overland Stage, pretty little Alanna watched in horror as the two drivers were fatally attacked and murdered by outlaws. She was forced by circumstances to spend three nights with a young and dashing cavalry officer, Captain Nicholas Ballinger, who is also from Fairfax County, Virginia. It seems the two of them had been traveling together at the time of the attack.

Nicholas felt sick inside at what the story implied. Without reading further, he wadded up the newspaper and tossed it on the floor. He did not need to read any more to know the kind of picture Frank Shelby had painted for his readers. He had taken the truth and distorted it to fit his own aim, not caring that he had just ruined an innocent young girl's reputation!

Nicholas stood in stunned silence, trying to decide how to proceed. His first thought was to go to the office of the *Missouri Republican* and demand satisfaction from Frank Shelby, but common sense told him that would accomplish nothing and would only fuel the rumors.

He thought of Alanna, who was already faced with insurmountable problems, and this would be the final blow. When this story got out, as it surely would, she would be shunned by her father's neighbors, and perhaps by her family as well.

Nicholas's jaw set in a grim line. Had he not been crucified by the very same society after his mother's disgrace? Yes, those people would destroy gentle, sweet Alanna.

"No, by God, this will not happen to her!" he swore aloud. "I will not let Alanna be destroyed by gossip, as I was. Not if I can help it."

Angrily, he pulled open the door and walked across the hallway to Alanna's door. No one would hurt her, he would see to that!

Alanna was seated near the window, peering down at the street below, amazed by what she saw. Since the hour was late, very few people were about, but those that were seemed to be in a hurry. Shopkeepers were locking their doors and scurrying away to their homes, she supposed.

The outer door was suddenly thrust open, and Nicholas stood there, his expression livid, his green eyes sparkling with an inner light.

Alanna slowly rose to her feet, holding out her hand in a pleading gesture. "I am truly sorry, Nicholas. I have been sitting here thinking about what I could have done that was wrong when I went to your room. I believe I know. I should never have gone to your room wearing only the nightgown. Is that it? Is that why you are angry?"

Her eyes flickered, and she waited as if she needed his confirmation. "Why don't you answer me?"

There was such misery on her little face that he wanted to assure her everything was going to be all right.

When she walked toward him, he saw she had removed the transparent gown and was now dressed in the brown frock she had worn earlier.

His eyes softened as they swept her upturned face. "How do you feel about me, Alanna?"

She stopped in her tracks and cocked her head so she could study him closely, wondering why he should ask such a strange question. "I trust you more than anyone I know."

"How would you react if I were to ask you to become my wife?"

She blinked in astonishment—had he lost his senses? "Your wife? No, I cannot be your wife."

"Why not? There is no one else in your life. In fact, I am all you have at the moment. Would it be so bad to be married to me?"

"I belong to Gray Falcon." Her words did not sound convincing, even to herself.

"He's dead, Blue Eyes, and what you require at the moment is a live husband."

"You said that you would never marry," she reminded him.

"I changed my mind."

She inspected him closely and found there was sincerity in the depths of his green eyes. "You . . . I had not thought . . . I do not know."

"In that case, since you have no definite objections, we shall be married tonight." He moved to the chair where her new cloak was draped, then picked it up and held it out for her. "Shall we go, Alanna?"

Her footsteps were wooden as she walked to him. Alanna felt numb from the suddenness of his decision, and she was trying to decide why he would want to marry her. She was certain he had no deep love for her. She was not beautiful, and he did not even desire her as a woman. What could be his reason for wanting to make her his bride?

Draped snugly in the warm folds of the cloak,

Alanna allowed Nicholas to lead her out the door.

They were both silent as they moved down the stairs. Nicholas stopped just long enough to ask the desk clerk where to find a preacher.

Out they went into the cold night air, but Alanna did not feel anything, she was still too numb. How could this be happening to her? Why had Nicholas suddenly decided to make her his wife?

Nicholas stood stiffly beside Alanna, and in a clear, clipped tone responded to Reverend Millard's questions as to whether he would love, honor, and cherish Alanna Caldwell all his life, while Mrs. Millard looked on with a serene expression on her face.

"Nicholas Ballinger, do you take this woman to be your lawfully wedded wife?"

"I do."

"And you, Alanna Caldwell, do you take this man to be your lawfully wedded husband?"

"I . . . do."

"Then, by the power vested in me, I now pronounce you husband and wife. What God has joined together, let no man put asunder."

The kindly preacher smiled. "You may now kiss the bride."

Nicholas pressed a cool kiss on Alanna's forehead. She could not help comparing the sterile kiss Nicholas gave her now with the passionate kiss they had exchanged in the coach. She could not see much enthusiasm in her new husband.

After several handshakes and good wishes from the Reverend Millard and his wife, Nicholas took Alanna's arm and led her out into the street.

The wind was bitterly cold, and it had begun to rain as they made their way slowly back to the hotel.

Nicholas paused at the door of the *Missouri Republican* and reluctantly entered, propelling Alanna before him.

Frank Shelby would not be happy about the marriage, because it would kill his story. No one was interested in reading about a married couple.

There was a man behind the desk who was shuffling papers. "Can I help you?"

Placing money on the desk, Nicholas said in a heavy voice: "I would like an announcement placed in tomorrow's newspaper."

The man with thick glasses and straw-colored hair nodded, dipping his pen in ink. "Yes, sir, what would you like the advertisement to say?"

"Just write that on this day, Captain Nicholas Ballinger and Alanna Caldwell were married."

The man's eyes lit up with recognition. "Aren't you the man and woman who Mr. Shelby—"

"If you want any other details," Nicholas broke in with a commanding voice, "I suggest you contact Reverend Millard. He will help you out."

"Do you want me to find Mr. Shelby so he can do a story on your wedding?"

"There will be no story, is that clear? Just print the announcement."

"But Mr. Shelby won't like it if I don't tell him right away."

Without another word, Nicholas took Alanna's arm and steered her outside. They were silent as they made their way back to the hotel. Many questions whirled around in Alanna's mind, but Nicholas's strange mood silenced her.

She glanced up at her new husband, who looked more like a man about to go to war than a new bridegroom.

"What is happening, Nicholas?" she asked at last.

"Why are you so angry? I know you did not want to make me your wife—why did you?"

He looked at her through veiled lashes. "At least we have quieted the gossip-mongers for now."

"I am not certain I understand, Nicholas. To me, marriage is something that is sacred between two people who love one another."

"It's quite simple. Fate has played a cruel joke on us both, Blue Eyes. You'll have no bargain in me as a husband. And you do not need to worry that I will try to compete with your Gray Falcon for your affections."

Chapter Seventeen

Alanna stared at the flickering flames of the lamp that made an eerie pattern on the wall. Her mind wandered back in time to another wedding night. She had spent that night alone also.

Nicholas had escorted her back to her room and left abruptly. Two men in stiff white coats had brought her dinner, but she had not wanted to eat alone, so later, when the men returned, she sent the food away uneaten.

She had been watching out the window, hoping to catch a glimpse of Nicholas. Her back ached and her shoulders were stiff because she had been standing in one place for a long time, but still she would not give up her vigil.

Pressing her forehead against the cold glass, she watched the rain make a dusty trail down the windowpane.

It was difficult to think of herself as a wife, especially Nicholas Ballinger's wife. Going over in her mind the events of the day, she tried to find a reason for Nicholas's actions. She was certain that everything had begun to go wrong the moment she wore the nightgown into Nicholas's room to find that strange little woman there.

Alanna heard the door open, and she pivoted around to see Nicholas enter carrying his valise. He was followed by a man in uniform carrying a trunk.

She wanted to fly across the room and throw herself into his arms, but she dared not. She watched while the man placed Nicholas's trunk at the foot of the bed and then smiled at her. He left abruptly.

She looked at Nicholas with uncertainty reflected in her blue eyes. "Are you going to stay here?" she asked, almost afraid he would say no.

Nicholas nodded grimly. "It would seem the sensible thing to do, since we are man and wife. I took great pains to let the people in this hotel know that we are married. Because of the newspaper article about us, I thought it was imperative that we present the picture of the happily married couple."

"But why?"

He saw the confusion on her face. Sitting down in the chair, he held out his hand to her. "I will try and make you understand what has happened, Alanna."

She dropped down on the floor before him, and she could smell the slight scent of spirits on his breath. "I would like to understand."

"I have been in the saloon buying drinks for everyone and toasting my new bride. Because of the damage done by Frank Shelby's article on us in the newspaper, I thought the only way to retaliate was to let everyone know you are my wife. Do you understand?"

"You showed me the newspaper, but I do not really understand. How can this harm me?"

"In Virginia, more than anywhere else, Alanna, a woman is held up as an example of purity. If her name is besmirched, she is ruined socially. I did not want this for you."

"That seems a strange reason to marry me, Nicholas."

There was tension in his expression, and his green eyes were penetrating as he stared at her. "First of all, you should have no illusions about me, Alanna. I am not a man who knows how to woo a woman with pretty words. But I will tell you this: as my wife, you will never again know a cold or hungry day."

"No?"

"No. I feel I should be honest with you, however. Do not expect fidelity from me, because I am certain I would only disappoint you. There have been many women in my life, but none of them have mattered a damn. Neither of us married for love, do you understand me?"

"I believe so. Then you will not expect fidelity from me either?"

His brow knitted in a frown. "Of course I will."

"I see—fidelity from me, but not from you. I must have missed that part of the wedding ceremony."

He looked at her with measured patience. "Alanna, we should not be having this conversation."

She tried to hide the disappointment in her eyes. "Why did you marry me, Nicholas?"

"To state it simply and bluntly, to save your reputation—mine can no longer be saved."

"Why should you care about my reputation? I feel that I am responsible for my own mistakes."

"To the contrary, you are my responsibility now. You are a Ballinger."

"So this thing called a reputation is all-important? And you feel that you are to blame that mine is no longer intact?"

"I do not expect you to understand my reasons. You come from a different culture, and you cannot know the anguish you would have suffered if I had

172

not made you my wife. You will find that some people will be cruel, but you must not allow them to hurt you or to crush your wonderful spirit."

She moved forward and placed her hand on his knee. "You must care about me if you wanted to spare me hurt."

His eyes grew cold. "As I said, Alanna, have no illusions about me. And never fall in love with me, because you will only be hurt. Hold onto your Gray Falcon and keep him in your heart, but never put me there, Blue Eyes."

She tried to envision her lost love, but her new love was too strong and growing stronger every day. Her eyes moved to the bed and back again. "Will you expect nothing from our marriage?"

His lips twitched with amusement. "Nothing more than a warm body on a cold night. And we know that you can provide that. You need have no fear that I will want anything else from you."

Her eyes widened with hurt as she recalled Gray Falcon's eyes dark with desire for her, but there was no desire in the green eyes that stared at her now. "I wish you had not made me your wife. You have only complicated my life."

He clasped her hand, then laced his fingers through hers. "I have found you an admirable companion, more intelligent than any other woman of my acquaintance. You are braver than most men I know"—his smile deepened—"and you can fish better than anyone I know. We will be friends, you and I, Alanna. Will that be so hard for you?"

"And I am supposed to be your sweet little companion who turns a blind eye when you look at other women. No, thank you, Nicholas. You do not know me at all, if you think I am so addle-brained. I would rather live with my father."

173

His eyes dulled. "If that is your wish, you will go directly to your father's home. Later I will explain everything to Mr. Caldwell." Under his breath, he added, "I hope he will understand."

Alanna felt crushed that he had not insisted that she go to Ballinger Hall. "Will you tell me about my father's home?"

He stood up and pulled her up with him. "You will learn all you need to know when you arrive there."

"Will I meet your mother?"

His eyes hardened. "Yes, eventually. But you need not be concerned about her, she will not bother you. I will see to that."

She shrank from the intense coldness in his eyes. How could a man detest his own mother so thoroughly? She decided not to pursue the matter. "Will you not take me with you, since we are married?"

"No, I believe Miss Wickers can be persuaded to accompany you, now that I have made you respectable."

He stretched his arms up, cording the hard muscles across his back. "I don't know about you, but I could use a good night's sleep. Imagine sleeping in a bed again!"

She watched as he removed his jacket and began to unbutton his shirt. All at once she felt a tingling sensation in the pit of her stomach, and she was unable to catch a clear breath. She could not look away when with beautiful animal grace he removed his shirt; she saw his bare back flexed and muscled.

Suddenly overcome with embarrassment, Alanna moved to the window and stared out into the night. She could hear every move Nicholas made, and when she heard his boots hit the floor, she knew he was almost naked. The bed springs creaked, and he blew out the lamp, casting the room in darkness.

"Now you can undress, Blue Eyes. I promise not to look."

She discovered her hand was trembling when she unfastened the hook on her gown. She had slept beside Nicholas in the stagecoach. Why was this any different? Stepping out of her gown, she allowed it to drop to the floor. Next came her undergarments, and they, too, lay in a heap. She reached for the nightgown she had placed across the foot of the bed and slipped it over her head. She would sleep in it after all.

For a moment she stood, unsure of herself. Then, slowly, she pulled back the covers and slipped into bed beside Nicholas. Her leg brushed against his, and she quickly pulled away, as if the contact had burned her. She was so near him she could smell the pleasant, spicy aroma of his shaving soap.

She wanted more than anything to reach out to him, but she dared not. "Are you asleep?" she asked softly.

"No," came his reply.

"I do not know what is expected of me. You said I was only to keep you warm."

He laughed softly and drew her into his arms. "I will not force myself on you, little Blue Eyes, if that is what you are afraid of. Surely we know each other well enough by now that you do not fear me."

She stiffened in his arms. "I have never been afraid of you, Nicholas. I have told you that before."

He pulled her forward until her head rested in the crook of his arm. "I suppose, like every young lady, you dreamed of one day marrying a man who would love and cherish you. Did you, Blue Eyes?"

"Yes," she admitted, knowing that though she

loved him desperately, she dared not tell him. "I always thought I would marry for love."

"Can you ever forgive me for destroying your dream?"

"There is nothing to forgive. I am sure you think you married me for the best possible cause—*noblesse oblige.*"

He smiled. "How clever of you to use my own words against me. But I am not sure if it was a noble act that induced me to marry you. Perhaps I was selfish and wanted you all to myself. Anyway, had your reputation been ruined, no one of any consequence would have married you anyway. It seems you are stuck with me, Alanna."

She was reflective for a moment. "If I understand what you are saying, you saved my reputation at the expense of destroying my dream?"

"You are too damned intelligent for your own good. Unlike most women, you listen to what a man says, and then you use it against him."

He laughed, and unconsciously pulled her tighter into his arms. "I find I like being with you. You have not bored me one day since I met you."

What did he mean? Once again, she was not sure if he had complimented her or insulted her. "I do not mean to use anything against you, Nicholas."

"I know that. You have not yet learned to be devious and deceitful, but you will."

"I hope not."

He traced a pattern across her shoulder. "I hope not, too. I like you just the way you are."

How could he like her as she was, unattractive and too thin? Did he not wish she were more beautiful?

The storm clouds had moved away, and the moon now made a silent path across the bed so she could clearly see Nicholas's face. "I would ask only this one thing of you as my husband, Nicholas."

"This night is magic for you, Blue Eyes, because it's your wedding night. Ask, and I will gladly grant you your every wish."

"I found much pleasure in the kiss you gave me before. Will you give me another kiss?"

Silence hung heavily in the air. Then there was a hint of hidden humor in his eyes as he raised up to tower over her.

"So you will pester me until you get a kiss, like you did the last time, little savage?" He brought her closer, her body flattened against his. "Don't say you didn't ask for this," he warned. "Remember what almost happened the last time."

Alanna held her breath as he lowered his dark head. At first he held her loosely, his lips brushing hers softly. Warmth spread throughout her body, and she ached for closer contact with him.

"You little temptress," he murmured as she moved her arms about his neck and pressed her body tightly against him. "If you play with fire, you may get burned."

She gazed deeply into those wonderful green eyes, and felt like she was melting into nothingness. Again he brushed her lips, only this time her mouth followed his, and she pressed her lips against his.

Alanna felt him stiffen for a moment before he groaned and clasped his arms about her slight body, pressing her so she was molded tightly against him.

Her head was swimming and her heart was pounding like a drum. She had no will of her own, only a desire to get even closer to the hard, muscled body that was arched against hers.

"We can stop now before it goes too far," he offered in a deep voice. "But if you continue to tempt me, I will not be responsible for what happens between us."

She pulled back to look at him with eyes that were

open and honest. "I am not an innocent, Nicholas. I know about what happens between a husband and wife. My grandmother told me it was a good thing."

His body became rigid, and he grasped her chin in a firm hold, making her look at him. "Have you ever done this before, with Gray Falcon?"

"No. But I would have if Gray Falcon had lived, Nicholas."

He closed his eyes, knowing he was taking advantage of her innocence. "I see."

"I know more than you think I do, Nicholas. I have seen the beautiful mare frolic and play coy, tormenting the stallion until he breaks out of his pen to demonstrate how he feels about her." Her voice deepened as she reached up and touched his cheek. "Then the stallion takes command, and the beautiful mare is glad he did."

Nicholas was enchanted with her, and he wondered how a virginal young girl could stir his blood to the boiling point.

He had not intended to make love to her, but he knew that he would. He had never had a virgin before now, and had never wanted one, but the thought of taking Alanna made the blood run hot in his veins.

"Just remember," he told her, "you asked for this."

Chapter Eighteen

Alanna looked into his eyes, which were inflamed with passion. "Yes," she admitted boldly, "I want to become your true wife."

Nicholas placed his hands on her upper thigh and began slowly dragging her gown upward. With lightning quickness, he had drawn the gown over her head and tossed it on the floor.

With the silvery moonlight on her body, she was so lovely he felt something catch in his throat. There was no shyness in her blue eyes, only an innocence. And there was trust there.

Nicholas was overcome with an emotion he could not put a name to, but he felt a rush of tender feelings, and he found himself wanting to make this night unforgettable for her.

"Sweet Blue Eyes," he murmured, "I will introduce you to a world where you will touch me as you have never touched a man before, and I will give you what I have never given a woman before tonight."

His hand moved down her smooth neck, across her shoulder, and over her firm young breasts.

Alanna touched the hand that rested against her breasts, and raised it to place a kiss on the palm. "You may take all of me, husband, for it's all I have to give to you."

Excitement was building inside Nicholas, and yet he wanted to savor the moment, to make the memory of this night burn in Alanna's brain for all time. Slowly and deliberately, he lowered his head to touch his lips to her breast. When he heard her moan, he took the hardened nipple in his mouth and sucked it gently.

Her hand came up to rest against his back as he repeated the ritual with her other nipple. Rolling his tongue around the hardened rosebud tip, he felt her squirm and groan, and his heart raced with excitement.

Alanna felt all the breath leave her lungs, and she was lost on a sea of exquisite feelings. Nicholas became the instrument of her joy, and with each touch, each caress, he introduced her to a newer and deeper desire.

Like a tree branch that intertwines in the wind, she came to him. Catching his head in the palms of her hand, she brought his face even with hers.

He stared at her parted lips and slowly covered her mouth with his.

Nicholas felt as if a dam had broken inside him, and he was awash with feelings he had kept buried for too long. Like awaking from a nightmare and coming into the light, he gravitated toward his little Indian princess.

Spreading her legs, he could no longer hold himself back. He had to have her now. Thrusting forward, he burst through the invisible barrier and entered the soft velvet core of her body, burying deep inside her.

"Nicholas," she cried, turning her face against him. *"Nicholas."* With age-old instinct, she seemed to know how to move to please him.

As he slid forward and back inside her, he could feel his tensions melt away, and a new and deeper feeling began swirling around in his mind. He had never felt like this before with any woman. It was as if they had been made for each other. Through a blinding surge of passion, his body quivered, and he clasped Alanna to him, trying to hold onto the beauty of the moment.

He covered her lips with his and tasted the sweetness of her mouth. He could not explain the wonder of their coming together, but it did not matter. He knew the beauty would be there each time he took her.

"Sweet Blue Eyes," he murmured against her lips. "Sweet, sweet wife."

Alanna was breathlessly trying to draw air into her lungs. She clung to Nicholas, knowing she was giving herself to him completely. She loved him so deeply, and for this moment he was hers. No matter that soon they would be parted—for now, this moment, he belonged to her. He had made her his wife and created a woman where before there had been a young girl.

"Did I hurt you, Blue Eyes?" he asked with concern etched on his handsome face.

"No, Nicholas. It was a most wondrous feeling."

He stared into her face, seeing that a transformation had come over her. Her blue eyes were sparking with new knowledge. Her lips were swollen from his kisses, and her face was molded in perfect harmony with her little turned-up nose. How could he not have perceived her beauty when she was the most beautiful woman he had ever seen? His eyes moved down to her firm young body, and he knew that she was perfect.

181

Her body trembled as he bent to touch his lips to her nipples, and she opened up for him again. This time he would go slowly and love her lingeringly until they were both too exhausted to respond.

Nicholas stood over Alanna, feeling regret for taking advantage of her innocence the night before. He had not meant to, it had just happened. After holding her in his arms, it made it harder for him to do what he must. Last night he had been overcome with soft feelings and he had become a victim of his own unbound passion. This morning he was thinking clearly again, and he knew what he had to do.

Looking at Alanna now, he realized she looked so childlike, so innocent, he had a strong urge to take her in his arms and just hold her. Last night she had reached inside him and stirred his blood. She had almost made him forget his vow never to give his heart to any woman—almost, but not quite.

Anger burned in his heart as he turned his eyes away from her. Already the ugliness that had ruined his life had touched hers. Most probably he had harmed her more by marrying her, since his mother had disgraced the Ballinger name, which he had given Alanna to protect her.

With a feeling of regret, he picked up his valise and moved quietly across the room, knowing many weeks would pass before he would see Alanna again. He needed time to think, and he needed to put distance between himself and his new bride.

Alanna awakened to the sound of someone knocking on the door. Burying her head beneath the pillow, she tried to ignore whoever it was, but the caller was persistent.

She sat bolt upright, her full awareness returning. Her face lit up with happiness as she scanned the room for her husband, but Nicholas must have stepped out. Perhaps that was him at the door.

She leaped out of bed and flew across the room, but stopped short. Suppose the caller was not her husband! She did not have any clothes on.

Pulling the rumpled nightgown over her head, she reached for the coverlet and secured it about her before padding across the floor to the door. Her face fell when she saw that it was not Nicholas at all, but the woman who had been in his room the day before.

"Good morning, Mrs. Ballinger. I am Frances Wickers. May I come in?"

Alanna had not yet thought of herself as Mrs. Ballinger, and it took her a moment to remember her new married status. "Yes, please come in. But if you have come to see my husband, he is not here."

Frances Wickers placed her battered valise near the door and noted the tumbled condition of the bed. She blushed and looked away quickly. "It was your husband, Mr. Ballinger, who sent me around. He asked me to accompany you to your father's home in Virginia."

Alanna thought surely the woman had misunderstood. Yes, she had told Nicholas that she wanted to go to her father's house, but that was before Nicholas had made her his wife. Surely now he would want her to go to Ballinger Hall. "Are . . . you certain my husband said that I was to go to my father's house?"

"Yes, he was very definite about that point—he repeated it to me several times. Do you have any problem with his decision?"

"I just do not understand his reason. Where is my husband now?" Alanna simply could not believe he would make love to her and then send her off to her father.

Frances Wickers stripped off her gloves and surveyed the room. "He said to tell you he would be leaving for Washington at sunrise—it's past that now. He paid me a more than adequate salary to accompany you to your father's home, so I shall do as he said. The eastbound stage leaves at noon, so I'll help you pack."

Alanna was stunned into silence. How could Nicholas leave her after last night? She had thought he loved her. Her eyes filled with tears. Of course he did not love her. Had he not told her he was incapable of loving any woman? Why should she expect it of him?

Had last night been only an illusion—a beautiful dream that had faded with the sunrise? Oh, the love had been there, but it had been all on her side.

"There, that's done," Frances Wickers announced, firmly snapping Alanna's trunk shut. "I have left out the blue gown. Shall I order a bath for you?"

Alanna turned to her with only a trace of sadness in her eyes. "Yes, please do. We have not a moment to waste if the coach leaves at noon."

Miss Wickers was a quiet little woman, and that suited Alanna just fine in her present state of mind. She had much to think about. Her life had been changed dramatically, and she did not know where it would all end. She tried to imagine what life would be like in this Virginia. What kind of a people would her brother and sister be? Would they resent the fact that she was considered a half-breed?

Alanna was later to remember very little of the journey from St. Louis to Virginia. They traveled sometimes by boat, and once by barge, but mostly by coach. She had lost her enthusiasm, and cared little for the mode of transportation or the changing scenery. The closer she got to her destination, the more uneasy she became in her mind.

The bleak weather seemed to follow Alanna and Miss Wickers across the country. Plagued by snow, sleet, and rain, the weary travelers were in a state of near-exhaustion by the time they crossed the border into Virginia.

Once they were traveling across the Virginia countryside, the weather took a turn for the worse. Snow fell in heavy flakes and surrounded them in a dismal world of white.

As Alanna stared out the coach window, she felt tension knotting in her stomach. This was Nicholas's domain, and she felt like an intruder. Their worlds were so far apart, she wondered if they would ever be able to breech the gap that separated them . . . certainly not, if they lived in separate residences.

The blinding snowstorm impeded the horses' progress. The coach swayed and bumped over the rutted roads, while a cold wind seeped through the cracks beneath the door. Alanna and Frances Wickers huddled beneath woolen blankets, trying to keep warm as best they could.

By now Alanna and Frances had come to an unspoken understanding of one another, and Alanna found she liked the shy little woman very much. Peering at Frances now, and watching her fingers deftly manipulate the knitting needles, Alanna marveled to see a beautiful pattern take form.

Frances looked up to find Alanna watching her, and she smiled. She had grown to care for, and respect, this gentle girl who was confused by the world she had been thrust into by an unfeeling husband. Poor Alanna was lost in the ill-fitting green gown she wore, and her sweet little face, peeping out of the velvet-trimmed bonnet, held such a forlorn expression.

"Alanna, we should reach your destination by late afternoon if the weather doesn't worsen."

"I am frightened, Frances. What will I do if my family does not want me?"

"Nonsense! Not want you? I am certain you have nothing to fear on that account. Otherwise, your husband would not have sent you to them. It wouldn't surprise me if they welcome you with pomp."

Alanna was curious about many things, but mostly she wanted to know about Nicholas's world. "Do you know my husband's mother?" she asked at last.

"Heavens, no. We are not on the same social level, but like everyone else from Virginia, I have heard the gossip about her." Frances sniffed with indignation. "I care much less for those who do the gossiping than I do for the one being persecuted by them."

"Frances, Nicholas is very critical about his mother. I believe he does not like her at all."

The elder woman paused with her needle in midair. "I have always thought Mrs. Ballinger was to be pitied, but most people didn't agree with me. Perhaps if she had not been a born Yankee herself, or if her lover had not been a Yankee, her neighbors would have been far less severe on her. Then her husband was executed by the Yankees—you can see why the people shun her, Alanna."

"It must have been very difficult for Mrs. Ballinger, knowing she was responsible for her husband's death."

Frances peered over her glasses. "And the death of

186

her lover, don't forget."

"I would not know how to treat her if I were thrown into her company."

Frances patted Alanna's hand. "Just be yourself and you can't go wrong. I have a feeling the poor woman needs understanding. Perhaps you can become her friend."

Alanna smiled. "Frances, when we first met, I did not think I would like you. But you have become a dear friend to me. I will miss you when we are parted."

There was sincerity in Frances's eyes. "And I shall miss you, dear."

"Will we ever see each other again?"

"Perhaps not, Alanna. You are entering a world that I cannot be a part of." Suddenly her face brightened and she smiled. "However, if you and your husband should have children and find yourself in need of a capable governess, I would come to you at once."

Alanna stared at Frances in wonderment. She had not thought about having children. To have Nicholas's son or daughter would make her deliriously happy. That thought warmed her heart with overwhelming joy, until she realized that she and Nicholas would not be living as husband and wife.

"I am now in my forties, and I shall never marry, but I have always loved children," Frances continued. "While I was teaching the children at the mission, I became very fond of them. I believe I would be well qualified to be a governess."

"If I have children, I shall have no one but you as their governess," Alanna said, feeling pity for her friend, who was so kind-hearted, she would have made a wonderful wife and mother. "I wish you could stay with me, Frances," she said wistfully.

187

"I can't, Alanna. You need time to adjust to your new environment. It will be very different from anything you are accustomed to. But if later you need me for any reason, you have only to send me word and I'll come to you."

Alanna's eyes brimmed with tears. "You are a dear friend to me. I shall never forget your kindness."

Frances, to hide her own tears, turned her head away and stared out the window. She would miss this sweet girl. She prayed Alanna would not be destroyed by Nicholas Ballinger and the life that lay ahead of her. "Just remember what I told you. If you should ever need me, all you have to do is ask."

"I will remember, Frances." Alanna stared out the window, watching the snowflakes flutter past. "I have decided not to mention to anyone that Nicholas and I were married. If he wants it known, he can be the one to tell."

"But why?"

"I just prefer to keep it to myself until Nicholas comes from Washington." Alanna lowered her lashes. How could she tell Frances that Nicholas had married her only out of pity, or worse still, out of some feeling of duty. Since he had left her so abruptly after the wedding, he must have realized his mistake and fled.

The clicking sound of Frances's needles seemed to keep time with the clip-clopping of the horses' hooves. "If that's the way you want it," she agreed.

It was early afternoon when they reached the relay station in Arlington. The snow was still falling heavily as they stepped to the ground.

Frances steered Alanna inside the office to make inquiries about their transportation to Alanna's

188

destination. Without ceremony she spoke to the man behind the desk. "My good man, have you any orders concerning our transportation to Caldwell Plantation?"

"I don't know. Tell me your names, and I'll tell you if I have any orders concerning you," he said, looking at the pretty young girl and then at her older companion. His curious stare was so probing that Alanna stepped back behind Frances.

"This is Alanna . . . Caldwell. Any arrangements for her would have come from Nicholas Ballinger."

The chubby-cheeked man's mouth gaped open in surprise at the mention of the Ballinger name. Craning his long neck so he could see around Frances to where Alanna stood, he stared with open curiosity.

"No, I don't have any such orders. Will Captain Ballinger be coming home? What is this woman to him, and how is she connected with the people at Caldwell Plantation?"

Frances gave the man her most disapproving glance. "My good man, I am not standing here in this cold, drafty office to satisfy your curiosity. Are you certain that no arrangements have been made for us?"

The man shook his head, still trying to get a good look at the face of the pretty woman beneath the too-large bonnet. "None that I know of, ma'am."

Frances leaned across the desk, losing patience with the man's vagueness. "Then have you transportation and a driver to convey us to Caldwell Plantation at once?"

"Yes, ma'am. I'll see to it right away." He stood up, his glance still on Alanna, but his words were spoken to Frances. "Do you know when Captain Ballinger will be returning home? We haven't heard much about him these last few years."

189

Frances raised her chin and gave him a searing glance. "I'm sure that is none of your affair, sir. Just find us a carriage and driver at once."

Alanna felt as if the world was closing in on her. She was in a situation over which she had no control.

There was no looking back, and she was too frightened to look to the future.

Chapter Nineteen

Alanna felt her fear heighten with every turn of the carriage wheel. She would soon be walking into a house of strangers, and she would like to have had Nicholas beside her when she arrived.

She leaned back against the tapestry seat, wondering what awaited her at the end of the road. How soon would Nicholas conclude his business in Washington? After that, would he come to fetch her at her father's house?

"Have you ever been to Ballinger Hall, Frances?" she asked, somehow wishing Nicholas had sent her to his house rather than her father's. "I know very little about my husband's house."

"But surely Mr. Ballinger has told you how magnificent it is."

"No, not really."

"If there is a grander estate anywhere in this county, I have not seen it. The grounds are simply lovely in the spring and summer. The Ballinger family at one time opened the grounds to the public for one week each summer. I once went there as a child with my mother and father. I remember how lovely it was then." She was quiet for a moment. "Of course, that was long ago. It would have been before your Nicholas was born. I understand that as a result of the tragedy, the grounds have been closed to all outsiders."

"One can no longer visit the grounds?"

"No, and it's such a pity. It was a chance for the ordinary person to see how the elite live."

"Do you know my father?"

"I know him only by reputation. Your father is highly respected. Caldwell is also a lovely plantation, although it's not on the grand scale of Ballinger Hall."

"Will we pass anywhere near Ballinger Hall? I would like very much to see it."

"Yes. As a matter of fact, we will pass right in front of it. Would you like me to point it out to you?" Frances clasped her hands. "Oh, it will be such a nice surprise for you. Imagine, you will one day be mistress of that grand old estate. I only wish you were going there today."

Alanna pressed her forehead to the frosted window. "So do I," she said to herself.

After they had been traveling for an hour, Frances leaned forward, her voice filled with excitement as they came to a straight roadway with a great river in the distance. "This is where your husband's estate begins. It runs along as far as the eye can see and even beyond."

Alanna glanced at the snow-covered ground that gently sloped down toward the river. "What river is that?" she asked.

"That is the Potomac. At one time, it was a very busy seaport."

"But where is Nicholas's house? I cannot see it

The Publishers of Zebra Books Make This Special Offer to Zebra Romance Readers...

AFTER YOU HAVE READ THIS BOOK WE'D LIKE TO SEND YOU 4 MORE FOR *FREE* AN $18.00 VALUE

NO OBLIGATION!

MORE PASSION AND ADVENTURE AWAIT... YOUR TRIP TO A BIG ADVENTUROUS WORLD BEGINS WHEN YOU ACCEPT YOUR FIRST 4 NOVELS ABSOLUTELY *FREE* (AN $18.00 VALUE)

Accept your Free gift and start to experience more of the passion and adventure you like in a historical romance novel. Each Zebra novel is filled with proud men, spirited women and tempestuous love that you'll remember long after you turn the last page.

Zebra Historical Romances are the finest novels of their kind. They are written by authors who really know how to weave tales of romance and adventure in the historical settings you love. You'll feel like you've actually gone back in time with the thrilling stories that each Zebra novel offers.

GET YOUR FREE GIFT WITH THE START OF YOUR HOME SUBSCRIPTION

Our readers tell us that these books sell out very fast in book stores and often they miss the newest titles. So Zebra has made arrangements for you to receive the four newest novels published each month.

You'll be guaranteed that you'll never miss a title, and home delivery is so convenient. And to show you just how easy it is to get Zebra Historical Romances, we'll send you your first 4 books absolutely FREE! Our gift to you just for trying our home subscription service.

BIG SAVINGS AND FREE HOME DELIVERY

Each month, you'll receive the four newest titles as soon as they are published. You'll probably receive them even before the bookstores do. What's more, you may preview these exciting novels free for 10 days. If you like them as much as we think you will, just pay the low preferred subscriber's price of just $3.75 each. *You'll save $3.00 each month off the publisher's price.* AND, your savings are even greater because there are never any shipping, handling or other hidden charges—FREE Home Delivery. Of course you can return any shipment within 10 days for full credit, no questions asked. There is no minimum number of books you must buy.

4 FREE BOOKS

TO GET YOUR 4 FREE BOOKS WORTH $18.00 — MAIL IN THE FREE BOOK CERTIFICATE T O D A Y

Fill in the Free Book Certificate below, and we'll send your FREE BOOKS to you as soon as we receive it.

If the certificate is missing below, write to: Zebra Home Subscription Service, Inc., P.O. Box 5214, 120 Brighton Road, Clifton, New Jersey 07015-5214.

FREE BOOK CERTIFICATE

4 FREE BOOKS

ZEBRA HOME SUBSCRIPTION SERVICE, INC.

YES! Please start my subscription to Zebra Historical Romances and send me my first 4 books absolutely FREE. I understand that each month I may preview four new Zebra Historical Romances free for 10 days. If I'm not satisfied with them, I may return the four books within 10 days and owe nothing. Otherwise, I will pay the low preferred subscriber's price of just $3.75 each; a total of $15.00, *a savings off the publisher's price of $3.00.* I may return any shipment and I may cancel this subscription at any time. There is no obligation to buy any shipment and there are no shipping, handling or other hidden charges. Regardless of what I decide, the four free books are mine to keep.

NAME

ADDRESS   APT

CITY   STATE   ZIP

(   )
TELEPHONE

SIGNATURE   (if under 18, parent or guardian must sign)

Terms, offer and prices subject to change without notice. Subscription subject to acceptance by Zebra Books. Zebra Books reserves the right to reject any order or cancel any subscription.   ZBMSO2

from here."

"No, you cannot see it just now. But notice the wharves jutting out onto the river. At one time ships sailed all the way from England to the wharves of Ballinger Hall. You see, the Ballingers agreed to make their wharves into an exchange center so their neighbors could benefit as well."

"That was generous of the family."

"Yes, it was. No one could ever say a Ballinger was not public minded. In the past, Ballinger Hall supported more than two hundred slaves. Of course, the slaves are free now, and rightly so. The crops raised there are tobacco, rice, cotton, sugar, wheat, and corn. Before the war, the Ballingers raised the finest thoroughbred horses in the country."

Alanna's ears perked up. Since she loved horses, that was one thing she and Nicholas might have in common. She tried to think of them riding together across that lovely meadow in the distance.

In a rare moment of merriment, Frances gave an inane giggle. "I sound like one of the family, don't I? It's just that I have always admired the estate. When Captain Ballinger first wrote to me and asked me to accompany you to your father's house, one of the reasons I accepted was because it would give me another chance to view Ballinger Hall."

Alanna was watching the pine trees, which were beginning to thin out, giving her a better view of the estate. Suddenly, like a shimmering white mountain out of a soft blanket of drifting snowflakes, the house came into view. It was beyond anything she had expected—tall, imposing, majestic. Five acres of snow-blanketed lawn swept past the manor house all the way to the river.

Frances was watching Alanna's reaction before she started plying her with details about the grounds.

"To enter the main road," she began, "one would have to go beneath that gatehouse. The three-story mansion is built of white brick and has two wings. The columns are of white imported Italian marble. Even the doors and shutters are white. It is magnificent, is it not?"

Alanna could not follow half of what Frances was telling her, but to her, the house and grounds were so lovely it was like something out of a dream. How could Nicholas bear to be away from Ballinger Hall? Thinking about the small Indian lodge she had grown up in, she doubted this great house would ever feel like home to her—if indeed Nicholas ever acknowledged her to the rest of the world and brought her here to live as his wife.

When the carriage pulled past the gatehouse and down the winding road, Alanna was overcome with a feeling of loss. She could see now why Nicholas had agreed to send her to her father—she was not of his world.

"Just ahead, is the beginning of your father's property line," Frances said. "See, just there."

Alanna gripped Frances's hand. "Will you not change your mind and stay with me?"

Frances smiled at her with understanding. "I cannot. Captain Ballinger said I was to see you to the door, but I am not to get out of the carriage."

"But why?"

"I have wondered about that myself. Perhaps he thought you and I would not get along and you would be happy to be rid of me."

"The opposite is true, dear Frances. How can I be parted from you?"

Pointing to a tall, stately red-brick house situated on the right side of the road, Frances drew Alanna's attention. "That's your father's house."

Amid a flurry of drifting snowflakes, Alanna stared up the tree-lined avenue, feeling as if the hand of doom had just settled on her shoulders. She did not know the people who dwelled within, and she would always be an outsider. Even her father was a stranger to her now. She wished she could tell the driver to keep going.

Smoke curled from the chimney, warm and welcoming. She watched with pulses drumming as they rounded a curve in the road and the coach turned up the wide driveway.

Frances stowed her needlework in a tapestry bag and turned her attention to Alanna.

"Listen to me, and remember what I say. You are as good as, if not better than, anyone in this house, and don't let them make you feel otherwise. Hold your head up, and be proud of who you are. Fight for what you believe in!"

"I will, Frances."

By now the carriage had come to a halt, and the driver had leaped to the ground and was holding the door open. Alanna and Frances embraced, and Alanna brushed away her tears.

Frances raised Alanna's face and smiled. "God be with you, my sweet friend. Now, go before you have me crying. Go on, get inside."

Reluctantly, Alanna got out of the carriage. The house looked even larger than it had from the road. With a last glance at Frances, and after receiving an encouraging smile, Alanna walked bravely up the front steps.

Frances nodded to the driver, and the carriage moved away slowly. Alanna felt deserted as she stood forlornly on the steps of her father's house.

Turning quickly, she watched as the carriage bearing Frances disappeared beyond the trees. Her last friend in the world was gone—she was alone.

The front door opened suddenly, and it took Alanna by surprise. She stared at a man with a shiny black face and regal bearing.

His features were quizzical. "Yes, ma'am, how can I help you?"

Alanna took a step backward, hoping Nicholas had at least alerted her father that she was on her way. "Were you not expecting me?"

The servant glanced at the caller's modest wool cloak and judged her to be no one of importance. "Why, yes," he said, his face breaking into a smile. "If you're the new upstairs maid, you were expected two days ago. But don't you know enough to come to the back of the house?" He chuckled. "You hurry on around to the back door and the young miss need not know you made a mistake."

"I am not the maid," Alanna explained, wishing she were.

He looked at her, doubtful for a moment. "Then if you will tell me your name, I'll inquire within if you are expected, ma'am."

"I am . . . I am . . . Alanna . . . Caldwell," she answered, raising her chin with pride. "I have come here to see my father, Anson Caldwell."

For a moment the man seemed thunderstruck, but being well trained, he soon recovered. "Yes, ma'am, come right on in. I ask your pardon for keeping you standing in the cold." He turned back to her to make certain he had heard her correctly. "Did you say you was Anson Caldwell's daughter?"

She raised her head with as much dignity as she could summon. "Yes, I did."

The man quickly moved away, and stopped to rap on a door at the end of the hall. Alanna could hear him whisper to someone just beyond her view, but she could not hear what he was saying.

When the servant returned, he reached for Alanna's cloak, but she chose to keep it with her. "Miss Eliza has guests. She will attend you shortly."

The woman who moved purposefully down the hall had a hardness in her eyes. She loomed in front of Alanna, and her voice came out in a harsh whisper. "Who do you claim to be?"

Alanna stared at her half sister for a long moment. Eliza's hair, a soft brown, was drawn severely away from her face. Although she was pretty, she had a stingy little mouth that was drawn up in a frown, giving her a pinched look. Alanna smiled but received no smile in return.

"I am Alanna Caldwell. Were you expecting me?"

Eliza Caldwell would like to have denied that the beautiful young girl with the ill-fitting garments had any connection with her father, but with one look into those sapphire blue eyes, she knew the truth. This had to be her father's daughter from his connection with that Indian woman.

Eliza looked behind her to make certain none of her guests had followed her into the hall. "Of course, we were not expecting you. What are you doing here?" she asked in a cold whisper, as if she feared being overheard by whoever was behind that closed door.

Alanna felt the bitter disappointment of being rejected. She had always hoped her sister would like her—now that hope was dashed. She raised her chin just a little higher. "I . . . thought I might see my father."

Eliza had always hated the unknown girl that was her father's other daughter. But so far, their lives had never touched, so she could pretend this girl did not exist. But now the thing she had feared had come to pass, and Eliza felt threatened by Alanna's mere presence, and suddenly had a burning need to humble her father's half-breed daughter.

"My father is not at home. Tell me what you want, and I will relay the message to him when he returns."

Alanna felt the cruel sting of rejection, but she had always been able to present a calm appearance when she was her most devastated. "Please tell my father that I am here," she said challengingly. "Or shall I tell him myself?"

Eliza had expected her half sister to be a pitiful creature who could hardly speak English. She felt no gratification at finding out she was wrong—this girl spoke English as well as she did, and in spite of her awful gown, there was nothing pitiful about her.

"I told you, my father is not at home. And how do I know you are who you claim to be? Anyone could come in here professing to be Alanna Caldwell and expect to be taken into our home." Her eyes narrowed with spite. "I don't choose to believe you."

Alanna took a step backward at the sight of the cold hatred in Eliza's eyes. Her head came up with a proud tilt. "I *am* Alanna Caldwell, and I will remain here until my father comes home."

Eliza glanced back over her shoulder at the closed door behind her. "No, you will not. I have guests, and I won't be placed in a position of having to explain you to them. You are not wanted here," she hissed.

Alanna no longer wanted to talk to this woman. She was apparently not expected, and she would never stay where she was not welcome. "Then you will have to provide me with transportation, for I have no way of leaving."

Eliza nodded at the butler, Hamish, who still stood nearby. "See that the carriage is hitched at once." She

198

pointed at Alanna. "And see that she is transported wherever she wants to go."

With a last glance at Alanna, Eliza moved to the door. With a curt nod, she entered, but before she closed the door, her voice drifted back to Alanna. "Just a pesky problem I had to deal with. Shall we have our tea now?"

Old Hamish's eyes were filled with sympathy as he glanced at Alanna. "Don't you go worrying none, miss. When the master comes home, I'll tell him you were here. Now come with me, and I'll see you sent on your way. Have you got somewhere to go?"

She fought against the tears that blinded her eyes. "Yes," she whispered through trembling lips. "I have somewhere to go."

Alanna followed the man, wondering where that would be. She had no money, and she did not know anyone except Frances, and Frances would be miles away by now.

Her back was straight, her head held high as she moved out the door and down the steps, where she stood in the numbing cold while Hamish hurried to the stables.

There, standing on the doorstep of her father's house, Alanna felt a wetness on her cheeks. She did not like this white man's world she had been forced to enter.

When the coach drew up before her, she moved down the steps, vowing never again to come back to her father's house.

"Where to, miss?" the coachman asked as he held the door open for her and then handed her a woolen coverlet.

"Take me to Ballinger Hall," she said in a clear voice, unmindful of the man's startled glance.

Alanna was hardly aware that the coach jerked into

199

motion. She had been down before, but as of yet, she had never been defeated. And she was not going to be defeated today either!

The snowstorm had built up to a blinding swirl of whiteness as the carriage pulled beneath the gate-house of Ballinger Hall and stopped before the imposing mansion.

The coachman held the door for Alanna, and she swallowed the lump of fear that formed in her throat.

"Would you please," she asked the coachman, "tell Eliza Caldwell that you took me to the stage office in town? I do not want her to know where I am."

He eyed her with kind understanding. "Yes, ma'am. If she asks, I'll tell her just that."

Alanna nodded gratefully. Taking her courage in hand, she was ready to face Nicholas's mother. She mounted the steps, hoping she did not have to deal with another rejection today. She was just too weary and cold to think about anything but a warm shelter.

Her trunks were placed on the steps, and the driver tipped his hat to her before climbing back on the carriage and guiding the team of horses down the driveway.

Alanna's hand was trembling as she reached for the knocker and rapped at the door.

Suddenly a rush of warm air hit her in the face as the door was whisked open. The man barring her way was a stiff-mannered butler dressed in a black and gray uniform.

The man smiled and motioned for Alanna to come in out of the cold.

"How can I help you, young miss?" Askew asked, looking into a pair of the bluest and most frightened eyes he had ever seen.

Her voice was soft, almost pleading. "I am Alanna

200

Ballinger, Nicholas's wife."

Alanna was aware of a soft warm voice behind her. "Who is it, Askew?"

With a stoic expression he answered, "This is Alanna Ballinger, Madame. It seems Master Nicholas has sent his wife home to you!"

Chapter Twenty

Alanna could do no more than stare at the woman who moved gracefully into the great hall. Her raven-black hair was pulled away from her face and fastened in a loose knot at the nape of her neck. She wore a black velvet gown with a wide white lace collar. Her face was unlined, her features unspeakably lovely, and her green eyes, so like Nicholas's, were probing in disbelief.

She advanced a step in Alanna's direction and then paused. "What did Askew say, young lady? Did he mistake your meaning?"

Knowing she could not deal with another confrontation today, Alanna stammered wearily, "I . . . am Nicholas's wife . . . we were married in St. Louis. He . . . has sent me to my father's house, but I could not stay . . . not knowing where to go . . . I came to you. Please do not turn me away."

"Of course I will not turn you away." Still the woman searched Alanna's face as if she were looking for something. "I find it hard to fathom that Nicholas would not have made certain of your destination. Where is my son? Why didn't he come with you?"

"He . . . is in Washington."

"I see." Suddenly the lovely vision smiled and moved forward, trailing the sweet scent of an unknown fragrance. "Had I known you were coming, I would have prepared a more suitable welcome." She brushed her cool cheek against Alanna's. "You are cold. Come into the parlor and warm yourself while Askew sees to your trunks." She looked briefly at the servant. "Put her in my son's room."

Alanna, overcome with relief at being accepted by Nicholas's mother, looked about the great room, vaguely aware of the gilded mirrors and family portraits that adorned the paneled walls.

She followed Mrs. Ballinger, almost too weary to think coherently.

The room they entered was large and imposing, and the richness of the interior displayed great wealth. Like the outside of the house, this room was all white. A plush white rug lay over a shiny wooden floor. White walls and white couches and chairs lent their charm to the decor. A white marble fireplace glowed with a welcoming light.

Alanna had never thought to see such magnificence. No wonder Nicholas was unimpressed with the hotel in St. Louis! "Your house is very beautiful, Mrs. Ballinger."

Lillia Ballinger's smile was open and genuine. "You must call me Lillia. What shall I call you?"

"My name is Alanna."

"What a lovely name. We once had a neighbor by that name. But she died long ago."

"If her last name was Caldwell, I believe she may have been my grandmother."

Lillia looked puzzled. "Your grandmother? I never knew Alanna Ballinger had any grandchildren other than Anson's offspring." She looked puzzled for a moment. "But then I do not know the family very well."

Alanna was stiff and weary from so many days of traveling, and she still shivered from the cold. Not wanting to discuss her father, or to be reminded about being turned out of his house, she changed the subject.

"I am sorry that I came so unexpectedly. I had hoped Nicholas would have written you of our marriage."

Lillia ushered Alanna before the fire and seated her in an oversized chair. "No, my son has not written me in a very long time." Her eyes were soft as they ran over Alanna's features, and she smiled. "I cannot tell you how delighted I am that Nicholas has at last taken a wife." Her green eyes flickered with pain as she walked to the bell pull and gave it a strong tug. "I had feared he would never marry," she said wistfully.

Alanna untied the ribbons of her bonnet and removed it, allowing her braided hair to fall free. "You are not sorry he married me?"

Lillia sat down in the chair near Alanna, with a puzzled frown on her face. "No, my dear, I am not sorry my son married you. Why should I be? I have always thought, if and when my son married, he would choose someone exceptional. Therefore *you* must be exceptional."

Alanna felt tears of gratitude building up behind her eyes. She had not expected to be met with such warmth. Before she could speak, a cheery-faced maid with wisps of snow-white hair trailing from beneath a peached cap moved forward with lithe strides.

"Kitty, what do you think? Nicholas has sent me a daughter-in-law."

The older woman's eyes sparked with interest, and

her face creased in a smile. When she spoke, it was with a heavy Irish brogue: "Lord love you, child. I never thought I'd see the day my Nicholas would be married." She eyed Alanna closely. "And such a pretty little thing you are, too. But you would have to be to catch the eye of *that* handsome rogue."

Lillia laughed. "Alanna, Kitty has been with me since I was a girl in Philadelphia. When I married Nicholas's father, she came with me to Ballinger Hall. She runs everyone's life on the plantation, including mine. And if you don't watch out, she will be ordering you around as well."

Alanna glanced from one woman to the other, not knowing what to say.

"Now, don't be filling her head with wild notions about me, Madame," Kitty bantered with the warmth of someone who was more a valued friend than a servant. "You'll have her thinking I'm a tyrant."

Suddenly the maid noticed Alanna shiver. "Poor little one, she's frozen clear through, and us here talking her head off." She reached for Alanna's hand and pulled her to her feet. "It's into a hot bath and bed for you. Then I'll bring you a nice warm meal."

Lillia laughed in amusement. "Did I not warn you that Kitty would soon be in charge of your life, Alanna? But go along with her for now. We will become better acquainted tomorrow, after you have rested."

So many new emotions showed on Alanna's face. There was warmth here, she could feel it. How could Nicholas hate Lillia, when she was so wonderful? Too cold and weary to think about that at the moment, she allowed Kitty to lead her up the massive, winding stairs to the master suite.

By the time they reached the bedroom, Alanna was too tired to even examine the room.

Kitty, seeing this, clucked over her like a mother hen. "There, there, you're all done in. Just climb into bed and rest for a spell. Here, allow me to help you out of that gown, so you can lie down. Later on this evening, if you feel up to it, you can bathe and eat."

Alanna was perfectly willing to allow Kitty to undress her. When the maid pulled back the covers on the bed, Alanna climbed in, and was asleep almost before her head hit the soft pillow.

She did not even hear Kitty when she moved to the massive fireplace to lay a fire. She was also unaware that Lillia came in later and stood over her while she slept, staring with tears in her eyes at the young girl her son had married, and hoping this meant he would soon be coming home.

When Lillia tiptoed out of the room, Kitty followed her downstairs and into the parlor. Only when she moved to the window to watch the softly falling snowflakes did Lillia speak.

"What has my son done, Kitty? This lovely child was so lost and alone when she came in. She is an innocent. How can she be expected to deal with a complicated man like Nicholas? I do not understand. Is this some new torture he has sent me?"

"You're thinking he might have a bit of his father in him, aren't you?"

"Oh, no, he is nothing like Simeon, and you know it." Her eyes grew wistful. "Remember what a sweet and loving boy Nicholas was?"

"Yes, and I remember more than that too. I remember how he blamed you for his father's death, and how he goes on blaming you."

Lillia smiled sadly. "I can take his coldness, Kitty, because I deserve that. His father and I both played a part in making him bitter and disillusioned. I had hoped—that being away would give him time to adjust to what happened. But, I just don't know."

"I doubt if that little girl knows what she's got herself into. She ain't the kind of girl your son usually associates with."

"You are right, Kitty. His taste most often ran to a more wordly wise woman, or even the sophisticated and polished debutantes, but this girl is . . . young, innocent."

"Perhaps he loves her?"

"Perhaps." Lillia smiled. "She is lovely, Kitty. With the right clothes, and a little polishing, she will sparkle like a rare and beautiful jewel."

The maid chuckled. "Well, you always wanted a daughter, and it looks like you finally got your wish."

Lillia was thoughtful for a moment, and suddenly her eyes lit up. "Send someone into Alexandria and bring back the dressmaker, Mrs. Minion. Tell her to bring her extra seamstresses, and tell her they should expect to remain with us for at least two or three weeks."

"I'll attend to it, but have you thought Nicholas might want his bride to remain the way she is? Hadn't you better leave her be until he comes home?"

Lillia's eyes sparkled with excitement. "Yes, I have considered that possibility. I am not going to let what happened to me happen to her, Kitty. Nicholas left unchecked might develop some of his father's traits. I will arm that girl with confidence so she can stand toe-to-toe with my son and meet him on his own terms. If I had done so with Simeon in the beginning, things might have turned out differently between us."

Kitty snorted. "It wasn't anything you did that made Simeon Ballinger into the monster he was. His personality was already formed when you met him, and you know it. But I have no fear that Nicholas will be like him," she said with confidence. "He is more your son than he ever was Simeon's. Nicholas is just fighting against what he thinks you did to his father. The day will come when he realizes he is wrong."

Lillia's brow creased into a frown. "Do you suppose Nicholas told her about me?"

"No, how could he, 'cause he don't know the whole story. It makes me angry every time I remember how you took the blame for what happened, when it was his father who was at fault. I still think you should tell him what really happened. It isn't right that you bear all the blame and Nicholas believes his father was an innocent victim."

Tears gathered in Lillia's green eyes. "I cannot tell him the truth, Kitty. And I'm surely not innocent. I must protect Nicholas from finding out the kind of man his father was, and for that I will suffer my son's hatred, if need be."

Kitty walked across the room, mumbling under her breath. "You're too young for sainthood, but Simeon Ballinger was certainly one of the devil's disciples."

Upstairs, in the quiet serenity of Nicholas's bedroom, Alanna had the first peaceful night's sleep she had known since her grandmother's death. As the snowflakes silently drifted past the bedroom window, she sighed in her sleep and curled up warmly beneath the eiderdown comforter.

When Kitty pulled back the heavy curtains, sunlight flooded the bedroom and fell across Alanna's face. Coming awake swiftly, Alanna stretched her arms over her head and returned the housekeeper's smile.

"Madame said it was time for you to be up and about. The dressmaker's already here, and you still have to bathe and eat." She held a warm robe out to Alanna. "Come on, time's a-wasting."

Alanna blinked her eyes, not understanding half of what the little woman was saying. "Am I to have new gowns?"

"Indeed you are. And you can trust Madame to choose well for you. She is a wonder when it comes to fashion."

Alanna shook her head to clear it. "Did I sleep through the night?"

The housekeeper smiled. "You were all done in. You slept the clock around."

There was a knock at the door, and Kitty opened it and directed the servants to place the copper tub before the fireplace while she built up the fire. Steaming water was poured into the tub, and soft towels and perfumed soaps were placed nearby.

When one of the servant's curiosity got the better of her, and she glanced at Alanna, wanting to see the woman the master of the house had married, Kitty rushed the whole lot out of the room.

"Now that's the last of them, so you can be allowed to take your bath in peace."

Alanna slipped out of bed and padded across the floor. "Am I to bathe in that?"

Kitty watched the girl's eager face. "Of course, you are."

Alanna, who was still wearing her petticoat, quickly slipped it over her head and laid it on a chair. Stepping out of her underdrawers, she stood, unembarrassed and naked, before the startled Kitty. "Shall

I just step in? I have never bathed in one of these before."

Kitty's eyes widened in shock. "You mean you have never had a tub bath?"

"No. I have always bathed in the river. My grandmother was an oddity in the Cheyenne tribe because she insisted I bathe often, even in the winter."

Poor Kitty's mind was in a muddle as she tried to follow Alanna's conversation. "Just slip in the tub and have a good wash," she said, trying to get the naked girl into the water.

Tentatively, this was accomplished, and the house-keeper handed Alanna a bar of soap. "Would you like me to wash your hair for you?"

With her body immersed in the tub, Alanna dipped her hands in the water and felt it trickle through her fingers. "Yes, please."

Kitty lathered Alanna's midnight-black hair with the sweet-scented lilac soap. After she was certain it was clean, she poured water over the girl and stepped back.

"Will you be needing help with the rest of your bath, miss?"

"No, I can manage quite well."

Kitty moved to the door and paused with her hand on the knob. "I laid out the gray gown for you." She hesitated. "A moment ago, you spoke of the Cheyenne. Were you referring to Indians?"

Alanna looked into the seeking eyes of the little housekeeper. "Yes, I am an Indian and belong to the Cheyenne tribe."

Trying to keep her composure, and nearly suc-ceeding, Kitty nodded. "I'll bring your breakfast right away."

When the housekeeper had gone, Alanna leaned

her head against the edge of the tub and stared at the ceiling. As before, she could feel there was warmth and love in this house. She liked the perky Kitty, and she had found Nicholas's mother to be warm but somehow sad.

Her eyes moved around the room that she had been too weary to inspect on her arrival last night. It was a large room, decorated in warm colors that reminded her of Nicholas. The wine-colored rug matched the bed covering and curtains at the window. The massive bed was beautifully hand-carved, and against one wall a brown leather sofa sat near the fireplace.

She smiled, thinking about sharing this wonderful room with Nicholas.

The housekeeper rushed into the bedroom, where Lillia was propped up against several pillows. As she approached her mistress, a frown clouded Kitty's usually shining gray eyes.

"Kitty, did you make sure Nicholas's wife feels at home? Did you tell her the dressmaker is waiting to take her measurements?"

"Yes, I did all that, but I think you have one giant problem on your hands. Even now, I don't even know how to explain it to you."

"Whatever do you mean?"

Kitty shook her head. "Nicholas's wife just admitted to me that she grew up with Indians. And that's not all—she says she's an Indian, too!"

"Nonsense." Lillia looked doubtful. "How can that be? She has already admitted to being the granddaughter of the late Alanna Caldwell. Besides, she is light-complected and has blue eyes, so she can't be an Indian. Her manner of speech would indicate that she comes from an aristocratic Southern background. Of course, her clothing is appalling, but—"

"I'm telling you," Kitty broke in. "The girl says she's an Indian!"

Lillia threw the covers aside and pulled on her dressing gown. Pushing her feet into her slippers, she moved to the door.

"Set up a table in Nicholas's bedroom so I can have breakfast with the girl. I think I had better learn more about his bride. If this is my son's notion of how to strike back at me, he has badly misjudged me."

Chapter Twenty-One

Alanna had just pulled the gray gown over her head when the knock sounded at the door.

Barefoot, and clutching the front of the gown together, she opened the door to find Nicholas's mother standing there looking elegant in a flowing pink velvet dressing gown, and not a hair out of place.

"Good morning," Lillia said cheerfully. "If you have no objections, I have asked Kitty to set up a table in here. I thought it would be nice if we had breakfast together so we might get better acquainted on your first morning here. Would you like that?"

Alanna's eyes sparkled. "Yes, very much. I would like us to know one another."

As Lillia moved into the room, her dressing gown molded to the outline of her body. Alanna felt awkward and dowdy beside her stunning beauty.

Lillia looked around the bedroom with a wistful expression on her face. "I have always kept this room ready in case Nicholas should come home unexpectedly. It is cleaned and aired each week, with logs in the fireplace so it could be lit on a moment's notice."

She smiled at Alanna. "I am glad now that I did,

because it was ready to receive you when you arrived last evening. Did you have a restful sleep?"

"Yes, I did."

Alanna's fingers felt stiff as she fumbled with the hook of her gown and slipped hurriedly into her shoes. "It is a very nice room. It is not hard to imagine Nicholas in this environment."

Lillia listened to the girl speak. There was nothing in her voice that would indicate she had been raised by Indians. She spoke clearly and distinctly, with only the hint of a Southern accent.

By now Kitty had come into the room and was directing two maids to set up a table, while two others were placing food on the snow-white tablecloth. When the chairs had been placed at the table, Lillia motioned for Alanna to join her there. When Kitty was satisfied that everything was perfect, she motioned for the maids to leave, and she followed them out.

Lillia could sense Alanna's discomfort, and smiled to put her at ease. "I know how difficult it is to meet new people. I am rather shy by nature, although I have learned to hide it well."

"I cannot imagine you being afraid of anything, Mrs. Ballinger."

"We are on a first-name basis, remember? You will call me Lillia, and I shall call you Alanna."

"Yes, Lillia."

"First of all, tell me about yourself so I might get to know you."

Alanna raised her head and stared into bright green eyes. "I am the half-white daughter of Anson Caldwell," she said with defiance sparking in her eyes. "I will not apologize to you or to anyone else for who I am."

Lillia tried not to look shocked at the unsettling bit

214

of information. "Nor should you ever have to apologize for who you are. Tell me how your father and mother met," she said softly. "I wonder why I never heard of it. I knew that Anson had traveled west for some years, but I never knew of your mother."

"I suppose my father was ashamed of me and told no one of my existence."

"Tell me about your childhood and how you came to know my son."

The pot of hot tea cooled, and the breakfast went uneaten as Alanna fascinated Lillia with the story of her life. She told how her grandmother had died and how Nicholas had come into her life that cold wintry day.

Alanna stumbled over the part where Nicholas felt obligated to marry her. She did not mention their wedding night, but Lillia read between the lines. She could see the heartbreak in Alanna's face when she told about waking up in the hotel in St. Louis and finding Nicholas gone.

"And how did you happen to come to Ballinger Hall? You said something about going to your father's home first. Perhaps you had better tell me about that."

Alanna told Lillia about her confrontation with Eliza Caldwell, and Lillia could read the hurt in her daughter-in-law's eyes.

"We shall deal with her all in good time. In spite of Eliza's rudeness, I believe your father would like to know you are here. When we are ready, I will inform Anson of your whereabouts."

"I do not want to see him! You cannot imagine how strong that feeling is. I would not even know how to act with him. It has been too long since I have known him as a father."

"You think that now, dear, but you may change

215

your mind." Her smile was bright. "Whatever the reason, I am delighted to have you in the family."

Lillia reached across the table and clasped Alanna's hand. "Now, I am going to tell you what we are going to do, so you can win that handsome husband's heart. Although I fancy he is already enchanted with you." Her eyes took on a greener glow. "When my son comes home, he is not going to recognize his little bride. As you know, I have sent for the dressmaker, and you are going to be transformed into an elegant lady."

Alanna's eyes sparkled with hope. "I want to look and act like you."

"No, my dear, it is much better that you be yourself. You are far more beautiful than I ever was."

"No, I—"

Lillia held up her hand to halt Alanna's denial. "Your training will not stop with your wardrobe. With your permission, I will teach you all the tricks a woman should know to catch and hold a man's interest—and there are tricks. You have a natural beauty, and we shall merely call attention to it."

"Am I really pretty?"

"Alanna, you are stunning. No matter what my son said, he knew that when he married you. He will be forced to admit it to you before we are finished."

"I love Nicholas a great deal, but he has told me he will never love a woman. I do not expect him to change his mind just because I change my wardrobe."

Lillia's eyes narrowed. "So he told you that, did he? Well, Master Nicholas Ballinger has a shock coming to him. The very idea of marrying you under such circumstances! Sometimes a woman has to teach a man a lesson in manners."

Alanna drew in her breath. "Please help me to be a woman Nicholas can be proud of."

Lillia smiled. "All will be well, I promise you. But tell me, wherever did you get that awful gown? I know it isn't yours, because it is much too large for you."

Alanna smiled. "Nicholas purchased all the clothing in St. Louis. None of the gowns fit properly, but I did not want to complain."

"It sounds just like what a man would do, but then, they cannot be expected to pay attention to fashion. Let me tell you what I have observed about men. They very rarely pay heed to a woman's appearance if she is properly dressed, but let one hair be out of place and it draws their attention at once. Will you trust me to help you?"

Alanna felt a surge of joy. "I will do whatever you say."

Lillia looked at the table and shook her head. "First of all, let's go below to the kitchen and find out if cook has more blueberry muffins—these are cold. Then, after we have eaten, I am going to cut your hair."

Alanna's eyes rounded. "I have never had my hair cut before."

"Then it's high time you did."

The afternoon was spent with the dressmaker. Alanna had her measurements taken, then she and Lillia looked at fabrics and pored over the latest pattern books, deciding which gowns would be most flattering to Alanna.

It was late afternoon when an exhausted Alanna lay across her bed watching her mother-in-law go through her trunk.

"This won't do," Lillia said, tossing the last of the gowns Nicholas had bought her in St. Louis on the

217

floor. "Dispose of all these," she said to Kitty, who nodded in approval.

Reaching into the bottom of the trunk, Lillia lifted out the elkskin gown.

Alanna raised up, ready to protest if Lillia wanted to throw her gown away. "My grandmother made that for me."

"Oh," Lillia said in wonder. "This is exquisite. Such tiny stiches, and such lovely work. Your grandmother must have been a wonderful seamstress."

"Yes, she was," Alanna said, happy that Nicholas's mother appreciated her grandmother's craft.

"We shall have to do something special to preserve this. Your children will one day want to see it." Her eyes softened. "Nicholas's children." Suddenly her eyes became misty. "Only God knows what my grandchildren will think of me."

Before Alanna could answer, Lillia smiled. "Mrs. Minion says she will have nothing for you to wear for two days, but her creations are worth waiting for. Until then, I have brought you three of my gowns, which she shortened for you. Also there are a robe and several nightgowns. You will just have to suffer with the ill-fitting undergarments until we can go into Arlington to choose proper ones. As for footwear, I have brought you several pairs of my shoes. It appears we both wear the same size."

Alanna's head was swimming with gowns, shoes, and silken undergarments. "Thank you, Lillia," she said with sincerity.

Lillia smiled at Alanna's serious expression. "Come on, get off that bed. Dinner is ready, and afterward we have work to do."

Alanna groaned, but she slipped off the bed and followed her mother-in-law out the door. After all, she was hungry.

"We may not have much time until Nicholas comes home, Alanna."

"How can a wardrobe change how Nicholas feels about me, Lillia?"

"Not without your help. You see, if you feel good about yourself, that will be evident to anyone who sees you. Besides, you are so lovely, you deserve to be presented in the best possible light."

As Alanna sat across the formal dining room from Nicholas's mother, she listened to her instructions. "Now, when you are asked if you want a second helping of any food, you will graciously reply, 'No, thank you.' Is that understood?"

"Why? Suppose I am still hungry?"

A smile tugged at Lillia's lips. "Frankly, I don't know why. Where I was brought up in Philadelphia, men liked to see their women eat a healthy meal. However, here in the South, a woman must appear to be starving. It just doesn't make sense, does it?"

"Not to me it doesn't."

"Nor to me. Now, which fork do you use with the dessert? Yes, that's right, that one. You are a wonder, Alanna, you retain everything I explain to you, and I never have to tell you twice."

"Sometimes this ritual of manners, and all the do's and don'ts, seem very foolish to me. If you had come to my grandfather's lodge, you would have eaten with your fingers. It seems much more sensible to me."

Lillia leaned back in her chair. "I would have loved to have known your grandparents. I'm sure they were very special, because they have made you special."

Alanna's heart warmed to this gentle woman who had received her with such kindness. She was determined to be everything Lillia wanted her to be. She wondered how Nicholas could ever have turned away from his mother.

After dinner, the lessons continued in the parlor. Lillia was seated on the sofa, while Alanna stood before the fireplace. "Let me see you walk," Lillia commanded.

Alanna was wearing a soft pair of kid shoes that had been Lillia's. She moved across the room and back, becoming more accustomed to the high heels each time.

"Good!" Lillia exclaimed. "Now your walk cannot be improved on, so let me see you sit."

Alanna moved to a chair and sat down. "No, no. A lady always sits on the edge of her chair, with her ankles crossed and her hands clasped in her lap. Try it again. Yes, that is good, yes, yes. Another important thing I want to point out to you is that if someone inquires of you 'how are you doing?' it is not an invitation to tell them of your aches and pains, or that you did not sleep well the night before. It is merely a greeting and you are to answer, 'Fine, thank you.' Will you remember that?"

"I . . . believe I understand. If they ask how I am feeling, they do not really want to know."

Lillia laughed. "Now that I have looked at our rules through your eyes, I see how foolish we are. Like actors in a play, we act a part and move through our lives like strutting peacocks."

The clock struck ten, and Lillia motioned for Alanna to come and sit by her. "The first day we have

220

accomplished a lot, and you have done extremely well."

Alanna was pleased by her compliment. "I am exhausted," she admitted.

"And so you should be, because you have worked hard. Tomorrow, we shall continue."

Alanna groaned. "Will I ever be a lady?"

"You are already that. There is a grace and bearing about you that many women would envy. Some things cannot be taught, they are inbred, little Indian princess." Lillia looked troubled for a moment. "I want to ask you about your father. Have you reconsidered informing him that you are here?"

"I . . . no, I do not want to see him."

"Alanna, I wish you would relent and allow me to send for him. I know you resent him, but you don't know the whole story of what happened to him after your mother died." Lillia thought of how Nicholas had turned away from her. "Give him a chance to explain. See him and talk to him. Perhaps you will find him to be a nice person."

Lillia saw the doubt in Alanna's eyes. "Think about it, my dear. You don't have to decide anything now. But everyone deserves to be heard, because circumstances are not always what they seem."

Alanna had the feeling Lillia was talking about herself and her son. "I will think about it," she agreed.

Alanna found herself wide awake. The longer she lay staring at the ceiling, the more awake she became. She had been thinking about what Lillia said, and she could not make a decision about seeing her father.

At last she moved off the bed and slipped into the

221

warm robe Lillia had given her. For some reason her footsteps took her out of the bedroom and down the stairs to the parlor.

A bright moon shone through the window, and Alanna saw that she was not alone. Lillia stood at the window, staring out into the night. She must have sensed Alanna's presence, for she turned to face her.

"So, Alanna, you could not sleep either."

"I suppose my head was too filled with thoughts of beautiful gowns."

"I find it strange that you should come to this room, because you see, very often I cannot sleep, and I come here. For some reason, it seems to comfort me. It has since I first came to live here."

"It is a lovely room, Lillia."

"I have known many happy hours here, and some sad ones as well."

Alanna moved closer to her mother-in-law, and they both stared out the window. "Life is unkind sometimes, Lillia. I suppose we must balance the good against the bad, and hopefully the good will win."

Lillia's soft laughter filled the room. "Do you know something, my serious little friend? I am so grateful that you have come into my life. You have filled a void that has been too long empty. My son is going to know many happy days with you as his wife."

"I hope so. But Nicholas may not agree. I believe he would far rather have remained unwed."

For a long time the two of them stood there until at last Lillia spoke: "What, if anything, did Nicholas tell you about me, Alanna?"

Alanna tried to avoid Lillia's eyes. "He . . . spoke very little of you."

Lillia gripped Alanna's shoulder and made her

222

look at her. "You know about what happened to Nicholas's father, don't you?"

"I know what Nicholas *thinks* happened to his father. After meeting you, I realize there is more to it than he knows. I feel that you must be protecting Nicholas from something. I also know you could never be unkind to anyone, or do the things you are accused of."

Lillia took in a deep breath. This dear little girl had just set her free with her open trust. "I want to thank you for not assuming that I am guilty. You are the first person who thought there might be more to the tragedy than was told. No one else even asked me for my side of it."

"Would you like to talk about it, Lillia? You can trust me, you know."

"Yes, my dear, I know I can trust you. But to tell you would only put a great burden on your young shoulders, for you see, you could never tell Nicholas the truth."

"Have you told no one about the night that your husband died?"

"No, no one. Only my faithful Kitty knows what really happened."

"I'll leave you now, Lillia, but if you ever want to talk—"

Suddenly the older woman sat down on the window seat, and Alanna saw the tears streaming down her face.

"I have changed my mind, Alanna. I have decided to take you into my confidence. It may be selfish to burden you with the horrible truth, but I feel you will understand. I don't want to die without someone knowing what really happened that night. I can only hope you will not hate me after you know the truth, for you see, I was not the monster Nicholas thinks I

223

am—but neither am I blameless."

Alanna sat down beside Lillia, sympathy shining in her blue eyes. "Tell me whatever you want to, and I will never betray your confidence."

Lillia felt as if a great load had been lifted; she was about to transfer some of her pain to younger, more capable shoulders.

Chapter Twenty-Two

Lillia did not want to remember the circumstances surrounding her husband's death. Indeed, she had fought for years to forget about the incident. But the time had come to tell someone, and she trusted Alanna never to tell Nicholas. She clutched her hands together as pictures of the past moved through her mind like a kaleidoscope of flashing colors.

"Alanna, I grew up in Philadelphia. Ours was a happy home, with my mother and father and three older sisters. After my sisters had married and moved away, I was content to remain at home with my parents."

She smiled as if remembering something pleasant. "You may not believe this, but I was considered beautiful, and many suitors called on me, although I did not give my heart to any of them. I did not want to leave home."

"I think you are still lovely," Alanna said. "But please do not speak of this if it is too painful to you."

Lillia shook her head sadly. "No, you must hear what happened. Perhaps if I had been less beautiful, my life would have taken a different turn." She was quiet for a moment, as if she was considering that thought. At last she spoke, and it was as if she were talking to herself. "I will never forget the day Simeon Ballinger came into my life. It would have been far better for him and me if I had never laid eyes on him."

"How did the two of you meet?"

"Simeon Ballinger was a dashingly handsome Southerner. Although Nicholas has my hair and eye coloring, he looks very like his father. Of course, Simeon was much older than me when I met him. He was forty-three, and I was seventeen."

Lillia looked into Alanna's eyes. "You will have to understand that Simeon swept me off my feet. I was raised in a modest home. My father was a dear man, but a poor manager. He needed money to pay off some debts, so he was selling off his livestock. That's why Simeon came to Philadelphia. Simeon had heard that my father was selling his string of Arabian horses, and he had come to look them over."

Lillia's eyes were swimming with tears, and she looked at the ceiling, trying to gather her composure.

Alanna dropped down on her knees and clasped her mother-in-law's hand. "Do not distress yourself with this ordeal. Let us speak of other matters."

Lillia laid her hand on Alanna's head. "Even though it is painful, bear with me to the end. The truth should be heard, if nothing else, so you can tell my grandchildren when they are old enough to understand. I would not like them to believe their grandmother was the kind of woman the gossips would have you believe."

Alanna realized that Lillia needed to talk about her past, so she nodded. "You talk, and I will listen."

Lillia's heart swelled with love for her newly acquired daughter. She only hoped that Nicholas would know what a jewel he had in Alanna before it was too late. She gathered her courage and looked into the trusting blue eyes. "When I first laid eyes on Simeon, stars were dancing in my head. He was handsome, aristocratic, and very much a gentleman. Later, he told me that when he saw me, he knew I would be his wife. The wedding was the social event of the season in Philadelphia. Simeon was generous and settled enough money on my parents to help keep them from financial ruin."

Lillia's eyes clouded. "I was to learn that Simeon could be very generous. He was free with money, always willing to help a friend or neighbor. I thought he did it out of the kindness of his heart, but I was later to learn that that was not the case. He was an extremely wealthy man and could afford to be generous with money, but he was a selfish and stingy person when it came to giving of himself." She shook her head. "But we will not get into that. Simeon's one love was Ballinger Hall, and he would do anything to preserve it. Just how far he would go would not become clear to me until the outbreak of the Civil War."

"Were you happy for a time?"

"Yes. Can you imagine how I felt when he brought me here? Oh, it was grand to know that I would be the mistress of the finest estate in Virginia." Her shoulders slumped. "How naive I was to think I had Simeon's love! He lavished me with lovely gowns, jewels, everything money could buy . . . but it was for show. You see, the mistress of Ballinger Hall must be a shining example for the rest of Virginia to look up to. Actually, at the time I came here we were putting on an exhibition once a year so everyone could see how grandly we lived. The gates were thrown open, and anyone who wanted to could come in and gawk at us."

"I know about that. The woman who escorted me

227

here, Frances Wickers, told me she had been allowed to visit Ballinger Hall when she was a child."

Lillia was reflective. "I had not been settled in Ballinger Hall for much over four months when Simeon began to disappear for days at a time, and he would never tell me where he was going. It took three years until I found out, from a well-meaning but mean-spirited neighbor, that Simeon had a mistress in Arlington and one in Richmond. I cannot tell you how tormented I was. I refused to believe it until I faced Simeon and he took pleasure in admitting the truth to me."

Lillia glanced out the window. "It was a winter night, very much like this one. I stood over there near the fireplace, and he was seated on the sofa. Oh, how cruelly it hurt me when he laughingly admitted he had many lovers, and that I was the least of them."

Lillia looked in Alanna's eyes, as if searching for understanding. "Can you imagine how I felt?"

Tears were building up in Alanna's eyes. "I am sorry you were so grievously treated."

"I don't want you to think I am placing all the blame on Simeon. For one thing, I believe he did not realize when he married me that his neighbors would think of me as 'that Yankee from Philadelphia.' He was always conscious of his neighbors' opinions, and he was affected by their dislike of me."

"I do not understand prejudice."

"Neither did I. Anyway, being young and unsophisticated, I am sure I must have been a disappointment to Simeon. I was to find out that he preferred a more mature and experienced partner. He told me that I was dull and unexciting, and he sought more desirable . . . lovers." She grasped Alanna's hand. "I wanted to die, but I didn't. At that time, I discovered I was going to have a baby, and I was happy about that."

Lillia took a trembling breath and rested her head on the back of the windowseat. "I wanted that baby so badly. In my naive way, I thought having his child would make Simeon love me. He was kind to me while I was carrying the baby, but when I miscarried, it was if he blamed me, and from there matters only worsened. He was never home, and when he was, he shut himself in the library and drank. His valet had orders to bar me from the room."

She sighed as if it was painful for her to continue. "One night, I was awakened from a sound sleep and Simeon was . . . he had drunk too much. . . ." Her eyes filled with pain. "I wish I did not have to tell you this, but I need to tell someone. He stayed with me that night and was very . . . abusive. That was the night Nicholas was conceived. I often wondered how someone so wonderful as my son could have come from such a dreadful night."

Lillia dabbed at her eyes with her handkerchief. "Simeon was delighted to have a son, and things got better. Nicholas was a loving and sensitive boy, and he became his father's shadow. For all his faults, I believe Simeon was a good father. Since Nicholas would one day be master of Ballinger Hall, he taught him all he would need to know about running the estate."

"I do so wish I had known Nicholas as a boy, Lillia. What was he like?"

"He was loving to me, and like all little boys, he thought his mother was special. The time came when Simeon became possessive of our son and tried to keep him away from me as much as he could. I tried to be the kind of wife Simeon wanted, for Nicholas's sake, but by that time he had lost complete interest in me. I had heard that his mistresses were plentiful. For many years I thought the fault lay with me, and I had very little confidence."

From what Lillia avoided saying, Alanna guessed there were many unspeakable things Simeon Ballinger had done to her that she could not talk about. She could only guess how difficult it was for Lillia to say as much as she had.

"I am so sorry, Lillia. I know how I would feel in your place."

"That will never happen to you, Alanna. Not as long as I'm alive." Her eyes flamed with determination, and then she smiled slightly. "But to go on with my story, the war came, and Simeon became obsessed with saving Ballinger Hall. Nicholas, being young and idealistic, joined the Virginia Regiment, against his father's wishes. The time came when fighting was all around us. Everyday we saw the telltale black smoke that warned us that the Yankees were advancing and burning as they went."

"Were you frightened of the Yankees?"

"I would have been, if I had not been more afraid of Simeon. His personality swung back and forth like a pendulum. At times he would be silent and brooding, and at other times he would be . . . abusive . . . screaming and carrying on like a madman. I thank God that Nicholas never witnessed this in his father. Of course, at this time Nicholas was a colonel in the Confederacy, so he was away from home."

Lillia's eyes brimmed with tears that finally spilled down her cheeks. She gripped the side of the chair, fighting for control of her feelings, and finally she succeeded. "The day the Yankee troop rode up to Ballinger Hall was the worst day of my life."

Lillia was silent for such a long time that Alanna was not sure she would continue. Her voice was a mere whisper as she spoke: "Captain Barnard Sanderson was their commander. His announcement that he was going to use Ballinger Hall as his headquarters had a certain calming effect on my husband. I now believe that he saw from the beginning that Barnard was attracted to me, and he began to use that attraction to save Ballinger Hall."

Lillia's eyelashes fluttered. "I am not blameless in this, for I was also attracted to Barnard. He was everything that Simeon was not, and eventually I fell in love with him. I have paid a high price for loving Barnard. Every day of my life I must live with the fact that he died because of me."

"Oh, Lillia, my heart aches for you."

Lillia looked into compassionate eyes that swam with tears. "Do not weep for me, dear little Alanna, weep instead for your husband who has had to suffer for what his father and I did to him."

"Did Captain Sanderson know that you loved him, Lillia?"

"Oh, yes, but not at first. Barnard and his two aides took up residence in the house. He used Simeon's library for his headquarters while his men were camped near the barns. Simeon very cleverly began to manipulate both of us. He would find reasons to be away from home for days at a time."

"To leave you alone with Captain Sanderson?"

"Yes. At first Barnard and I avoided any contact with each other, for the attraction was growing between us daily. Simeon must have had someone watching us, because after returning from one of his excursions, he began ranting and raging at me. I was shocked and appalled to find that his anger came because I had not allowed Barnard to make love to me. He thought that if Barnard cared about me, he would not burn Ballinger Hall."

Lillia paused and looked at Alanna. "I was ashamed and horrified to learn that he was using me to save the house. He ordered me to go to Barnard's

231

room that night and offer myself to him. I should have fought him or run away, but that's looking back. It may be hard for you to realize this, but I was so much under Simeon's power that I could not break free, and I did what he said."

Alanna's face drained of color. "You went to Captain Sanderson?"

"Yes, and I will swear before you and God that nothing happened between us but one kiss and a declaration of our love. We talked all night. Barnard had somehow guessed that Simeon had forced me to come to him. He was . . . he was so kind, and I fell more desperately in love with him. We decided that night that it would not be wise to be together, because the attraction between us was so great. The one night we had together was enough to last me a lifetime, for I had someone who thought I was beautiful and who loved me—I know he did. He was gentle and understanding, and I have little doubt that had he lived, I would have gone to him after the war. I am very much to blame for what happened later, and I alone am responsible for the deaths of my husband and Barnard."

Alanna had a vision of Lillia falling in love with the kind and gentle Barnard after the cruelties she had suffered from her husband. "But how were you to blame? How can you think you were?"

"My biggest mistake was allowing Simeon to see that I loved Barnard. Oh, I tried to cover it up, but I'm sure it showed in my eyes. Even though I tried to avoid Barnard whenever I could, Simeon knew—he knew. You see, we could not be around each other without wanting to be together. Barnard loved me as desperately as I loved him. We were miserable being apart, but we knew it would be worse if we saw one another. No matter how much Simeon ordered me to go to Barnard and offer myself to him, I refused."

Lillia stared into the firelight as her mind turned backward in time. "The real trouble came one day when I least expected it. Kitty and I were in the kitchen preparing the noon meal, because by this time the slaves had all been freed and the cook had been one of the first to leave Ballinger Hall. When Simeon came in, I could tell by the wild look in his eyes that something had upset him. He was angry and accusing. This must have been building inside him for a long time. When he asked me what my feelings were for Barnard, I admitted that I loved him and that he was coming back for me after the war. Simeon raged at me, swearing no man would take me away from him. I tried to calm him . . . but . . ."

She took a deep breath. "How was I to know that Simeon would lose all control? He found a gun he had hidden away in his bedroom. He went directly to the library, where Barnard was seated at the desk. My love never knew what hit him, for Simeon . . . shot him, I was told later, point-blank. I don't know where the bullet struck, I was never told." She sighed. "Everything was so confused, and I never saw Barnard's body, for his men took him away."

Lillia shuddered. "But his blood was all over the floor, and I would not allow anyone else to clean it up."

Her eyes were wild with grief. "After that day, I have never gone into that library. And I never will."

Alanna was horrified by Lillia's tragic tale. "What happened next?"

"What you might expect. Barnard's aide had been in the room and had witnessed the whole event. Tempers ran high with Barnard's men. My husband was immediately taken out to the barn and shot." Lillia shivered. "I never knew what they did with his

233

body. Dark days followed, and as the story came out, or rather a distorted version of it, my neighbors began to shun me, and rightly so, for I deserved their contempt. What almost destroyed me was that my son should turn away from me in disgust. Do not mistake me, Nicholas has every right to despise me, and I don't blame him, but the hurt is like an open wound that will never heal. So many tragedies, so many lives ruined."

Lillia smiled. "Now you know the worst of me. Perhaps you will not want to stay under the same roof with a woman of such a tarnished character."

Alanna's eyes burned with admiration and loyalty. "I will always be proud to know you, Lillia. I know there is more to the story than you are telling. I am almost certain that you have played down your husband's faults."

Lillia touched Alanna's cheek. "Dear, sweet Alanna, God has at last given me some sign that he has forgiven me, by sending you to me." The green of her eyes deepened. "But you must remember your promise to me that you will never tell Nicholas what I have told you tonight!"

"You have my word, Lillia. I do wish, though, that he knew the truth. Then perhaps he would be more forgiving."

"No, he must never know what happened. This way he can look back on his father and believe he was a great man. But if he knew that both his mother and father were less than perfect, it might destroy him."

"One thing I do not understand, Lillia. Why did you not leave Simeon Ballinger before things got so bad?"

"I wish I had been stronger, then perhaps I would have left. My parents, being informed of Simeon's brutal nature by a concerned Kitty, left their home and property to me so I would always have a place to go, should I so desire. There have been many times when I yearned to seek that haven. But I didn't. After Simeon died and I had to endure being shunned by my neighbors and friends, I wanted to run away."

"But you stayed."

Lillia turned tear-bright eyes on her daughter-in-law. "But I stayed, Alanna. When I saw the disillusionment in my son's eyes, I wanted to flee, but I had to think of his future, because, in his state of mind, he didn't care if Ballinger Hall was burned to the ground. In a way, you might say his father died to preserve Ballinger Hall for Nicholas, so I had to see that it passed on to him intact. I put my time and energy into running this plantation for Nicholas. The neighboring plantations had fallen to ruin with no crops and no money. I was determined that when my son came home, he would have something to come home to."

"Lillia, it has been my experience that the guilty do not always get punished. Even worthy people like yourself do not always win. I do not believe you deserved any of the things that happened to you. Nicholas's father was the fortunate one, because he really won. Everyone thinks he died a hero, when indeed he did not."

Lillia smiled and rose to her feet. "Nicholas is the winner in this, Alanna, because he has you. I pray he will be worthy of your love."

Alanna's eyes shone with hope. "I hope I will be what he needs in a wife."

Lillia suddenly looked weary. "Alanna, have you thought any more about seeing your father?"

"Yes, and I have decided to see him, but only if he comes here."

Lillia frowned. "I am not certain Anson Caldwell

would want to come to this house, my dear. You see, no one of good family ever comes here anymore."

Alanna raised her chin and smiled sadly at her mother-in-law. "If my father wants to see me, he will come to Ballinger Hall. I will not visit his house again, and I will not see him if he shuns you."

"Your loyalty does you credit, Alanna, but it may not gain you any friends. Come, it is time for you to rest, my new champion."

Chapter Twenty-Three

Alanna was seated at the vanity, seeing Lillia arrange her hair in the reflection of the mirror.

"Now that we have cut your hair, Alanna, see how nicely it curls? I have pulled it away from your face so the curls fall down your back in the latest style."

Lillia stood back and observed her handiwork. "Something is missing, though." She rummaged around in her ivory jewelry box and smiled. "These pearl combs should add just the right touch."

Alanna stared at the stranger in the mirror. Could that really be her? She wore a soft pink day gown that fit high at her neck. The long sleeves came down to a vee across her wrists. A frothy waterfall bustle fell to the floor in back. On her feet were soft kid slippers, and she was surprised to find how comfortable they were.

Lillia leaned forward to fasten a strand of lustrous pearls about Alanna's neck. "Now, that's finished. Stand up and let us see what we have, my dear."

Alanna stood up slowly, hardly daring to breathe. "I cannot believe this is me, Lillia! I am pretty!"

"Not pretty, Alanna, breathtakingly beautiful. There is not a girl or a woman in this county or state

237

who can hold a candle to you."

Alanna's eyes were glowing as she looked at her full reflection in the floor mirror. The gown hugged her small waist, and the color was perfect for her complexion, for it gave her a somewhat ethereal look.

"I wish . . . I wish Nicholas could see me now."

Lillia patted her arm. "Never mind that, when my son sees you, he is going to know how wonderful you are, if he hasn't already come to that conclusion."

"Lillia, what time did my father's note say he would arrive?"

Lillia glanced at the mantel clock. "At three, and that's only fifteen minutes from now. From what I remember of your father, he was always punctual, so we had better go below."

Lillia looked Alanna over again. "In my note, I omitted telling your father that you and Nicholas are married. I thought that announcement should come from you."

"I am nervous about meeting him."

"You need not be. Just look at that pretty face in the mirror. There's only one thing missing."

"What is that?"

Lillia tilted Alanna's chin up and smiled. "Remember, I told you to hold your head high. Meet your father's eyes, and do not flinch. Show him that you are proud of who you are."

"All right, I will try."

"There is one other thing I want to warn you about. In your father's note, he mentioned that your brother, Donald, and your sister, Eliza, would be coming with him. I didn't tell you before now because I didn't know if you would object to seeing your sister. I believe it is necessary for you to face her sooner or later, and today is as good a time as any. It's always best to face an adversary on your own ground."

Alanna felt as if hundreds of butterflies were fluttering their wings in her stomach. "I do not like her, Lillia, and she does not like me."

"Don't worry about that. Just remember that Eliza is in your home today. And if at any time during the visit she begins to make you angry, you can ask her to leave. It might help if you remember that you are a Cheyenne princess, and that should give you the courage you need to face her down."

Lillia extended her arm to her daughter-in-law. "Now, shall we go below?"

Lillia had been correct about Anson Caldwell's punctuality. Just as the hall clock chimed the third hour, they heard the sound of a carriage pulling up in the driveway.

As Askew walked to the door, his manner stiff and formal, Alanna had the strongest urge to fly to the window so she could see her father, but instead, she did as Lillia had instructed her to do. Standing straight and proud, she waited for the visitors to be announced.

She was aware of the ticking of the clock, the opening and closing of the door, and the sound of footsteps coming down the hallway.

"Courage," Lillia said in a whisper. "Raise your head and show Eliza Caldwell how proud you are."

At her prodding, Alanna raised her head, but she could scarcely breathe past the beating of her heart. She heard Askew's formal voice as he announced the visitors, "Madame, Mr. Caldwell, Miss Eliza and Master Donald have arrived."

Lillia seemed to float across the floor to greet their

239

guests. "Anson, how long it has been since you have visited Ballinger Hall. You are always welcome. And Eliza, how lovely you look; your gown is perfect. Donald, you are looking well. I was so delighted to hear that you won your seat in Congress."

Alanna, with the aloofness of a disinterested spectator, watched Lillia greet her family. Her eyes were cool as they met her father's probing glance, until suddenly she was reminded of when she had loved him very much. She had thought the years would have changed his appearance, but they had not. Except for a few gray hairs at his temples and the tiny wrinkles around his eyes and mouth, he was the same man.

For the first time in many years, Alanna heard her father's deep voice, and it brought back many fond childhood memories of when he had been her whole world.

"Lillia, how can I thank you and Nicholas for looking after my daughter? I am puzzled, though, as to how she came to be in your house, and not in mine."

"Alanna will tell you how that came about," Lillia assured him.

Alanna's eyes moved on to her half-sister, Eliza, and she was met with the same icy glare as before. There would never be any love between Alanna and her father's other daughter.

Alanna, refusing to look at her father, turned her glance to her half-brother, Donald. She had often wondered if he would look anything like their father, and she was not disappointed. He looked very much like she remembered her father when she had been a child.

Lillia was moving toward the door. "I'll just leave you alone to get reacquainted with your daughter."

240

As Lillia disappeared out the door, Alanna wanted to call her back.

Anson moved slowly across the room, his blue eyes soft yet pleading. "Can this polished and beautiful woman be my dear little girl?" he asked, smiling.

Alanna could only stare at him. She had waited a long time for this moment, and now she could think of nothing to say to her father. His blue eyes were anxious and seeking.

Anson looked at his daughter for some show of warmth or recognition. The last time he had seen her she had been crying and clinging to his neck, begging him not to leave her. His breath became trapped in his lungs—except for her blue eyes and her creamy white skin, she could have been her mother standing there.

"Will you not greet your father, my sweet Alanna?" He reached out his hand and she drew back. He tried to hide the hurt in his eyes. "I see you are all grown up now. The last time I saw you, you were but a child."

When she still made no reply, he glanced to either side of him, where his older offspring now stood waiting to be presented to her. "I would like you to meet your brother, Donald, and your sister, Eliza. They both insisted on coming here today to meet you."

Alanna was trembling on the inside, but outwardly she presented the picture of calm serenity. "I am pleased to meet you both," she said, her eyes coldly raking Eliza's face. "I have heard much about you both."

Eliza's mouth thinned. "You always told us that she was raised by Indians, Papa. I expected to meet a dirty, uncivilized—"

"That's enough," Donald spoke up, cutting his

sister short and stepping forward. With a bright smile, he held both hands out to Alanna. "I, for one, am delighted to meet my sister at long last."

Alanna looked into dancing blue eyes and found acceptance shining there. She offered her hands, and he warmly squeezed them. "Like Eliza, I didn't know what to expect. Our father didn't tell me you were a beauty." Suddenly he pulled her forward and she found herself clutched in a warm embrace. She had not wanted to like any of them, but she could not help liking Donald.

When Donald released her, he nodded toward his father, who looked somehow dejected and uncomfortable. "Will you not give your father a warm greeting? I can assure you he has been looking forward to this afternoon with great anticipation."

Suddenly Alanna saw her father reach forward, and she was drawn tightly into his embrace. "My little girl," he said in a broken voice. "My Alanna. At last to look upon your face and know you came to no harm! When I heard what had happened to the Cheyenne, I was desperate to know your fate."

She was trembling with some long-suppressed emotion. His words touched her heart and stirred up a flood of emotions.

There was desperation in her voice when she spoke. "I thought you did not care about me, Father. I waited and waited, but you never returned."

"God forgive me for what I did to you, Alanna." He held her at arm's length and looked at her with pleading eyes. "I loved your mother so much, and when she died, I didn't want anything or anyone to remind me of her. I know it was wrong and unfair to you, but her death almost destroyed me."

"What he's trying to tell you," Eliza spoke up, "is that he didn't love my mother. He shed very few tears

242

when she died."

Anson's face lost its color. "Eliza, you will keep a civil tongue in your head. This is not the time or place to discuss family grievances."

"Humph, and why not? Lillia Ballinger won't mind. She hung out her dirty laundry for everyone else to see—but then, what would you expect from a Yankee? I'd say this is the perfect place to dredge up family dishonor."

Alanna glared at her half-sister, her anger barely in check, her eyes flaming with indignation. "While you are in Nicholas Ballinger's home, you will not again insult his mother." Her warning hung in the air, and it was apparent to the occupants of the room how easily the mask of civilization could be stripped from Alanna's face.

Ignoring the disapproving glances from her father and brother, Eliza took a cautious step backward before she answered. "Just what makes you think you have the right to answer for Nicholas Ballinger?"

Alanna raised her chin and replied proudly: "As Nicholas's wife, I claim that right."

Three pairs of astonished eyes studied Alanna. At last her father spoke. "That explains why you did not come home to me when you arrived in Virginia."

Alanna glanced at Eliza. "If I had come to your home, would you have welcomed me?"

Eliza turned her head away, but not before Alanna saw the fear in her eyes. The woman was afraid that Alanna was going to tell their father that she had thrown his daughter out of his house.

"Of course, you would have been welcomed. I should have sent for you long ago." Anson looked around. "Where is Nicholas now?"

Alanna still watched her sister. "He is in Washington on business."

Donald laughingly took Alanna's hand. "Do you know what you did? You came along and snared the most eligible bachelor in all Virginia. Women will want to scratch your eyes out for taking Nicholas from under their noses. As for myself, I'm glad to have him out of circulation."

There was pure hatred in Eliza's eyes as she stared at her half-sister. "I always suspected likes are drawn to likes. Nicholas, a man who joined the enemy army, a scandal-ridden mother, and a half-breed wife, a most unholy threesome."

"Eliza," Anson threatened, "you will either remember your manners, or leave at once." His eyes were filled with sorrow as he looked at Alanna. "I can only ask you to forgive your sister."

"Pay no attention to Eliza," Donald said, eyeing his sister with disgust. "She is one of the jealous women who has long hoped to catch Nicholas's eye."

"Lies!" Eliza shrieked, her hands flexing into claws as she sprang at her brother. "All lies. You would take her side against me, your own sister!"

Donald gave Alanna an apologetic look while he restrained Eliza.

Anson pulled Alanna aside, while Donald gripped Eliza's arm and moved her across the room. "Take your sister out of here," he ordered.

"We'll just wait for you in the carriage," Donald said. He smiled at Alanna. "We will have time to talk later on. I have many questions to ask you about your years growing up in an Indian village."

Alanna watched in horror as Eliza was forcibly led away, knowing she had an enemy. But why had Eliza reacted so violently toward her when she did not even know her?

Anson looked at Alanna with remorse written on his face. "I am grieved that our first meeting in so many years had to be clouded with such ugliness. I had some crazy notion that all my children would be united under one roof. I can see that is not possible. You see, Eliza . . . is very like her mother who was, selfish and spoiled—but that's a different story. I can only offer you my most humble apology for bringing her here today. Had I known how she would react, I would not have done so."

"She and I will never be friends. I do not want to see her again."

"Will you not try to forgive Eliza for her unkindness? She grew up without a mother to soften her ways."

"Why should I?" Bitterness threaded her words. "I also grew up without a mother, but Eliza at least had a father."

"Yes, you are right." His eyes ran over her face. "How are you? Are you happy?"

Her voice still had an edge to it. "I am married to the man I love."

"I never suspected when I asked Nicholas to find you that the two of you would end up married."

"He was bringing me to you. I might add that it was against my will. We were married in St. Louis."

"When I came here today, it was with the hope of taking you home with me." His blue eyes flickered. "But since you are married to Nicholas, you will want to remain at Ballinger Hall."

"We are neighbors. Perhaps we can come to know one another." Suddenly her eyes hardened, and she stared at her father. "Unless you are one of those who have been unkind to Lillia. I will not tolerate anyone who is unfeeling toward her."

"I believe Lillia will tell you that I was not one of those who shunned her." He smiled. "How very like your mother you looked as you were defending

Lillia—the way your eyes sparkled, the haughty expression. Seeing you today, I am reminded why I loved her so much."

"I loved her too," Alanna said sadly. "I am proud to be her daughter."

"And so you should be, for she was an exceptional person. She gave me years of happiness, and that is more than I deserved." He smiled. "She gave you to me."

"Yes," Alanna said dully.

He felt uncomfortable discussing the past, so he asked, "How are your grandmother and grandfather?"

Her voice was dull and devoid of feeling. "They are both dead."

"I feared as much when I heard about the Cheyenne joining forces with the Sioux to attack the Seventh Cavalry. That's when I realized you were in danger. It was Donald who used his influence in Washington to try to locate you, but we were unsuccessful until I received the letter Blue Flower Woman had sent to me. Knowing Nicholas Ballinger was nearby, I asked him to find you. The rest you know."

Suddenly Alanna could no longer hold her emotions in check, and they came spilling out in a flood. "All those years, I waited for you to come back for me. You said you would. Everyday I practiced my English as you told me to, just so you would be proud of me."

He touched her hair. "I am so very proud of you, Alanna. I want the whole world to know that you are my daughter. As for the reason I never came back for you, it was as I told you before. I wanted nothing to remind me of your mother. I now know I was wrong. I have missed out on knowing you, and that is a great pity."

"I wanted you to come back. There was a time when I watched for you every day. Then as the weeks and months passed and you did not come, I gave up hope."

"My sweet daughter, can you ever forgive me for all the years of neglect?"

Alanna thought about what Lillia would do in her place, and it became clear to her what she must do. "Yes, I will forgive you, Father."

He drew in a deep breath. "It's more than I deserve. May I come to see you again?"

Alanna smiled. "Yes, of course. You will always be welcome here."

"I am glad you have Nicholas to look after you. He is a good man."

He drew her into his arms again, and the two of them stood for a long moment as they tried to recapture something very precious they had lost. But it was not to be. Alanna was the first to move away. "You should not keep your family waiting any longer. Go to them."

Anson felt pain in his heart. She had said she would forgive him, but his neglect of her over the years had robbed him of her respect and her love.

"I will call again," he said, kissing her on the forehead and moving across the room.

After he had gone, Alanna stood silently, remembering how wonderful life had been when she had lived with her father and mother as a family. Now that she had seen him again, he was not so important in her life.

She felt pity for him, because the years had destroyed something fragile and rare between them. There was no going back. One could never bring back yesterday.

247

Chapter Twenty-Four

The frosty winds of March gave way to the brisk warm breezes of April. Spring was heavy in the air, and Ballinger Hall was coming to life after a long winter's sleep. Newborn colts frolicked in the meadow, while calves joined their mothers to graze on the new grass in the pastures. Majestic white swans floated over the mirror-bright five-acre pond, followed closely by an entourage of downy offspring.

As Alanna moved along the grassy pathway, the scent of green hay perfumed the air. Bees fluttered among the lilac bushes, and mockingbirds sang in the magnolia trees. She moved past the formal gardens through an orchard awash with pink and white blossoms.

She had been told that the extensive woods to the south was a haven for wild game. The deer were so gentle that they would come up and eat out of her hand. It was a new notion to her that deer could be raised as pets.

A strange sound caught her attention, and she glanced in awe at a grandly plumed peacock that strutted majestically among the less-favored female peahens.

Her footsteps hastened as she approached the

ornamental bridge that spanned the pond, breathing in the wonderful scent of honeysuckle.

Surely this was paradise. She could not imagine anyplace more lovely. It was right that Nicholas should have come from such a land.

She paused in the middle of the bridge and glanced down at her reflection in the water. It was hard to see any resemblance between her and the frail person she had been after her illness. Her face had filled out and her complexion glowed with health. She knew she was pretty, and she hoped Nicholas would think so too.

Each day, she watched the road and listened for Nicholas's return, but no word came from him, and he did not come himself.

Alanna's days were not uneventful. She liked being with Lillia, and of course there were the stables to visit. By now she knew all the horses by name, and the trainer, Glenn Hubbard, was amazed at how the horses almost kicked down their stalls to get to Alanna when she visited. It appeared as if she had some strange power over the animals, as if they were drawn to her in some unexplained way.

Her father had come to visit several times, as had Donald, but of course Eliza had not attempted to see Alanna, and she was grateful for that.

The sun was dropping beyond the western horizon as she walked leisurely back to the house. She paused for a long time to stare at the meandering Potomac River, watching the reflection of the dying sun dance across its crystal-bright water.

Her footsteps were hesitant as she entered the house. Another day without any word from Nicholas. Ballinger Hall, and everyone in it, was waiting, as she was—waiting for the master to come home.

*　　*　　*

Lillia had gone to bed hours ago, and the household servants had settled in for the night and all was quiet.

A crescent moon lent its dim light to the bedroom where Alanna lay, somewhere between sleep and wakefulness as the nightmare took hold of her. She was dreaming that she was cold—so cold she would never feel warm again. She felt as if the life was draining out of her. With a sob she flailed her arms, trying to ward off the dark hand of death.

Suddenly they were caught, and she found herself being crushed in two strong arms. Nicholas's voice came to her at first from a long way off, and then closer as she tried to decide if she was asleep or awake.

"Easy, Blue Eyes. It's just a dream. Remember, I made you a promise that as my wife you would never be cold or hungry again."

Suddenly she came fully awake. She had not dreamed Nicholas's voice, for she could feel the strength of his arms about her. He had come home!

Her arms went around his neck, and she pulled him down to her. His soft chuckle met her ears.

"How fortunate I am to come home and find such a tempting female in my bed. I had not expected you to be here. I thought you would be with your father."

She was reluctant to tell him how her sister had ordered her out of her father's house. "I decided that a wife should be in her husband's home."

"Did you?" He smiled. "I wasn't certain if you would want to see me."

"I should be angry with you," she admitted, "after you left me without a word. But I have decided to forgive you," she breathed against his neck. "What kept you so long? Why did you not come sooner?"

"Just like a woman," he said lightly. "You marry them, and right away they think that gives them the right to ply you with questions."

She did not mind if he teased her. All that mattered was that he was here now, and that he appeared to be glad to see her. "You do not mind that I am in your bed?"

"Where else would you be?" His voice deepened. "I have had only one night with you, but it was enough to keep you on my mind the whole time I was in Washington. You cannot guess how I hurried home." He moved off the bed and began undressing. "I could hardly keep my mind on what I was doing."

His words sent a thrill down her body, all the way to her toes. "I am glad you are home," she admitted in a breathless voice.

He lay down beside her and pulled her into his arms. "Are you?"

"Yes. Your mother will be glad also."

She felt him stiffen at the mention of his mother's name, and Alanna knew that now was not the time to talk about his feelings for Lillia.

His hand moved across her silken hair, and he curled a strand around his finger. "You cut your hair?"

"Yes, your mother cut it herself. Do you like it, Nicholas?"

"No more braids?"

"No more braids."

"I kind of liked my little Indian princess. I don't want you to change too much." There was a hint of warning in his voice. "Stay as you are."

"I look different, but I am the same on the inside. Lillia said many people groom the outer person but neglect to groom their inner self."

His voice became hard. "Did she? I would not have thought her an authority on the inner self."

Alanna wisely turned the conversation back to her

251

hair. "My hair is still long."

He smiled and allowed his hand to drift over her hips. "I'd say your hair isn't the only thing that's changed about you. Someone has been fattening you up."

She raised her head to look at him with concern on her face. "Do you think I am too fat?"

He tried to keep his tone serious as he ran his hand across her flat stomach. "You feel just about right to me."

The touch of his hand and the sound of his voice invoked memories of the joy he had awakened in her body on their wedding night in St. Louis. Her senses were reeling, and her heart was filled with love.

The shutters had been thrown open, and the night was awash with the smells of spring mixed with the fresh earthy smell of newly fallen rain. To Alanna it felt right to be in Nicholas's arms, for this man was her husband, and the giver of life to her.

Tossing her head back, she allowed him access to her creamy neck. "Nicholas," she murmured. "I have missed you so desperately."

She was filling his senses with each tantalizing move she made, and it clouded his reason. He felt excitement shoot through his body at the mere notion of possessing her again. He raised her gown over her head and tossed it aside. In no time his own clothing lay in a heap.

When he took her in his arms again, her soft lips became even softer under the pressure of his mouth, and her sweetly scented skin molded to him like an extension of his own body.

"I need you," he said in a thick, passionate voice. "Blue Eyes, how I need you!"

That was all Alanna needed to hear. She arched her body toward his and shivered with delight when his mouth toyed and teased with the tips of her swollen breasts. She was being wrapped in a veil of sweetness, and her body tingled wherever his hand touched.

When he at last entered the softness of her body, she shivered with pleasurable feelings. Nicholas strained to drive deeper inside her, to reach a part of her that had not been touched before.

As Nicholas filled Alanna's body, he also filled her heart. All she could think of was him. He had said he had missed her, and even if that was not an admission of love, it was a confession of need. At the moment she was as important to him as life. His body was taking from her all she was willing to give. She clung to him as glorious passion fused them together.

Nicholas became the perfect lover, deriving pleasure from her body, yet giving pleasure in return. He was adoring and patient, showing her how to derive the most pleasure from his touch. He made love to her slowly and lingeringly, and when he had evoked the ultimate response in her, their bodies trembled together, caught up in wave after wave of searing passion.

With their bodies still pressed together, they lay in the soft moon-glow, neither able to speak of what they felt. Nicholas ran his hand down her smooth hair and tilted her face up to his.

"I wondered if it would be the same between us as it was the first time. When I could not get you out of my mind, I convinced myself that it was only a dream." He touched her lips with his, then drew back to look into her luminous eyes. "Nothing I have imagined could have matched this strong tie between us."

She rested her head against his chest, listening to the beating of his heart. "I never knew about these feelings between a man and a woman." She tossed back her head and looked at him questioningly. "Is it always like this?"

Her sweetness filled his mind and his body. "Not with me, Blue Eyes." His voice became laced with bitterness. "Of course, I cannot speak for a woman. Perhaps you should ask my mother—she seems to be the authority—"

She clamped her hand over his mouth. "Nicholas, do not say anything you may regret later. Your mother is a gentle and loving woman, and she does not deserve disrespect from her only son."

His glance became searching. "So, my mother has found an ally in you. I wonder how she was able to justify her behavior." He took a deep breath. "But then my mother can make anyone see what she wants them to see."

Alanna did not want to hear him criticize his mother, so she artfully moved on to another subject. "Did you complete your work in Washington?"

He smiled down at her. "Yes I did, little Blue Eyes. In fact, I have some news which I believe will please you. I visited the Bureau of Indian Affairs and reported my first-hand knowledge of the government's abominable neglect of the Cheyenne on the reservations. I was assured that the matter would be corrected immediately."

"Can the government send help swiftly enough to help my starving people?"

"Indeed they can. I was there when they telegraphed a message to Wiley Chappell in which they assured him supplies were on the way."

"Oh, the singing wires," she said thoughtfully. "I have heard about that."

"Yes," he laughed, "the singing wires."

She got to her knees as happiness spread over her face. "You are a worker of miracles, my husband. I would like to know that my people will never go hungry again."

"I cannot promise that, Alanna." He was mesmerized by the sight of her.

Nicholas could not believe the change that had come over Alanna in such a short time. Her eyes sparkled with an inner light, her face was beautiful. Her midnight-colored hair cascaded down her back to her waist, swinging gracefully with each move of her body. His eyes moved down her creamy shoulders, across her firm young breasts, taking in her narrow hips and her long legs. He held his arms out to her, thinking she was the picture of the perfect woman. Why had he not seen it before?

When she came into his arms, he held her to him tightly, remembering the day he had first seen her. He had little doubt that if he had not come along that day she would have died. That thought caused him to hold her even tighter. What was happening to him? Perhaps she was enchanting to him because she was different from the other women he knew. She was innocent, fresh, and unspoiled, unlike her white counterparts. He wanted above all to keep her that way—to keep the world from tarnishing her.

His hands spanned her tiny waist, and he drew her upward until his mouth closed around a soft white nipple. Excitement flowed through his body, and he knew he would take her again. He turned her over to her back and hovered above her for just a moment, drinking in her loveliness. Caught in the magic of her smile, he moved between her legs and found the waiting heaven of her softness.

Afterward, Alanna sighed contentedly. Curling her body around his, she fell asleep, basking in the warm feelings that surrounded her heart.

While Nicholas held his sleeping wife, feelings of doubt plagued him. Yes, Alanna was exciting in his bed, but how would she cope in a world of which she knew nothing about? How would he be able to protect her from the hurt that was bound to come her way?

He turned his back on her, wondering what in hell he was doing married to a woman who would never fit into his world. In St. Louis it had seemed the only solution. Now he was not so sure. A man could not keep a woman in bed all the time. Alanna would still have to function in a world she could not even comprehend.

With these and other troubled thoughts nagging at his mind, he finally fell asleep.

Chapter Twenty-Five

When Alanna awoke, she found Nicholas was not beside her. He was nowhere in the room.

She got out of bed and quickly slipped into an orchard-colored gown with stiff white lace at the collar. She tied her hair back with a silk ribbon and dashed downstairs.

Remembering the night before, she felt joy in her heart—Nicholas had finally come home!

Askew, his manner stiff and formal, met her in the entryway and directed her to the dining room, where Nicholas was seated across the table from his mother.

Both pairs of green eyes settled on Alanna when she came into the room. Nicholas came to his feet to hold the chair for her to be seated at his right.

Alanna stared at her husband. This was the first time she had seen him without his uniform. He wore a gray coat and a snow-white shirt. Gray pants hugged his long, lean legs, and his black boots were polished to a high sheen.

Seeing Alanna's puzzlement, Nicholas shrugged. "I am a civilian now. You will not be seeing the uniform again."

"Lillia, your prayers have been answered. Your son is home," Alanna beamed.

Lillia nodded, a sadness reflected in her eyes. "Yes, we can always be thankful for that."

Alanna smiled up at her husband, remembering how he had held her in his arms and had been so sweet and gentle. When Nicholas did not return her smile, she looked at him in confusion. There was no evidence of the tender lover of the night before. Nicholas's eyes were cold and hard as he stared back at Alanna, his eyes sweeping her from head to toe. "What in the hell do you have on? What have you done to yourself?"

Alanna glanced down at her new gown, knowing it was becoming to her. She was crushed that Nicholas did not think so. "Do you not like the color?"

Nicholas's eyes flamed as he looked at his mother, but his voice was cold. "I do not want you filling Alanna's head with any of your notions, Mother. She is unspoiled, and I want to keep her that way—is that understood?"

"What you mean is she is innocent, and you want to keep her *that* way," his mother stated.

"Whatever you say," he answered indifferently, his eyes challenging his mother to say more. He then turned stiffly to his wife. "I have business to tend to, so I will be gone most of the day."

Alanna watched in confusion as Nicholas moved out of the room. Glancing at Lillia, she saw that her mother-in-law's eyes were swimming with tears.

"What is the matter with him, Lillia? I had hoped he would—"

Lillia shook her head. "If I thought time would soften my son's heart toward me, I was only deluding myself. He still blames me for his father's death.

258

There is no forgiveness in him."

Alanna reached out her hand and laid it on Lillia's. "Perhaps if you give him a little more time, he will come to realize he is wrong."

"No, that will never happen. Nicholas is slow to anger, but even slower to forgive. Once a person has made an enemy of him, they can expect never to get back within his good graces again."

"Lillia, I beg you, please tell him the truth of what happened to his father. It's the only way you can make him understand."

Her face paled. "No, I cannot do that, and you must not either."

"I have to confess that I do not understand Nicholas very well. He is a complicated man, Lillia."

"Yes, complicated and unbending. But there is a good side to him also, Alanna. If he ever buries the past, I am sure he will make a wonderful husband. I want to warn you though, he can be ruthless. Do not let him hurt you."

Alanna stared out the dining room window, feeling like a fool. It was as though Nicholas was two different men: one the adoring lover, the other the cold stranger he had been this morning.

Nicholas breathed in the spring-scented air, thinking how good it was to be home. His self-imposed exile from his beloved Ballinger Hall had been a difficult punishment to endure. This land was all that really mattered—this was all that would endure after the last Ballingers had been placed in the crypt.

He had spent most of the morning riding across the estate with his overseer, Albert, who had once been a slave at Ballinger Hall. After the war ended, his mother had placed Albert in charge, and Nicholas had to admit that it had been a wise decision.

He was surprised and relieved to learn that Ballinger Hall was thriving. The spring crops had been laid in, the barns were filled with hay and feed. There was a new roof on the stable, and the barns and house were in good repair. He was less grateful when he learned that Ballinger Hall thrived because of his mother's tireless management.

As Nicholas and Albert rode in the direction of the stable, Nicholas dismounted and threw the reins of his horse to a young stablehand.

"Albert, I want you to look at the horse I bought in Arlington. It has been a long time since I have seen horseflesh to match this red mare. I purchased it from a man called Poteet Garvey, who runs the livery stable."

Albert's black eyes rounded. "That Poteet Garvey is a Yankee, come to make money on the misery of others, and he cleaned lots of folks out of their pocket change. He's bad to do business with, Mr. Ballinger."

"That may be, but this horse he sold me is worth every cent I paid for her and more. It doesn't take a trained eye to know she is excellent horseflesh! I expect she will also be a good breeder."

Albert stopped in his tracks, his jaw slack. "Did you say she's a red mare?"

"Yes, I did. Her name's—"

"Don't tell me, let me guess, Mr. Nicholas—it's Red Betty, ain't it?"

"So you've heard of the horse?"

Albert looked grim. "Yessir, most folks here abouts has heard of Red Betty. She's just pure down ornery, and there ain't nobody that can tame her. Poteet makes a living out of selling her and buying her back when the owner finds out he can't even saddle her. Course he never buys her back for as much as he sells her for."

Nicholas's eyebrows came together in a frown. "Are you saying I have been swindled by a Yankee?"

"Yessir, that's what I'm a-saying. Poteet must be busting his sides out laughing at you. Ain't too many plantations down the Potomac where they ain't thought they could break that horse, and they paid for the privilege of finding out they was wrong."

Nicholas's features were grim as his footsteps hastened in the direction of the stables. Even before he entered the white-brick structure, he could hear the sound of splintering wood and obscenities shouted out by Glenn Hubbard, the trainer.

"Hold her boys, or she'll destroy the whole damned place."

When Nicholas entered the stables, Glenn glanced up at him. "Red Betty arrived about an hour ago, Mr. Ballinger, and she's managed to set the other horses on their tails. Don't know how to calm her down. She's about busted out of her stall and already sent one of my stableboys up to the big house for doctoring."

Nicholas's eyes narrowed. "She was calm enough when I bought her two days ago."

"Yeh," Glenn stated, "I suspect that Poteet puts something in her feed to make her appear docile, but when it wears off, she's a hellion. She ain't even no good for breeding 'cause she won't allow a stud to go near her. It would be death or broken bones for any man that's fool enough to think he can tame her— and Mr. Ballinger, I am not a fool. I may work for you, but I won't go near that horse."

By now Albert stood beside his boss, and all three men watched the red mare. A frightened stableboy cringed in the far corner as Red Betty kicked up her heels, splintering another panel of wood, her eyes

261

rolling, her sides heaving.

Nicholas's voice revealed his anger. "It galls me to think that I allowed a slick-talking Yankee to get the better of me, Glenn. I'll shoot that horse before I let that damn swindler have her back."

Glenn nodded his head in agreement. "It would be a pity to destroy such a beautiful animal, but once in a while a horse will come along that just can't be rode, and they ain't no good to no one."

To demonstrate that Glenn was right, Red Betty reared out, and with hooves flying, tried to reach the cowed stableboy, sending the frightened lad racing out of the stable.

The unmanageable red Arabian was rearing up on her hind legs, her pointed ears laid straight back, her eyes rolling in her head.

"I'm afraid this one's just plain no good to anyone, Mr. Nicholas," the overseer said. "It's a blessing she ain't already killed someone."

It was early afternoon when Alanna put on her silver-gray riding habit and made her way to the stable. It had become her custom to ride every day about this time. Lillia had taught her how to ride a horse sidesaddle like a lady, but secretly Alanna thought riding astride like an Indian was better.

As she approached the doorway of the stable, she could hear the sound of men's voices raised in excitement and the frightened neighing of a horse.

Alanna recognized her husband's deep voice. "Glenn, get the rifle, I'm going to put that animal out of her misery and save myself a lot of trouble. God only knows what a laughingstock I am for buying her in the first place!"

Alanna stepped inside the cool stable, her eyes

going immediately to the terrified mare in the corner stall. The poor animal was rearing and bucking, trying to get free.

She glanced at Nicholas, thinking she must have misunderstood his words. "Surely you do not intend to shoot that animal," Alanna said in horror. "No one would kill such a fine animal."

Nicholas quickly assessed his wife's appearance, noting grimly how lovely she looked in the stylish riding habit. That, and the fact that he had been duped by a Yankee, made his temper flare. "Get back to the house at once, Alanna. This is no place for a woman."

Alanna, ignoring his order, stepped around him and headed toward Red Betty's stall. "I cannot believe you three brave men would stand around talking about destroying such a fine little filly as this."

Nicholas started after Alanna, when Glenn stopped him. "Let her be, Mr. Ballinger. I've seen animals react strangely to your wife. She has a way with them, kinda talks their language, I guess."

"She'll be crushed," Nicholas said, furiously shaking Glenn's restraining hand off his arm. When he would have rushed for Alanna, a strange thing happened—the mare stopped kicking and perked up her ears.

The three men watched spellbound as Alanna talked soothingly to the mare in the language of the Cheyenne, at the same time taking several hesitant steps in the animal's direction.

The overseer and the trainer stared in disbelief, for they did not understand Mrs. Ballinger. Nicholas, however, realized that Alanna had lapsed into her own language.

"There, there, pretty girl," she said soothingly.

"You have no reason to be frightened. You are far more beautiful than the other mares in the stable." She approached even closer, reaching out her hand, but the mare pulled back just at the last moment.

"I will not hurt you, pretty girl. You and I are going to be friends." This time when Alanna reached out her hand, the mare did not pull away.

Nicholas watched in disbelief as his wife ran her hand down the wild animal's neck.

Alanna reached into a nearby oatbag and filled her hand, then held it out to the mare. Slowly at first, the mare tasted the oats, but she looked as if she might bolt at any moment. "What is her name?" Alanna called out in English.

"Red Betty," Glenn answered, smiling. He glanced up at his tall boss. "I told you she had a way with animals. Has that one eating out of her hand."

"If I'm not careful, she'll have me eating out of her hand as well," Nicholas muttered beneath his breath, a statement that brought a snicker from Glenn, while Albert pretended to count the boards in the ceiling.

"Well, will you look at that!" Glenn exclaimed. "That killer horse is as gentle as a lamb with Mrs. Ballinger."

Still doubtful, Nicholas stated sourly, "Feeding an animal's one thing, but that horse will never be tamed."

"Someone toss me a halter," Alanna said in a soft voice. "This little lady would just love to be ridden."

"Now, Alanna, don't do anything foolish," Nicholas warned, feeling helpless. He knew that if he advanced near enough to get Alanna away, the horse might spook and Alanna could be crushed. "That horse is dangerous, damn it. Move away from her," he hissed furiously.

When Nicholas tried to move cautiously to

Alanna's side, the horse lay back her ears and moved away nervously, stopping Nicholas's advance.

"Stay where you are, Nicholas," Alanna cautioned. "I will have to win her confidence before I can allow you to come near her."

Nicholas had no choice other than to do as Alanna said, for at that moment it appeared as if the animal had accepted her and no one else.

Glenn tossed Alanna a halter. She caught it in her outstretched hand and quickly slipped it over Red Betty's head, talking soothingly to the animal all the while.

All three men and two stableboys were shocked into silence as Alanna grasped the halter on both sides of the horse's head and blew her breath into the horse's nostrils. Several times this was repeated. "This will give her my scent," she explained in a quiet voice. "See, how she responds to kindness, Nicholas." She patted the horse. "Now we have an understanding of one another, do we not, Red Betty?"

The mare stretched her head forward and nudged Alanna's hand. Alanna laughed and laid her cheek against the side of Red Betty's face. "See, she likes me."

Nicholas, who was nervous the whole time Alanna was near the horse, moved forward. "She may have accepted you, but that does not make her any less dangerous. Glenn has already informed me that she can't be ridden."

Alanna smiled as she moved to the railing and lifted Lillia's sidesaddle, while her eyes challenged the trainer. "You are wrong on this one, Glenn. I will not only get on her back, but Red Betty will welcome me."

Nicholas, still afraid his movements might endanger Alanna, took a cautious step nearer. Now that he could reach his wife, he grabbed her arm and pulled her back. "I will not allow you to do this, Alanna. That horse is a killer." His voice told everyone watching that he would brook no opposition.

"Nonsense, Nicholas. There is no such thing as a killer horse, there are only men who do not know how to properly handle a high-strung little filly like this one."

Alanna jerked free of Nicholas's grip, and before he could stop her—in a show of petticoats—she was over the gate and in the stall with Red Betty.

Nicholas dared not move, lest his movement spook the horse and it trample Alanna to death. He watched helplessly as she slung the saddle over the mare's back and fastened the cinch.

"Of course, it would be better if I did not have to ride sidesaddle," she said, unlatching the gate and leading the horse forward.

"Alanna, I'm warning you, don't do this," Nicholas said through clenched teeth. "Don't defy me in this." He had visions of her body lying broken and bleeding beneath the devil horse's deadly prancing hooves.

Alanna chose to ignore Nicholas's orders. Out of the stable she marched, leading the seemingly docile Red Betty. While her audience watched, she climbed upon the mounting block and eased herself into the saddle.

At first Red Betty stood stark still, and no one breathed.

Alanna leaned over and whispered something in the mare's ear. When she straightened up, she nudged the animal in the flanks, and they moved slowly around in a circle. She trotted the animal around, gradually making the circle wider and wider. Then Alanna urged Red Betty into a gallop.

As the mare became more accustomed to having a rider on her back, Alanna would urge her to a faster pace.

Nicholas had almost relaxed when suddenly Alanna headed the animal for the fence. For one breathtaking moment, it appeared as if horse and rider were suspended in the air. Over the fence Red Betty sailed, racing across the meadow beyond, with Alanna laughing in delight.

"Well, I'll be damned," Glenn stated, scratching his head in amazement. "I've seen horsemen come and I've seen them go, but I ain't never seen the likes of this horsewoman before." His faded blue eyes sparkled with admiration. "Mrs. Ballinger is truly magnificent. Look at the way that animal obeys her every command!"

Albert chuckled. "Mr. Poteet Garvey is gonna be mighty put out when he learns he won't be getting that horse back. I'd like to see his face when he finds out. Imagine him being bested by a wom—by Mrs. Ballinger!"

Nicholas moved to the fence and stared after his wife as she raced up a hill. Her dark hair had come free of its confines and was rippling out behind her. It appeared as if she and the horse were one as they raced through a cluster of brightly colored wildflowers.

His eyes gleamed, and he smiled to himself. There was no woman he knew who could have performed such a feat, and no man either, for that matter.

Alanna was exceptional, and Nicholas felt the sudden pride of ownership. Not only did the horse belong to him, but the woman who had mastered it was his as well.

He smiled to himself. It seemed only fair that he make Alanna a gift of Red Betty. Most likely no one but her could ride the animal anyway.

Alanna raced the wind, feeling all her cares and woes fall away. This was a magnificent horse, and today was a beautiful day. She was unaware that the three men closely watched her, amazed at her accomplishment. She only knew it was good to be mounted on such a spirited and powerful animal.

Chapter Twenty-Six

Several days had passed since Alanna had tamed Red Betty. Word had swiftly spread up and down the valley, and neighbors were secretly pleased that the Yankee upstart Poteet Garvey was about to receive his just desserts.

The incident lost nothing in the telling and spurred the county's interest in the new Mrs. Nicholas Ballinger. When it was learned that she was also the daughter of Anson Caldwell, invitations for parties and afternoon teas began to trickle in at Ballinger Hall—invitations that Alanna declined because they did not include Lillia.

Alanna saw very little of Nicholas in the daytime, since he was kept busy on the plantation. At night when she, Nicholas, and Lillia sat around the dining room table, it was a tense afffair. Nicholas was never openly rude to his mother. Instead, he ignored her for the most part, talking to her only when she spoke directly to him.

It broke Alanna's heart to see Lillia treated so coldly by her only son. If only there was something she could do, something to change the situation, but any time she mentioned Lillia to Nicholas, she was met with frosty silence.

At night Nicholas always took Alanna into his arms and their passions would ignite, but there was no closeness, no sharing of each other's thoughts. Alanna wondered how much longer things could go on as they were.

It was a beautiful morning. Spring now had a firm grip on the land, and Ballinger Hall was wondrous to behold.

Nicholas had been gone from the house since before sunrise, which was his habit these days.

Alanna was standing at the parlor window observing a noisy sparrow chattering and scolding the other birds in the spreading branches of the stately magnolia tree.

Hearing footsteps behind her, she turned to find Lillia entering the room.

"It's a glorious day, Lillia. Not a cloud in the sky. Will you ride with me this afternoon?"

Lillia seemed preoccupied with something. "No, not today." Her eyes sought Alanna's as if she were asking for understanding. "I wanted to tell you that I have decided to move back to Philadelphia."

Alanna's eyes widened in disbelief. "But you cannot leave," she protested. "Ballinger Hall is your home. What would I do without you?"

"It was not an easy decision to make, but I feel the time has come for me to leave. Ballinger Hall belongs to you and Nicholas now. My home is in Philadelphia. I have stayed here too long."

Alanna had not expected that Nicholas's mother would want to leave them, and she was confused and saddened. "Will you return to the house your father left you?"

"Yes. I hope nothing has changed. I find I am quite happily looking forward to seeing old friends. And it will be good to see my sisters and their families."

Alanna felt her heart sink. "How long will you be away?"

Her mother-in-law moved to her side and stood looking out the window. "Indefinitely. I am making no plans to return to Ballinger Hall."

Alanna shook her head. "But I do not understand. You love this house. It is your home, Lillia. You cannot just move away."

Lillia smiled sadly. "I have given it a lot of thought, and it would be far better for everyone if I left. I stayed this long only to keep Ballinger Hall in good repair until my son returned. Now it is time to find a life for myself. I confess to looking forward to some peace and quiet."

"I do not want you to leave, Lillia. I feel certain that Nicholas will not want you to go."

"He already knows I am leaving. He understands my reasons."

"Please stay just a little longer," Alanna pleaded.

Lillia touched Alanna's soft cheek. "No, dear, I cannot. And after I am gone, I want you to accept some of those invitations you have been turning down because of me. If not for your sake or Nicholas's, you must make an effort to mend the fences between old neighbors for the sake of your children."

"If you will stay, I promise I will accept every invitation that comes to the house. I will be kind and gracious to everyone, just as you taught me. I will do anything to keep you here." There was eagerness in her eyes. "Besides, I could never control the servants as you do. I would not know the first thing about running this house."

Lillia smiled sadly. "That is why I will be leaving Kitty with you. Just place everything in her capable hands." She hugged Alanna. "I am going to miss you sorely, my dear. No mother-in-law could ask for a more loving daughter. I have a feeling that when I am gone, you and Nicholas will come to a happy understanding."

Alanna realized that nothing she could say would change Lillia's mind. "When will you be leaving?"

"I have already talked to Nicholas about it. I will be leaving in the morning, and he has consented to drive me into town so I can take a northbound coach."

"But tomorrow is too soon!"

"I feel like a quick break is best. There is just one thing I would ask of you—"

"Ask anything of me, and I will do it."

Lillia smiled. "I would like you to accompany me and my son to Arlington tomorrow. I fear if we are alone, the silence between us would be unbearable."

Alanna wondered what she would do without her gentle mother-in-law. But it could not be easy for Lillia, having to face Nicholas's cold, accusing glances each day. She realized she must not be selfish by trying to cling to her—she must let her go to find a life of her own.

She clasped Lillia's hand. "I would not think of allowing you to leave without seeing you off."

"Fine. Now how about if you come upstairs and help me finish packing?"

The coach ride into town was uncomfortable, to say the least. Nicholas was stiff and silent, while Alanna and Lillia tried to keep a conversation flowing, but failed miserably. At last Lillia lasped into silence and sat back to watch the passing scenery.

"I will miss this," she said, almost to herself. "It has been my home for a very long time."

"No one has asked you to leave, Mother," Nicholas said in an annoyed tone. "Ballinger Hall is still your home. It always will be."

Lillia reached across and laid her gloved hand on her son's arm. "Nicholas . . . I . . . will miss you."

He was still unyielding, and no flicker of softness showed in his green eyes. "If you find it intolerable in Philadelphia, you can always return."

She withdrew her hand, trying to hide her disappointment. "Yes, I can always return."

"Ask her not to go," Alanna suddenly burst out. "Ask her to stay, Nicholas."

He turned cold green eyes on Alanna. "My mother is old enough to know what she wants."

Alanna glanced at Lillia, who was trying to conceal the fact that she was crying. She felt her heart break for Nicholas's mother, but there was nothing she could do to help her. What Lillia needed could come only from her son.

When the coach pulled up to the stage office, Nicholas helped his mother down. "You know, you could take the traveling coach to Philadelphia and save yourself the discomfort of public conveyance."

She shook her head. "I don't mind the discomfort. Besides, I will have Albert to look after me on the trip. I will send him back to you as soon as he's rested. I know you will be needing him." She smiled sadly. "Good-bye, Nicholas. Take care of Alanna."

"You will let us know that you have arrived safely," he said coldly, before turning away.

Alanna hugged Lillia. "I will miss you."

Her mother-in-law smiled. "And I shall miss you, too. You and Nicholas take care of one another."

Alanna nodded and watched Lillia move away, to be helped into the waiting stage by Albert. She stood silently as the stage moved away and long after it had rounded a corner and was lost from view. She would miss Lillia very much.

Nicholas stood beside her stiffly, still silent and brooding. "You would think just once she would say how sorry she is that my father is dead because of her," he said, almost against his will. "Not once has she displayed any remorse for what happened to him."

"What do you want from her, Nicholas? Should she beseech your forgiveness on bended knees, or write her repentance in blood?"

His features were stormy. "Little do you know about an event that took place when you were residing in an Indian lodge, Alanna. This does not concern you."

"Perhaps not, but I would never have treated my mother in such a shabby fashion."

He arched an eyebrow. "I had not noticed you holding out the hand of friendship to your own father."

Before Alanna could answer, Nicholas took her arm and steered her down the street. "Come, let us not talk of my mother or your father. I have a score to settle with someone." His mouth thinned and his eyes darkened. "A certain Yankee needs to be taught a lesson."

Alanna was puzzled as to what Nicholas was talking about until they neared Poteet Garvey's livery stables.

It would seem her husband was not a man to allow anyone to take advantage of him. She was finding out that retribution from him could be swift and thorough. She wondered what he had in mind for the unfortunate Poteet.

Alanna's hand rested on Nicholas's arm as they entered the stables. Several fine horses occupied the stalls, but not one of them compared with the magnificent Red Betty.

When Poteet, a fat little man with thinning gray hair, recognized the master of Ballinger Hall, his eyes gleamed, and he came forward with a knowing smile on his face.

"Ah, Mr. Ballinger, so nice to see you again. How can I be of service to you on this fine day?"

Nicholas glanced around, as if pondering the man's words. "I'll take three pounds of horseshoe nails, and four new bridles—those," he said, indicating the black leather bridles which hung on the wall.

Poteet's eyes danced with anticipation. "And what else would you like?"

Nicholas glanced down at Alanna. "That will be all for today."

The livery stable owner glanced from the lady to her husband. "Are you sure?"

"Yes, quite sure."

Poteet looked befuddled for just a moment. "How's the red mare?" he ventured.

Nicholas exchanged glances with his wife. "Red Betty couldn't be better. I'm thinking she might be a contender in the races at the county fair this year. I can't thank you enough for parting with such a fine animal. If she runs as well as I think she will, her purse alone will double what I paid you for her."

Poteet looked disbelieving. "You ain't had no trouble with her? She had a real stubborn streak, and could be downright mean on occasion."

275

"Really? That is strange. As a matter of fact, Red Betty is so gentle I have given her to my wife as her own personal mount. I myself prefer a horse with more spirit."

Poteet, still not convinced, since no one thus far had been able to tame or even gentle the animal, tried another tactic. "If you are of a mind to, I'll take her off your hands. I had a buyer interested in her just the other day. Course, I couldn't give you what you paid for her, but I'll not be far off."

Nicholas's eyes narrowed, and his voice was dangerous. "You wouldn't be trying to cheat me, would you, Garvey?"

By now several men had gathered around, and they were watching with interest.

Poteet grinned nervously. "Now that I think about it, I'll give you back the exact amount of money you paid for the mare. No, I'll give you a hundred dollars more than you paid for her. You can't say I'm not a fair man."

"Back off, Poteet," Nicholas said, his eyes hardening. Suddenly his voice took on a warning tone. "In the future, you might want to remember this: no one, especially not a Yankee, can take advantage of a Ballinger."

Poteet's eyes narrowed. "That's not what I hear," he said sarcastically. "I heard a Yankee took advantage of your mother."

Before the foolish man knew what was happening, Nicholas grabbed him by his shirtfront. "You will curse the day you said that, Yankee," he hissed. With a powerful upper cut, he clipped Poteet Garvey in the jaw, and the man went tumbling backward, over several pails, until he slammed against a horse trough and slid to the ground.

By now more than a dozen men were watching,

each with a satisfied expression at seeing the Yankee, Poteet Garvey, on the ground.

"Don't ever mention any member of my family again," Nicholas warned. "Is that understood?"

Poteet's little eyes darted sideways as if he were looking for an escape in case Nicholas decided to take the fight further.

Nicholas, with calm dignity, led his wife out into the sunlight without a backward glance.

Alanna's eyes were shining with admiration as she glanced into her husband's green eyes, thinking that Mr. Garvey got just what he deserved. The man had simply chosen the wrong person to try to take advantage of. Most probably the man had not been born who could get the better of her husband.

"Nicholas, do you think Poteet Garvey will give up trying to swindle his neighbors after today?"

He looked down at her with a serious reflection in his eyes. "Probably not, Alanna. Garvey will soon come up with another scheme to make a dishonest dollar. But when the word gets out about today, he will have a hard time finding anyone who will do business with him."

As Nicholas sat across the table from Alanna in the hotel dining room, he could not help but notice that she was the center of attention. Men looked at her with admiration, and women studied her closely, as if hoping to find a flaw.

He looked at his wife for the first time through other people's eyes, and discovered that she was fair indeed. With her sapphire-blue eyes that still held a hint of innocence, a small upturned nose, full mouth, and even, white teeth, she was stunning. She wore a bonnet edged with lace and a velvet coat trimmed with fur. Rays of sunlight filtered through the window and made her ebony hair appear as soft as black velvet.

He was suddenly hit with a new feeling: he felt proud to be her husband. Marriage was not as tedious as he had thought it would be.

He was glad that Alanna was so easily accepted, but he wondered what these people would think if they knew that the object of their adoration was a half-breed, a Cheyenne princess.

Alanna caught Nicholas staring at her, and she reached up to straighten her bonnet, thinking it must be crooked.

He caught her hand and smiled. "Have I told you that you were magnificent with Red Betty?"

She warmed to his praise. "She was only frightened. Once she saw I was not going to hurt her, it was easy to gentle her and win her over."

"Do you apply that same theory to me? Did you break and gentle me as you did Red Betty?"

She smiled. "I cannot imagine any woman gentling you, much less breaking you, Nicholas."

Nicholas fell silent, and Alanna watched him with a worried frown, knowing that he was brooding about the man who had insulted his mother.

She took a sip of her water and placed the glass down firmly on the table. "He was a despicable man and deserved what he got."

He reached across the table and squeezed her hand. "And you gave it to him, Alanna. I wonder how he would feel to know a woman got the better of him."

"I think he is the kind of man who will never be convinced he did anything wrong. Those that swindle others have to distort the truth so they can live with themselves."

Nicholas stared into sapphire-blue eyes and felt his

278

heart rate increase. "You have a wonderful sense of honor, Mrs. Ballinger. I am a very fortunate man."

She nodded. "Indeed you are. Red Betty is a horse that comes along but once in a lifetime. I have never seen one to match her."

He smiled. "That is not exactly what I meant, Blue Eyes."

Nicholas suddenly wanted to go home. He wanted to take his wife in his arms and prove to her and to himself that she belonged to him.

Chapter Twenty-Seven

The former mistress of Ballinger Hall was missed by one and all. Even the servants were saddened by her absence. Now a strange quiet overcame the house.

Alanna found herself ill equipped to step into Lillia's shoes as the mistress of Ballinger Hall, so she relied heavily on Kitty's good judgment. The housekeeper gently made suggestions to Alanna, and after several days Alanna felt confident enough to plan the daily menus by herself.

It was a morning when everything had gone wrong: one of the colts had broken through the fence and trampled the vegetable garden; then the cook had scalded her hand, and the doctor had to be summoned.

Alanna was seated on the sofa, with Lillia's sewing basket in her lap, trying to decide how to mend the jagged rip she had torn in her gown when she'd tried to help catch the mischievous colt.

Askew approached her in his usual formal manner to announce that Miss Eliza Caldwell wished to see her.

Without waiting for permission to enter, Eliza pushed past Askew and stood before Alanna, resentment burning in her eyes. "I have grave news for you," she blurted out without feeling. "My father is dead!"

Alanna came to her feet, spilling the sewing basket and sending its contents scattering across the floor. "What did you say, Eliza?"

Eliza was working her fingers out of her gloves. "I said, My father is dead," Eliza announced in a harsh voice, as if it pleased her to be the bearer of such sad tidings.

Alanna suddenly felt numb. It was difficult to think of her father as dead. She moistened her lips before she spoke. "How did it happen?" she asked in a trembling voice.

Now Alanna could see the traces of grief in Eliza's eyes. "The doctor said it was his heart. One moment he was talking to me, and the next, he fell over— dead."

Alanna reached out her hand to Eliza, but the woman backed away. "I did my duty by telling you about the death, but do not pretend you had any feelings for my father. You didn't know him, and he didn't know you."

"Eliza, you look pale. Sit down and allow me to get you a cool glass of water."

Eliza whirled on her. "I want nothing from you. You came here hoping to take my father away from me—well, now you can't. You don't have him, and neither do I."

Alanna shook her head. "You do not know what you are saying. I wanted nothing from my father. I stopped expecting things from him a long time ago."

Her half-sister's eyes hardened. "He was always talking about you and your mother, telling stories

281

about what a beautiful child you were." Her eyes were wild with grief. "Well, let me tell you, I was more of a daughter to him than you will ever be. You, who are little more than a savage!"

Again Alanna attempted to calm Eliza. "You are overwrought. Let me help you."

Eliza backed away, shaking her head. "Just stay away from me. You came here to Virginia, and my father died. You are to blame."

"I do not see how—"

"He was upset because you were cold to him." She shredded her handkerchief with nervous fingers. "I tried to show him that I loved him, but he didn't care. All he loved was you and his precious Donald."

"I am certain that he loved you."

"How would you know . . . you . . . half-breed!" Eliza glanced around the parlor. "You think you have it all, but you'll find out you're wrong. Nicholas Ballinger will never be satisfied with you for long. I happen to know that his appetite for women is insatiable. He will soon tire of you."

Alanna shook her head, wondering what she had done to stir up so much hatred in this woman. "I think you had better leave now, Eliza. I have tried to be patient, but you have no right to speak ill of my husband."

The spiteful woman stared at Alanna for a long moment with malice gleaming in her eyes. Alanna was wondering how hatred could be the dominant emotion in Eliza when she should be feeling grief for her dead father.

Animosity laced Eliza's heated words. "I looked at my father's will, and he left you nothing, Alanna. Does that hurt just a bit?"

"No, I have never expected anything from Anson Caldwell. My heart aches for you, though, Eliza, for you just lost him today, while I lost him a long time ago."

Alanna's kindness only served to make Eliza more resentful.

"Pray spare me your pity, Alanna. You will be the one who needs pity when Nicholas Ballinger tires of you and turns to other women."

Without another word, Eliza gathered up her skirts and moved across the room and out the door, leaving a dazed Alanna staring after her.

It was an hour after Eliza's visit, and Alanna still sat in the parlor, trying to come to terms with her feelings. Great waves of grief welled up inside her, and she wanted to cry, but she could not. Dark shadows fell across the room when she heard voices in the hallway. Quick steps rushed in her direction, and she was soon wrapped in Donald's warm embrace.

She felt her brother's shoulders quake with emotion, and it triggered an answering emotion within her; tears poured down her face. For a long moment the brother and sister stood there, locked in a comforting embrace. At last Donald looked into her face.

"It was quick, Alanna, our father didn't suffer at all."

"I . . . wish I had known him better."

"I realize that. I believe he had many regrets where you were concerned, mostly in these last days. I am not trying to make excuses for him, but he felt great remorse for the way he neglected you."

"None of this matters, Donald. I am sorry for you and Eliza."

"I understand she was here today."

Alanna frowned. "Yes, she was here."

"Try not to think about her, Alanna. She is a hard and bitter woman. Someone with your sweetness could never understand a person like her. There was a time when I pitied her. Now I just dislike her, even if she *is* my sister."

"I find that I do not like her either. I wish I never had to see her again."

Donald smiled slightly. "And why should you?" His expression became serious. "Except that we are having a memorial service tomorrow. Will you come?"

"Yes, I shall be there for you."

Pain reflected in his eyes. "We shall be there for one another," he told her. "I must go now and make the final preparations."

He kissed her cheek and left abruptly.

When Nicholas entered the parlor, he found Alanna sitting near the window. The only light came from the moon, which fell across her face and revealed the sadness in her eyes.

He pulled her up to him and enfolded her in his arms. "I was in Arlington when I heard. I came as quickly as I could. I'm sorry that your father died, Alanna. I know how it feels to lose a father."

"I wish I had known him better. I cry for what could have been, and I cry for Donald and his sister. But I found it hard to cry for my father, because I lost him a long time ago."

He held her trembling body, suddenly feeling very protective toward her. "Cry for your father, for he was a good and worthy man."

Alanna was suddenly overcome with grief. Nicholas held her until the wracking sobs subsided and she lay exhausted in his arms.

Several times Kitty stuck her head in the door to see if Alanna was all right, but each time, Nicholas waved her away. At last, too exhausted to think, she fell asleep, and he carried her upstairs to their bedroom.

Gently he undressed her and pulled the covers over her. He then lay beside her and held her in his arms all night. She slept fitfully, and when she awakened, he talked to her soothingly until she fell asleep again.

The next day the sun rose like a glorious ball of fire. Alanna, her face hidden behind the black veil Kitty had given her, stood beside Nicholas and Donald while the minister spoke a glowing tribute to her father. She was numb and unaware that the many people who attended the service were straining to get a look at her.

Eliza was vocal in her grief, throwing herself across the closed coffin and crying for her father. After the service had ended and before the onlookers could approach Alanna, Nicholas spirited her away to a waiting carriage, while Donald tried to comfort Eliza.

Alanna slipped out of the house and walked alone down to the Potomac River, unaware that the sky had darkened with storm clouds. When she felt the first drops of rain, she continued to stand there until she was soaked to the skin. Like the Indians she came from, she had cleansed her soul of grief. The dead were buried, their ghosts put to rest.

Night had fallen over Ballinger Hall. Alanna, wearing one of the transparent nightgowns the seamstress had made for her, walked across the bedroom to stand before Nicholas, who was already in bed.

Her soul-searching today had led her to the conclusion that broken fences must be mended before a person died—afterward all one had left were the recriminations. If only she had reached out to her father while he lived! She thought of Nicholas and the breech between him and his mother. The two of them should resolve their differences before it was too late.

In a bold move, she bent, taking his face between her hands, and raised it up to her. "I have been thinking about your mother all day. Nicholas, why could you not have asked Lillia to stay? I feel certain she would not have gone if you had indicated you wanted her to remain. Why not write her a letter and ask her to come home?"

His voice was dull. "My mother knows how I feel. I am certain she did the right thing by leaving. At any rate, the choice was not mine, but my mother's."

Alanna's eyes shimmered with tears. "I wanted her to stay. This is her home. This is where she gave birth to you, do not forget that."

"Am I to take it that you would rather not be alone with me at Ballinger Hall?"

She shook her head and pressed her lips against his, trying to show him how she felt about him. When she got no response, she laced her fingers through his dark hair.

A low sound tore from his throat, as he tasted the saltiness of her lips. He pulled back, noticing she was still crying.

"You should know before you try this ploy again, Alanna, that a woman's tears will not soften me." In spite of his words to the contrary, all the while his

286

hands were kneading her back as if he were trying to give her comfort.

He came to his feet and took her in his arms. "Let us not talk of others. Let me make love to you," he groaned, reaching for the fastenings on her gown. "Come to me, and I will die a happy man."

Alanna melted against him as his burning lips settled on hers. She felt everything else leave her mind as he put tenderness into the kiss. Surely he must care something for her, or he could not be so loving.

She parted her lips, and his tongue slid into her mouth, tasting the sweetness, while he ignited a fire inside her. When his tongue danced in and out of her mouth, the heat was building in her veins. Reminded of the pleasure he could give, she could not control her impatience.

Nicholas pulled her so tightly against him that she could scarcely breathe. His hard, muscled body craved the satiny soft body. "You belong to me," he stated in a voice of possession. "You are my wife."

"Yes," she whispered as he slipped her gown off her shoulders.

It took him little time to dispose of his own clothing. His mouth moved slowly downward to her slender neck to taunt and suckle her rosebud nipples. His tongue circled, tasted, probed, and tantalized with velvet softness.

Now Nicholas had a driving need to possess the soft body that was rendering him mindless.

Alanna was like a fever in his brain, a fire in his blood. Each night when he took her in his arms, he became more firmly tied to her, but still he craved what only she could give him.

Chapter Twenty-Eight

Lifting Alanna into his arms, Nicholas laid her on the bed and joined her there. "You grow more beautiful each time I see you, Blue Eyes." He ran his hand over her smooth hips. "How is it possible that one so beautiful belongs to me?"

She smiled with warmth. "I want to be pretty for you, Nicholas."

He frowned and looked deeply into her eyes. "Tell me, do you ever think of Gray Falcon?"

She knew she had to tell him the truth. "Sometimes I do. At times I feel like I am being disloyal to his memory."

"When do you feel that?"

"Like now, when I am in your arms."

"Do you still love him?"

She lowered her lashes. "I will always want to keep his memory in my heart."

His eyes were flashing as he pulled her to him, silencing her with a burning kiss.

When he pulled back, she followed him, seeking the heat of his mouth. She clung to him, feeling the muscles bulging beneath her hand.

Nicholas's hand moved across Alanna's hips, and

she felt a painful ache deep inside. She wiggled her hips, trying to get closer to him, and his breath came out in a hiss.

His voice was made deeper by his passion. "Do you know what you are doing to me?"

"I want to please you," she said. Her hand slid across his back, and she felt the muscles go taut. "I have always wanted that."

The core of her softness touched against his swollen, throbbing hardness, and she felt faint with desire.

Each seductive move on her part would make his eyes flame with unleashed passion. Her grandmother had failed to tell her that a woman could have so much power over a man—but she was learning that for herself.

Nicholas gathered Alanna to him, pressing her into the soft mattress. "If you play the seductress, you must expect to be seduced, Blue Eyes."

His wonderful hand was moving across her abdomen, and he spread her legs apart. Suddenly, he jabbed forward inside her moist opening, arousing, teasing, making her helpless with need.

His breath fanned her cheek, and she groaned with pleasure, thinking she never wanted him to stop.

He teased her with gentle massaging motions, and all she wanted was for him to put out the fire he had ignited inside her.

"Sweet, sweet Blue Eyes," he murmured in her ear, his hot breath making her shiver. "Grant me permission to enter further into paradise."

"Yes, please, Nicholas," she answered him in a breathless voice.

She was overcome with wild pleasure as his swollen member pierced deeper inside her. By now they were both caught up in a searing passion which neither of them could control.

Nicholas's movements caused a greater longing, and he increased the tempo. Wilder, deeper, he reached within her, bringing them both pleasure beyond reason.

With a strangled cry, she felt her body erupt. But that was not to be the end. Time after time, he brought her body to a fevered pitch, and joy sang inside her. At last his body trembled, and he reached the pleasurable plateau with her.

Alanna wanted to hold onto him so the magic would endure forever. She wanted to speak of the joy that filled her heart, but she dared not.

When the tremor left Nicholas's body, he realized he had never felt so vulnerable with a woman before. He could not stop himself from clasping her tightly to him while he sprinkled burning kisses over her face.

"I'll have to be more careful with you, Blue Eyes," he murmured, "or you will have me begging at your feet for scraps of affection."

He ran his fingers through her tangled hair, then dipped his head to kiss her lips.

"I am a wife," she whispered in a confused voice. "I would never make you beg."

"Yes, you are my wife, and you belong to me alone, Alanna."

"Yes, of course I do," she answered, wondering why he should feel the need to remind her.

Nicholas gripped her chin and made her look into his eyes. "Will you miss me while I am away?"

She frowned, hoping she had misunderstood. "Are you going somewhere?"

"Yes, an old friend of mine, Madeline Arthur, is selling off her stable in Charlotte, North Carolina. Her husband died recently, and she needs the money to settle her debts. I am interested in the bloodline of several of her mares."

Alanna felt her heart sink. "An old friend that is a woman?"

"Yes." He touched his lips briefly to hers and smiled slightly. "I know what you are thinking, but I have no feelings for Madeline besides friendship."

Hope sprang to life within her. "Will you take me with you?"

"No, Blue Eyes. You would be far more comfortable here at Ballinger Hall."

"Was this woman once your lover?"

He looked irritated. "I will not discuss this with you."

"Was she?" Alanna demanded.

"Yes, she was. But that was a long time ago. Didn't my mother tell you that no woman should ask such questions of her husband?"

Alanna remembered what Lillia had told her about Nicholas's father having mistresses, but she had promised not to tell Nicholas about his father. Was this woman, Madeline, Nicholas's mistress? Was he following in his father's footsteps?

Her eyes were pleading. "I will not mind the discomfort as long as I can be with you."

His lips thinned. "I am going on business, and I do not wish to be encumbered by a woman."

Alanna felt her temper start to burn with intensity. "You did not think of me as an encumbrance when we were stranded together."

He drew in an impatient breath. "Alanna, this subject is closed."

"Is the woman pretty? Is that why you are going to her?"

He was suddenly amused by her question. "What's the matter, Blue Eyes? Can it be that you are jealous?"

She lowered her lashes. "I do not know. Perhaps I am." She gazed up at him. "Should I be?"

He held his arms out to her. "No. You are my wife, and she is not. Put all your doubts aside and come to me."

She wanted to go to him, but she sensed something in him that stopped her. "Perhaps, in some cases it is better to be the lover, who is desired, rather than the wife, who is left at home and neglected."

His firmly molded mouth curved into a smile. "You have an imaginative mind, Blue Eyes. Surely you don't think I am going all that way to see a woman?"

He rubbed his hand over the dark bristle that shadowed his face. "You, Alanna, are the only woman I would go out of my way to see."

Her answering smile was tremulous, and she was lost in the vivid green of his eyes. Then doubt tugged at her again. "Sometimes I feel as though you are ashamed of who I am, and that you think yourself high above me."

He looked thunderstruck. "The opposite is true, for so long I have cared about no one, thought about no one. I lived in a world where I didn't have to feel. Then one day you came into my life and made me smile a lot. It is you who are high above me, Alanna."

She realized for the first time how lonely he must have been. "I wish I could believe you."

"Why should you not? This woman means nothing to me anymore?"

"But she once did."

He shrugged. "She is less of a threat to you than Gray Falcon is to me. It has been years since I have seen her."

"Were you as close to her as I was to Gray Falcon?"

His eyes were half-veiled. "Perhaps. But we were

young then," he admitted, wishing he had never mentioned Madeline Arthur to his wife.

"I remember the night we were married, you as much as said you would not be a faithful husband. What am I supposed to think when you go off to that woman?"

"Think what you will. I am weary of this conversation."

"Swear to me that you will not touch that woman," Alanna demanded.

"I will not take this from you, Alanna," he warned.

"Swear," she said again.

"No, I will not." He moved away from her, his steps purposeful and determined. "You don't want to be a wife—you want to be a jailer."

Alanna moved away from him, feeling a strange transformation within her mind. She raised her head and looked back at him coldly. With her Indian background, she had always had the unsettling ability to close a person out of her heart with surprising ease—as she had with her father. Regrettably, she had not let him back in her heart until it was too late.

"I promise you that I will never stand by meekly while you flaunt a mistress in my face, Nicholas Ballinger. Do not forget that I am that uncivilized little half-breed you married. I do not live by the same rules your white women abide by. Do not give me reason to doubt you. All I ask is your word."

His smile faded and jaw line hardened, while his amusement disappeared. "Is that a threat?"

She was coldly beautiful as she stared up at him. "No, Nicholas, not a threat—a statement of fact. All you have to do is give me your word that you and that woman are not lovers."

He moved to stand beside her, then gripped her by

the arm. "Be warned, Alanna, I am master of this house, and you are my wife. I will not be bullied by you."

There was a proud tilt to her head. "Be warned about this, Nicholas, I am my own person before I am your wife. Go to that woman, but do not expect to come back and find me waiting for you."

His mouth set in a severe line of disapproval. "You go too far, Alanna."

"Regrettably so, Nicholas, but know in your heart that if you shame me, I will never forgive you." Silence encroached, hanging heavily in the air.

He paled beneath his tan, looked like he would say more, then reconsidered. He walked across the room and turned back to her at the door. "I will leave you with your thoughts, Alanna. When I return from Charlotte, I expect you to beg my pardon."

She watched him leave, knowing he was as angry as she was. If she was wrong, she would beg his pardon, but she did not feel like she was wrong. One thing was certain, she would never be a docile little wife who turned a blind eye to her husband's indiscretions. Never!

All night long Alanna lay in the big bed, dry-eyed and wondering where Nicholas was sleeping. He did not return to her, and she did not seek him out.

Alanna was miserable. Nicholas might say that woman was not a threat to their marriage, but the difference between Madeline Arthur and Gray Falcon was that Gray Falcon was dead and Madeline Arthur was very much alive.

When dawn came, Alanna still had not slept. She moved to the window and watched Nicholas and the trainer Glenn Hubbard ride away.

There was a deep ache in her heart. "No, Nicholas," she whispered in a painful voice, "you will not break my heart as your father broke your mother's."

Two weeks had passed without word from Nicholas, and still he remained in North Carolina. Alanna had not expected him to be gone so long, and she wondered if he stayed away to punish her for being such a demanding wife.

Her days were spent in search of an activity to fill the lonely hours. Riding Red Betty and training her was pleasant, but one could not ride all day.

She tried not to think of Nicholas, because in her imagination she could see him holding that woman in his arms, and it made her physically ill. Why did she have to love Nicholas? If she were like him, if she looked on their marriage as one of convenience, she would have been better off. She shook herself mentally and pushed her troubled thoughts aside.

She missed Lillia even more than she'd thought she would and wished she would come back to Ballinger Hall. Alanna needed her wise advice. She was sorry that she had argued with Nicholas, and she decided that she would beg his pardon when he returned.

It had been raining all day, adding to Alanna's feeling of gloom. Now as she stood under the shelter of the veranda, she watched the rain beating down on the Potomac.

She thought of the green meadows of her homeland and the clear Powder River, and she was overcome with homesickness. She reminded herself that the land which she had once called home no longer belonged to the Cheyenne people, but that did not ease her longing to see it again.

It was sad that the once proud Cheyenne people had been forced to leave their lands. All they had now was straw-colored dirt, few horses, no weapons with which to hunt, and dwellings which were no better than hovels.

She heard the back door open, and she turned to see Askew step out onto the veranda.

"Madame," he said stiffly, "Mr. Donald Caldwell to see you. Shall I show him to the parlor, or shall I show him out here?"

Alanna's eyes lit up with joy. She had not seen her brother since the day their father had been buried. "Show him out here, Askew."

Chapter Twenty-Nine

A jovial Donald joined Alanna on the veranda. "Well, little sister, how are you faring as the mistress of Ballinger Hall?"

She smiled brightly, liking Donald more every time she saw him. He reminded her of their father when she had been a young girl. He had a way of putting people at ease, and she was grateful that he had accepted her as his sister.

"You look well," he observed, taking her hands and moving her around so he could see her from head to toe.

She wrinkled her nose. "I thank you, gallant sir, but being mistress of all this," she waved her hand in a wide circle, "can be a lonely existence. Besides, I do not feel like the mistress. The servants are so well trained, they need no direction from me."

Donald bent over and kissed her cheek, a move that startled as well as pleased her. "I know little about a woman's duties," he said, "but I feel sure the servants should never be allowed to have the run of the house."

She smiled weakly. "Actually, Kitty is a great help to me. I do not know what I would do without her."

As if to prove her correct, Kitty appeared, carrying a silver serving tray. "I remembered that you liked popovers, Mr. Caldwell," she said, placing the tray on the wooden table.

"You remembered correctly, Kitty. It's been many a day since I've tasted popovers from Ballinger Hall."

Kitty sniffed and eyed him with a look of gentle reprimand. "A mite too long, to my way of thinking." Without another word, she turned and disappeared into the house.

Donald frowned. "She's right, you know. I should never have allowed gossip to keep me away from Ballinger Hall. Of course, I shall be a regular visitor, now that you are here."

Alanna reached out and touched his hand. "Oh, Donald, how sorely Lillia has suffered because of the neighbors shunning her. If only I could tell you . . . but no, I cannot. I gave her my word to keep silent."

Donald sat down on one of the chairs and smiled at her. "Are you going to hint at secrets you cannot divulge, or play hostess and pour me a cup of tea?"

She placed her hand over her mouth to smother a laugh. "Just watch what a proper lady I am." To demonstrate her abilities, she became sober-faced and picked up a delicate china cup. With expert ease, she poured the hot brew into the cup and handed it to Donald.

He took a sip, watching her all the while. "Won't you join me?"

"I'll sit with you, but I have not developed a liking for tea."

Still he watched her. "How have you been?"

She shrugged. "All right."

"So you miss Lillia?"

"Yes, I do, and Nicholas is away also."

"I had heard that. In North Carolina, I believe."

298

Alanna did not want to talk about Nicholas. "How is your sister?"

Donald leaned back and roared with laughter. "I like the way you say 'my sister.' I assure you, I take neither credit nor responsibility for Eliza."

Her eyes sparkled with a mischievous light. "She *is* your sister, so therefore, you are cut from the same cloth."

It was the first he had ever known her to tease, and it took him by surprise. "If I am, then so are you."

"Only half," she reminded him.

Suddenly his features settled into seriousness. "I have come to ask a favor."

She met his eyes. "If I can help you in any way, you know I will."

"Even if it involves a trip to Washington?"

She looked puzzled, and then excitement stirred within her. "Tell me what you want of me."

"It's simple. I am heading a committee to investigate the treatment of the Indians in Indian Territory. As you know, since George Custer's massacre—"

"You mean since George Custer met his death on the field of dishonor," she corrected him, her head held proudly, her eyes gleaming with anguish.

"As you will," he said, "but if you go with me to Washington, that's just the kind of thing you mustn't say to the committee."

"Go on with what you were saying. I promise not to interrupt."

"Since the death of Custer," he began again, "hatred for the Indian has flourished. I want to do something to set the record right, and with your help, I think I can."

Her interest grew. "How can I help?"

"Come with me to Washington and talk to the

299

committee. Allow them to question you. Be honest with them, and tell them what you have witnessed first-hand."

She looked doubtful. "Will they listen to me?"

"I can assure you they will."

A look of joy spread over her face—then indecision crept into her eyes, and she shook her head. "How can I go with you, Donald? Nicholas is away from home, and he may disapprove of my going."

"That is up to you, of course, but this will be a good chance for you to do something for your people. How could he object to that?"

She laid her hand on his, and desperation threaded her words. "If only I could."

"All you have to do is say yes. I have a very dear friend you can stay with, and you will be gone a week at the most."

Suddenly her face brightened. "I'll do it!"

He took a sip of tea, crammed a popover in his mouth, and stood up. "Then get packing, little sister. I'll pick you up tomorrow morning before sunrise."

"What shall I wear?"

"Ask Kitty. And by the way, bring her with you, it'll give you more respectability than my patronage ever could."

Washington, D.C. was a bustling city with a continuous stream of buggies and coaches moving at a snail's pace down Pennsylvania Avenue. The sound of the horses' clip-clopping hooves echoed against the brick buildings as they rode along.

The dome of the Capitol shone brightly in the noonday sun, and Alanna could not help feeling a sense of pride. This was the city her grandfather and the chiefs of the Cheyenne Nation had once talked

300

about with awe and reverence.

There had been a time when the Indian had trusted the man who occupied the White House, but that trust had fallen into dust, just like the broken promises that had come to naught.

Donald called her attention to the different points of interest, and she craned her neck to see each building. It seemed construction was going on everywhere, and Alanna thought the city had a feeling of newness.

The driver guided the horses down a slanted tree-lined street and brought them to a halt before a charming red-brick mansion.

"This is where you will be staying," Donald told her. "I sent a rider ahead last night to inform Dotty Singleton to expect you and Kitty. I know she'll be delighted."

"Are you certain we will not be imposing?" Alanna asked, fearful of meeting new people.

"Not a bit. In fact, when I told Dotty about you, she suggested that I bring you to Washington. It was also Dotty who suggested you stay with her. You will like her, everyone does. She is a widow, I'd say in her late fifties. She can make a party a success just by attending it, and ruin one by leaving too early."

"Her function is to give parties?"

"In a way. You see, she is the most powerful hostess in Washington, even though her Democratic Party is out of favor at the moment and is likely to be so for many years to come."

"I do not understand."

"Well, you see, since the war the Republicans have been in power. Dotty represents the Democrats, even though she is a woman and can't belong to the Democratic Party."

"You are confusing me."

"Never mind, it confuses me as well." He signaled for the driver to open the carriage door, and he helped Alanna alight.

Her hand rested on Donald's arm as they moved up the brick walkway, followed closely by Kitty and the driver, who carried one of the heavy trunks.

As they climbed the steps, the door was swept open, and they were met by a cheery-faced, plump little lady, with gray curls bobbing every time she moved her head. Dressed in bright pink, Dolly Singleton smiled in welcome.

"Oh, my dear, I am so delighted you have come," she gushed, pushing past Donald and latching onto Alanna's arm. "You will entertain me for hours with stories about your childhood in an Indian village."

"Alanna, this charming lady is your hostess, Dotty Singleton. Dotty, my sister, Alanna Ballinger."

"Let's dispense with formalities," Dotty said, waving her hand above her head. "I'm Dotty, and you're Alanna."

Alanna smiled at the little woman, charmed by her easy grace. She had not expected to feel so welcome.

Donald followed them inside. "Now, Dotty, don't expect to monopolize my sister's time. Remember, I have a purpose for bringing her to Washington."

"Oh, posh. I intend to hold a party to introduce her to Washington society." Her face crinkled into laughter. "Loretta Gibbens will be pea-green with envy, but I'll invite her to the party anyway."

Alanna got a sense of openness as she glanced around the room, which reminded her of its owner. It was filled with old and valuable furnishings. Masterpieces hung on the wall, and the scent of fresh roses spilled from the sides of a silver bowl on the entry table and filled the room with perfume.

Donald took Alanna's hand and pulled her to the

302

door, while Dotty was directing the driver with Alanna's trunks. "I leave you in Dotty's capable hands for now, but I shall see you later tonight."

"I'll be waiting for you," she said, going up on tiptoe to plant a kiss on his cheek. Donald looked pleased. With a slight bow, he was out the door, closing it behind him.

Alanna sat on the edge of the rose-colored chair, enchanted by the sound of music that drifted through the room. She watched the magic hands of the woman harpist and was fascinated by the man who played the flute. Their music blended sweetly into a haunting melody. She had never heard anything so lovely, and it brought tears to her eyes. When the music stopped, she wished that they would play on and on.

Dotty, seeing her guest was moved to tears, bent to whisper in her ear. "I am glad you have an appreciation for music, my dear. I fear many of us have begun to take it for granted. It is wonderful to rediscover its beauty through your eyes tonight."

"It is truly wonderful, Dotty. I have never heard anything more lovely."

The older woman frowned. "Of course, you would have had no musicals at Ballinger Hall." She was thoughtful for a moment. "I was thinking about the scandal." Dotty patted her hand fondly. "I do not wish to be unkind, dear."

"For reasons I am sure you know, there have been no visitors to Ballinger Hall for a very long time. Although lately there have been an influx of invitations."

Dotty haughtily tapped her fan on the mahogany arm of the chair. "Which you declined, I trust."

Alanna stared into soft, understanding eyes. "Yes, I declined them all."

"Good for you," Dotty said with determination. "Now, let me warn you about something. I, in my modest way, am not without influence. I have decided to be your patroness, so to speak, and to put you forward. Get ready to be a raving success."

"What does that mean, Dotty?" Alanna asked in confusion.

"That will mean, my dear sister," Donald said, joining in the conversation, "you will be the rage in Washington society. Hostesses will vie for your attention, and everyone will want to be seen with you. In other words, with Dotty as your benefactress, you become not only accepted, but sought-after."

"I am not sure I understand."

Dotty patted her curls into place and looked Alanna over carefully. "Yes, you will be my new project." Her eyes almost disappeared beneath rolls of fat when she smiled. "What fun. You are going to be a sensation!"

"Will this help my people, the Cheyenne?"

Dotty nodded. "Indeed it will. I will raise you up so high, people will listen when you talk. If you are wise, you will be able to convince the people who hold the power and control the purse strings to help the Indians."

Alanna's eyes sought her brother's. "Would Nicholas approve of this?"

"I can assure you that he would be delighted to learn that Dotty has taken you under her wing."

Dotty smiled. "I'd like to see more of that handsome husband of yours. I know he was in Washington some weeks ago, but he stayed very much to himself. Now, it would really be a feather in my cap if I could convince your Nicholas Ballinger to attend one of my parties."

Alanna's head was filled with confusing notions. What had a party to do with one being accepted by others? She tried to digest what she had been told, but the thing that stuck in her mind was the fact that she might be able to help the Cheyenne. For that reason alone she would do whatever was necessary.

Dolly was walking around Alanna, looking at her with a practiced eye. "From what I have seen of your wardrobe, it is sensational. I see Lillia's fine hand in this. She always had excellent taste."

"Do you know my mother-in-law well?"

"At one time I did. But that was a long time ago."

Alanna raised her head, and defiance sparked in her blue eyes. "I am very fond of Lillia. She is more wonderful than you can imagine."

Dolly chuckled. "If you think so, it must be. Later, I want to hear all about why you feel as you do. But now I am thinking of how to present you."

Alanna's eyes became stormy. "I will not allow anyone to speak ill of Lillia."

Dotty's eyes brightened. "My dear, you cannot imagine how refreshing it is to see loyalty in one so young."

Donald winked at his sister. He was proud of her, and he had a feeling her honesty would set Washington on its ear.

Chapter Thirty

Alanna's footsteps were silent as Donald led her into the small chamber located within the confines of the Capitol. Her eyes moved across the faces of the three men seated at the long table, and she felt relief that Donald was with her because they seemed so still and unsmiling.

"Gentlemen," Donald began, "I would like you to meet my sister, Alanna Ballinger. As I told you, she is half Cheyenne, and she spent most of her life in a Cheyenne village in Montana Territory." He smiled at her warmly. "Alanna, these men are all colleagues of mine who share an interest in seeing justice for the Indians of this country."

Donald indicated each man by name: Oliver Redburn, Paul Ross, Sidney Udell. "This will be an informal hearing, Alanna, so just relax. Feel free to ask questions if there's anything you don't understand."

Alanna could not know how regally beautiful she looked as she stood before the panel dressed in her wine-colored silk gown. Her dark hair was unadorned. Her blue eyes were large and expressive, and her head was held at a proud tilt.

After Donald had seated Alanna at one side of the table, he joined the other gentlemen on the opposite side.

Oliver Redburn, a man with a crop of snowy-white hair and thick bifocals, began the questioning.

"Were you aware of the massacre of Colonel Custer and the men of the Seventh Cavalry at the time it occurred, Mrs. Ballinger?"

She threaded her gloved fingers together and placed them on the table, looking Redburn in the eye. "I was aware that a state of war existed between the Sioux and Cheyenne and any whites who trespassed on our lands."

"Your lands?"

"Yes, my brother has told you that I am half Cheyenne." Without blinking she added. "I like to think the better half of me is Cheyenne."

Congressman Redburn felt his lips twitch, and he tried not to smile at her quick wit. "Tell us," he said, clearing his throat, "what your thoughts were on the day the Cheyenne rode out to intercept the Seventh Cavalry."

"I thought about what my grandfather had told me. He, like many of the Cheyenne, did not want war. He knew if the Cheyenne met the soldiers in combat, it would signal the beginning of the end for our tribe. He knew it was a war we could never win."

"Then why did he fight?"

Alanna lowered her eyes. "I wonder what you would have done in my grandfather's place, Congressman. Suppose your family had lived on your land for many hundreds of years, and then one day a strange people, with different-colored skin and a different view on life, invaded your land and told you that you must leave because some man in Washington said you had no right to be there. Would you meekly pack your belongings and leave?"

Her eyes moved over each man's face, seeking an answer. "I do not think any one of you would have done differently than my grandfather did."

"No, damn it," Paul Ross shouted, bringing his fist down so forcefully on the table that his water glass rattled. "I would drive the bastards out!" His face suddenly reddened, and he looked at Alanna apologetically. "I beg your pardon, Mrs. Ballinger. It's just that, like your brother, I have long thought the Indian deserved better than he got from us."

When she smiled, a lovely transformation came over her face, and it almost took Congressman Ross's breath away.

"Well, Congressman, from here on out, I shall be a champion of yours, especially if you will help my people."

Donald sat back and watched Alanna work her magic on the panel. For over an hour they fired questions at her, and she answered clearly and honestly.

Now it was Donald's turn to ask her questions. "Tell us, Alanna. What was the state of the Cheyenne people when Nicholas Ballinger first saw you? This was after you had been uprooted and forced to move hundreds of miles from your lands."

For the first time, her eyes showed her distress. "We were cold and hungry, and many starved to death. You cannot imagine how degraded we felt having to go to the Indian agent and beg for food, only to have him tell us there was no food. Our weapons had been taken away, as had our horses. We had nothing left but our pride. I knew of one family of seven who were too proud to ask for food. They just lay in their pitiful lodge, with holes in the walls where the cold was seeping through, holding hands and waiting for death to claim them—which it did. Death was a constant companion on the reservation."

Alanna waited for them to digest what she had told them. "Gentlemen, the youngest member of that family was a six-month-old baby girl. I was not as brave as they were, and I am ashamed to admit to you that I begged for food to feed my starving grandmother."

Tears sparkled in her eyes, but she refused to let go of her composure. "Can you imagine the helplessness you would feel if your beloved grandmother was dying of starvation and there was nothing you could do to save her?" She lowered her head, and when she finally looked up, her eyes were clear. "My grandmother died on a bitterly cold day. When Nicholas Ballinger found me, I was trying to dig a hole in the frozen earth to bury her. I do not remember much about that time, for I was ill."

Alanna's account of the death of her grandmother touched the hearts of all four men. Donald rose, thinking his sister had been questioned enough. "Gentlemen, I believe my sister has given us enough to go on for one day. Are there any further questions you want to ask her before we adjourn?"

There was mumbling and muttering among the congressmen. Finally Sidney Udell spoke up. "I have just one question, Mrs. Ballinger."

She nodded.

"Do you hate the whites for what they did to the Cheyenne?"

"No, how could I? My husband is white, my brother is white. There was a time when I was ashamed of the part of me that was white. But since then I have met some very wonderful people, and many of them are white. I have at last come to terms with the part of me that is white."

Paul Ross gave her a warm glance. "We in this room all want to help you and your people, Mrs. Ballinger. But what would you have us say to our opponents who will be only too willing to dismiss the Indians as unimportant?"

"How could anyone dismiss my grandfather, Wolf Dreamer, who was wise counsel to his people? He was a man who loved and nurtured me, while teaching me about such things as honor and truth."

Her eyes gleamed with indignation. "Tell the people who think the Cheyenne are not important about my grandmother, Blue Flower Woman. Like most grandmothers, she had a heart so big that everyone in our village was the recipient of her goodwill and kindness. No, gentlemen, you cannot dismiss a people who have lived and loved in the shadow of the wide sky for farther back than your history was recorded."

Paul Ross nodded. "I wish the ones who oppose us could hear you speak, Mrs. Ballinger. I feel certain you would win many of them over to our side."

Congressman Udell smiled. "May I say you are charming, Mrs. Ballinger? It is difficult to believe you were brought up in an Indian village, because you look just like any well-brought-up southern girl."

Her smile was soft. "If you could have seen me then, Congressman, you would have had difficulty imagining me in the gown I wear today."

She received warm smiles from the men around the table. Each one of them shook her hand and promised her they would do whatever they could to help the Indians.

Donald linked his arm with Alanna's and led her out of the room, leaving the three congressmen staring after her in admiration.

As they moved down the wide carpeted halls, he steered her around a corner and smiled down at her.

"You impressed them even beyond what I had hoped, Alanna. I believe you helped the Indian cause today. Of course, we must bear in mind that there are so few of us who want to help the Indian at this time—we have strong opposition. But we should be able to get food and supplies to your Cheyenne right away."

"That will be wonderful, Donald."

He was leading her through the main part of the rotunda when Alanna's attention was drawn to a man in a military uniform who limped toward them, leaning heavily on his silver-handled cane. The man was tall and distinguished. His sandy-colored hair was sprinkled with gray, and as he drew near, she could see he had bright blue eyes.

Donald smiled at the man in recognition as he drew even with them. "Colonel Sanderson, how good to see you. I had heard you were back in Washington."

The soldier offered his hand to Donald, but his manner was somehow stiff and withdrawn. "It's good to be back, Congressman. It is gratifying to see you won your election. I was certain you would beat your opponent to become the congressman from Virginia."

Alanna caught the man's eyes, trying to still her pounding heart. Did Donald address the man as Sanderson? Could he be a relative of Captain Barnard Sanderson, the man that Lillia had loved? No, she dismissed the notion as wishful thinking on her part. Sanderson must be a common name, and there was probably nothing that would link this man to Lillia's captain.

"Colonel Sanderson, I'd like to present you to my

sister, Mrs. Nicholas Ballinger." Donald's eyes were watchful as he looked at his sister. "Alanna, Colonel Sanderson has just returned from an extended tour of duty out west in California."

The Colonel's eyes seemed to turn cold as he quickly glanced away from Alanna. "Well, I have an appointment, Congressman," he remarked, rudely brushing past Alanna without acknowledging the introduction.

Alanna watched the man's retreating back with a certain amount of excitement. "Donald, tell me quickly, is that man a relative of Captain Barnard Sanderson?"

Her brother took her arm and led her out the front door of the Capitol before he answered. He turned her to face him. "That was Barnard Sanderson, at one time a captain, but lately promoted to Colonel."

"But how can that be?"

"I apologize for his rudeness to you. I should have predicted he would not take kindly to the Ballinger name—I think you already know why."

Alanna grasped his coat front, and desperation threaded her words. "Is that the same man who was supposed to have been killed by Nicholas's father?"

"Yes, it is. For a time everyone thought he was dead. I don't know any of the particulars because he isn't talking. He's very much a private man. You saw how rude he was to you just now. I am told that is his way with everyone."

Exhilaration throbbed through Alanna's body. "Donald, I have to talk to him. Take me to see him at once."

He looked at her, puzzled. "We can't do that now. The Colonel must be here on business."

"How can I see him?"

Donald was thoughtful. "He did have a house in

Georgetown, perhaps he still does."

There was an urgency about her. "Will you take me to see him?"

"Can't. I'm leaving for home this afternoon. But I should be back in a couple of days. I could take you then, if it's so important."

"Must I wait so long?"

"Well, perhaps you could have Dotty invite him to the party tomorrow night."

Alanna's face brightened. "Yes, Dotty will help me." She felt laughter bubbling up from inside. "Oh, Donald, this is going to make someone I care about very happy!"

"Are you going to tease me, or enlighten me?"

"I cannot say any more just now. But if everything turns out the way I hope it will, you will know."

It was a ball the likes of which Washington had not seen since the inauguration of President Rutherford B. Hayes. Dotty had thrown wide her doors and welcomed the most prominent people of Washington.

Unlike the social gatherings at the White House, since Mrs. Hayes, or "Lemonade Lucy," as she was called, would allow no strong spirits, wine and champagne flowed into delicate crystal glasses.

It was reputed that Dotty's honored guest, Mrs. Nicholas Ballinger, had taken Washington by storm, and if Dotty was sponsoring her, then surely it must be so.

Alanna, looking cool and elegant in a light blue organza gown with yards and yards of white lace flowing down the back, watched ladies dance by, their silk gowns whispering as they occasionally touched the ballroom floor.

Although Lillia had arranged dancing lessons for

Alanna, she chose not to dance since Nicholas was not present. However, she was always surrounded by ladies and gentlemen as she stood beside Dotty. A constant stream of people came up to the hostess, asking to be introduced to Alanna Ballinger of Ballinger Hall.

Dotty leaned close to Alanna and whispered behind her fan. "Well, you are 'in' with Washington Society, my dear. How many invitations have you received tonight?"

Alanna smiled. "I lost count of the people who invited me to one function or another." Her brow creased in a frown. "I have not seen Colonel Sanderson, have you?"

"Oh," Dotty said, shaking her head, "how remiss of me. I received his refusal in the form of a letter. He speaks of ill-health, but I know him well enough to guess he just did not want to come. The man is locked within some deep-dark secret and will allow no one to get close to him. I didn't think he would come tonight, but since it seemed to mean so much to you, I sent him the invitation."

"I have to see him and talk to him as soon as possible," Alanna said in a voice threaded with desperation. "It is most important!"

Dotty was mildly shocked.

"Yes, my dear, I can see that it is important to you. Later, when we are alone, I want to hear why you feel the need to see Colonel Sanderson. I suspect it has something to do with your mother-in-law."

Alanna nodded. Even though Lillia had asked her not to tell Nicholas about Barnard, she did not say she could not tell anyone else. Perhaps Lillia would forgive her if she told Dotty only enough to make her understand how vital it was that she see the Colonel.

*　　　*　　　*

Nicholas had been riding since before dawn. When Ballinger Hall came into view, he felt a rush of happiness, knowing Alanna would be there waiting for him. He would hold her in his arms and make her forgive him for that foolish quarrel they had had the night before he left.

Nicholas was met at the front door by Askew. Handing the butler his hat, he asked: "Where is my wife? Is she in the parlor?"

"No, sir, she is not here. Madame left word for you that she had gone to Washington with her brother, Mr. Donald Caldwell."

Nicholas frowned. "Why should she have done such a thing?"

Askew, who had been well-trained not to state his own opinion, now broke the rule. "The madame was lonesome, being left so much to herself. I feel sure her brother will look after her and see that she is protected."

Nicholas arched a dark eyebrow. "So, you think she has been lonely, do you?"

"I should not have said so, Mr. Nicholas, but yes, I do. All of us who serve Ballinger Hall have seen the young mistress's loneliness."

Nicholas muttered under his breath as he took the stairs two at a time. "Damn you, Alanna, for not being here when I arrived home."

He had missed her more than he'd thought he would. Unable to get her out of his mind, he had cut his trip short by several days, just to return to her.

Even the allure of an old love had not appealed to him. When Madeline Arthur had made it quite clear that she would not spurn any advance he might make, he had kept his distance, his mind always on his wife, who he thought would be waiting for him to return.

He dismissed the argument that had taken place

the night before he'd left for North Carolina as unimportant. But why had she left him?

He flung open the door to his bedroom and found it strangely empty. In fact the whole house seemed empty. Why had she gone without first consulting him?

He retraced his steps downstairs, pushed past a startled Askew, and left the house.

It took Nicholas no time at all to saddle his horse and head in the direction of the Caldwell Plantation, feeling certain he would get the answers he needed there.

Chapter Thirty-One

It was long after midnight. The house seemed strangely silent after the noise and commotion that had been created by the hoards of merrymakers who had attended Dotty's ball.

Alanna and Dotty were seated on a corner sofa in the now almost deserted ballroom while Dotty, looking as bright and fresh as she had at the beginning of the evening, kept a wary eye on the eleven servants who were cleaning floors and waxing furniture.

"I find that when I keep watch, the domestics always clean much better, and it saves me the grief of having to call them back."

Alanna covered a yawn, wondering where Dotty got all her energy; she was always up early and was never in bed until after midnight. "I heard several people remarking this evening that your ball was a success," she offered sleepily.

"Indeed it was! And you, my dear, were the reason. Again I salute your mother-in-law for her good taste in dressing you. You outshone everyone here tonight."

Alanna warmed under the older woman's compliment. "I have you to thank for introducing me. But I do not feel like I belong here."

Dotty chuckled. "My dear, that is one reason you were such a sensation. You were coldly aloof, as if you were high above us all, and that is always intriguing. If I know Washington—and I do—by tomorrow you will have more invitations than you can possibly accept."

"I was neither cold nor aloof, Dotty. I was merely frightened out of my wits," Alanna admitted.

"Be that as it may, you were a success."

"Dotty, I do not want to appear ungrateful, but all I could think about tonight was talking to Barnard Sanderson. Then I want to go home."

Dotty's eyes shone with the light of curiosity. "I want to hear about Barnard Sanderson. I admit you have kept me on tenterhooks all evening."

"Actually, Dotty, the story is not mine to tell. As you guessed, the story is Lillia's. But under these dire circumstances, I believe she will understand that I have to confide in you."

Dolly's eyes were bright and clear. "You can trust me, Alanna. I have never divulged anything that was told to me in confidence."

"I know that, Dotty, and that is why I am going to tell you a very tragic story and hope you will understand better why I have to help Lillia."

Dotty became so completely enthralled by the bittersweet story that had ended in such tragedy that she even forgot about keeping an eye on the servants.

Alanna's voice was calm as she told her of the events leading up to the tragic night when Nicholas's father had been killed.

When Alanna had come to the end of her tale, her eyes were sparkling with tears, and Dotty dabbed at her eyes with a lace handkerchief. "So you see, Dotty, Lillia believes Barnard Sanderson is dead."

"Yes, but have you considered that he may have allowed her to go on believing he was dead because he didn't really love her and wanted to be rid of her?"

"Yes, that is always a possibility. That is why I must talk to him. If I find that he did not care for Lillia, then she need never know he is still alive."

Dotty nodded her head. "That seems sensible, my dear." Her eyes sparkled with delight. "Just suppose they were both madly in love and you can help them find one another again after all these years."

"I just want to see Lillia happy. She does not deserve what happened to her."

Dotty stood up, tapping her fan against the palm of her hand. "Tomorrow we shall call on Colonel Sanderson. We shan't give him a chance to turn us away, so we will not ask to see him, we'll just show up on his doorstep." Her eyes deepened in color as she planned her strategy. "Yes, I have it!"

Alanna laughed at Dotty's enthusiasm. "Tell me how you think we can get in to see a man who will not welcome either of us—least of all me?"

Dotty winked. "It's quite simple, my dear. It is known far and wide that I serve the best chicken stew in Washington D.C., if I do say so myself. Since the Colonel informed me last night that he was too ill to attend the ball, would it not be an act of kindness on my part if I hand-delivered a pot of my chicken stew?"

A slow smile touched Alanna's lips. "You are devious and sly, Dolly Singleton."

The older woman's eyes danced merrily. "That's the truth, and if anyone ever tells you anything to the contrary, I hope you will defend me." She looked thoughtful for a moment. "We shall become co-conspirators and play Cupid, Alanna. But keep in mind that we may stir up a hornets' nest and do your mother-in-law more harm than good."

"I am willing to take that chance. One of the reasons that Lillia is so guilt-ridden is because she feels responsible for the Colonel's death. At least we can free her of that guilt. Whatever happens, I will at least have tried."

Dotty stared into Alanna's face. "How do you think your husband will feel about this?"

Alanna blinked and looked away. "I do not believe he will ever forgive me when he finds out."

Dotty dropped down beside her and took her hand. "Then do you think you should go through with this?"

"Yes, I will see it through to the end, and deal with the consequences as they develop."

Dotty shook her head. "You may find you have bought your mother-in-law's happiness at the cost of your own."

"That is the chance I will have to take. I must do this—I have no choice."

Nicholas climbed the three steps to the porch at Caldwell Plantation. Although the plantation was much smaller than Ballinger Hall, it was blessed with rich bottomland, and the crops were always the best in this part of the county. During the war, the house had been partially burned and the barns destroyed, but they had since been rebuilt, and it appeared the family was prospering.

He rapped on the door and waited impatiently for an answer. After a few moments, the door was opened by the aged butler, and when he saw Nicholas, his wrinkled black face broke into a smile. "Master Nicholas, come right on in. I haven't seen you in many a year."

Nicholas stepped into the entry hall, trying to remember how many years it had been since he had last been at Caldwell Plantation. "It's good to see you, Hamish. Is Donald at home."

"No, sir. He was till this morning, then he went back to Washington. Miss Eliza's still here, though. Do you want to see her?"

"Yes, I'll see her."

Nicholas followed Hamish into the cream-and-green-colored sitting room, where Eliza sat near the window, her sewing in her lap.

When she saw Nicholas, she rose to her feet and moved quickly across the room, offering him her hand. Her heart was thundering as his eyes settled on her, for she had secretly loved the master of Ballinger Hall for many years. "Nicholas, how wonderful of you to call! It's been so long."

He searched her face for a moment, trying to discover if there was any resemblance between her and Alanna. Surprisingly, there was. The same eyes, though Alanna's were a deeper blue—more like Donald's. The same turned-up nose, the same creamy skin, but there the resemblance ended. While Eliza was pretty, Alanna was beautiful. Eliza was only a pale imitation of her half-sister.

He remembered the reason for the visit. "Hamish informed me that Donald left this morning. I was told that he took Alanna to Washington—is that true?"

Eliza's eyes blazed with jealousy. "Yes, and she stayed with Dotty Singleton. I cannot imagine why she would do such a thing."

"Dotty Singleton?" he asked in confusion. "Isn't she the famous hostess?"

"The same." Malice crept into her voice. "It seems

321

Donald asked Alanna to go to Washington with him to be questioned by a committee he was heading. Something to do with Indians," she said vaguely. "I'm not quite sure of the reason."

"Why would Donald take it upon himself to transport my wife to Washington without my permission?"

Eliza waved her hand in disgust. "You know Donald. Lately he has come to believe that he's been put here on earth to save the Indian from us all."

Nicholas understood Alanna's reason for going to Washington, but he was still not satisfied. "Did Donald say when he would bring Alanna home?"

Eliza linked her arm through Nicholas's and led him to the sofa. When he was seated, she sat down beside him. "He doesn't confide in me anymore. Since he has his precious Alanna, he hardly has time for anyone but her. She has already spoken to the panel, and still she remains in Washington."

Nicholas frowned. He was astonished by the depth of Eliza's spitefulness. She certainly had no sisterly affection for Alanna.

There was a controlled tone to his voice. "What could be her reason for remaining in a town where she knows so few people?"

Eliza felt a tumult inside her. It was not fair that Alanna had it all. Their father had loved Alanna best. Yes, Alanna had everything: Ballinger Hall, Nicholas, Donald, and now, according to Donald, she would be accepted by Washington society, something Eliza could never hope to accomplish.

"Why don't you go to Washington and find out for yourself? Donald let slip a fascinating bit of information that might be of interest to you." Eliza's eyes gleamed. She was like a spider luring her kill into her web.

Now Nicholas showed a lack of interest in what she had to tell him. In fact, he appeared to be uncomfortable, as if he could not wait to leave.

"Yes," she said in a low voice. "A strange happening indeed. We all thought that Barnard Sanderson was . . . dead. It now appears he is not, and your little wife even went so far as to get Dotty Singleton to invite him to a ball she was giving in her honor." Eliza dared to go even farther in her spite. "Perhaps the Ballinger women are drawn to the Yankee."

Nicholas came to his feet, his eyes blazing, his words laced with ice. "You go too far, Eliza. I don't like what you are implying."

She shrugged. "I'm sure there is much speculation in Washington about your wife and that Yankee."

His jaw clamped together tightly, and his eyes were hard. "I will wish you a good day, Eliza."

Without a backward glance, he moved out of the room while Eliza smiled to herself. She had managed to plant the seeds of doubt in his mind—she was sure of it.

She stood at the window and watched him ride away. Yes, she thought, Alanna was not going to have an easy time explaining her actions when Nicholas caught up with her.

As Nicholas rode back to Ballinger Hall, anger was burning inside him. He would go to Washington and see for himself what or who was keeping Alanna there.

He disregarded Eliza's accusations and passed them off as the ravings of a jealous woman. Barnard Sanderson could not be alive! No, it wasn't possible, since his father had been condemned to death for killing the Yankee.

When Nicholas reached home, he dismounted and

323

rushed toward the house. As he entered the front door, he called to Askew. "Pack my valise and have Glenn make the carriage ready for a journey to Washington."

After Askew disappeared up the stairs, Nicholas moved into the parlor and stood in the middle of the floor, not really conscious of his surroundings.

God, how he hoped Eliza was wrong. There had to be a reasonable explanation for why Alanna had not come home.

Alanna tiptoed across Dotty's bedroom and silently approached her friend, who was propped up on two pillows, looking pale and listless.

"Has your headache eased any, Dotty?" she asked with concern.

"No, dear. If anything, it's worse. I have learned that when these headaches come upon me there is nothing to do except go to bed."

"I am so sorry. Perhaps you will feel better this afternoon."

"No, this will linger until tomorrow morning. I'm sorry I spoiled your plans to visit Colonel Sanderson. We will just have to postpone our outing until tomorrow afternoon."

Alanna smiled down at Dotty. "Just close your eyes and rest."

Dotty agreed with a nod.

Alanna walked quietly out of the room, knowing what she must do. Anything as important as Lillia's happiness could not be put off for another day.

With hesitant steps, she moved downstairs, then out the back door to the carriage house. This was going to be easier than she thought. Dotty's coachman had not been informed that his mistress was ill, so the horses were harnessed and waiting in the driveway.

"I will be going alone this afternoon," Alanna informed the driver.

He nodded respectfully and helped her into the buggy. Alanna's heart was beating fast as the horses moved down the street. She hoped she was not making a mistake by going to see Barnard Sanderson without Dotty.

When the driver reached Georgetown, he turned the buggy onto a quiet street lined with tall, stately townhouses. As the driver pulled over and stopped before a red brick house, Alanna almost lost her nerve. What would she do if Barnard Sanderson refused to see her?

When the coachman assisted her to the ground, she took a moment before gathering up her courage. "Wait for me here," she told the coachman. "I may not be long."

Her timid knock on the door was answered almost immediately. She was surprised to see Barnard Sanderson himself standing there.

"Yes, what can I do for you?" he growled.

Now that Alanna stood face to face with him, she almost lost her courage. Her voice was hardly above a whisper. "Colonel Sanderson, I have something very important to speak to you about. I hope you will not throw me out until you have heard what I have to say."

He looked startled for a moment, but he quickly recovered. "Do I know you?"

"We were introduced, but apparently you do not remember me." Boldly, she moved past him, fearing she would lose her courage, or that he might insist she leave when she revealed her identity to him.

Reluctantly, he shut the door and turned to her. "If you are here because you have some undying declaration of love for me, I can assure you I have never met you before. If, on the other hand, you are here on behalf of some charity, I make it a habit not to contribute to every notable cause that comes along—and I don't entertain ladies, young enough to be my daughter, in my home."

"Sir, I am not here for any of those reasons. I am Alanna Ballinger," she blurted out.

Her announcement seemed to hang in the air between them. His eyes hardened, and his hand gripped the cane he was leaning on.

"Please hear what I have to say," she beseeched him. "Then if you want me to leave, I will."

His features molded into a frown, and the dark reflection in his eyes sent a chill down her spine. "No Ballinger would have anything to say that would be of interest to me."

"But there you are wrong. Unless I am mistaken, you will certainly want to hear what I have to tell you."

Suddenly Barnard was intrigued in spite of himself.

"But let's not stand in the hallway bantering," Alanna said.

He nodded in silent submission and held out his hand for her to precede him into the parlor.

After she was seated, he spoke. "Don't you know it's unwise for you to come here alone? In Washington there are eyes and ears everywhere."

"What I have to say to you was too important for me to worry about what people will say." There was desperation in her words. "I had to come!"

His hand gripped the cane. "Then tell me what is

on your mind, Mrs. Ballinger."

She clasped her hands, wishing Dotty had been able to come with her. How would she ever be able to convince him of her sincerity?

He looked at her doubtfully. "Well, I'm waiting to hear what you have to say."

Chapter Thirty-Two

After a long silence, Barnard Sanderson spoke again, but his eyes were ever-watchful and suspicious. "All right, you gained entrance to my house and managed to get my attention. Now tell me what you want and then leave."

Her question was blurted out. "Are you aware that Lillia Ballinger believes you are dead?"

"Of course she thinks I'm dead. That is what she wanted all along. I feel sure she expected her husband to succeed at his task. She played us both against each other. Pity Simeon Ballinger was such a bad aim, even at close range."

He glanced down at his leg and tapped it with his cane. "I have the Ballingers to thank for this."

"No, no, you do not understand. Lillia never wanted any harm to come to you. Why do you suppose I am here?"

He seemed to droop right before her eyes. "I don't know. Suppose you tell me."

"Please sit down," she urged, since she felt at such a disadvantage having to crane her neck to look up at him.

"There," he said, dropping down on the chair next

to hers. "Tell me what your connection is with Lillia. I know she had no daughter, unless she lied to me about that also."

"I am her son, Nicholas's, wife."

He nodded in understanding. "Ah, yes, the son. I never met him, unless it was on the battlefield—in which case we would have been on opposite sides."

"I have not come here to tell you about myself or my husband. I am only concerned about you and Lillia."

Suddenly his eyes filled with anguish, as if the mere mention of her name was too much for him. "If it will give her any satisfaction, you can tell Lillia for me, there were many times when I wished I had died. Since knowing her, and in spite of her dishonor and deceit, I have not been able to get her out of my mind. The years have been long, and the bitterness deep, but at last I am able to live with the memory of being betrayed."

Alanna shook her head. "You do not understand. Lillia never betrayed you, she loves you. She has suffered grievously, thinking she is responsible for your death."

Again he looked skeptical. "I find that hard to believe. She is the one who wanted me dead."

"She never wanted you dead. I do not know where you got that absurd notion."

"You still haven't explained why you sought me out, Mrs. Ballinger."

"Because I love Lillia and it pains me to see her so unhappy. She has paid a thousand times over for daring to love one of the enemy. Her neighbors blame her for her husband's death and will have nothing to do with her. She has been cut off from the world for so long that one would think she would be bitter, but she is not. Oh, please believe me, she is

329

devoted to your memory. She has told me that you are the only man she ever loved. I swear to you, it is the truth!"

Hope sprang to life within Barnard, but quickly turned to scorn. "If only I could believe that."

"You can. I would not have come here to tell you a falsehood."

Still he was not convinced. "Another thing I cannot believe is that your husband allowed you to come to see me. Surely Nicholas Ballinger would not condone your consorting with one of the enemy."

"My husband does not know I am here, but even if he did, it would not change anything. Lillia needs you, and I have a feeling that you need her, too."

His eyes took on a glow, as if he were remembering. "I never felt about any woman the way I felt about Lillia. Despite what her neighbors may think, she never dishonored her husband. I wanted to marry her after the war was over." He shook his head. "But then her husband confronted me. When he told me that Lillia had urged him to shoot me, I was so devastated that I prayed his shot would be accurate."

"Do you not see that Lillia would never have asked her husband to kill you? From what I understand, Simeon Ballinger was a hard and cruel man. His cruelest deed was to let you think Lillia would want your death."

Barnard shook his head. "Many times I have ridden past Ballinger Hall. One time I thought I saw Lillia riding in an open carriage, but she was so far away I couldn't be sure." His face lit up with hope. "If only . . . if only."

Alanna jumped to her feet and knelt before him. "Please, I beseech you, go to Lillia, talk to her. What can it hurt?"

330

There was still a note of doubt in his tone. "My men did kill her husband without benefit of a trial."

"Yes, and Lillia has suffered for that long enough. Go to her now, today."

His brow furrowed. "Is she at Ballinger Hall?"

Alanna stood up. "No. She is at her family home in Philadelphia."

"Yes, I know the place." Barnard looked into Alanna's face. "Will this go hard on you when your husband finds out that you have been fraternizing with the enemy?"

"I do not think Nicholas would approve, but sometimes a person has to do what is right, regardless of the consequences."

He moved forward, struggling with his lame leg. Taking her hand, he raised it to his lips. "You Ballinger women are remarkable."

"Then you will go to Lillia as soon as possible?"

Joy sprang to life in his eyes. "You have won me over, and I believe you are telling the truth. Without reservations or hesitation, I will go to her today."

Alanna's eyes danced with happiness. "Oh, Colonel Sanderson, you will not regret it."

He took her arm and led her toward the door. "You must leave now, little matchmaker. I would not like for you to be the object of gossiping tongues."

She gave him a brilliant smile and rushed out the door, to the waiting buggy. "Please give Lillia my love when you see her," she called over her shoulder.

Barnard watched her with a smile on his face and the first happiness he had known in years. His long nightmare had come to an end. For years he had believed that Lillia had betrayed him, but she had not. As incredible as it sounded, Lillia still loved him. "I will," he replied, though Alanna was already in the carriage and could not hear him. "But first I will give her mine."

Alanna could hardly wait to tell Dotty what had happened during her visit with Barnard Sanderson. Of course, she would have to wait until the morning, when Dotty was over her headache.

As the horses pulled into the back drive, she tried to imagine the meeting between Lillia and Barnard. The two of them loved each other so much that it was only right that they should be together.

Alanna's brow knitted when she thought about Nicholas. He would not be at all pleased, but she would not think about that now.

As she entered the house, Dotty's maid met her at the front door. "Mrs. Singleton would like you to join her in the study right away, Madame."

Alanna was surprised. "She has come downstairs? She must be feeling better."

"Yes, Madame."

Without pausing to think, Alanna hurried toward the study. Now she could tell Dotty about her afternoon.

Pushing open the door, she saw Dolly seated at her desk, and she rushed forward, her eyes dancing with joy.

"You cannot imagine how wonderful it all turned out, Dolly." She noticed that Dolly was looking at her strangely, but she continued breathlessly. "I know what you are thinking, and you are right. I should never have gone to see Barnard Sanderson without you, but I just had—"

Dolly interrupted, cutting Alanna short. "Can you imagine my surprise when your *husband* arrived just an hour ago, Alanna?" Dotty gave a warning nod just

332

behind Alanna. "Won't you greet your husband, my dear?"

Since the chair Nicholas was sitting in had a high-back, Alanna had not seen him when she entered the room. She turned to him slowly, with a feeling of dread in her heart.

Nicholas had not risen, and from all outward appearances he seemed calm. But she looked into green eyes that were ice-cold, but held a fire of anger in their shimmering depths.

Alanna said the first thing that came to her mind. "Nicholas, I wasn't expecting you. What are you doing here?"

His voice was measured and even, his movement unconcerned, almost detached, as he straightened the cuff of his sleeve.

"Such a strange greeting for a husband you have not seen in a while! But to answer your question, I came to get my wife. Apparently it's a good thing I did."

Dotty rubbed her temples, and her face paled. "Mr. Ballinger, I know what you must be thinking, but your wife is innocent of any wrongdoing. If it looks bad, it's just that she has not learned the rules we impose on one another."

Nicholas's glance was cool. "What particular rule were you referring to, Mrs. Singleton?"

Before Dotty could answer, Nicholas held up his hand. "Don't tell me. What I have to say to my wife is better said in private." He turned to Alanna. "I have instructed Kitty to pack your belongings. May I assume that you will leave with me?"

She glanced at Dotty. "I . . . do not know. I . . ."

Dotty came to her feet and moved around the desk to stand beside Alanna. "You don't have to leave if you don't want to, Alanna." She then looked at

Nicholas. "I will say again, she has done nothing wrong."

Nicholas took Alanna's arm and led her to the door. "I'll send the carriage back for Kitty and my wife's trunk. Good day, Mrs. Singleton."

Alanna glanced back at Dotty. "I . . . I'm sorry."

Dotty, unwilling to let Nicholas go until she knew what would be her little friend's fate, rushed after them and forestalled them at the door. "Where are you taking Alanna?" she demanded.

Nicholas was surprisingly patient as he turned to Dotty. "I am taking her to the hotel for tonight. Tomorrow we will go home to Ballinger Hall." He smiled tightly as Dotty still barred the exit. "Have no fear that I shall harm her physically, Madame. It is not my habit to hit women." He smiled slightly. "And if you know my wife, you cannot imagine her cowering before any man. No, Madame, if anyone is to be pitied, it is I."

Dotty moved aside, struck by Nicholas Barringer's charm and handsomeness. "No, Mr. Ballinger, you are not to be pitied. You are to be commended for having the good sense to marry Alanna. She is exceptional, and she should be treated as such by you."

Nicholas's jaw line hardened. "We will wish you good day, Madame."

Dotty moved aside and watched as Nicholas led his wife out of the house. When they had both disappeared into the carriage, she closed the front door and leaned against it with a smile playing on her lips.

"You handsome rogue, Nicholas Ballinger. You have a wife who doesn't play by your rules. You are going to have to suffer some before you tame Alanna, if you ever do tame her, which I doubt."

*　　　*　　　*

Alanna peeped at Nicholas through lowered lashes. "Why did you come for me?"

He glanced down at her. "Isn't that apparent?"

"Not to me."

The muscle in his jaw tightened. "I had been told that you were seeing a man by the name of Barnard Sanderson. Of course, I didn't really believe it, because Barnard Sanderson is supposed to be dead, and even if he wasn't, my wife would never betray me by associating with him."

He reached for her chin and forced her face up to his. "But he is alive, isn't he, Alanna, and you did go to see him, didn't you?"

"I . . . yes."

His eyes were unreadable. "Why?"

Alanna remembered her promise to Lillia. She could not tell Nicholas the real reason she had gone to see Barnard Sanderson, because it would mean breaking her word. "I cannot tell you, Nicholas."

"Can't, or won't?"

She pushed his hand away roughly, knowing this was going to be difficult. "I cannot, and I will not."

"I see." He turned to stare out the window. "Then the only thing I can infer from your silence is that you have something to hide."

"Infer what you will, Nicholas, I have nothing to tell."

When he turned to face her, there was leashed anger blazing in his eyes. "I never thought you would deceive me, Alanna. But why should I be surprised? All women are the same. But why with Barnard Sanderson? Why with the man who is responsible for my father's death?"

"I did nothing wrong, Nicholas. I cannot believe you would think I had. Do you have so little faith in me?"

"About as much faith as you had in me before I left

for North Carolina, Alanna. If I recall, you were certain I would betray you."

"This is different, Nicholas."

"Tell me how it is different."

She wanted to throw herself into his arms and have him hold her closely, but she dared not. "Please trust me in this, Nicholas."

"I want to. All you have to do is tell me what you did with that man today."

She bit her trembling lips. "I cannot, Nicholas. Do not ask it of me."

His face became a hard mask of fury, and his eyes burned into her. "So be it, Alanna. By not telling me, you have proved yourself guilty."

"Of what?"

By now the carriage had pulled up before a glass-fronted hotel, and the doorman opened their carriage door and smiled in greeting.

Nicholas gripped his wife's arm and pulled her forward. "Do not mistake me for a fool, Alanna," he hissed. "I have known enough harlots to recognize one when I see one."

She was deeply wounded. How could he believe the worst of her? As he roughly helped her out of the carriage and then led her into the hotel, her hurt turned to anger.

She allowed Nicholas to guide her up the stairs, and she did not balk when he inserted a key in the lock and pushed her into the room.

Walking over to the window, she tangled her fingers in the lace curtains, trying to gather her wits so she would not strike out at him in anger.

When she turned to face him, she caught a surprisingly agonized expression on his face which caused her to speak to him in a soft voice.

"You must trust me, Nicholas," she pleaded,

reaching out to him, only to have him pull away from her. "As I told you before," she said sadly, "I have done nothing to shame either you or me."

His eyes narrowed, and he moved toward her. "I suppose that would depend on one's point of view. From where I stand, you have committed the ultimate sin a wife can commit against her husband."

He silently assessed her for a moment, wanting to believe her. "Tell me something, Alanna. I asked you to trust me when I left to buy horses, but you didn't, did you?"

"No, because you told me the night we were married that I should not expect fidelity from you."

He grabbed her chin and forced her to look at him. "Every time I made love to you, you betrayed me. I know you would close your eyes and pretend I was your Gray Falcon. Deny that if you can," he challenged, hoping she would do just that and put to rest the fears that had been tormenting him.

She shook her head, not realizing before now that he had felt that way. "You are wrong, Nicholas. I knew whose hands caressed me, just as I knew Gray Falcon was dead. I could never pretend with you, because you are nothing like Gray Falcon. He understood me."

She saw a hardness in him now that caused her to take a step backward, where she came up against the window.

He stood before her, and she flinched as his hand reached out to touch her cheek. "Would your Gray Falcon have understood betrayal?"

Her eyes stung with unshed tears, and she refused to answer him.

Nicholas looked deeply into her eyes, as if he were hoping he could read the truth in the blue depths. "Tell me where I can find Barnard Sanderson, and I will ask him the questions you are so reluctant to answer."

"No, I cannot, Nicholas."

With a muttered oath, he turned away and moved across the room. "I am a Ballinger, and unlike my father, I am an excellent shot."

Without another word, he pulled the door open and slammed it behind him, leaving Alanna stunned and feeling very alone.

Chapter Thirty-Three

Darkness fell across the streets and byways of the capital city. Alanna stood at the window watching as the lights of Washington came on one by one. She tensely watched each carriage that came by, hoping one of them would be Nicholas.

She prayed that Barnard had already left for Philadelphia, because she did not know what Nicholas would do in his state of mind if he found the man at home.

She could not really blame Nicholas for being angry. He had every right to demand an answer to her behavior, she just did not have the right to give him the answers.

A bright moon gave a splendid view of the White House in the distance, but Alanna hardly noticed. Deep within her heart, she felt such a loneliness that it was almost like a physical pain. It was apparent that she did not belong here.

Today both Nicholas and Dotty had talked about rules which she had apparently broken. But if she was able to help Lillia and her Barnard find one another, what did rules matter? Surely Nicholas could not have believed there was anything between her and Barnard Sanderson?

If only she had been able to tell Nicholas the truth, but she could not break her promise to Lillia.

She had been so deep in thought that she had not heard Nicholas when he returned. A heavy hand fell on her shoulder, and she was spun around to face his towering height and to deal with the scowl on his face.

"Your friend, Colonel Sanderson, was gone, Alanna, so you will just have to supply me with the answers I want."

He placed his hand on either side of her face and forced her to look at him. "I need answers, damn it, and you are going to give them to me."

His hand gripped her wrist, and he jerked her forward. "Do not try to lie to me, Alanna, because if you do, I'll know."

"Nicholas, you are hurting me," she protested, trying to loosen his grip.

He pulled her across the room and forced her to sit on the bed. "Now, you will tell me everything that happened between you and that man today."

Alanna bit her lip to keep her resentment from showing. She just wanted to be left alone. She tossed her head, and her blue eyes met his defiant green eyes. "I do not have to tell you anything, Nicholas."

Jumping to her feet, she moved to the window to put some distance between them. When she felt Nicholas come up behind her, she stiffened. How could she answer any questions to his satisfaction without betraying Lillia?

"Did you think you could make a fool out of me, Alanna?" he bit out.

She turned around and met his green gaze. "You have misjudged the whole situation, Nicholas."

"If that's the case, tell me where I'm wrong. Tell

me why you were with my mother's old lover."

"Why do you insist on believing the worst of your mother and me?"

"Why do you insist on keeping secrets from me? You say you are innocent, and yet you will not tell me what you were doing with Barnard Sanderson. What am I supposed to think? Did you let that man put his hands all over you?"

"No, it was not like that! Colonel Sanderson is a gentleman. He is really to be pitied."

"I am fresh out of pity for him. If you will recall, my father is dead for supposedly killing that man. My God, what do you expect from me?" he cried out in agony.

"I wish . . . I wish you could know . . ." her voice trailed off. "Sometimes things are not as they seem. That is all I can say, Nicholas."

He let out an impatient breath. "I haven't got the vaguest notion what you are talking about. I did some checking on Barnard Sanderson, and I found that the ladies like him quite a lot. Rumor has it that some woman from his past broke his heart, and he treats all women with contempt. But not you, Alanna. He did not despise you, did he?"

Her eyes widened. "Nicholas, you need not be jealous of Colonel Sanderson."

"You will never see that man again, Alanna. I am taking you back to Ballinger Hall, and you will not be allowed to leave without me to accompany you."

Her temper flared. "You are my husband, not my prison guard. I will not have you telling me who I can see and who I cannot."

He stared into her eyes. "Damn you, Alanna, do you know what a fool I felt when you explained to Dotty where you had been today? It was as if time had turned backward and I was walking in my father's shadow."

Before she could protest, he pulled her tightly into his arms.

"I went for a walk tonight so I could clear my head. Can you imagine the hell I have been through, thinking of you in that man's arms? I wanted to find him and cut out his treacherous heart, but he had already left Washington." He clamped his jaw together tightly. "Where did he go, Alanna?"

"I cannot tell you where he went."

"Is it that you don't know, or that you just won't say?"

"I won't say."

Suddenly his features softened, and he reached out to touch Alanna's face.

"You cannot know what I have been living through, can you, Alanna? When I came home today and discovered you had gone, I couldn't rest until I found you. Why did you leave Ballinger Hall?"

"Surely you know I came to Washington at Donald's request."

"Yes, I saw your sister, Eliza, and she told me . . . well, never mind what she said."

Before she could question Nicholas, he crushed her in his arms. Her heart was drumming loudly, and her breath came out in a deep groan.

"Did that bastard touch you, Alanna?"

Alanna could feel the tenseness in him as the implication of his words sunk in. How could he think so little of her to imagine she would betray her wedding vows? She wanted to scream at him, to pound against his chest. But his grip on her was too tight, and his mouth ground against hers, silencing her protest.

She felt his body tremble, but she knew it was not with passion, but with rage against her and what he thought she had done.

"Alanna, oh, God, if I had been able to get my hands on him today, he would be dead."

She shook her head in protest, just as he dipped his head and his mouth brutalized her tender lips.

"If I make love to you tonight, do I go where another man has been?" he asked, raising his head and staring into her eyes. "Do I, Alanna?"

Alanna bit her trembling lips and shook her head, causing her midnight-black hair to swirl out about her shoulders. "How can you ask such a thing of me?"

He wanted more than anything to believe in her innocence, but with what Eliza had told him, and then hearing from Alanna's own lips that she had been with Barnard Sanderson today, what was he to believe?

"You are mine, Alanna. No matter if you don't want to be, you belong to me."

She felt her anger melt away. Perhaps it was not unreasonable that Nicholas could have drawn the wrong conclusion. "Nicholas, why can you not trust me?"

His face was half hidden in shadow as a cloud passed over the moon. "I want to, Alanna."

"Then do."

"How can you know how much I ache for you, Alanna? My days are haunted with the sound of your laughter, and my nights are spent wanting to make love to you."

"Are you saying you love me?" She waited breathlessly for his answer.

His features hardened. "I once told you that I am not capable of loving a woman, but I desire you, can you not be satisfied with that?"

Alanna felt a sob building up in her throat. How

could lust be a substitute for love? Feeling as if her heart had just been crushed, she turned her face away from him, her pride coming once more to her rescue.

"Love is but a word that fools and poets talk about." She raised her head and met his eyes. "You and I do not need words, do we, Nicholas?"

Nicholas groaned and crushed her to him. "Half the time you have me running mindlessly after you, and the other half, you have me wondering what the hell you are talking about. Will I ever understand you?"

"I doubt that we will ever understand each other."

He smiled, but there was no humor in his green eyes. "Surely we understand some things about one another." His hand went to the back of her gown. "I understand what it takes to make you writhe with pleasure." His lips touched her ear, sending shivers of delight dancing on her skin, as if he wanted to prove his point. "I know what you like, Alanna."

Unfastening her gown, he pushed it off her shoulders, where it fell to lie in a heap on the floor.

"You are trembling," he whispered, pulling her into his arms with a knowing smile. "Surely you are not frightened of me. No, you know I would never hurt you, don't you, Alanna, no matter how angry I am with you?"

While he was speaking, he was expertly removing the rest of her garments, then he kissed and caressed her into mindless surrender.

Alanna felt his hot kisses burn her skin. The cloud that had been covering the moon moved away, and she realized, in a daze of passion, that she and Nicholas were both naked.

When he reached out and pulled her against his body, she momentarily pulled back, knowing that if she gave in to him, she would lose her ability to fight him. When his hand drifted down to gently caress between her legs, her breathing seemed suddenly to stick in her throat, and there was no fight left in her.

His hard, lean body was pressed so tightly against her now that she could feel his swollen manhood, and her world tilted upside down.

Nicholas knew he was now in control. It suited him that Alanna was so easy to manipulate. He stepped back a pace and held her at arms' length. His eyes swept down her sweet curves, and he felt his body tremble with desire for her.

"The time has come," he said harshly, "when I will take you for my pleasure." His voice was velvet-smooth, and his green eyes sparked with the flame of passion.

"Nicholas, I do not want—"

"Shh, do not speak."

Alanna held her arms out to him. She heard Nicholas's breath come out in a soft hiss. When he took her in his arms, they both sank down to their knees. Alanna pressed her body tightly against him, and he jerked her head up and covered her mouth with a burning kiss.

Neither of them cared that a cloud had moved across the face of the moon, casting the room in soft darkness. As they sank down on the floor, Nicholas ran his hands over her hips, molding her to his contour.

"This is better than love," he murmured. "We are in each other's blood. Tonight I will fill you so full of myself that you will never think of another man."

As Nicholas rolled her over on the soft rug and positioned himself between her legs, Alanna knew she would never stop loving him. She was in torment, wanting to feel him inside her, but he seemed to be taking his time.

"So, Blue Eyes, you want me, don't you?"

She swallowed past the lump in her throat. "Yes."

"You know what it feels like to have a yearning so strong in your gut that it tears you apart?"

"Yes, Nicholas." She realized he was deliberately trying to torture her. Her hand moved down and enclosed his pulsating manhood. A hiss escaped his lips, and he groaned as she turned her head so her lips touched his. With daring, she thrust her tongue into his mouth and was satisfied when another gasp escaped his lips.

"Wildcat," he whispered hotly in her ear. "You like torturing me, don't you? You want a part of me that you can never have, Alanna."

Alanna knew in her heart that Nicholas would never belong to her or to any woman. Her pride would not allow her to admit to him that she loved him.

Nicholas's hand traveled the lines of her silken body. When his lips settled on her creamy white breasts, Alanna thought she would die from some new, unknown hunger that burst to life deep within her.

Now he positioned her hips, and he thrust forward inside her as if he were driven to possess her. A tremor shook his body as he rested deeply inside her velvet softness.

Alanna closed her eyes and bit her lips to keep from crying out at the wonderful feelings that swept through her body. How easily Nicholas could overcome her anger, with just the touch of his hand. She was his mindless puppet, aching for his lovemaking.

When she opened her eyes, she found him staring at her. The muscle in his temple was throbbing, and she knew he was trying to control his unleashed desire.

"Damn you, Alanna . . . damn you," he muttered. "You won't be satisfied until you have all of me, will you?"

She did not understand what he meant, but it didn't matter, for at that moment she held him close to her, and she could not mistake the desire that flamed in his eyes.

Her hands slid up to his shoulders, and she gently touched his cheek. "Kiss me, Nicholas," she pleaded.

She saw indecision on his face. When she moved her hips forward, he cried out her name. She pulled his head down and covered his mouth with hers, and had the satisfaction of feeling him melt against her.

Alanna knew that tonight he would make love to her against his will. She was learning that she could make him want her, and even though there was no comfort in that thought, she would use it to keep him near her. Tonight Nicholas belonged to her and she to him.

"Nicholas, kiss me," she whispered, moving beneath him in such a way that caused him to roll his head in agony. She would use her charms to keep him with her tonight. Tomorrow would be another story, but she would face that when it came.

Nicholas drove deeply inside her, rhythmically stirring her blood.

Then suddenly, when she thought she could not stand the pleasurable feelings he aroused within her, he gentled his movements, and soft, sensuous feelings swirled around in her mind, carrying her on a soft bed of desire.

Afterward, she lay in his arms while the silvery moon spread its light across them.

Finally he turned her to face him. "Even if we loathed one another, this would be good between us. So you see, love is not important."

Her blue eyes widened. "Are you trying to convince me or yourself?"

"I am merely pointing out to you that there will be no love between us. But also, know that I will not tolerate you being with another man. You are my wife, and it's time you went home and acted the part."

She raised up on her elbow. "Just what do you want in a wife, Nicholas?"

"A son and heir," he said coldly. "Nothing more, nothing less."

"Let me see if I have this right. You want me to return to Ballinger Hall and play the good little wife, fall into your bed when you snap your fingers, and give you a son on demand."

A smile played on his lips. "That's right. When I summon you to my bed, will you come?"

Feeling crushed and defeated, Alanna sat up. "I will go home with you, Nicholas, and I will come to your bed when you demand it, I will even hope I give you the son you want, but never as long as you live, speak to me of love. It is an emotion I can well do without."

He reached out to her, but then dropped his hand. "Now we understand one another."

Suddenly she thought of his mother sitting at home while his father visited his mistresses. "What will you be doing while I am waiting at Ballinger Hall?"

"What do you mean?"

"I mean, will you take unto yourself a mistress or two, or three?"

A smile tugged at his lips. "I haven't thus far, but then you keep me too well-satisfied. I have no need of another woman."

"Is that a warning?"

He looked at her with a serious expression on his

face. "No, I do not play games, Alanna. I have no plans to take a mistress."

His eyes were seeking. "Can you swear to me that you have never been with any man other than me?"

"Of course I have not." When she stood up, his eyes followed her. "I am insulted that you should think so little of me."

He stood up and pulled her into his arms. "I don't have a great deal of confidence in women. My mother was an example of how a man can love a woman so much he is willing to commit murder for her."

Alanna threw her head back. "You do not know your mother, and you do not know me. Why must you always assume your father was guiltless?"

He watched her closely. "Do you know anything to the contrary? If you do, tell me."

She lowered her head. "I just think you should have more faith in your mother, that's all."

He pulled her stiff body into his arms. Lifting her into his arms, he carried her to the bed.

"I have a need of you again, only this time I crave the softness of a bed."

He tossed her on the bed, and before she could scramble to her knees, he was on top of her. Holding her hands above her head, he moved his lips close to hers.

"Say you need me too, Blue Eyes. You are breath and life to me. Say you want me to fill your body with mine."

"Yes," she breathed, under his spell once more. "Oh, yes, Nicholas."

Chapter Thirty-Four

Philadelphia

Lillia dusted the Chinese figurine and placed it back on the shelf. Looking about the room with its bright yellow decor and its many windows that welcomed the sun, she was almost at peace with herself.

Here in the modest house where she was born, she had come to terms with her past and had laid old ghosts to rest. There was no host of servants here to see to her every need. There was only a cook, but Lillia was content.

She moved to the double doors that led to the garden and threw them open. It was a golden day with bright sun shining down on a row of daffodils. As she moved down the narrow path toward the gazebo at the far end of the garden, she also had her regrets. She would always be a fugitive from her son's life, and he would always have contempt for her, but she would have to live with that.

She thought of Alanna and smiled. That lovely young girl just might be her son's salvation. If only Nicholas would come to see what a treasure he had in

Alanna before it was too late.

Lillia heard a carriage pull up at the front of the house, and she smiled. Since she had come home to Philadelphia, there had been a steady stream of old friends who dropped by to pay their respects.

Knowing the cook was hard of hearing and would not hear the callers when they knocked on the door, Lillia moved back into the house. Her footsteps were noiseless as she made her way across the shiny wood floor to the door.

Opening the door, she was momentarily blinded by the afternoon sun shining off the brass buttons of a blue army uniform. "Yes," she said, shading her eyes with her hand. "May I help you?"

There was a long silence from Barnard as he stared at his lovely Lillia. Time had been kind to her, and she was as beautiful as ever. His eyes feasted on her, for he had never forgotten a single detail of her face.

"Hello, Lillia," he said at last. "Have you forgotten me so soon?"

Lillia shook her head in disbelief and took a backward step, clutching her hand over her mouth. "It can't be . . . you are . . . dead!"

"I knew coming here would be a shock to you, Lillia, but I knew of no other way to present myself to you."

Tears were running down her face, and still she could not believe her eyes. Here, standing before her, somewhat older, but still the same, was her Barnard! But no, this had to be some cruel jest. Barnard could not have come back from the dead.

"Who . . . are you?" she choked out.

Barnard removed his hat, tucked it beneath his arm, and took a step inside the house. "Lillia, it's me. You know who I am."

She felt the floor tilt, and she reached out her hand

351

to him as she fell forward. He caught her in his arms and felt her go limp against him.

Quickly carrying her into the first room he came to, he laid her on a sofa and dashed to the brandy bottle on the side table and poured some of the liquor into a glass. Bending down beside Lillia, he lifted her head. "Here," he urged, "take a sip of this."

Her eyes fluttered open, and she did as he instructed. Slowly she sat up, staring at him all the while. "Who did my husband kill that day in the library?"

He dropped down beside her, knowing how confused she must be. "I was gravely wounded that day, but I did not die, Lillia."

She was afraid this was all a dream and that he would disappear again. She reached out a trembling hand, and he clasped it in his warm hand. "Barnard," she whispered through her tears. "My dearest Barnard."

His arms went around her, and he held her to him as if he would never let her go. "My love, my love," he murmured, "How grievously I have suffered, thinking you did not love me."

She pulled back and looked at him. "How could you think such a thing? I told you I loved you."

He smiled and reached out a finger to trace her jawline as he became reacquainted with her every feature. "That doesn't matter now. All that matters is that we are together, and I will never let you go."

She lay her head on his shoulder, still not sure this was not a dream. "How did you find me?" she wanted to know.

He smiled and touched his lips to her cheek. "A lovely little cupid by the name of Alanna Ballinger insisted that you still loved me. It is because of her that I am here."

Lillia looked puzzled. "My Alanna?"

"No, my love, our Alanna." His smile touched his eyes, and they danced with happiness. "I will tell you all about that later. Right now, I want to know—will you marry me, Lillia?"

She brushed the tears away and nodded. "Oh, yes, Barnard. I would feel honored to be your wife."

Barnard took her face between his strong hands and lowered his head. Soon they were lost in a burning kiss that returned them to that night so long ago when they had first professed their love for one another.

Lillia's happiness sung in her heart. Life was never perfect, but her love for this man had endured mountainous opposition, and she would cherish him for the rest of her life.

Alanna sat huddled in the corner of the carriage, feeling miserable, while Nicholas sat beside her, cold and brooding.

"I wanted to tell Dotty good-bye and to thank her for all she did for me," she said in a soft voice. "You could have granted me that one concession."

His eyes swept her face. "You can write her a letter," he said dryly. "The less contact you have with her, the better off you will be."

Her blood boiled. "Does being my husband give you the right to choose my friends?"

He studied the tip of his boot. "Let's just say that I have removed you from an environment that I felt was detrimental to your well-being."

Alanna lapsed into silence feeling, like she was a prisoner. "You may not be the Indian agent, but you will keep me confined as surely as if I were on a reservation," she said, turning to look out the window.

He drew in an impatient breath. "You will have the run of Ballinger Hall, and you can have your brother and sister over whenever you want, but I will not allow you to leave unless I accompany you."

She turned away from him, wishing she had the means to escape. Her spirit was wild and free, and she felt like a bird in a cage. She leaned back and closed her eyes, wishing this tedious trip was over.

Nicholas's eyes were blazing storm centers. The seeds of doubt had been planted in his mind, and they had begun to fester and grow. Alanna had done something wrong in Washington, otherwise she would not be so secretive. He turned his face away from her, not wanting to look at her. He should never have forgotten that a beautiful woman can be the most deceitful of all.

It was almost dark when the carriage pulled up at Ballinger Hall. Nicholas helped Alanna to alight, so he could shepherd her up the stairs. Instead of leading her to the master suite, he took her to a room down the hall and threw open the door.

"This will be your room from now on."

She tried not to look surprised or hurt as she swept past him. The room was done in cool greens and was very beautiful, but to Alanna, it might as well have been a small cell with bars, because she knew there was no escape for her.

Walking to the window, she saw the view from this room was of the Potomac River. Shivering, she crossed her arms, thinking she knew how Lillia must have felt when Simeon Ballinger first turned away from her.

"If you require anything, Kitty will help you," Nicholas said.

Alanna whirled around to find him still standing in the doorway. "Am I to be locked in?"

His mouth thinned. "My God, Alanna, do you think me such a monster?"

"Do not do this to me Nicholas," she pleaded.

He did not pretend to misunderstand. "It is already done, Madame."

She turned away, wishing he would leave. She was crushed in spirit and mind, and she needed time to be alone. Her only satisfaction was in knowing that Lillia and her Barnard had most probably found one another by now.

Her mind was in a bitter turmoil. Everything she had done since coming to Ballinger Hall had been a mistake. Why had she married Nicholas in the first place? She knew he did not love her—that he would never love her. Her father was dead, her sister Eliza despised her. What was the rest of her life supposed to be like?

Kitty came in, carrying a tray, her eyes filled with sympathy as she looked at Alanna. "I was told to bring your dinner in here. Will you come and eat?"

"I don't want anything, Kitty."

The housekeeper crossed her arms over her breasts. "Well, I'm not going to leave until you eat. Something's going on around here, and you had best fortify yourself to meet it head on."

"I am not hungry, Kitty. Besides, just the sight of food makes me feel sick."

Kitty raised an inquiring eyebrow. "How long has this been going on?"

"I don't know, a week, perhaps more. Yes, perhaps several weeks."

The wise gray eyes sparkled. "In that case, I believe you had better climb into bed and let me bring you some hot milk, then off to sleep you go."

Before Alanna could protest, Kitty had picked up the tray and sailed out of the room.

She was weary, so she began to undress. Opening the trunk, she found a nightgown and pulled it on. Now tiredness really hit her, and she moved to the bed, pulled back the green coverlet, and climbed between the cool white bedsheets.

By the time Kitty had returned, she was feeling drowsy. "Here," the housekeeper said, shoving the milk at Alanna. "You can't go off to sleep without something warm in your stomach."

"I'm just too weary, Kitty. Besides, I have something to tell you."

"Drink the milk," Kitty insisted, "and then I'll listen to what you have to say."

Alanna quickly drank half the warm liquid, and then she smiled at Kitty. "I have some wonderful news for you."

Kitty handed her a napkin to wipe the milk from her upper lip. "We could use some good news around here." She waited expectantly. "You tell me yours, and then I'll tell you mine."

Alanna watched the housekeeper's face. "I saw Barnard Sanderson while I was in Washington. He is not dead, and by now he should be with Lillia."

Kitty looked disbelieving. "How can that be?"

"Barnard Sanderson was not killed that night, but only wounded. I do not know the whole story, but he still loves Lillia, and she loves him. I told him where to find her, and he has already gone to her."

"The saints be praised," she beamed. "I have waited a long time for my sweet Lillia to be happy."

"You said you had some good news," Alanna

356

reminded Kitty.

"Well, actually it's more of a suspicion." She studied Alanna's face closely. "I will need a doctor to confirm what I believe."

Alanna looked quizzical. "What is it? You are not ill, are you?"

"I never felt better in my life. It's you that's sick to your stomach. I suspect you are going to have a baby."

Alanna looked dumbfounded for a moment. "Me! A baby. Surely not—" Her face lost its color. "Yes, now that I think about the signs, it is possible. I have just been so busy I did not notice." Her eyes brightened with happiness. "I wonder what kind of a mother I will be."

Kitty clasped her hands together. "What a glorious day this has turned out to be after all. Lillia will be so happy."

Alanna's face fell. "I suppose Nicholas will have to be told."

"It would seem the proper thing to do, seeing that he's the father."

"I cannot tell him, Kitty. I just cannot."

Kitty put her arms around Alanna and found she was trembling. "Now, now, love, just lay back and do not distress yourself. There will be plenty of time to tell the proud papa."

Alanna clasped the maid's hand. "You tell him for me. Please."

Kitty stood up, wondering what had happened to cause the young miss to be reduced to such a state. The maid could only guess that it had something to do with Colonel Barnard Sanderson. "It's not something that can't wait until morning. You can tell him then."

"No, I cannot. You tell him now—tonight."

Kitty nodded, her face grim. "If it'll get you to rest, I'll let the subject lie for now. But I feel sure he would like such joyous news to come from you. I cannot be the one to tell him. Wait a little longer, until you are certain, and then you can let him know he is to be a father."

Alanna turned her head toward the window and squeezed her eyes together tightly. She was going to have Nicholas's baby, yet there was no joy in her heart.

Chapter Thirty-Five

As it turned out, several weeks had passed since Alanna discovered she was going to have a baby, and still she had not told Nicholas.

The two of them continued to occupy separate bedrooms and they never dined together anymore. When they did chance to meet in passing, their conversation was stiff and polite. Alanna realized Nicholas had not yet forgiven her.

It was a lonely existence for Alanna, for now, fearing she would harm her unborn child, she had given up riding.

It was a warm day, with lazy clouds floating in the azure sky. Alanna moved down the steps to the stables, thinking she would look in on Red Betty and see how the mare was faring. When she entered the stables, Glenn greeted her by doffing his cap and giving her a warm smile.

"Your horse has been looking for you every day," he told her. "She watches the door for you, and I declare she is nervous and fidgety."

Alanna approached the red mare. "Has she been out to pasture?"

"Yes, but she's still listless." He nodded at the sleek

animal. "Look how she perks up when she sees you."

Alanna ran her hand over the animal's flank. "She needs exercise, Glenn. Will you ride her for me?"

A deep voice came from behind Alanna. "Why don't you ride her yourself? I gave her to you, therefore she's your horse."

Alanna spun around to face her husband. "I did not hear you come in."

"You're slipping, little Indian. Has civilization robbed you of your sharp instincts?"

She moved to brush past him, but he caught her arm and stalled her. "You didn't answer me. Why aren't you riding your horse lately?"

"I just do not feel like it," she said, prying his hand away from her arm under the watchful eye of the horse trainer.

"Walk with me," Nicholas said, moving out of the stable at a leisurely pace so she would be able to catch up with him.

Alanna smiled at Glenn. "Will you exercise Red Betty for me? It will be several months before I will be able to ride her."

"I'll do just that, Madame," he answered, wondering why her husband didn't seem to notice that she was with child.

Alanna moved out of the stables and found Nicholas waiting for her. When she drew even with him, he moved toward the river, expecting her to come along.

"I never thought I would see the day when you would neglect a horse, Alanna. Surely you don't think that acting like a spiteful child will gain you any sympathy?"

"I do not understand what you are accusing me of."

He frowned. "Don't you?"

360

"No. How can my not riding Red Betty be interpreted by you as a childish act?"

He let out an impatient breath. "You are sulking because I have been neglecting you lately, and you think you will gain the attention of the others if you—"

She stopped in her tracks. "How dare you! If I choose to ride Red Betty or not to ride, it has nothing to do with you."

He arched a dark eyebrow. "Have it your way."

"If you have nothing further to say to me, I will wish you a good day."

He took her arm and prevented her from leaving. "How are you doing?"

She stared into his eyes. Now would be the time to tell him about the baby, but she could not. "I have been feeling well of late," she said stiffly.

His hand moved up her arm. "I am told that you received a letter from Washington today. Was it important?"

She nodded. "It was from Donald. He was just inquiring about my health."

He looked at her. "Why should he be concerned about your health? You haven't been ill."

"No, I have not been ill. I intend to write and tell him just that." With a weak smile, she moved away toward the house, thus ending their conversation.

It was later in the afternoon when a loud rap came on Alanna's bedroom door. Without waiting for her to answer, Nicholas flung the door open and stood there, his face a mask of fury.

"I have decided that you will no longer sulk in your room. Get into your riding habit; you are going riding with me."

Alanna had been lying on the bed, and she sat up to look at him. "I would rather not."

He was across the room in five paces, and he pulled her off the bed roughly. "I said you are going riding, and by God you are going riding. Get dressed."

Her heart was pounding in her throat as he spun her around and unfastened her gown. She moved to the wardrobe and took out her riding habit and clutched it to her.

"I will be waiting for you out front. Don't make me come after you."

Alanna had never seen Nicholas so distant and cold. Her hands trembled as she fastened her gown up the front and pushed her foot into her black riding boots.

When she came down the front steps, Nicholas was standing beside Red Betty. With a cold glare, he lifted her into the saddle and handed her the reins. Once he was mounted, they rode away from the house in the direction of the far meadow.

They had been riding for some time when Nicholas pulled up his horse and indicated that Alanna should do the same. He helped her to the ground and studied her face before he released her.

"I have something for you." He reached into the inside pocket and withdrew an envelope with her name written across the front. "I was in Arlington this morning and checked in with the post office to pick up a package I had ordered. This had come for you. I believe you will find it is from my mother, although if you will look at the return address, she writes from Georgetown. The address is the same as Barnard Sanderson's."

Alanna stared at the letter, which was still sealed. "I wonder that it did not come to the house."

"I wondered about that myself." He handed the

letter to her and moved away in the direction of the river. "Perhaps she did not want me to read it."

Alanna ripped open the letter and began to read.

Dearest Alanna,
How can Barnard and I ever thank you for all you have done for us? I thank God every night before I go to bed that you came into our lives; otherwise, we might never have found one another again. When you read this, I shall be Mrs. Barnard Sanderson, and I am already the happiest of women. I received a letter from Dotty Singleton, and she told me about your trouble with Nicholas. Since I know my son, I can imagine the anger you have had to face. That is why I am setting you free of the promise I made you swear. You are at liberty to tell my son as much as you deem necessary so he will know that you did nothing wrong when you were in Washington. Coward that I am, I am also leaving it up to you to tell Nicholas of my married status. I love you both and pray that you find the happiness that dear Barnard and I have found together.

Alanna folded the letter and placed it back in the envelope. She was so glad that everything had turned out well for Lillia. She glanced down at the riverbank and saw Nicholas silently standing there. With a heavy heart, she walked toward him slowly, knowing she would have to tell him about his mother and Barnard.

Nicholas spoke to her without looking up. "Is my mother well?"

"Yes, and she is happy, Nicholas."

"Well, that is something, anyway. Happiness is such a fleeting emotion, I suppose one should catch it where one can."

"Nicholas . . . I do not know how to tell you this, although you already may suspect. Your mother . . . has married Barnard Sanderson."

His head jerked up, and he looked at her as if she had taken leave of her senses. "Are you saying my mother married the man who is responsible for my father's death?"

"No, Nicholas, that is not true. Barnard Sanderson had nothing to do with your father's death. You just do not know what happened."

"And you do?"

"Your mother is not like you said she was, Nicholas. She is a good person. I cannot tell you any more. You either believe in her, or you continue to believe the lies you heard about her. Nothing I can say will change your mind."

There was pain in his eyes. "You cannot make me believe that my mother was innocent and my father was the guilty one."

"I will not *make* you believe anything. You will have to examine your mind and come to a conclusion on your own. I will tell you this, however: your mother loves you, and you have broken her heart just as your father did. I am glad she has found happiness at last."

"So the reason you went to see Barnard Sanderson was at the request of my mother?"

"No, Nicholas. Like you, your mother thought Barnard Sanderson was dead."

"And my father died for a crime he did not commit."

"I suppose that is true, but he did shoot Sanderson."

Nicholas's eyes were dull. "He paid a high price for shooting the Yankee. Pity his aim was not better."

"You do not mean that, Nicholas."

364

He turned away from her to stare at the restless river. "I apologize if I seemed overbearing when I came to your room, insisting that you ride with me. It is not good for you to stay cooped up in your room all day. You are accustomed to the outdoors."

"Will you go to see your mother? At least to talk to her, Nicholas."

"No. I have nothing to say to my mother."

He leaned against a red maple tree and looked at her. As always, he was struck with how lovely she was. Now there was a sadness in her blue eyes, and he knew he was the one responsible for her unhappiness. He had married her, he had thought for her own good, but he had ended up hurting her.

"What am I to do about you and me, Alanna?"

"I do not know, Nicholas. You seem to have found a solution by banishing me from your bedroom."

He took a hesitant step toward her and then another. She stood perfectly still, unwilling to meet him halfway. When he reached out his arms and enfolded her, he found her rigid and unyielding.

"I have missed you. Banishing you from my bed has been torment for me."

She was still too hurt to relent. "I have noticed that you have been away from home most of the time. I have not seen you pining away because of my absence."

He pulled her into his arms and stared into her eyes. "Suppose I told you that I burn for you every night, but I have too much pride to go begging to you? Suppose I said I needed you, Alanna?"

She tossed her head. "You have never needed anyone in your whole life, Nicholas. You are a man who is alone from his own choosing, and I would say that you like it that way."

His green eyes narrowed. "Does one ever choose to

be lonely?"

Alanna's attention was drawn to his lips, and she knew he was going to kiss her.

Her lips parted, and he jerked her to him. "How do I reach you?" he murmured, just before he ground his mouth against hers. Alanna felt her knees going weak, and she clung to him to keep from falling.

When his hands moved about her waist to bring her closer to his body, he froze. As he raised his head, she saw bewilderment in his eyes; his face drained of color. "What is this?" His hand moved down to her stomach, and he felt the firm roundness there. "My, God, why didn't you tell me you are going to have a baby?"

Her eyes became cold. "You are my husband, you should not have to be told."

He shook his head. "What a fool I have been. This explains why you gave up horseback riding."

"Yes, Kitty thought it would be harmful to the baby if I rode a horse."

His eyes softened, and his touch on her cheek was gentle. "Have you seen a doctor?"

"No. Kitty urged me to, but I did not want to until I could tell you about the baby."

"When were you going to tell me—after the baby was born?"

She turned back to Red Betty and laid her face against the mare's neck. "I do not know if I would ever have told you. I do not want to have your baby, Nicholas."

She did not see the pain in his eyes. "We didn't plan on this, did we?"

"You never considered that your son or daughter would have Cheyenne blood running in its veins, did you? Imagine a Ballinger of Ballinger Hall, with Indian blood."

He reached for her and gently placed her in the saddle. "I had already told you I wanted a son. This changes many things between us, Alanna."

He mounted his horse and nudged it forward. "We shall return to the house slowly, and you will not ride again until after the baby is born. I will send someone this afternoon for Doctor Goodman. You must have the best of care."

Alanna remembered Lillia telling her how kind and considerate Simeon was to her while she was carrying his child. Evidently the Ballingers of Ballinger Hall prized their offspring, whether they loved the mother or not.

When they reached the house, Alanna slid from Red Betty's back and ran into the house.

When she reached her room she leaned against the door and placed her hand on her stomach. "I did not mean it when I said I did not want you," she said to her unborn baby. "I want you more than I have ever wanted anything—except, perhaps, your father's love."

She was glad Nicholas finally knew about the baby, but he was wrong, it would not change anything between them. She and Nicholas had set their feet on separate paths, and they would never walk as one. How sad it was, she thought.

Chapter Thirty-Six

Alanna had been seen by the doctor, and he announced that she was healthy and the baby would be born in the early part of the fall.

It seemed to her that all the servants had been alerted to her condition, for they were most solicitous. Bowls of fruit were kept in her room so she could have easy access to them. The meals were prepared with the child she was carrying in mind. Vegetables, milk products, and fresh fish had been added to her diet at the doctor's insistence.

Nicholas was always at home now that he knew about the baby. He made a point of taking his meals with Alanna. She was the recipient of his kind attention, and she was aware that he watched her every move.

Nicholas had been in his study since dinner, and it was now late in the evening.

Alanna had been reclining in a chair near the garden window, and she found herself nodding off. She tired so easily. Her eyes were heavy, and she thought she would close them for just a short while.

Alanna awoke with a start as Nicholas knelt beside her. He gently touched her forehead. "You look tired," he said in a soft voice.

She looked into his green eyes and had the strangest feeling that she was drowning in their shimmering depths. "I am a little tired," she admitted. Then she moved forward. "I think I will go up to bed now."

Before Alanna knew what was happening, Nicholas scooped her up in his arms. "I will take you to your room."

She laid her head against his shoulder as he mounted the stairs with ease. His kindness made her even more vulnerable than she already was.

When he entered her room, he laid her on the bed and stood staring down at her for a long moment. His eyes moving over her slightly swollen stomach.

"Are you feeling well, Alanna?"

"Yes. Just clumsy, and I do not like all the fuss everyone is making over me."

He sat down on the edge of the bed and picked up her hand. "You will have to contend with being spoiled, Alanna. You are carrying the next heir of Ballinger Hall."

"Nicholas, I have tried to think why that would make a difference to you. We both know why you married me. I do not think you considered that there might be a child from our union."

"Did you?"

"Yes, sometimes."

His eyes seemed to look right through her. "I wanted to tell you that I will be gone for a few days. Kitty will see to your welfare while I am away."

She nodded, wishing she dared beg him not to leave her. She did not ask where he was going, although she was eaten up with curiosity.

He laid his hand against her cheek. "Have you been so unhappy here, Alanna?"

"I have never felt like I really belonged in your world, Nicholas. I sometimes long for the carefree days that I knew in my Cheyenne village. I suppose it is because life was so uncomplicated then."

"You were never meant to live in an Indian lodge, Alanna. You are bright and intelligent, and the time would have come when you would have been discontented with such a simple existence."

"I do not think so, Nicholas. I knew love, and that is what would have kept me happy for the rest of my life." She waved her hand around the grandly furnished room. "These superficial trappings do not make me happy."

His eyes became greener when he looked at her. "Do you still think of Gray Falcon?"

"Yes, Nicholas, I do."

She could not stop the tears from gathering in her eyes. She often thought of Gray Falcon, but it was with sadness. She knew that what she had felt for the brave young Indian warrior could not be compared with the love she had for Nicholas, which was all-consuming.

Nicholas blinked as if in pain. "Is there room in your heart for my baby and me?"

"My grandmother always told me that love was like a lodge with many rooms. She believed that love had no beginning and no end. I like to think that she was right."

He gave Alanna an exasperated look. "Again, you have me confused."

"I know," she said simply. "I do not think you understand love."

He turned his head away from her. "You may be right. I have forgotten what it is to love."

Sadness encased her heart, for she could feel his torment. How could she tell him that her heart was so filled with loving him that there was little room for anything else?

Alanna was startled when Nicholas pulled her into his arms and silently held her to him. "I have missed you in my bed, Alanna. I regret my decision to move you here."

He waited, as if hoping she would agree with him, but she said nothing, because her throat was suddenly dry. She closed her eyes, feeling the corded strength of him in every fiber of her body.

His shoulders seemed to sag. "Don't shut me out of your life, Alanna. I am trying to deal with misconceptions and guilt that I have lived with for years. You have made me see that I have made many mistakes."

She pulled back and looked at him. "Nicholas, the mistakes are not always yours. In our situation, I should never have agreed to marry you—that was my mistake. But you were so different before we came to Ballinger Hall, and I thought we could be happy together."

The muscle in his jaw twitched, and he looked away. "Mistake or no, you are carrying my child." He stood up and walked to the door. "But have no fear that I will make any demands on you, Alanna."

She reached out her hand to him, but already he had turned to the door.

"Take care of your health," he said over his shoulder, just before he disappeared through the door and closed it softly behind him.

Lillia was dusting the books in the small library when the housekeeper announced a visitor. Since Barnard had brought her to Washington, several of his friends had called at the Georgetown house to wish them well in their marriage.

Lillia looked down at her dusty apron and quickly removed it. "I will see the visitor in the parlor," she said, patting her hair into place.

"Hello, Mother," Nicholas spoke up from behind the housekeeper.

Lillia pressed her hand over her heart when she saw her son standing there. "Nicholas," was all she could manage to say.

His footsteps were slow as he approached her. He noted the blush of health on her cheeks and the way her eyes shone with expectancy when she looked at him.

"You are looking well, Mother."

"Happiness has a way of making a woman look prettier than she really is," she said, her eyes searching his face.

He nodded at the chair behind her. After she was seated, he stood over her, looking undecided. "I have come for several reasons. First of all, to congratulate you on your marriage."

She looked for a sign of sarcasm in his eyes, but saw none. "I am happy, Nicholas. I don't expect you to understand or forgive me for marrying Barnard. But life is too short for us not to reach out for happiness. I lived my whole life for your father, and then for you. I now live for myself."

His expression was noncommittal. "I have had a chance to do some soul-searching lately, and I have remembered many things about my father that I had buried deep within my mind. I tried to recall a time when he spoke kindly to you. He never did, to my knowledge. But I recall that you were always smiling and trying to please him."

She reached out her hand to him. "This isn't necessary, Nicholas. I want you to remember that you

372

were your father's whole world. He was a good father to you."

"I also recall that he would use me to hurt you. I don't know why, and I had forgotten that also. I suppose one strives to cover over the faults of the dead. At least, I think that is what I did with my father."

"Nicholas, don't do this to yourself. It isn't necessary."

He looked at her as if he had come out of a daze. "I am not saying I will embrace your new husband as a father, or that I can even accept him as a friend. But I suppose there must be something special about him if you care for him."

Her eyes were swimming with tears. "Oh, Nicholas, I love him, and he loves me. If only you could know him."

"Not just yet, Mother. Give me some time on this."

He laced his fingers through hers. "I know I have caused you much heartache. All I can say is I'll try and make it up to you in the future."

"There is nothing for you to make up. All I ask is to see you once in a while." She searched his face. "Did Alanna tell you about the night your father died?"

"No. She has been very secretive about everything concerning you. But she has forced me to see many things that I have tried not to see."

"She is an exceptional person. Everywhere she goes she leaves her mark on the people she meets. Dotty swears she loves her like a daughter, and I feel fortunate that she is like a daughter to me."

Suddenly there was pain in Nicholas's green eyes. "Those that are fortunate enough to win Alanna's love are lucky indeed. Me, she merely tolerates."

"No, you are wrong, Nicholas. I am certain

373

Alanna loves you."

He dislodged his hand from hers and stood up. "I did not come here to have you convince me of Alanna's feelings. I have some news which I believe will please you."

She waited expectantly.

"I am going to be a father in the autumn."

Her eyes brightened with tears, and she jumped up to hug him. She feared for a moment that he would push her away, but his arms went around her, and he held her tightly.

"I never thought much about becoming a parent. When I learned about the baby, it made me remember what my own mother meant in my life. I had to come here and tell you this."

She looked up at him. "I love you, Nicholas, and I thank you for being so generous and forgiving."

He touched his lips to her cheek. "Let us forgive one another, shall we?"

"Oh, yes, son."

He stepped away from her. "I will be leaving now. I have business to attend to before I can leave for Ballinger Hall tomorrow."

"Nicholas?"

"Yes."

"Tell Alanna I am happy for her." She looked at him questioningly. "And if you will permit it, I would like to visit her before the baby comes."

He moved to the door and turned back to look at her. "You are welcome any time at Ballinger Hall. But I do not want to see Sanderson there, not yet— perhaps someday."

Lillia knew her son had already made a great concession in coming to see her today, she would not ask for any more of him. "I understand, and I know Barnard will too."

"Good-bye, Mother."

Her eyes were dancing with happiness. "Until later, my son."

On the ride back to Ballinger Hall, Nicholas had much to reflect on. Alanna had made him realize that he had been unfair to his mother, and it was almost a relief that he had put the bitterness behind him. He could go home now and prepare for the birth of his child.

His eyes gleamed with pride. A new heir for Ballinger Hall! The cycle would go on, and another Ballinger would be born in the fall. The Ballingers were a part of this beautiful land. They lived here, worked here and were buried here—and so it would always be, he hoped.

Chapter Thirty-Seven

"Kitty, this will be wonderful," Alanna said, running her hand over the smooth cherrywood cradle that had been Nicholas's as a baby. It brought a smile to her lips to think of their child lying in the same cradle.

Kitty had ushered Alanna to the attic, where they had spent the morning looking at baby clothing that had been stored away in trunks.

"I'll have Askew carry these to the room that was once the nursery," Kitty said. "Let's get you out of this dust."

Alanna nodded, gathering up a tiny gown that had been her husband's.

The housekeeper's gaze softened. "Madame made that gown. She will be happy to know it will be used again."

When Alanna passed the grand staircase, on the way to her bedroom, she could hear Askew greeting someone below. She paused at the top of the landing and glanced at the lovely woman dressed in a wine-colored traveling gown. The woman had black hair and a flawless complexion. She was about Alanna's height, but she was slender and willowy, while

Alanna felt clumsy and misshapen.

"Is Nicholas at home?" the lady inquired.

"No, Mrs. Arthur," Askew told her. "We don't expect him back until tomorrow."

Alanna stared at the woman. So this was Madeline Arthur. She could understand why Nicholas had gone to North Carolina to see her. The woman was lovely.

Then anger burned in her heart that the woman would come to this house. Surely she was not here at Nicholas's invitation. Even he would not be so ill advised as to allow his mistress to stay under the same roof as his wife.

Slowly, Alanna, who had the blood of Cheyenne war chiefs in her veins, came down the stairs, ready to do battle with the woman.

When Askew saw Alanna, he politely made the introduction.

"Madame, this is Mrs. Arthur. She has come to see Mr. Ballinger. I told her that he was away."

Alanna's face was a polite mask, which did not show her displeasure. "Yes, my husband is away. Perhaps I can help you, Mrs. Arthur?"

Madeline smiled, speaking in a soft southern accent. "So you are the woman who made Nicholas give up his bachelorhood. You are even prettier than I thought." Her eyes traveled down to Alanna's rounded stomach. "I had no idea that you were with child."

Alanna's eyes turned cold. "You must have had a tedious journey, Mrs. Arthur. Can I perhaps offer you a refreshing drink?"

"It has been rather an arduous trip from Charlotte. I would not say no to something cool."

"Askew, have Kitty serve lemon coolers in the parlor," Alanna told the butler, who nodded and went to do her bidding.

As the two women sized up one another, Alanna felt at a disadvantage. Glancing down, she saw that her white gown was dusty from being in the attic. She wished she had seen to her appearance before coming downstairs to confront Madeline Arthur.

When both women were seated, there was a long and uncomfortable silence before Alanna spoke. "I believe my husband purchased horses from you, Mrs. Arthur."

"Yes, that's why I'm here. There are several valuable mares in the herd, that I would not trust to anyone but myself to transport."

Alanna was in no mood to play games with this woman. "Is it your practice to accompany the horses you sell to their destination?"

Madeline smiled while working her fingers out of her black leather gloves. "I believe you have seen through me, Mrs. Ballinger. You guessed from the first that I came to see Nicholas, didn't you?"

"Yes, I know that, but what I do not understand is why you took it upon yourself to come here. Knowing my husband as I do, I cannot believe he would approve."

A slow smile softened Madeline's features. "I believe you have a few misconceptions, Mrs. Ballinger. While it is true that I have a more than passing interest in Nicholas, I can assure you he has no interest in me. There was a time when we were both young that I thought he might care about me—but that was merely wishful thinking on my part."

Alanna arched a doubtful brow.

"It's true. I would stand on my head if I thought it would get Nicholas's attention, but it wouldn't. Since he married you, he's become far too serious about life. When Nicholas came to North Carolina, he was like a cold stranger to me. I used the excuse of accompanying the horses to Ballinger Hall in hopes of meeting the woman who had succeeded in snaring Nicholas Ballinger where all others have failed."

Alanna was not willing to believe the woman. "And now that you have seen me?"

Madeline looked at her assessingly. "You are just the kind of woman he would choose. Beautiful, well-educated, soft-spoken. I would venture a guess that you don't make life too easy for him. I had a chance to observe him while he was at my plantation. He could hardly wait to get back to you. He brushed me aside as if we were strangers."

Alanna searched the woman's clear gray eyes, and even though Mrs. Arthur had flattered her at every turn, she was feeling less than charitable toward her. "Appearances can be deceiving, Mrs. Arthur. Perhaps he was not so much in a hurry to come home to me as he was to leave you."

Madeline came to her feet, working her fingers back into her gloves. "I can see that I made a mistake in coming here. I knew when I started out that I was on a fool's errand. I can only apologize for my presumption."

"I can see that you are in love with my husband, Mrs. Arthur, and I do not appreciate your coming into this house under false pretenses."

Madeline smiled stiffly. "I will wish you a good day, Mrs. Ballinger. Don't be too hard on Nicholas when he returns, because we both know he would not have approved of my coming here today, any more than you have."

Alanna was cool and distant. "Good day, Mrs. Arthur. Have a pleasant trip back to your home."

Without another word, Madeline Arthur moved to the door. She paused and looked back at Alanna.

379

"For whatever the reason, you are a fortunate woman because you have Nicholas's love. I wonder if you know that."

Alanna said nothing as the woman left. Of course, Madeline Arthur was wrong. Nicholas did not love her, and she had his assurance that he never would.

Alanna watched Madeline Arthur climb into her carriage, and watched as it rode out of sight. She was angry that the woman had invaded Ballinger Hall. In her society, such an affront would not have been tolerated.

She had believed Madeline Arthur when she'd told her that Nicholas had had no part in her coming here today. But in her mind, that did not excuse him.

With deliberate steps, she moved out of the parlor and up the steps to her bedroom. Gone was her enthusiasm for decorating the baby's nursery. All she wanted to do was lie on her bed and stare at the ceiling.

Nicholas saw the unfamiliar carriage pulling away from the house. As the carriage drew even, he was suprised to see that the passenger was Madeline Arthur.

He motioned for his driver to stop. Opening his door, he moved to her carriage and leaned against the door.

"I had not expected to see you here, Madeline. You are a long way from home."

"I accompanied my horses. I wanted to make certain that they reached you without mishap."

He looked at her doubtfully. "Was that really your reason?"

She laughed. "All right, so I came to see you. Little good it did me, though. And I fear my visit may have

380

caused you trouble with your wife."

His eyebrows furrowed into a frown. "You should not have come here, Madeline."

"I know that now. I suppose I was just curious as to what your wife would be like."

His eyes had turned cold. "She is going to have my child. I hope your visit did not upset her."

"I fear I *did* upset her. Will you forgive me?"

He merely stared at her. "Do not come here again. I thought we already said our good-byes."

Her eyes grew sad. "We did. I guess I just didn't believe it until now." She reached out her hand to him, but he pulled away from her.

"Good-bye, Nicholas."

He tipped his hat to her and signaled her driver to move on. He got back in his carriage, and even before Madeline had disappeared from sight, he had dismissed her from his mind.

He tried to curb his impatience to see his wife. He had so much to tell her! He wanted her to know that he now understood about his mother, and that Alanna had made him see how wrong he had been about many things.

As soon as the carriage came to a halt, he leaped out and rushed across the lawn to the stables. He knew how he could prove to Alanna how he felt about her.

It was almost dark as Alanna came down the stairs and walked into the parlor. She dreaded the thought of eating another solitary meal. She was tired of her own company and longed for intelligent conversation.

The evening was hot, and the windows had been thrown open wide to catch the evening breeze. She caught the wonderful fresh fragrance of the roses that grew alone the pathway. Overcome with melancholy, she stepped outside and stood on the path.

As she bent to pluck a velvety-soft red rose, she heard footsteps behind her, and she whirled around to see Askew approaching.

"Madame, you are wanted at the front of the house," he said, his dark eyes dancing.

She stared at Askew, unable to recall a time when she had seen him smile.

"By whom?" she inquired.

"By your husband, Madame."

Alanna gathered up her gown and rushed back into the house, with her heart racing. Nicholas had come home!

Nicholas witnessed Alanna's astonishment as she stepped out the front door. Her eyes went to him as he dismounted and walked slowly up the steps to her.

She looked from him back to the numerous horses that were tied at the hitching post. With a confused smile, she spoke: "Are those the horses you bought in North Carolina?"

"Yes, they are." He took her hand and raised it to his lips.

"You were right, Nicholas. They are fine horse-flesh," she said admiringly.

His expression was serious. "Alanna, if your grandfather were here, I would have come to him this evening, asking permission to speak to him about you."

Her eyes rounded with surprise, but she could not speak because her throat seemed to have closed off.

He laid her hand against his cheek. "Since Wolf Dreamer is not here, I will have to speak directly to the object of my affection." His eyes were soft, and she saw a light in them that she had never noticed before.

"Alanna," he continued in a deep voice, which was laced with earnestness, "I offer as your bride's price twenty horses, hoping you will not turn me down."

Tears were swimming in her eyes as she glanced away from him. She could not bring herself to look into those green eyes that were so filled with love. "It is a great price," she said, pretending to examine the horses.

"Will you accept them from me, Alanna?"

"But I am already your wife."

"Yes, but will you be my love?" There was no mockery in his eyes—only sincerity.

She reached out and laid her hand against his face, and he closed his eyes against her gentle touch. "I have loved you for a very long time, Nicholas. The love was always here, you had only to reach out for it."

He gathered her into his arms and said in a voice that was filled with wonder, "If you loved me, why did I not know it before now?"

Alanna glanced up into his face. "I don't know, Nicholas. I believe everyone but you knew."

She still needed to hear him say how he felt about her. "Usually, when a warrior pays twenty horses for a maiden, it is because he loves her."

He pressed his face against hers. "My dearest love, I believe I have loved you since the morning I awoke to find you had removed the bullet from my shoulder. You have sorely tested my patience, you have humbled me." His arms tightened about her. "You have taught me how to love—you have shown me how to live."

His breath fanned her cheek. "I love you, Blue Eyes."

She was not ashamed of the tears that sparkled in her eyes, nor did she try to hide them from him. "I will accept the horses, Nicholas, because I love you with all my heart."

With a loud whoop that was uncharacteristic of him, he scooped her up in his arms and carried her inside. He brushed past the startled Askew on his way to the stairs.

"I am taking you to my bedroom, where you belong," Nicholas told Alanna.

Happiness burst forth in her heart. She looked into green eyes that spoke to her with a deep love. She pressed her face against his chest, returning that love from the depths of her being.

When Nicholas reached his bedroom, he set her on her feet, but he kept her in his arms. "Come here, Blue Eyes, tell me again that you love me."

She looked into his face, knowing how fortunate she was to have known the love of two noble men.

Gray Falcon was nothing more than a fleeting memory of another time in her life. With him she would have known happiness, but she might not have known a love so deep it could touch the soul. With Nicholas, she would know great joy, because she had also known great sorrow.

This tall master of Ballinger Hall was arrogant, and sometimes demanding, but he had humbled himself for love, and had shown that he was human after all, and very capable of loving a woman.